PRAISE FOR *THE LAST GIRL*

'Fast-paced and reading like the script of a movie you really want to see.'
HERALD SUN

'Brings class to teen-lit.'
ROLLING STONE

'Doesn't skimp on smart intrigue or sharp menace ... magnificent.
Bring on the trilogy.'
EMPIRE

'A very different end-of-the-world scenario. Forget vampires and zombies,
thoughts are the refreshing Big Bad in this tense page-turner of a YA series.'
YEN

'An explosive sci-fi thriller, with an original premise and a plot
that reads like an action movie, this book is a mad –
almost literally mad – race to the end.'
THE NEW ZEALAND HERALD

'Gripping and fast-paced, with exciting action scenes.
Danby is a strong and resourceful character.'
BOOKS + PUBLISHING

'Danby is a sharp, witty narrator and the pace is fast. *The Last Girl* has the
potential to be for a new generation of readers what John Marsden's
Tomorrow series was in the 1990s.'
AUSTRALIAN BOOK REVIEW

'Full of pop-culture references, sly humour, out-of-the-blue violence,
and challenges to narrative conventions.'
Kirsten Krauth, author of JUST_A_GIRL

'Danby is Australia's answer to Katniss Everdeen, a kick-ass reluctant
heroine that you just keep rooting for.'
Evie, GOODREADS

'Everyone needs to run out and grab a copy of this
epic book as soon as possible!'
SPECULATING ON SPECFIC

JUL - - 2017

Also by Michael Adams

The Last Shot
The Last Place

MICHAEL ADAMS

the last girl

ALLEN & UNWIN

SYDNEY · MELBOURNE · AUCKLAND · LONDON

Allen & Unwin – Australia
83 Alexander Street
Crows Nest NSW 2065
Australia
Phone:(61 2) 8425 0100
Email: info@allenandunwin.com
Web: www.allenandunwin.com

Allen & Unwin – UK
Ormond House, 26–27 Boswell Street,
London WC1N 3JZ, UK
Phone: +44 (0) 20 8785 5995
Email: info@murdochbooks.co.uk
Web: www.murdochbooks.co.uk

A Cataloguing-in-Publication entry is available from the
National Library of Australia www.trove.nla.gov.au
A catalogue record for this book is available from the British Library.

ISBN (AUS) 978 1 76029 340 6
ISBN (UK) 978 1 74336 941 8

Cover and internal design by i2i Design
Cover and internal artwork, *The Wall of Sound*, © Marika Järv, 2013
Cover and internal images (cityscape, girl and flames) by iStockphoto.com
Set in Minion by Midland Typesetters, Australia
Printed in Australia by McPherson's Printing Group

10 9 8 7 6 5 4 3 2 1

The paper in this book is FSC® certified.
FSC® promotes environmentally responsible,
socially beneficial and economically viable
management of the world's forests.

For Clare and Ava

PROLOGUE

I always knew I'd see the end of the world.

Being born under a bad sign could've had something to do with that. But I didn't need an omen to tell me we were headed for oblivion. My screens were so constantly filled with cataclysmic scenarios that it seemed obvious the question wasn't *if* but *when*.

Not *if* but *when* we'd be wiped out by climate change, superflu contagion, solar surge, rogue meteor, nanotech terror, nuclear madmen, alien invasion, robot uprising, zombie outbreak or just the good old wrath of God. Hell—we were so used to contemplating the end of the world as we knew it that we'd even given it an acronym. But the one thing all of our TEOTWAWKIs had in common was that they'd be caused by something outside of us.

Maybe I should've seen what was about to happen. Right up until those last moments I didn't put the pieces together any better than anyone else. I certainly never thought novelty socks would trigger the apocalypse.

But for me they were the beginning of the end.

1

the snap

ONE

'The Content Planet.' Dad lifted the book from its reindeer gift bag, tilting it this way and that, like there was some angle he wasn't getting.

Stephanie—his wife, my stepmother—nodded sagely. 'I thought you really should read it.'

Dad *had* read it. Months ago. On his tablet. I remembered because I'd thought the title referred to a world in a state of peaceful happiness. Dad had scoffed and set 'silly me' straight. Not con*tent*. *Con*tent. Stephanie had been right there at the breakfast table when he'd gone on about meeting the author at some conference. At least I had been listening. Well, *half* listening.

'I've been meaning to get this.' Dad pretended to read the back cover.

Stephanie beamed from beside our acrylic tree. Her platinum extensions cascaded from under her Santa hat and her boobs pushed against the fluffy trim of her Mrs Claus frock. The festive outfit wasn't for Dad's benefit. The curtains were wide open so anyone passing on Beautopia Point's promenade would be presented with my stepmother as the sexy centrepiece of our tacky Christmas card. Stephanie was literally window dressing.

'I'll read it on the flight,' Dad said. 'Thanks.'

The flight. Dad had offered to cancel his business trip. I told him I'd be fine. It wasn't like him being around would make any difference. Dad tried to hide his relief but I knew he was glad to be let off the hook. I reckoned that mentally he was already in the airport lounge, sipping scotch and rehearsing his sales pitches. But first, there was family business to conclude. So far he'd given me a skate-shop voucher enclosed in a card with wishes for a better New Year and love from Dad.

Now it was Stephanie's turn.

'Here you go,' Dad said, glancing up from his phone and giving her a silver envelope.

Stephanie sliced it open with a plastic nail and her eyes lit up on whatever figure was inscribed on her BestU gift card. Dad had given her the same present last year but I guessed the numbers needed to improve with age.

'Oh, nice,' she cooed, planting lipstick on his cheek.

He conjured a smile. 'Not that you need it.'

As much as I was into recycling, it was pretty lame that Dad had used that line last year, too.

Eyes puffy, hair everywhere, crumpled in my pyjamas: I just wanted to be back in bed. But it was my turn again.

'Here, Danbyn,' Stephanie said, passing me an identical reindeer gift bag.

She never called me Dan or Danby. Payback for me never embracing her as Steph back when she thought we'd be horseriding BFFs. What I did call her was Stepfordy and Stepphoney—at least when I dissed her to my friends.

'Thanks, Stephanie.'

I appraised the gift. A compact disc. *Eye In The Sky* by Distant Affliction.

'They do neo-covers, they're post-hipster,' Stephanie said, echoing something she'd heard somewhere. 'So, y'know, very cool. I think you should like them.'

Stephanie didn't mean she hoped I *liked* the band. She really meant I *should* like them. If I agreed with her that they rocked it meant she at thirty-whatever was as cool as sixteen-year-old me. If I told her they sucked it meant she was cooler than me. Stephanie couldn't lose. But I was pretty good at not letting her win.

'They're very popular,' I said evenly. 'Thanks.'

'I hope you don't mind it's not a download,' she replied. 'But the old-school sound from a CD is so much warmer, don't you think?'

I grinned at her totally bogus retro aesthetics, just managing to not ROTFLMFAO, as they used to say. Madly cackling on the lounge-room floor would've been like nuking myself for her enjoyment. The last thing I needed was any sort of scene. Better to give her this petty victory.

'You know,' I said, still trying not to laugh. 'That is so true.'

Stephanie nodded with satisfaction.

I wasn't just keeping the peace for myself but also for Evan, their six-year-old son, my beautiful little half-brother, who was swinging one of his new kiddie golf clubs too close to a spray of marigolds arranged in a vase on a side table.

'Goof!' he yelped.

'Careful!' Stephanie said way too harshly.

While she played the role of dutiful handmaiden to Dad and condescending big sister to me, sometimes she reacted to her own boy like what he suffered wasn't a condition but a compulsion to annoy her. Evan usually didn't notice her anger. That just made her madder.

'Goof!'

Evan let the club clatter to the floor, plunged his hand into a bucket of golf balls and guffawed as he clacked them around. Stephanie vented an exasperated sigh. Dad glanced up from an app and aped something like amusement.

'Goof!' I said, grinning at Evan.

He was a goof all right, nature as golden as his complexion, and his mother's antipathy and our father's ambivalence made me love him all the more.

'Goof!'

'Golf!' Stephanie steamed. '*Golf!* Golf, Evan, for godsake!'

It was such an overreaction that I wanted to laugh right in Stephanie's face. What stopped me was I was suddenly right inside her head.

Goddamnit-Evan-understood-golf-Now-he's-back-to-the-full-retard!

This was far beyond her usual transparency. Far beyond my usual bitchy guessing at her every awful motive.

This was me tuning in to what she was thinking and feeling and remembering. I was with her as she flashed to the afternoon she'd found Evan upstairs staring intently into the 3-D broadcast of a PGA game.

'Golf,' he'd said, executing the perfect imitation of a pro's power swing. 'What a tremendous drive that is.' Evan was transfixed, copying plays, parroting commentary.

Such mimicry would come out of nowhere and disappear just as abruptly. But every single time Stephanie couldn't help thinking *savant*. Since that afternoon she had daydreamed about chaperoning her little champion to lucrative tournaments. She'd be newly single, still young and courted by rich men. But another desire curled under her lust for fame and power. Someone would see her. Really see her. *Love* her.

Now Evan held two golf balls like big fly eyes and her fantasy evaporated. *Not-going-to-happen-At-least-Brendan's-going-soon-No-not-David-I—*

I snapped out of it. Stephanie wasn't saying anything, hadn't said anything. But it had been so real in my head.

Shit.

Dr Jenny said the Lucidiphil would silence the voices. Keep me stable until I could see the specialist. I'd taken the medication three times yesterday and once this morning as directed. But it was happening again. At least my family didn't notice my face go white or my eyes go wide. I made a conscious effort to close my mouth.

My plan had been to call Jacinta this morning, wish her Merry Christmas, apologise for everything and ask her to get the word out that I was okay. I wondered if I could still do that. I felt pretty freakin' far from okay.

'Here, Brendan,' Stephanie said, handing over Dad's last Christmas gift. 'You should love these.'

Her voice matched her lips. I wasn't imagining emotional mind movies for her anymore. Maybe what had just happened was a minor relapse, residual madness, nothing to worry about, resolved now. Dad dragged his gaze from his phone and squished his little reindeer bag.

'A bottle of single malt?'

A desperate dad joke, even by his standards.

'Socks,' he said as he lifted the footwear from the gift bag, face screwed up like a soothsayer getting bad entrails.

'No,' said Stephanie. 'They're Soxies!'

She pointed at the cursive stitching. 'See, it says So Soxy!, Too Soxy!, and, my favourite, Sox On Legs!'

Dad tried for a grin but came up with a grimace. 'You shouldn't have.'

I guess those stupid socks *were* physical manifestations of what ailed the planet and I could've seen the apocalypse in them any time I cared to look. Thirty per cent cotton grown from patented corporate seeds and harvested by peasant kids. Seventy per cent polyester spun from the war and corruption of Middle Eastern oilfields. Chemically dyed and machine-woven in some belching factory whose toxic waste gushed into freshwater rivers. Sorted and packed by serf workers deprived of democracy. Pallets piled into containers and trucked to cargo ships that ploughed across dying oceans in clouds of particulate. Process reversed at ports of destination: containers and pallets and boxes and packets broken down so Soxies could fulfil their destiny as stocking filler destined to become landfill.

You-shouldn't-have.

As Dad said it again, I knew the socks didn't trouble him politically, socially or environmentally. They troubled him economically. Not as items of global trade but of personal trade. His and Stephanie's relationship was a series of transactions based around sex, status and stuff—and she wasn't keeping her end of the bargain.

Except I couldn't know any of that. Dad hadn't spoken again. Wasn't speaking now.

Haven't-touched-me-in-months-This-some-sort-of-joke?-Nothing-but-time-and-my-money-to-spend-First-the-book-Now-this-crap-This-is-what-I'm-worth?

I rubbed my eyes. This was like accidentally pushing the wrong button on the remote so the director's commentary comes on.

You-shouldn't-have!-You-stupid-shallow—

'I thought you'd think—' Stephanie started to say. *It-was-funny.*

Her mouth tightened. Her eyes narrowed. 'What did you call me?'

Behind her venom I heard—*thought* I heard—whispers of desperation.

I-should've-gotten-him-something-better!-Should've-left David-earlier!

Lightning-etched flashes of my stepmother with her personal trainer bombarded my mind. Yesterday afternoon, while I'd been crying in bed and Dad had been working and Evan had been at special care, Stephanie had gone to David's city apartment. Her plan had been to break it off and get busy with Christmas shopping. But him listening to her so beautifully was like a form of seduction and the hours had gotten away from them. Stephanie raced home, feeling guilty as hell, swearing never again, his bouquet of marigolds on the front seat. She was nearly through the front door when she realised she didn't have gifts for me or Dad. So she rushed to The Grocery, grateful my episode meant I wouldn't be on the checkout, and grabbed the book, the socks, my CD and the reindeer bags, telling herself she could spin these last-minute purchases into thoughtful-sounding presents.

Dad, Stephanie, me: my hallucination had us all hooking in and out of her tumble of thoughts and emotions in the nanosecond it takes to light up a neural network.

But my delusion didn't just include the three of us.

Man-nude-Mummy-Daddy-silly-angry . . .

I couldn't believe it. My mental illness had taken me inside Evan's head. I was inventing a reaction to him being in *their* minds. There was no coping with this crazy. No way to hide it. Did Dr Jenny make Christmas Day house calls with her straitjacket? I laughed loudly like the mad girl I'd become.

Dad and Stephanie didn't hear me.

Or Evan as he announced, 'Goof! Goof! Goof!' and tipped his bucket of golf balls across the floor.

My father and stepmother only had hate-filled eyes for each other.

Dad spasmed and for a second I thought he'd been electrocuted by a wayward Christmas light.

'You're having an affair?' he whispered. 'With some *gym* guy?'

My mind had his thoughts screaming with self-righteous hurt and anger at Stephanie's mental picture of David. *I-gave-you-everything!-This-is-how-you-repay—*

Beneath Dad's fury was the big regret. *Robyn-wouldn't-cheat-Should-never-have-let-her-go.*

My mum: Robyn. My secret hope: Dad and her would get back together. My poor sick brain: creating this wish-fulfilment fantasy. But knowing it wasn't real didn't stop my skull from echoing with Stephanie's scorn and Dad's fury.

Her: *I-knew-it-You-still-love-that-druggy-psycho!*

Him: *How-long-you-been-slutting-behind-my-back?*

Her: *Now-I-know-why-you-don't-talk-to-me-or . . .*

Him: *Is-he-better-in-bed-is-that-why?*

'Well, you've never—' Stephanie shouted. *Satisfied-me-like-he—*

Dad launched himself at her. They hurtled across the floor. Tumbled into the French doors in a crunch of splintering wood and shattering glass. The Christmas tree slumped against a wall, baubles breaking, lights flickering. Whatever was wrong with me had gotten so much worse. Auditory delusions had become visual hallucinations.

Dad was on top of Stephanie. Maybe in reality he was tickling her as payback for the Soxies. Maybe they were laughing instead of screaming. It's not what I was seeing and hearing. He looked like he was killing her.

13

'Stop!' I yelled at them and myself. 'Stop!'

Stop!-Stop!-Stop!

They didn't hear me. They didn't stop.

Dad throttled. Stephanie scratched.

I-gave-you-everything-You-cheated-you-cheap—

Get-off-This-is-assault-You're-hurting-Can't-breathe.

Her face turned purple as he clamped his hands tighter around her throat.

Evan was crying or laughing, I couldn't tell which. Either way, I had to make this stop. Without thinking, I snatched a golf club from the floor.

'Dad, stop!'

He shuddered as he pressed his weight down.

I-hope-it-hurts-you . . .

Stephanie's bloodshot eyes bulged over his shoulder. *Please-Danby-hit-him-hit—*

Dad turned his head just as I swung the putter and cracked him hard across the temple.

TWO

With just a dozen shopping days till Christmas, we worker bees were abuzz with activity in The Grocery. Slicing ham in the deli. Spritzing fruit for that dewy look. Gift-wrapping cosmetics. Ensuring the imported towels were properly fluffed. Manning and traffic directing the checkout. Not that I was complaining. Working at The Grocery was my ticket to freedom and added two hundred dollars to my name each week that had nothing to do with Dad or Stephanie. Other GenZees might be stuck in the nest until they were thirty but I'd be flying the coop as soon I finished school. Destination? As & Es, baby. Asia. Americas. Africa. Europe. Everywhere Else.

Work was more fun than it had any right to be because Jacinta had started there the same time as me. Faced with oh-so-serious supervisors and even more self-important customers, my best friend and I amused ourselves with a furtive semaphore of rolled eyes, cheesy grins and spirit fingers. We made it our mission to make fun of The Grocery.

y theory was that its name had been contrived so the by clientele could sound down to earth when they said, 'I'm just popping out to The Grocery for a few things.' But the place was far from humble. This consumer temple had fake marble columns and banners along the colonnade that celebrated the excess of success. Big lips smooched a strawberry, a Champagne cork rocketed from bubbly froth and silver platters glistened with sashimi and caviar. Jacinta and I joked that The Grocery would sell panda prosciutto and whale wagyu if it was legal—and that Beautopian gourmands would gobble up the endangered delicacies just because they were so deliciously expensive.

Those seduced through The Grocery's sliding doors entered a cornucopia where they weren't 'customers' but 'clients' to be waited upon by the finest teenage 'consultants' that minimum wages could buy. Soft downlights, polished floorboards, scented candles and a classical violinist in the liquor enclave convinced them they'd rewarded themselves with a shopping destination superior to the plebian tap-app-scan-it-yourselfmarts. Beautopians bought it—literally. Coiffed women and their moisturised men purred up in European hybrids and wafted through the store sipping complimentary coffees as they hunted and gathered organic strawnanas and wild-farmed salmon.

But on a mid-December Saturday afternoon The Grocery's usual tranquillity was disturbed by a young couple arguing a few feet from where I was arranging cans of Canine Cuisine.

'What do you mean I'll get fat?' Blonde gym bunny. Tight abs on crop-top display. Pretty face twisted into an ugly snarl. 'You bastard!'

'I didn't say anything!' Sleepy dude. Board shorts. Barely looked awake.

'I heard you!'

'I didn't say a word.' The guy looked guilty as charged. 'Seriously, Patty, I didn't.'

'You're such an asshole!'

'Sssh! You're only two months along. You look great.'

She wasn't having any of it. 'I'm going to my mum's. You can go to hell.'

Ponytail swinging, she stalked off, leaving the dude stroking a box of Celebrity Cat. He hadn't said she was fat. He hadn't said anything. Crazy pregnant-lady hormones: that was my guess. But then two similar spats erupted in the next three hours.

At the end of my shift, Jacinta was already in the staff room. Plonked in a beanbag with her head twitching behind Shades she could've been mistaken for a teen rock star in the throes of an overdose. But her rhythmic tics said she was playing *Snots 'N' Bots*, her head and eye movements and alpha and beta waves harnessed to fire gooey boogers at the robot army marching across the inside of her lenses.

'Jax.'

'Yo.'

'The weirdest thing's been happening.'

I told her about the freaks who'd been squabbling about nothing.

Wet sneezes from my friend's Shades announced that her Nasal Base was wiped. Game over.

'Clear.' Jacinta's lenses went from tinted to translucent. She was looking at me now—albeit through an overlap of app info. 'Are we outta here or what?'

We walked across Beautopia Point towards TYZ.

'Well, it's weird, right?' I said.

Jacinta couldn't have been less amazed. 'People argue.'

'I was there. I didn't hear any insults.'

'So you're half deaf from all your mum's punk crap.'

I gave her the finger. 'It was spooky.'

She smirked and shook her head. 'So you've taken too many knocks. Brain-damaged kids imagine the darnedest things.'

Looking at her dead-eyed, I adopted a drone voice. 'You. Are. Correct.'

With a stiff cyborg hand, I showcased our suburb's luxury residences blazing orange in the setting sun. 'No one. Argues. In. Beautopia.'

Jacinta nodded sombrely. 'To. Do. So.' She genuflected at the fake colonial church steeple that rose over the Commons. 'Angers. The. Mighty. Phallus.'

Our artificial paradise was good for a ton of laughs.

Beautopia Point was for squibs but TYZ helped make it bearable. Thankfully the place's signage was overgrown by vines so we could ignore that our favourite hangout's naff official name was The Youth Zone. You know, for tha kidz.

Jacinta got us drinks while I put on my pads and helmet. Up on the half-pipe I popped in my earbuds and pressed play on the vintage Walkman that Mum had given me so I could appreciate the mix-tapes she loved making for my benefit. Lee Ving wailed about having a war as I dropped down the transition, crouched across the bottom, pumped up the opposing arc, caught enough air for a three-sixty and then dropped back in. I wasn't an innately talented skater but I'd gotten good because I'd give things a go and I bounced back from falls pretty fast.

Jacinta sat in the bleachers, head in social media. I joined her, gulping electrolytes.

'They might've been spamming a product,' she said, taking off her Shades.

I didn't get her drift. 'A sphincter says what?'

Jacinta grinned. 'You are. I'm talking about the couples who were arguing? They might've been spamming. SPonsored Argument Marketing. They get your attention by having a fight while they're standing near some product, or they mention it in passing. We absorb it subliminally. Pass it on. Next thing we know it's viral.'

'Are you for real?'

Jacinta nodded proudly. Marketing was how she was going to make her millions.

'It's not working very well,' I said. 'I didn't brand-drop when I told you. But I guess that first guy *was* kinda fondling Celebrity Cat.'

'There you go,' Jacinta said. 'You're welcome.'

Her Shades chirruped.

'But the others didn't—' I began.

'Check this out!'

Jacinta's lenses had the news: Mollie was throwing a VIP Christmas party.

'We are so going,' Jacinta said.

My heart was hitting speeds it never did skating. 'Do you think he'll be there?'

· • ·

Finn's movements were still the subject of conversation when we reached the gate to Goldrise.

'Dan, you're going,' Jacinta said. 'It's time to put yourself out there.'

I rolled my shoulders. 'It'd help if we were invited.'

'Don't worry about that. We're cool. Leave it to me.'

I laughed and offered her my fist. 'TBC?'

'TBC,' she agreed, giving me a bump.

Jacinta went into her apartment building. Chomping a piece of gum into submission, I skated down the hill towards my house. I passed beige towers and townhouses that rose behind precision hedges. The brass nameplates on the estates' serious fences always made me smile. Skybrook, Cloudvale, Sunshower: they sounded like retirement homes for gay hobbits.

I veered into Reflection Road. Stage Three's cranes filled the sky with concrete that cast more of Beautopia Point into shadow. Carving across the First Street walkway I passed an ornate red-brick building. A century ago this was company headquarters where dockside workers collected their meagre earnings for offloading coal and contracting black lung. Now it was the sales office where paper pushers pledged and borrowed millions to buy a piece of the city's most ambitious waterside development. Billboards showed sunny scenes of Blue

Ribbon Bliss™. A young mother bounced her baby in a crystal swimming pool. Families laughed in unison while enjoying a seafood picnic. Professional dads bonded as they rowed along the river. Fit seniors walked the water's edge.

I popped ollies along that promontory path and the foundation stones of the Beautopia Point dream came into view. This eastern shore was where the first dozen houses were built on rehabilitated wasteland. As the population had swollen Stephanie had insisted on calling us and our immediate neighbours 'The First Families' as though we'd landed with the *Mayflower* rather than just bought the development's first McMansions.

The layout, luxury and land size of our houses were almost identical. What provided the all-important status stratification was the quality of views. Only the three places nearest to the tip of Beautopia Point stared straight up the river at the city skyline. In recognition of such prestige, each was crowned with a widow's walk, though the little cupolas had been rebranded 'Captain's Nests' by some manly marketing genius. Not that Dad ever ventured up to his roost, which Stephanie had claimed as her own. Though it was barely big enough to swing a cat, she delighted in doing the downward dog up there each morning. She claimed she was saluting the sun but I'm pretty sure she was telling high-rise arrivistes to kiss her toned ass.

We, the Armstrong Family 2.0, lived at number three. Stephanie's cat, Upton, glared as I stepped over him on the path. Upstairs and downstairs, every light blazed. Infuriating but inevitable. For a long time I thought Dad and Stephanie were just forgetful. That was before I realised not caring about power bills or carbon in the atmosphere was a subliminal status symbol. Like being fat in pre-revolutionary France.

I slipped inside, turning off lights as I went. Dad wouldn't be home that night. He'd been away doing a corporate geotagging marathon. Or maybe it was a water archery adventure. He was always embracing some new sports fad and buying all the accompanying gear.

By now Evan would be tucked in bed. Stephanie had claimed the lounge room, curled up on the couch, purring into her phone. She didn't look up as I crept past to the kitchen. After making a sandwich, I retreated upstairs to sprawl on my bed underneath a painting Mum had done of me. Exaggerated black hair and saucer eyes. It wasn't a realistic portrait. More like a manga cartoon. I loved it anyway.

Facial recognition logged me into my screens so I was ready to chat, message, update, comment and stream. But first I wanted another *tiny* snoop of Finn's social self. We weren't friends but he was on everything and his privacy settings were just lax enough for me to keep tabs. Relationship status: still single, most excellently. Photo wall: new taco shot, uploaded at lunchtime. Interests: updated to include R.E.M. and 'general anarchy'. Mum had played me that band a couple of times and she'd been in my ear about countercultural stuff more often than I could remember. If and when Finn and I met at Mollie's party, I'd be sure to casually reference listening to *Document* on vinyl and try to remember Mum's theory that Resist had really only been a corporate-funded Occupy.

I was about to message Jacinta when my windows went wild with the news. Videos of a girl our age reciting her depressive poems had found their way onto a comedy aggregator and racked up millions of views in the past hour. Mashups already had her tortured verse autotuned and sung by zombie kittens. Exposure trolls had unleashed a torrent of her personal information. She'd slit her throat in front of her webcam a few minutes ago.

Sadness and shock were duly expressed. Then the 'conversation' really got going. She should've enjoyed the fame rather than feeling shame. She might've been happier if she lost weight. She clearly suffered from underlying depression. She died because the health establishment prescribed medication rather than meditation. She was damned because she didn't accept Jesus. She was an oxygen thief who did the world a favour. Geeks made mirror sites to ensure the death footage stayed online forever and comedians made cruel jokes and mockingly sought absolution by asking 'Too soon?' Sharing in her tragedy was a chance to be serious or controversial or religious or cynical or funny or techie or whatever.

I couldn't finish my sandwich. I felt sad for her and sick for us. The online world would mourn for a moment, make it all about our opinions and emotions and then move on like it had never mattered in the first place. I didn't want to be part of it again. So I used the off button on all my screens.

Connectivity cold turkey wasn't a completely alien concept for me. Mum's place in Shadow Valley was a black spot no matter what anyone said about total coverage and whenever I visited her I was obliged to do a few days without access. But this was different. This was voluntary. The phone, the tablet, the computer: they were all right there and a click or touch or word away from channelling the universe. Seconds, minutes, hours: it was tough. To stave off temptation I dipped into Dad's old book-form dictionary. Opening random pages and reading bite-sized definitions: it was a bit like web surfing.

Next morning Jacinta resorted to calling the landline I'd forgotten we had. Me dropping off our networks had worried her. *#suicidalsolidarity* had apparently trended overnight. I told her I was fine. Said that I'd dropped my phone in the bath and that our wi-fi was being buggy. I didn't want to hear that I'd overreacted to the girl's death—or that it was *me* personalising a distant tragedy. But being offline overnight left me feeling strangely liberated. A bit like Mum living proudly 'out of the loop'. So for shits and giggles I decided to see if I could last one week without logging back on.

•●•

That night Dad, Evan and I went to Rubber Thaime, Beautopia's slow-food–Asian-fusion experience. Stephanie didn't join us because she was catching up with an old schoolfriend who'd arrived in the city unexpectedly.

'What's everyone eating?' Dad asked, eyes on his phone as it whooshed like a missile. Either he'd just sent a message or he was piloting an American drone bombing Iran.

'Fririce!' Evan squealed, chewing on his napkin.

Dad disappeared behind his menu. 'Plate o' shrimp and a Miller for me. Danby?'

I told him green chicken curry.

'Sounds good. Beers for you guys, too?' It was a joke he'd been using since I can remember. He'd get a brew and we'd get lemonades. 'Where's that waiter?'

Silence filled the space between us.

'So,' Dad said, 'where's your phone?' He looked around the table as though it must be somewhere. My first no-screen day had been tough. I'd skated harder and longer, read an entire novel from start to finish. Now it was about to get tougher.

'At home,' I said. 'I'm trying to be less . . . connected.'

'Why?'

Dad wasn't being sarcastic. He genuinely had no idea.

After Dad and Mum split for the last time, Brendan adopted the idea that kids should be screened and not heard. My bedroom gradually came to resemble a NASA control room. At five I had a TV wider than I was tall. I got all the Disney princesses on DVD and then Blu-Ray and then 3-D UHD. Dad regularly upgraded my consoles and cameras and phones and tablets. I never needed a night-light. Going to sleep in my room was to drift off in a galaxy of stand-by stars.

Dad bought me things to buy himself time. Every hour that I was immersed in a screen was an hour he could use to brainstorm his business plans. But technology couldn't contain me all the time. After school and during term breaks, he relied on babysitters. When I was nine I woke up and found the latest one hadn't left, but was all made up and making him breakfast. A few days later Dad casually announced that this 'Stephanie' would be a live-in nanny. A few weeks later they told me they were getting married. A few months after that the newsflash was I'd be getting a new brother and we'd all be living in a big new house.

I hated Stephanie for all the usual reasons—she'd put the King under her spell, she'd shut the door on the Queen's return, she'd given him a Prince he loved more than me. If Dad had wanted me to give my stepmother a better chance, he shouldn't have deferred so much of my childhood to Disney.

Dad blinked at me across the restaurant table.

'So ... the last few days of the school year,' he ventured cautiously, a man feeling his way into a dark room. 'How's that all going?'

'Good.'

His eyes dipped to his phone. 'Have you got any grades back yet?'

'Well,' I said, 'I did get an A-plus in Aristotelian astronomy.'

I wasn't just being a smart ass. I was daring him to show he was listening.

Dad's phone burbled. He tapped away. Evan randomly clicked his Rubik's Cube.

I wished I had my phone. Then we could iGnore each other in peace. When Dad had returned email fire, I launched my next-best defence.

'How's work going?'

Show the tiniest interest in what Dad did and he'd talk for hours.

'Oh, right, good,' he said. 'Well, things will be great after the upcoming trip. I'm getting a lot of interest over there ...'

Dad's business was in the toilet. A sales joke I'd heard once if I'd heard it a million times. But now his company, Captive Audience, was embracing a new frontier by making sure people could safely stay digital when they sat down to take a dump.

After he started life as a single father, Dad faced up to the fact that his writing career was going nowhere and so he quit the bookstore to join an ad agency owned by an old schoolmate. Brendan quickly discovered his true talent didn't lie in the deep and meaningful, but in the short and superficial. He made more money in a month from writing catchphrases than he did in a year by selling books—and more than he would have in a lifetime spent writing them. He refined the art of the blurb and taught himself graphic design at night. After a year, he left to launch Captive Audience.

While Dad prided himself on 'thinking outside the cubicle', he had recently lost ground where it counted most. People were ignoring stall ads because so few had a problem using their phones and tablets in public toilets. So Dad gave them a problem. He commissioned studies whose results were a germophobe's nightmare and issued press releases that became news stories that bred public-health paranoia. Now he was ready to launch his solution. Enter a stall and Screen Door would sync with your device so you could sit and airswipe and airtype to your heart's content while absorbing banner ads and offers. Tagline: 'Enjoy everything E but the coli'.

'... think it's already been eclipsed by Shades and other glasses,' Dad was spieling. 'But older people won't abandon their handhelds. They'll use our system intuitively. It's about making the restroom part of the revenue stream and recreation experience. Resorts, cruise ships. Casinos, especially. Why stop playing poker just because you have to go! I'm pitching them with "Give Everyone A Royal Flush".'

I giggled. I'd always been partial to his dad jokes.

'Okay, let's order.'

The waiter had arrived balancing three plates.

'Hang on, I think you're at the wrong table.'

Our server frowned. 'Sorry, you're not plate o' shrimp? For madam, green chicken curry? Young man, fried rice. Drinks are coming too.'

Dad looked at me, eyebrows raised. 'Did I miss something?'

If he had I had. 'It must be another table with the same order?'

'No, madam,' the waiter said. 'You are table seventeen. Your order.'

We were table seventeen. But we hadn't ordered.

The waiter waited.

'Okay,' Dad said, shrugging at me. 'Well, what are we going to do? Send it away and reorder the same thing anyway?'

As we ate, we tried to work out what had happened. Did we order and forget? Did the waiter overhear us from a nearby table? Did some acoustic trick deliver our conversation to him inside? Did we have the same thing last time we were here? We couldn't answer those questions any more than Evan could make his Rubik's Cube show six solid sides of different colours. But it was fun trying.

I might've pondered the mystery longer if I hadn't been so blown away by what Dad said when we got home.

'Danby.' He looked at me sternly. 'We've got to look into a new school for you.'

'What? Why?'

'Aristotle said the sun revolved around the earth. An A-plus is great but they really shouldn't be teaching that stuff these days.' He grinned and kissed me on the cheek. 'Goodnight, smartypants.'

Dad went into the study to make a phone call. I stayed in the lounge room with a big smile on my face.

I had to speak to Mum. Not about anything in particular. But it was like talking to her would make this night about the three of us. Give me the same feeling I had whenever I thought about my most enduring image of them as a couple. Robyn in paint-flecked overalls, Brendan with ink-stained fingers, both drinking beer from bottles as they explained how they'd made my name from their own because we'd always be together. What sucked is that I didn't know if that was a memory or something I'd imagined.

I reached into my pocket—then remembered my phone was off limits and up in my room. So I used our landline to call Mum's landline. Talk about old-school.

'Hello?'

'Hi, Mum, it's—'

'. . . you've called Robyn.'

That damned pause got me every time.

'I don't want to get to the phone just now. If you know the meaning of life, leave it as a short message. If you saw my awesome flyer and are interested in turning your trash into treasure, please leave your name and number and I'll call you back. Namaste, yo.'

The answering machine was an ancient tape thing. It clunked and beeped.

'Hi Mum,' I said. 'Just calling to say hello. You're obviously out rummaging for my Christmas present. I'll see you on the twenty-seventh. Love ya.'

I waited till I sensed the machine was about to disconnect the call.

'Oh, I've been meaning to tell you, the meaning of life is—'

Screeeeech.

THREE

I had to come clean with my friends about my social media absence on the bus on Monday morning.

'I've been thinking the word "screen" has two meanings,' I started. 'I looked it up—it can mean to show or to conceal. My theory is that our whole lives we're—'

Blah-blah-blah: that's what they heard.

Jacinta said that with Finn on the horizon I'd picked the wrong week to give up social media. Emma couldn't believe I'd actually brought pens and notebooks to school. Madison sniffed that I was being quite rude. It was so unheard of they couldn't help spread the word. I gave up on trying to explain seriously. My friends rolled their eyes as I gave a different reason to each kid who asked me WTF. I told Marnie *Vogue* had called Disconnect Chic the New Black. Said to John that I was preparing for my new life in an Amish community. Claimed to Cybele that scientists had proved offline people produced more pheromones. Each of them looked at me funny and went off to make fun of me.

When the din had died down my friends went back to status updating, voting on *Instant Celebrity*, and watching *Amazing Coinkydinks*. Without a screen, my attention was free to drift to two little kids playing a game a few seats away.

'I spy with my—' the girl said singsong.

'Ambulance!' the boy blurted.

She laughed and nodded.

'Okay, my turn!'

He looked out the window at the world whizzing by. 'I spy—'

'Jogger,' she said. 'Too easy.'

He screwed up his face. 'Hey! You have to wait a little bit.'

'You didn't. My turn.'

The answers kept coming—'Hospital!', 'Helicopter!', 'Playground!', 'Gutter!', 'Clown!'—before either got to the letter clue.

Then they burst out laughing and blinked at each other like they'd just woken from a shared dream.

'That was awesome,' he said.

'I spy—' she said.

He shook his head. 'It's gone.'

I wondered how they'd done the trick and who they hoped to impress. They had no audience other than me. Virtually every kid on the bus had their face in a screen. I couldn't see how they'd planned such a routine. Sure, some of the landmarks we passed every day, but half of the things they'd spied had been random.

My mystery train of thought derailed when Emma poked me in the ribs because she couldn't do it online.

'Know what I saw in my newsfeed this morning?' she asked.

'No.'

'Well, you wouldn't,' Madison chimed in. 'Miss Exile.'

'That's Miss *Self*-Exile,' I corrected. 'And it's only for a week.'

'Whatever, anyway, like, some maths nerd somewhere,' Emma continued, 'reckons in maybe a year or something, we'll hit this tipping point and everyone on social media will know everyone else.'

'Maybe not Dan,' guffawed Jacinta. 'By then she'll be living on a desert island. Talking into a conch shell.'

I chortled along at that one.

'But, like, everyone knowing everyone,' said Emma. 'isn't that awesome?'

'Totally noisome!' I said.

At least one of Dad's dictionary words had stuck.

The girls blinked at me.

'It's means "nice" and "awesome",' I said with a smirk.

I could be a real smart ass sometimes.

That was the day Troy Burke got busted for copying Jacinta's A-minus English essay. The question had been, 'What's revealed about *Nineteen Eighty-Four* by George Orwell's original title *The Last Man In Europe*?' Rumour was that Troy had protested that, yo, everything he wrote, like, totally came out of his own head. His cause wasn't helped by his admission that he hadn't read beyond chapter three. The doofus wasn't even smart enough to claim he'd seen *Big Bro*, the recent hip-hop movie adaptation about rhymin' freedom-fighta Win-S. What no one could explain was how Troy had replicated Jacinta's essay word for word when he was at a desk four rows in front of her. Then it was officially decreed: some ghost in the machine had merged his file with hers. Jacinta's grade would stand. Troy would get a generous C.

My conspiracy scenario was he'd paid someone to hack the school's systems and the powers-that-be knew but didn't want to: a) admit a security breach; b) embroil the school in a scandal; c) expel their best sportsman. If I was really smart I might have been theorising that his bizarre plagiarism was linked to the I Spy game and the Rubber Thaime waiter and the squabbling Grocery clients. But I didn't even see them as dots to connect.

•••

After our last day at school, I took every shift I could at The Grocery, adding another five hundred dollars to my escape fund. When Jacinta and I weren't working, we were giddily discussing Mollie's party.

To avoid curfews cramping our style on the big night, I told Dad I was staying at Jacinta's and she told her folks we'd be at my place. Oldest trick in the book. The plan was to meet at TYZ and get changed into our party clothes. But first I had to endure an early pizza dinner with my family. At least I didn't have to worry about being interrogated. We were together in bodies only. Dad used his least-greasy finger to navigate his tablet. Stephanie read a gossip site on hers. Evan was lost in *Snots* on the Shades that seemed to connect with his mind better than we could.

Me? I'd lasted six very long days without my screens but caved when I heard that Finn had friended me. Since then we'd been sharing a few snarky laughs. Tonight we'd be finally face to face. As I ate my seafood slice, I hoped he liked my last comment about *LOLZ2* being for 'Lame-O-Loser-Z-Squared'.

Newsblurb burbled on the lounge-room wall, its fast-talking anchor taming current affairs into sixty-second segments with the help of her guest experts.

What did the Mercury mission mean for astrology? Best-selling skywatcher Bella said we were on the cusp of a transformation! Could the humble sardine turn the tide on the great oceanic extinction and save you dollars at the dinner table? Eco-economist-turned-celebrity-chef Tenzing Gumbo had just the recipe! Was it true that Hollywood babies were being born with gray hair? Celebrity stylist Zeus had teased out the truth!

The 'mad media minutes' raced by in a blur until one got my full attention.

'They say that dogs come to resemble their owners,' the anchor babbled, 'but could people come to think like their devices?'

The screen split to show another talking head.

'Research shows that people are increasingly able to predict who's calling or messaging them,' he said. 'We got friends to call other friends from private numbers.'

A third pop-up screen showed folks staring into MobiFfone flexis and tablets and Shades.

'Up to four times out of ten,' he continued, 'those on the receiving end correctly predicted who was calling or texting!'

A stat-strap appeared: *40% predict phone peeps!*

'The evidence suggests our senses are evolving to understand the electronic impulses given off by our favourite devices. The implications for the future of thought-comms are staggering.'

The newsticker summarised: *Science: we sync with fave fones!*

Then the anchor was back with a report about a new service that let people 3-D print their perfect match. But I was still wondering about the last story. If there was anything to the experiment—apart from MobiFfone's marketing dollars—then wasn't it possible we were tuning into people instead of products? I almost always knew it was Jacinta messaging before I saw her ID.

My phone tinkled. Finn liked my LOL comment and left a 'LOL'. Nice irony—at least I hoped he meant it ironically.

Then Finn's first-ever private message popped up on my screen. 'Wot U drink? @ Store.'

What did I drink? Only the occasional glass of wine with Mum because it made her happy.

'Pinot noir?' I messaged Finn, hoping that didn't sound stupid.

His response arrived a second later.

'Classy!'

I was off to a good start because classy was the theme of the party.

Mollie had initially tried to keep her big bash hush hush and exclusively for the interlocking flower of cool kids at the centre of our school's Venn circles of cliques. But the secret had quickly reached the likes of Jacinta and me and then spread to even more distant points on the social circumference. The word was that Mollie had said we were all welcome if we followed the dress code and behaved ourselves. Guess she was trying to cultivate a supernice attitude to go with the supermodel looks.

··•··

Mollie lived in an old-money suburb and she greeted us at her front door wearing a dazzling evening dress and diamond choker. She held a champagne flute in one hand and a cigarette with holder in the other. Over Mollie's creamy shoulder I noticed her mansion was packed and Princess Hellbanga throbbed from the stereo system.

'You look amazing,' I shouted. 'Thanks for this.'

'Upstairs is VIP only,' she said, inspecting our outfits. 'As long as that's clear.'

We nodded.

Mollie stepped aside to let us enter before shining her radiance on the next arrivals.

'Can't she afford a door bitch?' Jacinta whispered as we walked into the grand foyer.

I laughed. 'Every peasant must bask in the splendour.'

'Wow,' Jacinta said, doing just that.

I agreed. 'Wow.'

Where Stephanie had made our house look like a virtual mall, Mollie's parents had turned their place into an art gallery. The walls were adorned with huge abstract paintings. Furniture and sculpture flowed one to the other. Even the rugs looked like masterpieces. More amazing was that everyone had followed

Mollie's style directive. Hoodies and T-shirts and jeans and baseball caps had been swapped for designer dresses and high heels and suits and shirts with collars and ties. None of us looked as awesome as our hostess but we'd all scrubbed up nicely. Especially Finn, who was on the other side of the gleaming kitchen, being all handsome in a charcoal suit as he drank beer with some of the sports guys.

'Let's grab a seat,' I said.

'Uh-uh,' Jacinta replied. 'Gotta mingle if you wanna tingle.'

'Oh shut up!'

I dragged her back into the lounge room and we perched ourselves on a pop art sofa.

'Drink, ladies?'

A guy in waiter's whites materialised with a tray of what were maybe martinis. Jacinta and I clinked glasses. Mine tasted awful but I liked the warm glow of it going down. Drink in hand, boobs pushed up in my black gown, hair piled in a bun: all at once I felt very grown up. This time next year I'd be finished school and close to official adulthood. Maybe Finn and I would be celebrating our first anniversary. Maybe there'd be great angst about whether he'd go to university or travel the world with *moi*.

'Anyway, he was *soooooo* hot,' Jacinta was saying about the mechanic who'd fixed her dad's hybrid. '*I-totally-got-busy-on-myself-thinking-about-him-that-night.*'

'What?' I sputtered, looking at my friend.

'What "what"?'

'You . . . jilled off about some random?'

Jacinta jerked her head back. 'No! What? What're you talking about?'

'But you said—' I said.

'No, I didn't say,' Jacinta snapped.

'I'm sorry,' I said.

'Oh, I get it,' she said, cheeks red. 'You're being all crazy like those idiots at The Grocery. Not biting, sorry.'

Jacinta looked past me. Mischief twinkled in her eyes.

Delicious, I heard her say. Jacinta's lips didn't move, like she was trying to tell me secretly.

'What's delicious?'

'Dan, give it a rest.'

Jacinta pecked me on the cheek. *Snap-him-up-or-I-will*. It sounded like a whisper.

'What did you say?'

'Good luck, weirdo.'

Smiling innocently, Jacinta launched herself into the crowd and left me alone on the couch.

'Does madam approve?' Finn had appeared at my side with a wine bottle.

Trying not to blush, I busied myself reading the label. Not that the wine words meant anything to me. What mattered was it gave me time to string together a reply. Or, at least, rip one off.

'I'd rather have a bottle in front of me than a frontal lobotomy,' I said.

Finn smiled uncertainly. I tried not to go redder.

I patted the cushion beside me. 'What took you so long?'

His thigh pressed against mine as he joined me on the couch.

'Your friend looked like she was in a hurry.'

'Family emergency.'

He hoisted one eyebrow.

'Her mum called. Cat caught fire again.'

Finn nodded grimly. 'I hate when that happens.'

Like a magic trick, he produced two glasses for me to hold as he poured the wine.

'Nice to be face to face,' he said.

'It is.'

We clinked. We sipped.

'Hmm,' he said. 'It has a very clean finish.'

I didn't know what that meant. We sipped again.

'Really great to finally meet you, Danby.'

'Yes, it is. I mean, to meet you.'

We slipped into silence. This was embarrassing. Declaring my love for R.E.M. or professing anarchist tendencies would only sound desperate.

'Heavy penguin,' I blurted.

Finn frowned at me. 'What?'

'Just needed to say something that'd break the ice.'

Clunk.

But then he laughed at my heirloom humour. 'That's a good one.'

Finn infodumped while I drank. He was going to start a band called Godnot. He already had the logo: a crucifix question mark. He was going to write and sing really relevant songs. He had professional recording equipment. He would release everything independently. He would do it all while he got his law degree. He'd be a courtroom crusader by day and a rock 'n' roll revolutionary by night.

'I can't help thinking outside the dominant paradigm,' he said, refilling my glass. 'I get the sense you're like that too?'

Paradigm: one of those slippery words whose definition I could never quite remember. But it was cool that we were outside of whatever it was together.

'How about you, Danby? What're you going to do at university?'

Suddenly my plan to skip it and travel to all of those As and Es seemed aimless rather than adventurous.

'Communications.' It's what I was still telling everyone. 'Eventually.'

'Eventually?'

I took a deep breath. 'I'm going to travel first. See as much as I can. Where I'd like to go is—'

'South-East Asia,' Finn said.

'Well, yes, it's on the list.'

'I'm so going there,' he said, nodding seriously. 'Vietnam, Laos, Cambodia. There's just so much culture.'

I lowered my eyes and nodded and sipped my wine, trying to look so very thoughtful about culture.

Bullshit!-Only-place-I'm-going-is-Bali!-I'm-so-gonna-rip-shit-up-Get-my-draaaank-on!-Tap-me-some-fine-ass!

I guffawed up from my glass. If Finn had to interrupt me I was glad he was at least funny.

'What?' he asked, deadpan.

'Spot-on impression of Troy.'

'Danby,' he said, frowning. 'Troy couldn't find Asia with a map.' *But-he-sure-knows-his-Thai-stick!-Should-find-somewhere-to-blaze-up-before-I-tap-this-ass-Danby's-so-into-me-Chalk-up-another-V-card-for-the-F-Man!*

In a flash I knew Finn scored weed from Troy, that his radical rocker speech usually got him laid, that his ideal law job was corporate counsel pulling down seven figures.

But Finn had been quaffing wine as he said all that. Was he using *ventriloquism* to screw with me?

'Uggh,' I said, jumping up from the couch. 'Really?'

'What? What's the matter?'

'Leave me alone!'

Damn-she's-weird-like-they-said.

I swayed into the crowd as the room spun around me. Everyone looked like bad actors in a poorly dubbed movie. Their expressions didn't match their emotions and their lips didn't sync with what they were saying. But they were all so loud. The VIPs upstairs must have been shouting for me to hear them so clearly.

God-he-looks-hot-Can't-she's-my-best-friend-How'd-Hannah-lose-that-weight?-Bulimic-bitch-Man-look-at-her-She's-already-drunk-Yeah-chop-me-a-line-Marnie-would-kill-me-Can-Mark-tell-I-had-an-abortion?-Ah-that-hurts-Should-be-able-to-get-precursor-chemicals-from-Would-Mr-Rowland-do-it-with-me-now-school's-over?

Then I saw myself. Pale amid the party people. This wasn't outside the paradigm. This was outside my body. Wasn't that what happened when you were about to die? My heart thumped faster in my chest. Jacinta pushed through the crowd. I was seeing me through her—and her through me—and back again.

'Danby, are you okay?'

Suddenly I wasn't okay. I was absolutely fantastic. From Mollie to me: every cell and nerve and atom jumped up and down with the euphoria of existence.

Man-that-coke's-the-shit!

'Did you take something?' Jacinta asked.

She knew I didn't do drugs. Not after what happened with Mum.

'No,' I said, grinning and grinding my teeth.

'You look wired.' Jacinta handed me her drink. 'Calm down.' I took a mouthful of wine.

'Rachel had an *abortion* in August,' I whispered, wiping my mouth with my wrist. 'She's in the upstairs bathroom having sex with *Mark.*'

'Sssssshhhh!' Jacinta grabbed my shoulder.

I shrugged her off, slugged back more wine.

Someone's-spiked-her.

'What did she say?' shrieked Marnie, appearing from the throng. 'Mark?'

She rushed up the stairs, screaming her boyfriend's name.

All eyes and ears were on me. Someone had killed the music.

'What?' I said.

John, the leader of the geek clique, laughed snidely. 'You're wasted, Danby.'

43

'You should know,' I shot back. 'You're the one cooking meth over the holidays!'

I meant it to sound light-hearted. It didn't.

'You're drunk,' John snapped. 'Go home.' I heard his voice continue though his mouth was clamped in an angry line. *Who-told-her?-No-one-knows!*

'Let's go, Dan,' Jacinta said, trying to drag me away.

'No, stay!' said Paula, taking a break from sucking face with her rowing champ hook-up Jake. 'What else you got, Danby?'

It wasn't like what I knew were really secrets. They'd all been shouting about this stuff just seconds ago. My mouth seemed to motor by itself.

'Well, Paula,' I said, 'Jake-y Jake-y wants to play hide-the-snakey with Mr Rowland.'

A shockwave went through the crowd. Paula and Jake jolted apart as if they'd been electrocuted.

She's-lying!

Is-that-why-he-won't-have-sex-with-me?

The lounge room erupted in hoots of laughter and upstairs there was a tumult of shouting. Over all the noise I heard Finn like he was whispering in my ear.

Man-did-I-dodge-a-bullet-there.

I spun around. He was smiling and shaking his head with the sports guys who'd gathered for the show.

'Did you just dodge a bullet?' I yelled. 'Didn't you want to tap my ass, F-man?'

Finn looked around the room. *Mum's-crazy-too-That's-what-I-heard.* 'Someone call her father.'

I burst into tears. I couldn't understand what was happening. Was this some horrible prank? Was I about to be doused with a bucket of pig's blood?

Feet stomped down the stairs. *She's-lost-the-plot!-We've-got-your-back-Stupid-bitch-ruining-my-buzz-Thanks-I-get-for-inviting-plebs-they . . .*

The posse steamed into the room. Mollie first. Then Rachel, dishevelled and crying, backed up by big boyfriends, brute faces in fight mode.

'Get out!' Mollie pointed at me. 'Someone get this drunk bitch out of my house!'

My house: in a flash I knew that's how she'd come to think of it. Her parents had all but moved out. Her mother: in rehab with an eating disorder. Her father: cohabiting with his secretary. I knew how Mollie felt. Cocaine couldn't stave off that sadness.

'I'm sorry,' I said, meaning it, suddenly feeling very sick. 'I'm sorry about your mum and dad.'

You-bitch-you-f—

'You bitch!'

Mollie screamed as she shoved me hard. I went backwards over outstretched legs and then everything went black.

FOUR

When my lights came on, I was in a hospital gown.

'Hey,' Dad said from beside my bed. 'Welcome back.'

'What happened?' I asked.

'Don't you remember?'

I wished I didn't. But it was all there. I'd gone mental in front of everyone who mattered. I would never live it down.

'I'm sorry.'

Dad smiled the best he could.

'They call it the silly season for a reason,' he said. 'The good news is you're not concussed and you didn't break anything.'

He sank into his chair with a sigh that said the bad news was coming.

'Have you told Mum?'

Dad shook his head. 'I thought you'd want to do that.'

I nodded. 'What time is it?'

'Just after ten.'

Not even an hour since my freak-out. Now there were no

voices and no out-of-body trips. Whatever I'd been dosed with had worn off.

'Dad,' I said. 'I don't do drugs. I think I was spiked.'

Finn: it had to be. He had the wine and the glasses. I noticed there was a Band-Aid on my arm where they'd taken blood.

'That's what Jacinta said when she called me,' Dad said.

God, Jacinta would tease me about this until the sky fell.

'But they've done tests and there aren't any drugs in your system.'

It didn't make sense. Could I have had an adverse reaction to alcohol? I had to be totally honest. They would've told Dad anyway.

'I had a lot to drink.'

'Actually,' he said. 'Your blood alcohol wasn't very high at all.'

Dad's glum smile made my heart sink. Mum's problems had begun in a hospital bed like this. Nursing me for the first time she learned the news that the world had watched live while she'd been in labour. As her baby was being born thousands of people were dying in horrific circumstances that'd reshape the world. Mum couldn't shake the sense that the timing was significant and she'd sob until she was sedated. Dad reckoned the doctors created a pattern—depression alleviated by drugs—that took her years to break. Now he wore the same weary expression he'd had on the day he told me Mum was going away for good so she could get better. I didn't need to be telepathically deluded to know he was looking at me but seeing her.

'Danby,' he said. 'There's someone who'd like a word if you're up to it.'

I nodded.

•●•

'I'm Doctor Jenny Sales and I'm a psychiatrist.' The headshrinker looked like a tuck-shop mum and I liked her upfront manner. 'And you, Danby, are a special case.'

'Is that what you call it?'

'I'm not talking about what happened tonight,' she said, waving off what I'd done like it was no worse than farting at a formal gathering. 'Check this out.'

Jenny clicked a remote and a flat screen showed a body scan.

'This is you,' she said. 'We had to make sure you didn't have any internal injuries. Anyway, you're all fine. But do you notice anything?'

Only that the rainbow imaging made me look like a human piñata filled with jelly beans.

'See here,' Jenny said. 'Your heart's on the right side. Which is to say it's on the wrong side.'

I clutched at my chest. Left, right: I couldn't feel any heartbeat.

'Don't worry!' Jenny said. 'It's always been like that. But it can be hard to detect. It often doesn't show up until a test like this.'

'Am I sick?'

She shook her head. 'It's called *Situs inversus*. All the organs in your torso are on the opposite side to where they usually are. But they all work just perfectly. One in ten thousand people have it. Like I said, you're special.'

Special? I didn't feel special. I hadn't only been born under a bad sign—I'd been born goddamned back to front.

'Is this—thing—is it why I lost it?'

Jenny shook her head. 'No, it's just cool and I thought you'd like to see it.'

I looked at her, dumbfounded.

'Sorry!' She blushed and turned off the screen. 'I've always had terrible timing.'

I smiled. 'It's okay.'

'Your dad said you're real smart,' she said. 'So maybe there is a point to this, yeah? What I mean is sometimes you can be put together a bit differently but still be perfectly normal. Does that make sense?'

I nodded like it did.

Jenny took a seat. 'I don't want to keep you here all night,' she said. 'Tell me what happened at the party and then you can go home.'

It sounded like the best deal I'd get.

So I told her everything.

I finished by saying that Mollie had every right to push me.

'No, she didn't,' Jenny said. 'But that's it?'

I nodded.

'Has anything like this ever happened before?

'No.'

'Are you hearing voices now?'

'Just ours,' I said. 'So, what's wrong with me?'

'How the hell should I know?' Jenny grinned up from her notes. 'Adolescence is an anxious time. You were stressed about that guy. You've just done exams. You're not sure about the future—sex, peers, parents, jobs, travel, university, all of that stuff. It might've just been your subconscious letting off some steam.'

'But possibly not?'

'We have to follow up.'

'Because of my mum?'

Jenny nodded. 'That is one factor. But let's not jump to conclusions, okay?'

I nodded.

She crossed to the door. 'Brendan, you can come back in.'

Dad returned to the bedside.

'Danby and I have had a chat,' Jenny said. 'I'm referring her to Doctor Ryding. She's a specialist in young adult issues. I've put in a priority appointment request so you'll be able to see her in early January. For now I'm prescribing Lucidiphil. It's fast-acting and it should suppress any more episodes.'

Psychotic episodes.

Psychiatric appointments.

Prescription pills.

I was officially a head case.

FIVE

A head case looming over her father's unconscious body while her stepmother looked on in horror and her little brother whimpered. Lucidiphil hadn't kept my demons under lock and key. It was up to me to chain them back up.

'Oh my god,' I panted. 'Dad, I'm—Stephanie, are you—Are you okay?'

She spluttered amid the crushed Christmas presents, broken decorations and smashed glass.

Bastard-nearly-choked-me-to-death.

Stephanie's lips weren't moving. I saw a shimmer of myself through her eyes. My episode wasn't over yet. I didn't trust what I'd do next.

'Go upstairs, Evan!' I shouted.

Danby-hit-Daddy.

'Go, Evan! Go!'

He jolted. I never shouted at him. But it worked. As he bolted up the stairs, I imagined him thinking: *Cave-cave-cave.*

'Are you all right?' I asked Stephanie again.

Only when I spoke did I become clearer to her—as though I'd emerged from camouflage. Such a freaky delusion: myself through her eyes. Hair askew, eyes wild—and still brandishing the golf club.

Stay-away-from-me-with-that-you-little-bitch!

Shit. I let the weapon fall to the floorboards.

'I'm not going to hurt you,' I said. 'I've got to help Dad.'

I dropped to his side. She propped herself on her elbows.

Attempted-murder-that's-what-this—

'I didn't try to murder him!' I said, responding to my hallucination like a card-carrying crazy person.

Not-you— 'Not you, him,' Stephanie rasped. 'He's gonna pay. I'll—' *take-him-for-every-cent.*

The world turned inside out and took me with it. Unless I was in a rubber room and imagining this entire thing from start to finish, Stephanie was saying that Dad had just tried to strangle her. If that was true the rest of it was real.

I wasn't crazy. I was tuning into her. Like she'd heard Dad and he'd heard her.

But her and I being in each other's minds frightened me more than being out of my own.

Brendan-you-bastard-You're-going-to-jail.

Stephanie's shock was wearing off. She wasn't scared now, she was furious. She'd been scorned and she'd been assaulted. She looked at Dad's slumped form. Ugliness blasted from her in waves.

Limp-dick-loser-Attack-me-You-coward-Jail-that's-where-Hope-someone-beats-you . . .

'I'll, I'll—' I started. *Tell the police you attacked him*—

I wanted to take back my unspoken lie. But I didn't have to.

'You'll what?' Stephanie snarled.

She hadn't heard me.

Can you hear me?

Nothing. Thank God.

Stephanie didn't react to my relief. *Goddamn-you-Danby-you-better*—

She wasn't in my mind. How and why didn't matter right now.

'I'll—I'll help him,' I said. 'Help me.'

I felt sick at the red bump rising from his hairline. But I felt sicker at what was rising from Stephanie's head. *Help-him?-She's-kidding-For-all-I-care-he-can-go-and-f*—

'Maybe you killed him!'

Brendan-dead-Danbyn-jailed-Not-so-bad: she didn't feel too guilty thinking it.

I shot her a look.

'Just because you can't hear me,' I hissed, 'doesn't mean I can't hear you.'

Stephanie recoiled like I'd spat at her.

'Lalalalalalalala.' *Lalalalalalala*.

She sang it, thought it: hoping it'd keep me out.

I'd done First Aid at school. Remembered the mnemonic DRABCD.

D for danger. I'd neutralised that by knocking Dad out.

'Dad, Dad?'

I shook his shoulder. No R of Response.

His tongue and teeth were in place. Nothing obstructed the A of his Airway. Listening and watching his chest rise and fall confirmed the B of his Breathing. I moved him into the recovery position, thankful there would be no need for the C of CPR or the D of a Defibrillator jerry-rigged from Christmas lights.

'Dad, I'm sorry,' I said. 'Hang on I'm going to—'

Yes-operator-I-need-help . . .

'I'm phoning the police,' Stephanie yelled. 'You saw him try to kill me.'

She wanted her emergency call fresh and panicked when it was played in court.

Come-quick-my-husband's-gone-crazy-and . . .

'He needs an ambulance,' I yelled over her silent rehearsal.

I looked around for Dad's phone.

Gotcha: Stephanie thought as she beat me to it and snatched it from the floor.

'Police!' she screamed.

I lunged to grab the phone from her. Stephanie swerved away into Evan's scattered golf balls. Her silly heels shot out from under her. For a second my stepmother windmilled like a cartoon character as her emotions tumbled inside a black thought bubble. Afraid she wasn't pretty enough. Angry that Dad had pushed her away. Resentful I never gave her a chance. Hopeful Evan might someday be cured. Sure she had a lot more to do with her life.

Then Stephanie's body smacked hard onto the polished floor-boards and her head smashed harder onto the marble hearth.

'Steph—' I said.

But in that instant she ceased. I was in her mind and then her mind was gone. No bright light, no heavenly chorus: just gone. I scrambled to her side. My stepmother's eyes were open, fixed on the ceiling, and her lips were parted, as if she wanted to say something. Blood flowed from under her hair, bright against the marble, oily on the floorboards. I opened her mouth, breathed into her. I did compressions, counting them off loudly. Knew it was useless. Had to try. If I hadn't lunged she wouldn't have fallen.

Stephanie's fingers were curled around the phone. I gave her two more breaths and grabbed it. I punched the emergency number and put it on speaker by her shoulder. I continued compressions as the call went through.

'You've reached emergency services,' a calm recorded voice said. 'We are unable to answer at this time. Please try again or call your local police, ambulance or fire service directly.'

How was that possible? Weren't there enough operators willing to work Christmas?

I gave Stephanie two more breaths, grabbed the phone and hit redial, cradled it between my chin and shoulder as I kept doing compressions. This time I didn't get the recorded message. My call just terminated in a high-pitched squeal that sounded like the end of all things.

I let the phone fall away and I rocked back on my heels away from Stephanie. My air escaped her in a lifeless wheeze. Tears streamed down my cheeks. For a moment I was aware only of my trembling limbs and my own ragged breaths and my heartbeat in my temples. Then my mind went spiralling out around me, streaming from next door to the next street to the next suburb, sweeping in every thought from the screaming city.

Did-I-think-that?-Or-did-I-say-that-out-loud?-How-funny-Weird-like-a-dream-Man-what-a-strange-feeling-Can-you-hear-me?-This-is-what-it-feels-like-to-be-a-guy-Wow-so-strong-but-I-smell-different-You-can't-believe-this-Daddy-I'm-so-tall-What-do-mean-you've-just-had-a-few-drinks?-Wish-Sarah-would-come-to-Christmas-lunch-You-lied!-Santa's-not-real!-You're-Santa?-You're-the-Easter-Bunny?-Tooth-Fairy?-You-lied!-Calm-down-No-I-didn't-say-that-It's-not-what-I-meant-Robopony!-I-wanted-a-Robopony-Greedy-little-I-can-hear-what-she's-thinking-Who's-playing-Revolution-9?-Wow-this-is-cool-Do-I-really-look-like-that-to-him?-All-these-presents-how-will-I-pay?-Credit-card-God-just-stop-worrying-Can-she-hear-me?-Mea-culpa!-Help-me-somebody!-Yes-your-bum-looks-big-in-those!-You-feed-the-goddamned-cat-for-once!-Rather-be-watching-America-Is-Waiting-Hey-watch-what-you're-saying-Wow-it's-like-they're-my-boobs—你別管我-Can't-tell-him-it's-not-his-baby!-Bitch-can-pay-the-fare-in-trade-You-gross-pig!-I-can't-hear-myself-think-I-need-a-drink-and-cigarette-Dad's-gonna-kill-me!-Where's-all-the-noise-coming-from?-It's-like-Radio-waves-in-my-head-Esto-no-puede-estar-pasando-But-pictures-smells-feelings-too-これは悪夢です-Like-I'm-in-the-shower-with-Harry-No-as-Harry-Oh-I'm-touching-it-That-was-a-good-Christmas-before-I-No-I-didn't-I-never-did-Hey-shut-up-for-a-moment-No-son-of-mine's-gonna-be-a-fairy-I'm-not-talking-to-you-Leave-me-alone-Aš-užmušiu-jums-

kalé-Can't-tell-her-she's-I'm-adopted?-Where's-Danby?-
الـ-أستطيع-السمـع-نفسي-أعتقـدـIf-you-weren't-my-sister-
I-You've-got-Satan-in-you-Gotta-get-out-of-here-Screw-
you-all-Whatever-this-is-I-need-some-space-Down-to-the-
water-Must-be-a-dream-Some-hallucination-Gotta-block-
this-Shades-might-help-I-can't-believe-you-never-told-me-
Kjo-nuk-mund-të-ndodh-He-was-with-her-Knew-it!-Liar!-
No-don't-touch-me-Look-out-Shit-car's-gonna-flip-The-train's-
on-the-wrong-track-No-one-switching-Jump!-Jump!-Is-this-the-
end-of-the-Don't-say-that-Please-don't-think-that-Mustn't-let-
her-find-out-No-no-no-no . . .

Voices. Visions. Overlapping. Reverberating. For a second, people had a sense of wonder at tuning in the world as others experienced it. After that came their fear and panic when they realised they were laid bare to everyone. It was like a thousand channels screamed in all of their heads as their social statuses updated automatically and unfiltered from their darkest streams of consciousness. Language barriers offered little protection: thoughts and feelings behind foreign words needed no translation as they surged from head to head.

I pressed the heels of my hands into my eyes, plugged my ears with my thumbs. If I wasn't crazy then this was the world's worst nightmare.

'Wake up, Danby!' I screamed.

But I could barely hear myself over the noise getting louder and stronger.

I accidentally slipped into signals from the noise and entered spaces that should have been secret. Across the road

Ben was furious that Lisa was on the pill when they were supposed to be trying for a baby—and she was revolted that the file marked 'Scanned Tax Receipts' on his tablet held terabytes of porn. Next door to us another First Family was crumbling as details of Karen's drinking relapse, Doug's furtive gambling and their son Alex's homosexuality all poured out. In a house a few doors down Renee was shattered that Kenny really did think she was stupid and he was filthy that she'd been bored by him for years. Over on Second Street, elderly retirees Pete and Edie were going the other way as they realised beyond words that they really shared one soul and wordlessly exchanged regrets that they'd argued over nothing for decades. But like minds like theirs were the exception. Most people's desperation to suppress their secrets only blasted them louder. The elephants in every room had been set loose to stampede.

He ate greasy burgers despite last year's heart attack and hid his bonuses and sexted his secretary and pretended to believe in his wife's God and thought he deserved a bit of consideration and wished his boyfriend would lose some weight and gazed at his high school sweetheart's profile and had the divorce mapped out and knew those stocks had been toxic and she took his punches and pretended to deserve them and worked back to avoid the kids and felt bad still about cheating on her final-year exams and hated herself for hating her love handles and forgiving his and made faces at him under the burqa and really hated her girlfriend for backing out of IVF and left the baby in the bath alone while she was online dating and wished he'd have another heart attack.

I felt like I was swirling towards a whirlpool. Opening my eyes and ears again only made it more awful. Stephanie dead. Dad unconscious. My mind reeled away again.

This time I touched down somewhere familiar. Jacinta's bedroom. I wasn't just inside her teenage retreat. I was inside her terror and sorrow and anger and confusion as she sobbed convulsively with her back to her door.

Can't-be-happening-Not-adopted-A-bad-dream-I-hate-you . . .

Mr and Mrs Chang screamed at her and each other and themselves from other barricaded rooms.

Don't-be-stupid!-Wasn't-my-idea-to-hide-it-Your-father . . .

That's-a-lie!-You're-the-one-who . . .

'Jacinta,' I said. Jacinta.

She couldn't hear me, couldn't find me like I'd found her. It was as though I was in a cone of silence or on a different plane of existence.

Then Jacinta was gone as I ricocheted elsewhere. Alex knew Karen was thinking about a drink even as she mouthed words about loving him and they both hated Doug for promising God he'd give up gambling if He would cure his lush wife and ungay his son. Ben smashed windows as he stormed from the house ashamed and angry, but Lisa's mind was already suburbs away and brawling with her mother's self-pity at being denied a grandchild. Elsewhere, dark thoughts rapidly metastasised into darker actions. In horror, I witnessed Blago across the road punching demure Karina into unconsciousness just to get her out of his head.

You gutless bastard! I mentally screamed at Blago.

I was the one voice he *couldn't* hear. Not that it mattered with dozens or hundreds of others engulfing him in their hatred.

I tried to reach Karen and Doug and Ben and Lisa and Edie and Pete. No one could hear me and I couldn't hold anyone in my mind for more than a moment. But I shared their relief as a siren cut through the clutter. Although my emergency call had gone unanswered, the wailing getting louder and closer said my distress had been picked up anyway.

Any hope I had that first responders would rush in to save the day burned away when I locked onto the black mind behind the siren. Death grip on his steering wheel. Screaming through Beautopia Point's streets. Sound and signal so intense it sucked me and many others into his consciousness.

Those thoughts didn't compel me to run onto our front lawn and flag him down. But I also didn't want to believe what I was tuning from his mind. So I scrambled up the spiral staircase to our Captain's Nest to see with my own eyes.

Beneath me our enclave gleamed under a silken blue sky for one last second. Then the suburban still life shattered as the police cruiser screeched down First Street and skidded to a stop in front of number seven. The home of our neighbour: Harold.

Harry-you're-dead-You-mongrel-dog-Dead!

Constable Steve Daley had been a chilled kinda cop until he'd made a Christmas wake-up call to his wife. Without knowing what was happening he delved past her sleepy sweet nothings and slipped into the cellar of her memory.

'I'm gonna kill him,' Steve had thundered down the phone. *I'm-a-cop-I-should've-known!* 'Kill him.'

Sarah stopped murmuring. 'What?'

Then she knew that he knew. She shrieked and threw her phone against the bedroom wall. The call had ended—and there was a city between them—but that didn't stop Steve screaming and Sarah pleading.

He's-dead-baby-I'm-gonna-kill-him.

Don't-sweetheart-please-Don't-No-don't.

With that scene in mind—his, hers, mine, *ours*—Steve sprinted across his father-in-law's front lawn. Harold, Sarah's father, our neighbour in good standing, who'd often offered to babysit me and Evan, had locked himself in the upstairs bathroom, was watching helplessly as his world disintegrated and his death approached.

Moments ago Harold had been lathering himself in the shower when the water and steam seemed to evaporate. Somehow he was looking through his wife Martha's eyes as she marinated steaks for their lunch and daydreamed about how happy they'd been that Christmas in Rome when Sarah was five. Then Martha was mortified to see through Harry's eyes as he absently soaped himself. Worse, so much worse, was that in this sudden echo chamber she heard her husband telling himself he'd never done anything to make their daughter avoid Christmas with them. Then Harry knew Martha was sharing his mind—and that she knew the truth.

Martha's scream sent Harry spinning out of the shower. He saw his naked body in the mirror and knew he could never cover himself again. Martha sank to her knees and clawed at her eyes with chilli-smeared fingers.

Harry's heart pains started as Steve's hatred closed in. *Please-God-don't-Steve-I-was-sick-couldn't-help-it—*

He fell to the wet tiles, curled in a ball, clutched his chest.

Don't-die-before-I-kill-you.

Steve shouldered through the front door and stormed inside. He bounded up the stairs—and I saw it how he saw it, how it refracted from Harry and from Martha and from neighbours and strangers who were houses, blocks and suburbs away.

Drawing his service pistol, Steve paused outside the bathroom door.

Kill-him!-Kill-him!-Shoot-the-bastard!-What-he-did-was-unforgivable-Death's-too-good-If-it-was-my-daughter—

My stomach lurched at the communal consciousness cheering for cold-blooded murder. The mob baying for blood didn't even want to punish Harry or to avenge Sarah.

At-least-I'm-not . . . I-might-be-bad-but . . . There's-nothing-lower . . .

They thought persecuting and punishing the pederast could somehow minimise their own now-public transgressions.

Steve got flashes of support from brother officers spread across the city—

Do-it-mate-I-won't-arrest-you-Insanity-defence-You'll-get-off-Kill-the-f—

—even as he was appalled by their helpless mental confessions.

Not-like-the-money-belonged-to-any-Just-a-bit-of-recreational-use-Didn't-frame-him-not-really—

Then, above everything, Steve saw and heard and felt Sarah: clear and calm and strong. *I-love-you-I-need-you-Come-home-Please-don't—*

Steve didn't. He lurched away, banging off the walls, trying to get his head straight. *Sarah-I'm-coming-babe—*

Inches away, on the other side of the door, Harry thought he might live. Until he heard the violently outraged chorus of men and women screeching from near and far.

Drag-you-into-the-Rip-you-limb-from-Hang-you-up-by-your—

Then the screaming *really* started—screaming and scorching heavy metal. It was as if the blue sky was ripping open to let in the howling abyss of the universe. A massive airbus had materialised low over the river west of us. Surging from the dirty bloom of its jet engines, the plane was bearing down on Beautopia Point.

SIX

Captain Wahhaj Ahmad had been flying holiday-makers between Sydney and Bali for so long that he sometimes forgot why he'd been placed in the job. Days would go by without him checking the godsfist@freemail.com account for the only message it'd ever receive. That Christmas morning he *had* remembered—and found as usual he had no *jihadi* business. Getting ready for work he wondered for the millionth time if he was a puppet who didn't know his strings had been cut. His file could've been lost—a victim of drone bombings or simple clerical error—and he'd never be the wiser.

Wahhaj had once wanted it all—martyrdom, his father avenged, the virgins awaiting in Paradise—and had the patience to wait for his moment of glory. Back then other successful operations made him sure his turn would come soon. But months stacked into years. Those years piled into a decade and now it was nearly two. At this rate he'd be up for long-service leave. Not something a suicide pilot expected. But deep down Wahhaj gave thanks that God was not willing. He liked his life.

He liked drinking beer with his infidel colleagues. He liked the idea of changing his name to Wayne and settling down with a nice western girl.

Soon after this morning's take off Wahhaj suffered the mother of all communication meltdowns, his headset blasting what sounded like every air traffic controller in the world going totally mad.

'Can't you hear that?' he yelled to his first officer.

The young guy's lips didn't move but Wahhaj heard him above the craziness anyway. *Hear-what-old-man?*

That's when Wahhaj knew. This wasn't talk about vectors, turbulence, runways, coordinates.

Better-not-drink-too-much-Bikini-still-fits-nicely-She's-a-bit-of-all-right-Keep-cool-and-they-won't-find-it-Swim-up-bar-last-time-was-awesome . . .

These were passengers settling into the flight and anticipating hotel massages and sunset beaches and holiday hook-ups. 22E was pissed that the drinks service was taking so long. 15A was pretending he was in a spaceship. 34A had ecstasy pills hidden in his luggage. 34B thought 34A was cute and was wondering how she'd initiate conversation. The crew was going through the motions of the safety demo as they battled hangovers and thought about house deposits and planned New Year celebrations.

Wahhaj bounced uncontrollably between them. Then he wasn't alone in his mind anymore.

Hey-I'm-flying-the-rocket-ship, the kid in 15A thought as he saw the cockpit through the pilot's eyes.

22E: *How'd-I-get-in-the-cockpit?*

34A: *God-not-an-acid-flashback-not-now-please!*

In an instant they were inside the head Wahhaj had tried to turn into a fortress. They *knew*.

Suicide-pilot!-We-gotta-take-him-out!-Please-no!-Don't-want-to-die!

'What's going on?' the first officer said. *I've-got-to-take-him-out.*

Dude-I-would— 'never do anything,' Wahhaj said.

You-checked-that-email-this-morning. The younger man tried to get up. *Gotta-get-the-gun-from-the—*

Wahhaj's brutal elbow-crunch shattered his face and set him back in his seat unconscious. Everyone on board saw it and screamed.

Oh-my-God!-Please-God-no . . .

Wahhaj hit the emergency door-lock button. It'd stop them charging into the cockpit. But it couldn't block the stampede to judgement. All they saw was a suicide robot.

You-dirty-bastard-We-should've-nuked-We-gotta-take-him—

Anger burned in him. He'd prove them right.

God-is-Great! You-do-this-to-yourselves!

Wahhaj plugged his phone into the plane's audio system and toggled to his favourite track. Maybe if he played it loud enough it'd drown out the headbanging he was taking from all sides. AC/DC's 'Highway To Hell' blared through the cabin as he turned the airbus back to the silver harbour and shimmering skyline.

I knew all of that in the split-second it took me to drop, screaming, behind the Captain's Nest parapet. The plane roared so low overhead it shook me to my marrow and I feared the jet engines would suck me up and spray me out like wet confetti. Then the shadow and thunder receded. I staggered up, amazed to still be alive, and watched the plane race down the river, saw the city loom larger in the cockpit window. Wahhaj's intensity eclipsed all else for a few moments. Even through the AC/ DC, we all knew what he knew. Speed: six hundred kilometres an hour. Weight: half a million kilograms. Fuel: a quarter of a million litres. Result: the explosive force of a small nuclear weapon. Target: the Sydney Harbour Bridge.

'No, don't!' I yelled with the rest of the city. *No-don't!*

Wahhaj couldn't hear me. For a moment we couldn't hear him as he disappeared into the song he bellowed like a heavy metal mantra. The only noises were the pleas and prayers of the passengers and the people below watching from apartment windows, bobbing yachts and chaotic traffic. But in those few impenetrable seconds it seemed Wahhaj had a change of heart because the plane started a radically steep climb that'd see it soar high and safe over Sydney.

Relief rippled across the city and the faithful praised God.

God had nothing to do with what happened next.

Wahhaj silenced the hard-rock thunder so we could all share in his self-satisfied genius. He'd thought about his plan long and hard for years. Flying straight into the side of the bridge meant the fuselage, jet engines and burning fuel would explode through the lattice of cables and struts and spray into the eastern side of the harbor. That wasn't the way.

He pushed the controls forward. The airbus dropped into a death dive. Wings lined up with the bridge's eight-lane roadway. Nose centred on the apex of its steel arches. *Watch-this-bitches!* Wahhaj floated free in his seat, like the astronauts did in NASA's Vomit Comet, and saw this was going to be better than he'd dreamed. A truck driver had just jackknifed. Cars were jammed in both directions. Tiny people scrambled as the plane grew huge above them. There was only screaming: protesting jet engines, souls about to leave bodies.

God-is— But then Wahhaj was sitting in 15A.

This-is-a-rocket! The little boy's parents were scaredy cats. He knew the pilot didn't want to do anything bad. *This-is-awesome!*

Great-God-forgive— That's as far as Wahhaj thought before the plane exploded into the bridge in a white hot flash.

A shockwave pulsed. A tsunami washed across the harbour. People watching from windows screamed when flying glass shredded their eyes. An orange-and-black mushroom cloud unfurled over the city as the concussive punch raced up the river. I was knocked to the floor. The house shuddered beneath me. Everywhere alarms shrieked and were then lost in a roar so loud I thought my head would burst.

I screamed. I screamed for my mum.

My mind reached out to hers, a tendril stretching up and away from all of this, streaming west over the suburbs, cresting the Blue Mountains, soaring to the clouds then plunging over sandstone cliffs and surfing waves of eucalypts to arrive at her refuge in Shadow Valley. There she was, wandering between her Wollemi pines, the air tinged with reefer as she smiled and waved me down. But it was wishful thinking, a desperate conflation of how I'd seen her on my last visit and the magic-carpet ride

I'd taken to her place via Google Earth. I couldn't astral travel to Mum any more than I could see or hear her. I didn't know what that meant. Was she out of range? Had something happened to her? Or were her thoughts impenetrable like mine?

As the roaring subsided, it wasn't Mum I needed to worry about first.

'Dad?'

Dad's eyes blinked open and he instinctively rolled away from the terrible noise and straight into Stephanie's body and the pool of her blood. As he scrabbled away he remembered the blind hatred that had seized him as he attacked her. Then there was nothing. He figured he must have suffered a murderer's blackout.

Oh-my-God-I-killed-her.

Dad's head hurt. But it didn't just hurt. It seethed with voices.

Oh-my-God-He-killed-them-all.

The horizon was ablaze. It couldn't be a coincidence. He wasn't a forty-something marketing guy anymore. He was a biblical sinner whose blood crime had triggered the end of days. He could hear the heavenly host screaming its Last Judgement.

Killed-them-all-Bastard-Why-did-he—

'Dad!' I shouted. Dad!

He didn't hear my voice over the whirlwind of noise and he couldn't hear my thoughts. When I struggled to get up, my legs were like wet spaghetti.

Dad saw the police lights strobing against the lounge-room windows and heard the mob of angry minds clamouring in the street outside.

You-can't-escape-Pay-what-you-did-to-your-daughter-String-you-up . . .

Terrified, stunned, Dad thought the worst.

'Danby?' he cried. 'Evan?' *Danby? Evan?*

Without realising he was doing it, his mind searched for me and for Evan. I wasn't there. Evan was in darkness. Dad thought he was responsible. That he'd killed us in his fugue state.

'No!' I was on my feet, staggering to the stairs.

Dad had the wall-safe open. Unwrapping the .45 he'd bought during his brief dalliance with club pistol shooting. Kept because Stephanie feared home invasion.

I stumbled down the stairs. He'd have to hear me now.

'Don't, Dad, don't!'

But Steve was revving his cop car and blasting its sirens to scatter the mob. Dad didn't understand what was happening. He just wanted it to be over.

Pull-the-trigger! A troll voice surged out of the thoughts. *They'll-rip-you-to-pieces-You-gutless-bastard.*

So-sorry-Robyn-Steph-Evan-Danby.

Another millisecond and Dad might have processed that it was me tumbling off the landing, that the cop car was burning rubber away from our house, that the mob wanted to murder someone else. But he pulled the trigger. I experienced my father's exit from life before the gun's blast reached my ears, before the wisp of smoke escaped the scorched hole in his skull, before the abstraction of bone and blood sprayed onto the white wall behind him. Dad was there. Then he wasn't.

'No! No! No! No!'

Dad's body sagged and twisted and bumped off the couch as the gun spun across the floor and came to rest by those novelty socks. I stumbled backwards, heart shattering, fell against the stairs, barely able to breathe through choking sobs.

'Dad!' I couldn't even be alone with my shock and grief because the suffering and horror from the bridge smashed into me ceaselessly.

Can't-get-seatbelt-off-Door-won't-open-God-help-Can't-see-So-much-smoke . . .

People had been peeled and chopped and crushed. Scorched victims staggered amid burning luggage and beneath corpses hanging like hellish laundry from twisted girders. The roads had been punctured by debris and ripped by the shockwave. Survivors crawling from shattered cars found blazing fuel blocking what might've been escape routes. The only way off the bridge was to climb the walkway fences. Brave the barbed wire. Summon the courage to jump. But below them the harbour was on fire.

Gotta-let-go-Can't-jump-Can't-burn-Oh-God-not-this-Not-ready-to-die!-Not-like-this!

Almost as awful were all the *unconcerned* minds in unscathed bodies spread out across the city and suburbs.

Trivially focused. *Got-it-all-on-camera-Gotta-upload-Get-a-million-views-it'll* . . .

Told-ya so-ing. *Always-said-this-was-gonna-happen-Check-my-blog-I-knew* . . .

Thinking ahead. *I-don't-care-this-is-my-chance-to* . . .

Enjoying themselves. *Awesome-like-best-special-effects-ever* . . .

Everyone's everythink piled up and up—

Will-this-affect-the-post-Christmas-sales?-No-way-I'm-going-back-to-Iran!-Leave-me-alone!-Get-out-of-my-mind-Gotta-get-headphones-What's-going-on?-But-you're-my-brother-So-much-noise-Make-it-stop-Get-away-from-me-Car-stereo-Can't-hear-myself-think-Shut-this-out-Can't-breathe-So-much-blood-Oh-no-Please-please-wake-up-This-can't-be-real-Not-possible-I-have-to . . .

—and pushed me down, down, down.

Down through the stairs, through the house's foundations, through the dirt beneath and the clay under that, through the crust of the earth.

Killed-Danby-then-shot-himself-I-can't-believe-it-It's-true-Lock-myself-in-TV-room-This-is-my-house-You-get-out-Don't-take-the-car-They're-my-insides-coming-out-You-wouldn't-stab-I'll-freaking-kill-you-Can't-stop-the-bleeding-Where-is-she?-Can't-see-Hurts-so-much-Just-swallow-those-pills-and . . .

The thoughts followed me into the hole—

Help-us-please-Oh-my-God-She's-dead-I'm-bleeding-to-death-Better-this-way-How-dare-you?-Not-my-fault-Turn-the-volume-up-block-it-out-I'm-falling-I'm—

Not-like-this-not-like-not—

—and then they were gone and so was I.

Everything ended in the void. Moments passed like millennia. Maybe it was the other way. It wasn't light or dark. No macro or micro majesty. Stars didn't blaze and burn out with the grand turning of galactic gears. God particles didn't spark brilliantly reconfiguring cosmic building blocks. I was a fossilised grey bacterial speck. The merest shadow of the most marginal and meaningless life form. Embedded in a tiny dying planet. Forgotten and adrift forever in the frigid and infinite nothing.

Then there was the word—echoing across all of time and space—and the word was . . .

Chocopops!

SEVEN

Chocopops!-Chocopops!-Chocopops!

Evan's appetite often came on suddenly and now the purity of his hunger jolted me free of the endless static sea. I opened my eyes and gasped as though surfacing from deep under water. Across the room Dad's fingers twitched. I'd only been in that nothing place a few seconds. Seeing Dad like that hurt so much I wanted to go back.

Chocopops!-Chocopops!

I tuned into Evan upstairs, safe in his bedroom cupboard, oblivious to anything except the emptiness in his stomach. My little brother had shut out all the light and noise by burrowing into Big Bear and Sandypants and his other soft-toy guys. That was the darkness and silence Dad had mistaken for him being dead. Now he'd come up for air. Hugging his guys helped him block out the scary sounds outside and the strange scary voices that seemed to be inside him. But there was no way he could ignore the grumbling in his tummy. Mummy said breakfast would be after presents. It must be time now for *Chocopops!*

Dad's gun glinted at me from across the floor. It seemed to beckon me to do what he'd done. I knew he hadn't suffered. The bullet had ended his pain. It could be the same for me. Over in an instant. Countless others were killing themselves—swallowing pills, slicing veins, fashioning nooses—so they could be free. But I couldn't leave Evan behind to fend for himself any more than I could shoot him and turn the gun on myself.

Chocopops!

What I realised was that Evan was now out front of the million other minds. It was like being able to zero in on a single person speaking at a loud party. Tuning into him turned everyone else down. That gave me hope this thing might subside enough for us to survive.

I stumbled into the kitchen, trying to be single-minded like Evan, and concentrated on filling a plastic cup with the brown cereal and getting him the bottle of milk he'd use to wash it down.

'Evan?' I said softly, opening the cupboard door. 'Chocopops.'

He blinked up from Big Bear's embrace.

'You okay?' I asked.

I knew he was. The deep grooves of his mind had so far protected him from the worst of what had happened.

'I brought your Shades too.'

Chocopops-Snotbots!

'Chocopops!' he said. 'Snotbots!'

When Evan reached for his treats, I caught him in a hug. The closeness enveloped me, ushered me deep into his safe place, banished extrasensory sights and sounds. But it was more than that. In that moment I was somewhere that was the opposite of the lonely abyss. Connectedness, oneness, unity. It was a glimpse of what this phenomenon might offer—if only we could resist the power of negative thinking.

Chocopops-Snotbots-Let-go-squashy.

Evan nudged me out of his sphere and took the cup and bottle and Shades and retreated into his cave. He'd eat the little sugary pellets one by one as he replayed the game he'd mastered months ago. While he was occupied, I had to figure out what the hell I could do about whatever the hell was happening.

'You stay in there, okay?' I said, closing the door, wishing I could hide in there with him.

Through Evan's bedroom window, Sydney was much worse than it had been just minutes ago. Whatever was left of the bridge was lost inside smoke. When I sent my mind there I couldn't see or hear anything. The people had burned up, bled out or jumped into oblivion. But there was suffering across the city. The spectrum ranged from simple loneliness, swampy sadness and family anger to neighbourhood brawls, car crash agonies and house-fire horrors. Skipping around, like changing channels, brought weird flashes. The zoo maintenance guy running elatedly ahead of the frenzied chimpanzees he'd just set free. The nurse weeping with her own bravery as she switched off life-support systems. The professional clown slathering on make-up because he could surely save the world with a chain reaction of laughter.

Off Beautopia Point, the river was being swallowed up in a sooty haze. Bitter fumes stung my nostrils. But there was something worse underneath the synthetic smoke. Something charred and greasy. Then I knew. I was breathing people particles. My gut heaved and I spewed out the window until my stomach was empty.

I straightened up, wiped my mouth, staggered away from the smell and into my own room. I slumped onto my bed, sent my mind into the cloud of crazy for signs of sanity. They were there—people beaming care at family and friends, good Samaritans pleading for calm to strangers—but they could barely be heard above the human tabloids broadcasting the worst about themselves and others.

'Jacinta,' I said, trying to clear everything from my mind so I could find her. Jacinta.

My best friend was hiding under her bed, freaked out by much more than just her parents' confession and the plane hitting the bridge. In the chaos she saw my dad see Stephanie dead on the floor and think he'd killed her and me and Evan before he killed himself. Jacinta didn't want to believe I was dead but she couldn't find me anywhere. She couldn't believe her downstairs neighbour had sealed himself in his apartment with the gas turned on. She couldn't believe guys were stripping off in front of mirrors so everyone could see.

Jacinta started laughing. It was funny because none of it was real. She wasn't adopted. The bridge hadn't been blown up. Me and my family weren't dead. People weren't killing themselves. Perverts weren't using the mind-sharing to expose themselves. Jacinta knew what this was: a nightmare. She just couldn't wake up. She put on her Shades and figured if she couldn't stop the dream she'd fill it up with so much noise and light that nothing else could get in. Hellbanga Live In Rome blasted her ears and eyes. It helped only a bit. Even the three-dimensional pyrotechnics of the wimpled superstar belting out 'Papa La Nal' couldn't quell the thoughts rioting in my friend's head.

I grabbed my phone and messaged Jacinta.

I'M NOT DEAD popped up in a speech bubble from my profile photo hovering over Hellbanga.

Oh-thank-God-dream's-changing-Everything's-gonna-be-okay-Dan-why-can't-I—

I followed with: NOT A DREAM

'Message,' she said to make the Shades do their thing. 'What's happening, Dan? This is so—'

Even as the speech-recognised words flashed onto my screen I heard her thoughts going elsewhere.

*If-this-was-real-then-Dan-would-know-about-Finn-and-she'd—*Jacinta felt sick about going back into Mollie's party after the paramedics had left.

Oh, you bitch! My stomach roiled reflexively. I was so glad she couldn't hear my mind. This was the stupid shit that was spiralling out of control and making people insane. But it was easier for me to take the high road: Jacinta wasn't in my head and ferreting out that I'd been the one who dobbed her in for smoking last year.

DONT CARE—I sent the message, fighting to keep focus.

It appeared on her lenses. Jacinta felt relief—then more guilty panic for agreeing with Emma and Madison that I could be a self-righteous bitch.

SOMETIMES I AM! I tapped.

I sent my mind after Emma. Nothing. Her family had gone to Aspen. I couldn't find Madison. She was in Cairns with her mother. I got the sense this thing was like a wi-fi signal that weakened over distance. Either that or my friends were dead.

This-is-what-happened-to-you-at-Mollie's. Jacinta's thoughts burned helplessly across Beautopia Point. *You-you!-You-were-patient-zero-You-infected-everyone.*

'Sorry, Dan, don't mean it!' Jacinta said and that message hit my screen even as she thought, *Why-can't-I-hear-you?-This-isn't-fair.*

I called her.

'What's happening?' Jacinta cried in a ragged voice. *Am-I-going-to-die?* 'I'm so scared!'

'I don't know!' was all I could say. 'I don't know.'

How frightened I sounded to her wasn't helping. This echo chamber could drive you crazy in no time. I tried to avert my mind from hers. Listen only to what she was saying out loud.

'I can't wake up!' Jacinta yelled. 'It's all too much.'

She was struggling to hear herself above the torrential updates flooding her head. Her dad wishing he'd never even gotten married. Finn protesting to her and other girls that he wasn't a user. Mollie screaming at her mum at the rehab resort. The woman next door chanting 'Begone Satan!' as she held knives like a crucifix. The old fart downstairs hoping the gas cancelled him quickly.

'Jacinta, focus!' I said, trying to fake control. 'Don't worry about what other people are thinking!'

Generations of mums had offered it as standard operating advice. It applied now more than ever.

'There's nowhere to hide,' Jacinta whimpered. 'They're inside my mind! They know everything!'

'Calm down,' I said. 'Don't worry about—'

'I can't! I can't! I can't!' Jacinta screamed, barely able to hear herself over everything. 'I can't take this!'

She quit the call and disappeared back into her Shades with total blocking enabled.

'No!' I yelled.

COME OVER HERE! I messaged.

I saw it didn't get through. But I also saw Jacinta was having trouble seeing and hearing Princess Hellbanga. My friend was lost in what everyone else was thinking.

Leave-me-alone-Rapture's-not-coming-The-oven's-on-fire-Gotta-staunch-bleeding.

She's-so-scared-Don't-care-Nothing-matters-Stab-anyone-who-comes-in . . .

Our-Father-who-art-Petrol-tank-is-only-half-full-Won't-get-far . . .

At-least-food-in-fridge-Those-poor-people-on . . .

Swallow-this-and-it's-done-Sinking-down . . .

Might-be-okay-I'm-falling . . .

No-can't-let-go . . .

No-No-No!

Then Jacinta's mind went.

'No!' I shouted uselessly.

I called. Voicemail.

'Jacinta, please call me, please!'

I couldn't get through to her now and I couldn't get to her place without leaving Evan. All I could do was hope my friend rebooted as fast as I had.

I tried to find Mum again. Nothing. I called her landline.

'Hello?'

'Mum!'

'. . . you've called Robyn.'

Shit. I waited till the message finished.

'Mum, it's Danby!' I sobbed. 'Please pick up! Please! Dad's . . . oh God . . . Dad's . . . he's dead! Stephanie too. I don't know what's happening. Everything's going crazy. I don't know what to do! Please call me! I love you!'

I didn't know what it meant that she hadn't answered. What I hoped was that Shadow Valley wasn't being affected. I let out a dark little laugh as I imagined Mum out in her garden and oblivious to what was happening. Her pride at being so 'out of the loop' wasn't looking so loopy.

I wondered how far this thing had spread. Maybe other cities weren't affected. Maybe they were coming to help. 'On,' I said to my television and my tablet.

We'd taken it for granted that the apocalypse would be televised. In every scenario I'd ever imagined, when the end was nigh it was on every channel. Hazmat workers would torch plague victims as epidemiologists gave their terminal prognosis. Officials would tell us to duct-tape ourselves inside as the airborne toxic events claimed more capitals. Riots cops would shoot looters as the asteroid became bigger than the sun in the sky. Valiant news anchors would promise to stay on air until the very end. Yeah, there was none of that.

'I'll tell you what I'm hearing about the crisis,' shouted a red-faced host on the local news. She was only half in shot, framed by unfilled green screen, railing at an unseen someone. 'I'm hearing you're replacing me because I'm too—'

Another channel showed a live stream from inside a cathedral where churchgoers scuffled amid the pews. The national broadcaster had an unblinking grey-haired man whose spit-flecked lips made him look demonic. On Fox News two beefy blowhards slugged it out with Santa Claus. A CNN a journalist blubbered into his hands while the BBC's screen was simply empty.

My tablet gave me no comfort. Updates, feeds, posts, comments, tweets: they were at a trickle and that made horrible sense because our networks were now really peer-to-peer with no intermediary needed. Those who sent messages mostly replicated the mind-to-mind mashup: pleas for help, accusations, apologies, threats. But amid the mania I saw enough—

MoroccanMalia: Sisters all dead! Brother killed them 4 dishonr think. At my door now. Heard me 2.

GazaDove: War of all against all. PRAY!

LondonResist: Social media's been weaponised to suppress.

Amy777: Montmartre on fire. Repent.

DCDemocrat111: @NPR@NYT Gunfire at 1600 Penns Ave!

—to know that it was happening everywhere.

My timelines should've been filled with chatter and photos. Not one of my friends and acquaintances, near and far, real and never met, had posted anything—and many were people who usually didn't draw breath without letting the world know.

But when I scanned minds I saw how many were trying to disappear into other digital distractions. They had Shades on, faces buried in phones and tablets, noses up against plasma screens, earbuds pushed in so far they hurt. The music and movies and games barely made a difference except now the panicked thoughts came augmented with deafening sounds and dazzling vision. Letting myself drift into those heads it was hard to know which gibberish was people going mad and which was echoed jingles, which carnage was real and which was beamed from minds immersed in 3-D first-person shooters.

I went back to the Captain's Nest. Searching for hope in any direction. Everywhere black thoughts swirled so densely I was surprised they weren't visible, like ever-shifting flocks of starlings staining what was left of the sky. The vigilantes who'd slashed Harry to ribbons now slaughtered each other for their sins on his front lawn. Streets all around were full of people scattering and cars burning rubber with stereos blaring. Up on apartment balconies loners hunched over handhelds and belted booze and snorted stuff. Along the waterfront people were literally spaced out as they kept their distance from each other and tried to lose themselves in their devices. Unfortunates who'd escaped without a phone or tablet or Shades clamped their hands over their ears and shut their eyes tight and shouted crazily against what they couldn't help but hear and see. The sad, the mad, the bad: fragments of all their minds sprayed in all directions. I deflected them as best I could.

Amid the frenzy there were also terrifying stillnesses. So many people had crashed out. Just on the promontory there were a dozen who looked like their power cords had been pulled. Most were sitting or sprawled, but one woman stood on the breakwall with her arms out like she was expecting a hug. When I tried to find her mind she was as blank as the others. More and more went offline every moment. In the space of seconds a string of people screaming along a path dropped one after the other, as if they'd been roped together and pulled into the same psychic sinkhole.

The city had turned sepia. Like the start of *The Wizard of Oz*. Brown funnels of smoke rose like tornadoes. Everywhere my mind flashed, more fires were starting: spreading from dropped cigarettes, abandoned frying pans, smashed cars with ruptured fuel tanks, toppled power poles whose cables snaked in showers of sparks. Firefighters were helpless. Even if they had the presence of mind to get to stations and vehicles, there were far too many blazes and too few open roads. Whole streets were burning. Some people ran for safety but many were too consumed by arguments or devices to flee the flames and fumes. A terrified group of refugees disappeared in the orange flash of an exploding petrol station, its *whump* reaching me across the river as fire showered down to consume an entire block. The city was becoming a crematorium.

I scanned Beautopia Point's headspaces—amazed how quickly this new sense had become instinctive. My neighbours weren't fighting fires yet. Only themselves and each other. Booze and drugs and screens provided some diversion. But those thin defences would disappear when bottles and baggies and batteries ran dry. Then there'd be nothing to distract anyone from everyone.

Evan and I couldn't be here then. Or when fires broke out nearby. My mum's place. It might be safe. Shadow Valley was one hundred kilometres west. Trying to get there seemed a suicide mission. Staying here was a definite death sentence.

We had to go.

The BMW and Mercedes were in the garage. But I didn't know how to drive. Even if I managed to get us going it'd be a miracle if I could keep us on the road for long. Born-again Christians said the Rapture would create traffic hell when Jesus's biggest fans were sucked from their cars into heaven. What was happening was worse than that. A few motorists had pulled over. Were going mad in relative safety. Most were shouting and honking and freaking out. Slamming brakes. Jamming accelerators. Grinding cars. A demolition derby: multiplying exponentially in every direction.

I radared from head to head around the hood, tried to find a way through. Beautopia Point's streets were clear enough. But the avenues around our gated community were a maze of road rage. Bolder drivers made progress amid the chaos by mounting footpaths, mowing down fences, shunting aside other vehicles.

Escape was still possible. Just less likely with every second. Thousands of people were climbing into their cars. Some wanted to lock themselves in with a stereo. Or run the engine with the garage door down. Most were like me: ready to risk the only option that remained.

We had to hit the road.

But just as I resolved to drive out I heard someone else planning to break in.

EIGHT

Number-three-is-empty!

That's what he thought as he ran towards our front yard.

Kieran, I remembered. He'd been the guy at The Grocery who *hadn't* said his pregnant girlfriend, Patty, was going to get fat. Only now did I realise that her and me and the bus kids and Troy had all been glimpsing different tips of the same iceberg looming up ahead, the submerged juggernaut of each other. When she'd been given the full view of her boyfriend and everyone else, Patty had locked herself in the bathroom and turned the shower up to scalding. Kieran had fled their home to try to clear his head.

Distance didn't help. He couldn't avoid her doubts about the baby's paternity any more than avoiding eye contact and maintaining personal space stopped other street-wandering minds from smashing into his. Kieran wished he'd escaped with his phone—something, anything—and he'd been about to wrestle a tablet from a catatonic when angry voices—*Looter!-Thief!-It's-mine!*—sent him running towards the waterfront.

Kieran needed to plug into something with a screen and a volume control. But when his mind searched the row of McMansions it was repulsed each time.

My-house!-Got-a-knife!-Doors-locked-Step-in-here-you're-dead!

Until our place. Kieran couldn't sense my mind. Evan's registered only as the faintest blip of robots and boogers.

Number-three-is-empty!- Get-in-there-now!

As soon as Kieran thought it, so did a dozen other people.

Number-three-Empty!-Place-where-guy-killed-family-Then-himself!-Stereo-headphones-Booze-Go-go-go!

Mouths went dry and muscles twitched but the first person to make a break after Kieran was a bruiser named Boris.

House-is-mine!-Kill-anyone-who-tries-to-get-in!

Boris was a taxi driver who'd been dropping a blonde at Goldrise when suddenly she'd known he was picturing her naked.

Christmas-present-for-you-honey!-How-about-you-pay-the-fare-in-trade?

She felt the repulsive wave of lust and fled from the taxi. Since she'd gotten away Boris had drained his whiskey flask and been greatly amused by the misery around him. Gay sons, cheating wives, gambling husbands, sick daddies, suicidal husbands, vigilante cops, murderous crowds: it was like reality television beamed right into his head. That towelhead flying his plane into the bridge had been even better—like a movie but heaps gorier with better special effects—and that's when screaming idiots had started deserting their families and fancy houses. Anyone who got too close to Boris felt his fist or boot. Same went for anyone who thought shit about him. He loved that he could feel their fear and the pain he inflicted. But as awesome as this berserking was he needed a breather. All the stuff pouring into his brain was exhausting and he needed to blot it out.

Number-three-is-empty!

From the Captain's Nest, I saw Boris sprint along the waterfront, shoulder charging people out of his way.

Kieran felt him coming. *Oh-shit-oh-shit-that-guy's-an-animal.*

My adrenaline surged. I was in both minds—predator and prey—as Boris brought Kieran down with a flying tackle on our lawn.

'I *am* an animal!' the bully roared. 'I'm the dog of war!'

Boris's first punch broke Kieran's nose.

I was flooded with fight or flight chemicals. Kieran would've left our house if I'd so much as shouted at him. But if Boris got in here I'd be better off dead.

Fight: it's all I could do. I sped down from the Captain's Nest, feet barely skimming the stairs. When I reached the lounge room, I snatched up the .45 and trained it on the front door with shaking hands.

Boris sized up our house, recognised where he was.

The-gutless-shit's-place!-Pull-the-trigger-Ha-ha.

Him! He was the troll who'd been in Dad's head, urging him to kill himself out of nothing but pure malice. My fear turned to hate.

Boris stomped up our path, radiating fury to keep others away, feeding on their fear of him. Whatever had happened to the world was just fine in his book—if he could just shut up some of these pricks in his head. But I was the one prick whose thoughts were *not* in his head. Boris had no idea he was walking into an ambush. I saw how it'd play. When he bashed down the door, I'd pull the .45's trigger. Shots would ring out. He'd stumble back. Fall down dead on the lawn. Anyone else thinking about taking the house would get the message.

Someone-in-there-Can't-hear-them-Shot-him-down-Cold-blood-No-way-I'm-going-in-Number-three.

But I was full of shit. I wasn't a killer. I was a scared kid. I didn't need to take a stand. I needed to run like hell back up the stairs and hide with Evan in the cupboard. Problem was, even as it dawned on me that I'd left the door unlocked after letting the cat out, even as Boris's big bruised fist closed around the handle, even as my every nerve-ending prickled with electricity, I still couldn't move.

Boris yanked open the door. Stood there hulking and snorting. Backlit by hellfire on the horizon. I was right there on the other side of the lounge room. In seconds his eyes would adjust and my painful departure from this life would commence. Boris slammed the door, as if that could shut out the world, and stalked into our house.

'There you are,' he sniggered. 'What a loser.'

I saw what he saw: my dead father and dead stepmother.

I saw what he didn't see: me.

I was in plain view, not a dozen feet away, playing freeze tag for my life. All I could think was that Boris was like some fierce predator with bad eyesight that tracks prey by scent or vibrations. Because he didn't detect my thoughts he didn't perceive me.

I flashed to an experiment we'd done in a psychology module at school. Our science teacher Ms Carlson told us we were going to watch a short video and our job was to count how many times basketball players passed a ball back and forwards. The clip ran for about a minute as team members ducked and weaved and threw the ball this way and that. When it was done, Ms Carlson asked for our answers, which ranged from eight to sixteen.

'Anyone see anything peculiar?' she asked.

'The guy dressed as the gorilla,' class geek Cybele offered timidly.

Everyone guffawed until Ms Carlson rewound the video. There he was: a man in a monkey suit, strolling through the scene, stopping to beat his chest with his glove-paws. All but one of us had been concentrating so hard on what we'd been told was there that we hadn't seen what we didn't expect. But as soon as we knew the gorilla was there, we couldn't help see it. Surely my invisibility had similar limits. If Boris suspected my presence, he'd perceive me. If he decided to go upstairs, he'd walk right into me.

Boris stabbed at the TV remote angrily until he found a music channel to blast the house. Even the Fred Myers Experience yelling, 'Hell Is Other Peeps' wasn't enough to banish people completely from his head—and some of them wanted to take the house from him. Boris tried to respond with bellicose threats:

Come-in-here-Peeps-yo-tear-you-to-pieces-Peeps-yo-I'll-Hell-is . . .

What I tuned from Boris and the shared mind was—

Hell-is-other-peeps-yo-gotta-get-something-to-drink-Gotta-get-the-boat-out-to-sea-Player-one-game-over-Can't-stop-the-bleeding-Starts-New-Year's-Day-In-cinemas-and-VOD-Get-into-Number-three-Take-Boris-out-All-natural-sugar-free-Mum-always-used-to-say-That-chopper's-going-down-Only-Global-Finance-offers-interest-free-Can-out-run-the-fire . . .

—a desperate kaleidoscope of emotions and thoughts and memories and plans spinning with commercials and jingles and choruses and scenes. Mass distraction was amplifying the mental confusion.

Boris clutched his head—*Shut-up!*—and shouted so loud his lungs hurt. 'Shut up!'

I couldn't help but startle. Boris sniffed the air like a dog. I stood as stiff as an obelisk. After a moment he went back to threatening—*Stay-out-you-Hell-is-pricks-or-I-swear-I'll-peeps-yo*—the invaders out there who wanted in, wanted his TV, wanted him.

Gotta-be-booze-here. Boris spun up unsteadily and lurched towards me.

I didn't breathe and tried to will my heart into not beating as he passed a few feet from me and disappeared into the kitchen. When I turned to creep up the stairs, Boris registered my movement like a drop in air pressure. He froze by the open fridge. *Someone-in-here-Hell-is-Wow-vodka-brilliant-No-they're-still-outside-gutless-peeps-yo-Kill-you-all-yo.*

Stupid and thick-skinned Boris still felt pangs of inevitability. Out there—on the waterfront, across the suburbs and the city— were a million pricks who knew what he was about and hated him for it. Even he knew he couldn't fight them all.

Die-trying-Tastiest-fried-chicken-Better-to-die-on-your-feet-Limited-time-special-Than-live-on-your-knees. Boris saw Kieran recovering on the lawn. Idiot hadn't learned his lesson. Still wanted to get in. *Ready-when-you-are-Queeran.*

Boris chugged the vodka. The fire in his belly took the edge off everything and he stomped past me back to the couch. Gulped booze. Tried to find Fox News. They'd make sense of things. Except they weren't broadcasting. Hardly anyone was. He scanned cable channels. Wasn't sure what was on screen and what was in his mind from people outside. Dazzling toothpaste smiles. Black and white geeks in a cemetery. Number three looming like a haunted house. Princess Hellbanga strutting a stage. Blood spraying from a wrist. Fat juicy burger with fries.

You've-got-to-sleep-sometime-Boris-Micro-whitening-technology-They're-coming-to-get-you-Barbara-I-could-go-around-the-other-side-surprise-Boris-with-Papa-La-Nal-baby!-Suicide-might-be-a-sin-Two-for-the-price-of-one-Conditions-apply . . .

'Shut up!' Boris raged. 'Shut up!'

The world got louder and brighter.

What-do?-He's-taken-the-car?-Fresh-daily-guaranteed-Trapped-Got-to-be-another-way-Give-me-those-headphones-you-Burn-in-hell-for-what-you-Make-it-stop-Ha-ha-Boris-is-circling-the-drain-Hurts-so-much-So-loud-Make-it-stop . . .

'So loud,' Boris muttered, the empty vodka bottle falling to the floorboards.

He was going, going, about to be gone. This was my chance. If I didn't do something then Kieran or someone worse would be in here next.

I stepped towards Boris, raising the .45 at his fat face. There was just enough of him left to see me materialise out of thin air and to be seized by panic. That was good. I needed everyone outside to see me through his prism of fear.

I held the gun with two hands. Not shaking now. I knew the safety was off. Dad hadn't been able to put it back on. I blamed this bully for that. I remembered you weren't supposed to pull the trigger. You were supposed to squeeze. Where had I heard that? Some TV show probably. It was good advice.

The gun roared three times, kicking in my hands, making my ears ring. But I couldn't miss at such close range and with such large targets. Boris blanked out as my first bullet hole punched the framed Ken Done original above his head. My second shot killed the plasma with a satisfying pop. The final round went through the French doors and buzzed like an angry wasp past a guy in a tinfoil hat coming through our gate.

My theatre had the desired effect. The people outside saw me appear briefly like a gun-toting ghost girl before Boris's mind disappeared in a volley of shots. No one could be sure if he'd crashed out or if I'd blown his head clean off.

Gun-crazy-bitch!-Like-a-demon!-He-didn't-see-her!-I-can't-see-her-now!-Killed-him?-Totally-cold-blood!-Gotta-get-outta-here!

The news burned bright, getting hotter as it radiated outwards, an instant urban myth. Bitch had two guns. Bitch killed her whole family. Bitch got killed by her dad but came back to life. Bitch fed on the souls of those who crashed out. Bitch had been controlling minds for weeks. I didn't care. All that mattered was that people were fleeing our property. Kieran was crawling across the grass, praying I didn't end him with a bullet in the back.

It was like I'd put a force field around Number three. I knew it wouldn't last. At best I'd bought Evan and me some time. I looked at catatonic Boris. How long would he be out? A glance across the suburb told me that Jacinta was still offline. As far as I could tell—out on the promenade, in the other houses—no one else had yet come back from their blackouts.

But I'd resurfaced in seconds so I couldn't take any chances with Boris. In a lassoing motion, I unravelled the Christmas lights from the tree. Some had been broken in Dad and Stephanie's fight but about half still twinkled merrily. I wound the entire length around Boris, binding his wrists and ankles, wrapping him in black wire and blinking orange, red and green bulbs until he looked like a yuletide mummy.

NINE

I set the gun on the dresser in Dad and Stephanie's bedroom and rummaged through her handbag. Holding the BMW keys sent doubt spiralling up inside me. I forced it down. I had to be brave. But I also had to be realistic. I was pretty likely to crash the car. If we survived that, we'd have to go on foot with supplies that I could carry.

Leaving home had been my dream since Stephanie moved in. Striking out into the world, head held high, offering dignified goodbyes, taking a few treasured keepsakes, knowing I'd never look back: that's how I'd pictured it. This was a long way from that. I stood in the doorway of my bedroom with no idea what to take.

First thing I needed to take was a deep breath. I did that. Tried to keep calm.

My flannel pyjamas. Not the best outfit for a survival situation. I changed into jeans, a chunky woollen jumper, thick socks and leather boots. It might feel like I was melting in these clothes but at least they wouldn't melt to my skin if I had to face flames. I tied my hair into a ponytail and tucked it under a baseball cap. Pulling my backpack from the cupboard, I looked around for what else I needed.

My big bed was an expanse of stuffed animal friends carried over from childhood. More recent imaginary friends—Mary Shelley, Dorothy Parker, Ellen Ripley, Lisa Simpson, Elissa Steamer—gazed down from my corkboard collage. My beanbag was buried under a midden of clothes and my desk was strewn with magazines. My dressing table was a landscape of polishes, lipsticks and moisturisers and the wall shelves were stacked with books, games, gadgets and trinkets. I hadn't thought I was a materialistic girly-girl but now it hit me how much of my stuff was meaningless. Surely there had to be something I possessed that was useful for survival.

'Sneakers!' I said to myself, and packed them.

Spare jeans. A jacket. Sunglasses might be good. Ditto a notebook. I grabbed a clutch of pens. I ripped my cash roll out of its jar and stuffed it in my pocket. I didn't know if we were beyond money, but no sense being caught short. It pained me to leave Mum's painting, but lugging a canvas was hardly practical. She could do another one for me in Shadow Valley. My eyes fell on the Lucidiphil packet. Surely I didn't need the medication now that the world had given me a second opinion about my condition. I spun around: there was nothing else.

Downstairs I made sure Boris was still blacked out in blinking lights before I ransacked the pantry for packet noodles, tins of tuna, boxes of crackers, some fruit and a few bottles of water. I grabbed a lighter, torch, spare batteries, can-opener, cutlery. In the bathroom, I added a first-aid kit, sunblock, painkillers, tampons, soap and toilet paper. In all, I filled the backpack and two shopping bags.

I lugged the load through the internal entrance to the garage and put it in the boot of the BMW. Panting for breath, I looked around with fresh eyes. Dad's love of expensive sports had built up a survivalist repository of sorts. I grabbed the tent and a sleeping bag good enough to take to the summit of Mount Everest. I put them in beside my backpack and bags. I added his state-of-the-art fishing rod and tackle kit and the compound bow and quiver of arrows. I guessed I could learn how to use them. I was wondering whether I'd need my old horse saddle when I realised all I was doing was delaying our departure because I was so scared. The roads were only getting more dangerous and difficult. I slammed the boot shut.

I still had to load Evan. But I didn't want his last memory of the house to be horrific. So I went to the linen cupboard in the downstairs hallway and grabbed three big sheets. I draped one over Dad and then covered Stephanie. I stood by their shrouded bodies, trying to form a prayer. Only one word came.

'Goodbye.'

The third sheet was for Boris, still catatonic on the couch. Then I realised he was as good as dead if I left him tied up. He'd be at the mercy of whoever came in once we left. If the house burned he wouldn't have a chance. As I wondered what to do, Boris's Christmas lights winked out. I whirled around. The kitchen light was off. The electricity was gone.

Everywhere around Beautopia Point panic redoubled as televisions and stereos died and houses dropped into darkness.

Power's-out-I-need-that-tablet-Where's-the-flashlight?-Give-it-to-me!

Outside, the air was the colour of caramel, but the lounge room was almost black. I clicked on my phone's flashlight app, left Boris and headed upstairs.

I opened the cupboard doors. Evan was still in his Shades.

'Honey, we're going out for a while.'

'Luna?'

Luna Park was his favourite place in the world. We'd sometimes get the ferry there for the afternoon. Evan couldn't read my mind. I could still tell white lies. What a superpower.

'Yes, Luna Park!'

Evan hopped out of the cupboard and I quickly dressed him in corduroy trousers, sneakers and his little leather jacket.

Luna-night?-Dark-outside-ferry-Can-driver-see?

Evan had more going on than we'd given him credit for.

'Special surprise,' I said. 'I'm driving!'

Evan looked at me quizzically.

Danby-don't-drive.

'Dad and Stephanie said I could. For Christmas!'

Evan grinned.

'Big Bear! Shades!'

I nodded. 'Sure, we'll take them.'

He clapped. That was good. I needed him happy.

I carried Evan down the stairs and to the garage. He climbed up into his booster. As he resumed his game of *Snots*, I wedged the overstuffed toy between him and the back of the passenger seat. Shades would help keep his mind from wandering. Big Bear might help keep him safe if I crashed us.

'Be right back!'

There was one more thing to do before I got into the driver's seat.

Making my way back into the lounge room, I shone the phone on Boris. His chest rose and fell rhythmically. His mind wasn't anywhere. Nevertheless I approached him as though he was a tranquilised wolf. Unwrapped the Christmas lights just enough that he'd be able to free himself. When I pulled his arm clear I was stunned that it hung there in space. My heart thudded and I glanced at his face. Expected his eyes to flick open. For him to grin as his mind screamed *Gotcha!* But he was still a . . .

Goner.

The word had come from nowhere. I wanted it to go back there.

'No.'

Boris wasn't a Goner because Jacinta wasn't a Goner.

I sent myself out to her. She wasn't anywhere I could reach.

'Hold on,' I said. 'I'm coming.'

'*RIAAAAOW.*'

I spun around, heart smashing against my rib cage, to see Upton, the cat, flexing on the rug, eyes phosphoric in the phonelight.

'Jesus, you scared the shit out of me!'

'*Riaaaaaow,*' he said.

'Oh, come on,' I said, clomping to the kitchen, him following on little ninja feet.

I poured our entire supply of Celebrity Cat into the biggest bowl I could find.

When studying modern narrative in English, Mr Creighton had told us about a Hollywood guru who had his students Save the Cat early in scripts to get the audience's sympathy. But there was no way I was taking the little bastard with us. Upton would scratch my eyes out and slice open a vein before I got him anywhere near the car. I told myself he'd be okay, that he probably had a better chance than we did, and then shuddered when I thought about what he'd eat when he'd snuffled his way through that mountain of food.

I couldn't save Upton—or Dad or Stephanie—but I could save Jacinta.

The BMW's leather seats sighed as I slid behind the wheel. I found the clicker in the centre console and the garage door hummed up behind us. Turning the key in the ignition rewarded me with the engine purring to life. That was good. The car didn't know I couldn't drive it. I tried to look at the controls and instrument panel with a methodical mind. Billions of people drove. How hard could it be?

I found the lights, clicked them on and saw my skateboard propped against the back wall of the garage. No way I was leaving it behind. I got out, grabbed the deck, threw it in the back seat next to Evan and got back behind the wheel. In the rear-view mirror, Evan had the Shades translucent and was peering over Big Bear's polar fur.

Danby-drive-funny.

'You got that right.' I adjusted the mirror until my rear view was a rectangle of darkness tinged red by tail-lights. 'Now what?'

A rhetorical question, if ever there was one.

Mummy-foot-handbrake-gear-look-back-slowly-slowly.

I turned around. Evan wore a little smile but his eyes were far away.

Mummy-said-foot-brake—

I was in one of his disjointed memories. It made him feel happy but it was beyond freaky seeing Stephanie superimposed over me in my seat, smiling back at him as she reversed, describing what she was doing in a silly singsong. I just couldn't get a lock on the exact words.

'What?' I said. 'What did Mummy say?'

Evan's mouth took over from his mind: 'Foot down on brake, handbrake up, gear in reverse, look behind and then slowly, slowly like the sloth.' My little brother intoned his little mantra in the hollow tone he used when he parroted somebody. 'Foot down on brake, handbrake up, gear in reverse, look behind and then slowly, slowly like the sloth.'

Hearing it ripped my heart for him. If he ever asked what had happened to his mummy and daddy, I didn't know what I was going to say. No time to dwell on that. Only time to make use of what he'd said. I put my foot on the brake, lifted the handbrake, slipped the gearstick from P to R and then eased us back.

Once off the driveway, I turned the steering wheel so the car curved smoothly onto the road.

'Woo!'

Ridiculously proud, I smiled back at my little instructor. But Evan was behind his Shades. I was on my own.

Sliding the stick into D, I eased off the brake and leaned on the accelerator. The BMW crept along First Street and I steered us past a body on the road. Outside the halo of headlights, in gloomy yards and darkened footpaths, downcast faces were lit by digital glare. None of them looked up. But there were others in the shadows with enough awareness to see the BMW gliding past like a ghost vehicle.

Tinted-windows-No-one-driving?-Can't-hear-anyone-Gotta-get-the-car-Get-the-car.

Those thoughts fired like paparazzi flashes as the vehicle took on the strange allure of a celebrity's stretch limousine. People wanted to know who was inside. People wanted to be inside.

I jammed my foot down. We shot across Reflection Road. Left would-be attackers back down the hill. I drove us around a corner towards Jacinta's building. My eyes scanned left, right and all around for road hazards as my mind did the same to scan for imminent threats. The clamour everywhere was increasing but it wasn't directed at us for the moment.

I stopped the BMW outside Goldrise and turned to Evan.

He had his Shades off and was wide-eyed.

'Noisyscary!' *Noisy-scary-noisy.*

Evan was hooking into the minds. He didn't understand what they were saying and seeing but he was soaking up all their bad feelings.

Scary-noisy.

'I know,' I said as soothingly as possible, 'but it's all going to be okay.'

Luna-please.

'We'll go there in a minute but you've got to do something first.'

Do-something-first.

'All I need you to do is say, "Jacinta!" '

He looked at me uncertainly.

'Fairy floss at Luna if you can do it.'

That got him more interested.

'You know her. Ja-sin-ta,' I said slowly. 'Ja-sin-ta.'

Ja-sin-ta, he turned the word over in his mind, liking the sound of it.

That's what I wanted.

'Ja-sin-ta,' he whispered.

'That's right!' I beamed at him. 'JA-SIN-TA! JA-SIN-TA! JA-SIN-TA!'

Evan joined in, repeating her name, thinking her name.

Ja-sin-ta-Ja-sin-ta-Ja-sin-ta.

Jacinta couldn't hear my thoughts. But she might hear Evan's. If he could reach her, bring her back, then she'd see me through his eyes and I could tell her to get down here to the car.

Evan and I stared at each other, singing that one word, blocking out all else. I sent my mind out for Jacinta's, hoping she'd flicker back to consciousness. There was nothing. He wasn't getting through. But we had attracted the attention of other minds inside Goldrise and in neighbouring buildings.

Girl-and-kid-in-car-Can-deal-with-them-Still-get-away . . .

They'd heard Evan. Seen me through him. Coveted the BMW from darkened windows.

A warning shot would slow them down.

Shit!

I'd overpacked everything else but I'd left the gun on the dresser. It wasn't like I could whip the bow and arrow from the boot and learn archery in time to defend us. We had to get moving. First I had to make sure Jacinta knew my plan.

I grabbed my phone and hit redial.

'You've called Jacinta,' she said. 'You know what to do.'

Beep!

The guy who lived in Goldrise apartment 5C was barrelling down the fire-escape stairs with a baseball bat, prepared to beat me to death if that's what it took to take the car.

'Jax,' I said into her voicemail. 'I can't get to you. I'm . . . I'm going to Mum's. I'll call you again. I don't know—oh shit!'

I threw the phone on the passenger seat as 5C burst through the front doors. He stalked towards the car, pounding the bat against the palm of his hand.

I-will-smash-you-I-don't-want-to-but—

'Get out of the car and no one gets hurt!' he yelled.

I turned to Evan. He gaped, terrified, feeling the blast wave of the man's fury.

'Hang on!' I screamed.

I switched my foot from brake to accelerator and the BMW roared out of range just as 5C lunged. I didn't need to look back to know he'd landed rough on the road, had cracked a wrist bone and was howling in my exhaust.

Adrenaline rushed through me and I sped up with it. It was like the first time I braved the half pipe. Crash or crash through: that's all I could do. I couldn't think about leaving my best friend behind, about what had happened to Dad and Stephanie, about what was happening to however many millions of others. Mum, Evan, me: we were what mattered now.

I hit fifty as we hit Commercial Street, just missed an abandoned Jeep, veered around two teenagers brawling on the bitumen. Off to my left, The Grocery was in darkness and beset by bobbing flashlights. Looters. Their minds scared me. Not because they were stealing but because every single one of them was going at it alone. Though they were all there for the same reasons, could all read each other's thoughts, there was no cooperation or coordination, only competition and conflict. When wary distance failed, fights erupted. There was no coming back from this. I was living through the end of the world. 'Living through' was probably too much to hope for.

The BMW raced under Beautopia Point's archway entrance and into the real world—or what was left of it. I hit the brakes and we skidded to a stop in the middle of Boundary Road. We were in the working class suburb that bordered Beautopia. It'd be nice to report its residents were more down to earth than our estate's self-important elite and thus less susceptible to the mental meltdown. But that wasn't true. Behind the brick veneer and fibro facades, they were just as screwed as everyone else.

The phone burbled from the seat as a text arrived.

'Thank God!'

I snatched it up, overjoyed that I could swing the car around and go pick up Jacinta. But she hadn't messaged me. I'd missed a call. Private number. Mum!

I jabbed the key for voicemail.

'Danby! Danby!' She sounded terrified. 'Oh, baby, your dad! Stephanie! My God! Please be all right. Evan too. This is—this is—I love you. Please call me! I love you!'

Sobbing, I hit her number.

First time she'd ever answered first ring. 'Danby!'

'Mum! I'm so scared!'

'Me too, darling!' She yelled over whatever was in her mind. 'Wh—where are you?'

'I'm coming with Evan. Mum I'm—'

'So loud! I thought it was just me that I—'

Silence. I wished she wasn't out of range. That I could hear her mind and see she was really all right.

'Are you okay, Mum?'

'My mind . . . it's so loud.'

'Is it safe there?'

'It's not safe anywhere but at least here it's—'

Then she was gone in a *beep-beep-beep*.

I screamed at the thought of her beautiful mind catatonic.

Then I looked at the phone. Laughed with relief.

No bars. Mum wasn't gone. The network was.

'At least here it's—'

Safer: that's what she'd been going to say. I was sure of it. Shadow Valley was remote and sparsely populated. It had to better than here. All I had to do was get us there.

I wrenched the steering wheel and accelerated us away from the river and towards the freeway that connected the city to the mountains. Talking to Mum had given me hope that I didn't want to sully. So I didn't skip to minds in the smoke and haze ahead. This stretch of road looked clear of vehicles. Maybe this was the start of our clean getaway.

A wreck loomed out of the murk. White Kombi, flipped on its roof, billowing smoke, shredded corpse sprawling from a side window. After that, there was only total gridlock. Drivers bashed cars. Tried to funnel forwards. Trapped themselves tighter when they tried to reverse. I skidded to a stop. Cursed myself for being so stupid.

Now I did leapfrog from mind to mind. Traffic was at a standstill for kilometres. The freeway exit was blocked by a blazing pile-up. Every highway lane was blocked with crashed or abandoned cars. All around me drivers refused to believe these were all roads to nowhere.

Has-to-be-a-way-through-C'mon-move-Let's-go-At-least-got-the-stereo-screen-air-con-Oh-God-no-petrol-pouring . . .

Breaking news burned from mind to mind: a rainbow river of gasoline, spilling from drums in the cargo hold of a crashed Hegira, streaming down the road under vehicles.

It's-on-fire-Fire!-Oh-God!-Oh-God!

People were so parked-in they couldn't get free. Drivers kicked at windshields and then vehicles began bucking into the air on cushions of fire.

Rattling the gearstick, I stomped on the accelerator. We shot back wildly. Glanced off the fiery Kombi. Spun across the road until we crunched into a parked car. My face slammed into the airbag. It took a second to realise I was alive. Then I whirled to make sure Evan was okay. My little brother was cushioned by a side airbag and safe in Big Bear's embrace. But his screams were louder than the car alarm we'd set off. Evan's defences were crumbling.

Scary-Danby-scary!

'It's gonna be okay!' My shout only added to his terror. 'Hang on!'

The airbag deflated in a cloud of chalky dust. I shook the gearstick forward, twisted the steering wheel hard right and mashed the accelerator. We ripped down Boundary Road, side-swiping and scraping parked cars as we went.

The inferno receded in the rear-view mirror but keeping on towards the river offered no escape. A few blocks away a young *Hellwheels* fan was dying in a stolen V8. We'd never get past the carnage he'd created. Even if we could, a bigger disaster waited just around the corner where a speeding truck had flipped into oncoming traffic and turned that stretch of road into a pagan symmetry of bodies and debris. Trying to avoid *that* chaos by ducking into the side street would deliver us to a bearded guy in fatigues spraying his automatic rifle at the body-snatchers he believed were taking over. My mind raced beyond these obstacles, through more streets and other suburbs. Even where there was no violence, roads were all but impassable. Drivers had stopped to stare into devices. Or stalled or smashed when they'd succumbed to the nothingness. Near or far, there was no way out. The clear strip of asphalt in my headlights might have been the last open road left in the city.

Evan was still screaming. Only now did I hear what he was saying.

'Home!'

Home-home-home-home.

I'd stopped us outside Beautopia Point.

Back where we started. We were going home to die.

TEN

'Not on my watch!'

Wasn't that the sort of thing action-movie heroes always said? I swung the steering wheel and aimed the BMW back through Beautopia Point's gates. The place had gone even further to hell. The Grocery's banners were ablaze. Smoke billowed from Skybrook's roof. Flames danced in Sunshower's upper-floor windows.

I slowed as we approached Goldrise. Searched for Jacinta. Came up empty. Heard someone else.

I'm-coming-baby!

The woman let herself fall from the balcony of her penthouse apartment. Thinking about her husband. How horrible it'd been for him in that fireball. My foot went for the accelerator as she screamed into oblivion against the BMW's bonnet. All at once the car bucked and metal buckled and the windshield imploded and the headlights died as her body bounced away into the darkness. I swallowed my scream as steam gushed from the ruptured front end.

Noisy-scary-Sleep-sleep-sleepy.

'Evan!'

His eyes were closed and he shuddered in his child seat. My little brother was going down. Sucked under by so many souls circling in their own vortexes.

'Evan!'

I shook his shoulder hard. He couldn't hear me.

'Please,' I cried. 'Don't go.'

But he already had.

The car wasn't going anywhere. I shoved open my door and staggered onto the road. Every panel was scraped and dented. Tail-lights smashed. Bumper and muffler prised loose. None of that mattered. What killed me was that my crashes had accordioned the boot so much I couldn't get our supplies free. I fought the urge to scream. It wouldn't help.

My mind returned to our house. Kieran had gone in when we'd driven out. When he saw Boris was alive he smashed the bully's head with the vodka bottle. As much to have his revenge as to show minds out there that he was king of this castle. Seconds later Kieran realised he was just as vulnerable in our lounge room as he was out on the waterfront. None of the screens or stereos worked: there was no way to keep the minds out. But searching frantically for something—anything—paid off with the double jackpot of car keys and the forgotten .45. Now Kieran was backing Dad's Mercedes out of the garage, determined to use the gun on anyone who tried to carjack him and yelling along with the Astral Projectors on the stereo.

But I was grateful to be in Kieran's mind as he stole our car. That's because as he reversed down our driveway, the Mercedes' headlights lit on our possible salvation hanging on the garage wall. I waited until he'd roared past us and then yanked open the back passenger door.

'Evan?' I said softly.

No response. I took a moment to control my shaking and put my ear and hand to his nose and mouth to hear and feel his breath. Physically, my little brother was fine. Mentally, he was gone.

I grabbed my skateboard, set it down to the road. Unbuckled Evan's child seat, hefted him out of the car and into a fireman's carry. I planted one foot on my deck. It bent under our combined weight. But this was how we had to roll. I took the other foot off the ground and gravity began its work.

We picked up speed down the hill and I used Evan's arms and legs to keep us balanced. A woman watching from her upstairs window saw us as a six-limbed creature whirring through the dusk at supernatural speed. In an instant her vision of a giant insect alien sent a fresh wave of panic bristling through the suburb. A guy on an apartment balcony concurred we were a blurry extraterrestrial streak and let loose at us with his hunting rifle. Bullets whizzed off the bitumen but I kept us upright as we raced off the road and along our driveway.

Leaping from the board, I carried us into the shadows alongside the house and set Evan softly on the lawn. I crept across the yard. Knelt by the cabana. Peered through the lattice that divided the waterfront into dark diamonds. There weren't that many people between us and the river. I guess gunshots heralding a war between humanity and telepathic space cockroaches really helped to clear an area. Those still in the vicinity were fending each other off from inside their tablet trances or offline and oblivious like Jacinta and Evan. The one wild card was our next-door neighbour Doug. The bastard was oscillating along the waterfront. But he was so wrapped up with berating the world that I didn't think he'd notice us.

I grabbed Evan under his armpits and dragged him across our lawn and out the gate. No one saw me pull him down the breakwall's stone steps and onto the sand by the water's edge. With my little brother safe in the shadows, I hustled back to our garage. What I needed—what I'd seen through Kieran—was the lightweight kayak Dad had used for a month or so before he'd relegated it to a rack. I lifted it from the wall. It was built for one adult but Evan and I would have to squeeze into the cockpit. I hauled it up over my head and hustled across our lawn.

I was nearly at the water when someone grabbed my boot. Jerking away from the hand of a lady who'd crashed out made me stumble just enough that the kayak's hull dipped and banged against the promenade.

Thoughts sprayed from Doug as he whirled around.

That's-no-giant-cockroach-Someone-carrying-canoe.

Across the river, something exploded bright enough for him to see me.

Danby-I-heard-you-were-dead.

I threw the kayak off the breakwall and jumped down after it onto the little beach.

'Hey! Hang on!' he shouted, running after me, trying not to think *Get-her!* 'Danby, it's me, Doug!'

I grabbed Evan and plonked him in the cockpit. My phone! I couldn't let it get ruined by seawater. It'd be vital when the network came back so Jacinta and Mum could find me. I wrenched it from my jeans pocket and tucked it inside Evan's jacket.

Splashing alongside the kayak took me into thigh-deep water and then I used the little boat like a kickboard until I couldn't touch the bottom.

Come-back-here!

Doug waded behind us.

'Danby, come on, you know me,' he said. 'Just hear me out.'

That was the problem—I knew him and I had heard him. Doug didn't really want the kayak. Reckoned that if he couldn't hear me then I couldn't hear him. Keeping me with him might be the way to not go crazy and crash out. We could be good together.

I kicked hard, churning the water, and clung to a buoy. Hanging between it and the kayak, I looked back at Doug.

'Hey,' I panted. 'Some crazy shit, huh?'

'You got that right,' he said. *I'll-have-to-ditch-the-retard.* 'We need to stick together.'

Doug took another step. The water lapped his chest. He'd have to swim unless he could coax me to shore.

'We can help each other,' he said. 'You should come back.'

'You're right,' I said. 'Just let me do this first.'

Barnacles tore through my jeans as I shimmied up the buoy. With a boot, I pulled the kayak closer and lowered myself into the cockpit behind Evan.

'You bitch!' Doug shouted.

He dived into the inky river.

I yanked the paddle free of its bungee cords.

Doug popped up a few feet from the hull and I smacked the blade hard into the water beside his head.

'Danby, don't make me hurt you,' he said, treading water. 'Be reasonable.'

My impromptu weapon was six feet long. If he came closer, I'd slice open his skull.

'I killed my parents and Boris!' I blurted. 'You can be next if you want.'

Doug didn't believe me. He knew Stephanie had fallen, that Dad had shot himself and that Kieran had finished Boris. But as he was about to open his mouth to call bullshit I felt his blackest fear bubble up inside him.

'I've got my period,' I said. 'You're swimming in my blood.'

What?-Oh-you-dirty-Is-she-serious?-Oh-shit.

Doug froze as he helplessly imagined sharks zero-ing in on him. I quickly paddled into deeper water. Doug raced back to the beach.

'You can't get away!' He could barely hear himself over the minds pushing him down like plunging waves. 'You're gonna die.'

As I steered us away, Doug slumped down onto the sand as he was sucked into oblivion.

Paddling the kayak around Beautopia Point, my mind radared through the smoke on the water. No one swam towards us. We weren't in the path of a frantic speedboat. But the river was far from empty. Dinghies and yachts and cruisers skudded crazily as people climbed masts, hid in cabins and jumped overboard to escape each other. Solo skippers hoped their distance from other people would mean freedom from the madness, hoped they could hold out long enough to get past the bridge's ruined iron stalactites and reach the open ocean. I was heading the other way even though I knew the Parramatta River dwindled after it left the city that bore its name. But at least if I got that far I'd be fifteen kilometres closer to my mum.

A tide of boats swept towards me. I skipped across minds that overlapped like the choppy waves. I found no threats but my head filled with screams as the river flared, and shock and heat and spray pummelled the kayak.

'No,' I gasped. 'Please.'

But I knew. The explosion was Goldrise. Jacinta's building.

I sent my mind searching and looked back at the burning tower through stinging eyes.

Thank-God-I-got-out.

It wasn't Jacinta. It was 5C. Grateful he'd remained outside his building after he tried to take the car from me.

No-way-anyone's-getting-out-Stupid-suicidal-bastard.

I understood 5C's bitter conclusion. Jacinta's downstairs neighbour had turned on the gas to kill himself. But he'd set a time bomb that had turned Goldrise into an inferno.

There was no saving Jacinta. My best friend was dead. Gone. I didn't know how to go on—only that I had to or we'd die next. I paddled us forward mindlessly.

I don't know how we didn't run aground. Or go under the bow of some out-of-control boat. Next thing I knew, I had to stop and catch my breath. As we bobbed in the muck, I wiped my eyes and stared back at Sydney. All the skyscrapers had dissolved into the smoky horizon. Some harbourside suburbs still had power so that lights shone from windows and streetlamps warded off the daytime darkness. But swathes were blacked out from shore to hillside or only aglow at the mercy of unchecked blazes.

'Shit!' I snapped out of my stunned state.

A panicked weekend sailor spinning his wheel to avoid a phantom trawler looming from another mind put him on a direct course for us.

I paddled frantically. Got us out of his path. The man and his boat speared across the river behind us. Disintegrated amid a jetty's thick pylons.

Adrenaline rushing, fully alert, I paddled hard, pushing us upriver into fresh tortures. Every westward inch brought us in range of more people coming apart at the seams. Steering straight for them was insane. The only thing crazier would've been to stay put.

What maybe went in our favour was that we were invisible. Minds on the shores, and in other boats, couldn't tune into me or Evan and the kayak melted into the smoky mess of sky meeting water. But that could work against us if another boat came our way. All I could do about that was keep close to the shore where we were less likely to be hit.

Darkened suburbs scrolled by. Flashlights stabbed through the darkness. I steered between yachts at a marina, through the shallows alongside a bush reserve, across the burning frontage of a waterside apartment complex.

An iron bridge brooded from the gloaming. Its entire span was choked with cars. People cowered in smashed vehicles and tried to hide inside whatever wall of sound their stereos could conjure. Horns were honked by slumping heads. Headlights projected drivers as shadows in the smoke as they fled across cars. On the shores mobs who'd spilled from the bridge and down from the suburbs clashed in a punching, biting, kicking, cutting and bashing war of all against all. It was like everyone had decided that death was the only escape: it didn't matter whose.

I had to risk the middle of the river. Better to chance crashing with another boat than to go near whatever had replaced humanity inside that homicidal frenzy. There weren't any vessels that I could see. But that didn't mean we were safe. As we approached the middle pylons, I flicked across fevered minds, expecting to lock onto another suicidal swandiver. It wouldn't need to be a direct hit to kill us. Waves from a near-miss could capsize the kayak. We were wedged into the cockpit so tightly we'd drown before I got us free.

Then the horror was behind us. The river ahead was clear of boats and the industrial shoreline was uninhabited. Every muscle ached but I didn't slow for fear of losing momentum. I set an achievable goal. I'd rest when I got to the next flashing red channel marker. But when I reached it I promised myself a break at the next one. Then I forced myself on at the next one and the next one after that. That was how I kept going.

I paddled us past warehouses and depots. We slid beneath a disused railway bridge. Went by an eerily quiet apartment complex. The river opened into mangrove-lined Homebush Bay, crowned by Sydney Olympic Park's arches. My exhausted mind slipped away from me. Saw people streaming around a stadium. Heard what sounded like the roar of excited fans. Maybe some sporting event was finishing. Then I realised these were discombobulated souls trying *not* to become crowds as they wandered Olympic Park's arenas and boulevards.

My neck hurt from the car crash. My abdominals felt like they might snap and my thighs were burning. I'd tried to welcome this physical pain as a distraction. Now my body screamed in unison with the universe.

I couldn't go on. Then I didn't have to. I wasn't on the river anymore. I was in deep space. Being sucked towards a pulsing red dwarf. Except that wasn't right. In space you couldn't hear anything and you moved without effort. But I was being pulled through noise and friction. This was inner space. Had to be. Me being pumped through my own blood towards my own heart. Only I wasn't moving anymore. I was stuck in sludge that tasted of salt and copper. Everything pulsed red and black. Was I inside my own heart attack? No—this wasn't my death. It was the birth—of everything. Back in time, billions of years. I was part of the primordial soup being lit up by exploding lava. Lightning would strike and all life would start with me as the first organic molecule. Everything I thought I knew hadn't happened yet. But then it had—and I slammed back into myself.

I was Danby, dehydrated and delirious and slumped against my little brother's back in the kayak I'd just paddled straight into a muddy mangrove flat. I made myself sit up, rubbed river water out of my eyes, took what measure I could of the landscape from the red-black pulse of the channel marker behind me. Above where I'd landed was a walking track and beyond that was dense, dark bushland. There were millions of people in every direction but I couldn't sense anyone close by.

When I yoga-moved out of the cockpit, my feet sank into the mud. I tied one of the kayak's bungee cords to a mangrove branch so my ride wouldn't be carried off with the tide. I hauled Evan up and slopped us onto dry land. I checked his respiration and pulse. He was in better shape than me. Breathing easy while I rasped for air.

Looking around, I was met with a minor miracle: the shiny silver of a water fountain. I hauled myself up its plinth and took sips that were cold and revitalising. Then I splashed my face to wash off the salt and blood and mud.

A sign beside the fountain said that the black bushland behind the cyclone fence was Newington Nature Reserve. It didn't take long to find a flap of wire that'd been pulled back at ground level, probably by kids who treated this as their personal adventure park. I squeezed us through and dragged Evan into the shadows between the towering trees.

Everything hurt, everything was unfair, everything was wrong and everything had to be turned back the way it was. There was a simple way out of this. Had to be.

Wake up. Wake up. Wake. Up. Wake. Up.

I clicked my fingers in front of my face.

'Snap out of this, snap out of it.'

But I didn't.

Snap.

I turned the word in my head. It was the sound of something breaking in a split second—but it was also what people said when they thought or did something simultaneously.

The Snap—that's what had happened to us.

It wouldn't unhappen. You couldn't unsnap anything. I had to accept that. Denial was dangerous. So many people had died—were dying right now—because they couldn't or wouldn't face this new reality. Not having my thoughts exposed had given me a better chance. But I could never forget that death was on our heels if we were to stay far enough ahead to stay alive.

I cuddled Evan tight to me, my back against a tree trunk, and let my mind wander across our surroundings. We were lucky to have landed on this spot. The apartment complexes along the reserve's eastern side still had electricity and the residents who'd fought to stay didn't want to leave after witnessing the chaotic darkness elsewhere. But sooner or later their power would fail and batteries would die and then they'd only have each other and the walls to bounce off. That's when fleeing into shadowy parklands might become attractive.

Mosquitoes whined and dive-bombed. Wasn't smoke supposed to ward off the little bastards? There was enough of it in the air. Waving them away was useless so I stretched my jumper around Evan and rubbed mud from my boots on our exposed skin. It helped a little.

How long had it been since the Snap? The overload of bad shit and the prematurely dark sky had me all out of sync.

Waking up, opening Christmas presents: that was someone else's life, lived a long time ago in a galaxy far, far away. Even the phrase 'long time ago in a galaxy far, far away' seemed like it came from that ancient alien place. I wriggled around, got my phone from Evan's pocket and clicked it on. It was just after one in the afternoon. It felt surreal that less than four hours had passed. Maybe time had stopped working. Maybe it didn't matter now.

Except it did. More than ever before in my leisurely little life. That's because it was vital I kept track of how long Evan had been without fluids and food. I knew the time we could survive without life's essentials was roughly measured in threes: three minutes without oxygen; three days without water; three weeks without food. Evan had the cereal and milk not too long ago. He'd be okay for a while. But I had to find a way to wake him up—or at least get water into him.

I needed to keep scanning. Make sure we weren't about to be discovered. As much as I hated to, I delved into the nearest mind I found—and from there drilled down into what was the biggest danger nearby.

Gordy was eleven and balled up in a hollow log a few hundred metres away. He and his mum had been about to visit his dad in Silverwater Jail when other dressed-up families started yelling and tearing at each other. A klaxon screamed behind the razor wire and there were shouts and the *pop pop pop* of gunfire. Right then Gordy knew his whole life was lies. The man doing time for manslaughter wasn't really his father— and it hadn't really been manslaughter.

Gordy sprinted across the car park, already like a dodgem-car arena, and through the riverside park, where families trying out new bikes and kites were all snarling up at each other. He vaulted up and over the Newington Nature Reserve fence like an Olympic athlete. Stumbled into the trees and hid inside the log and blasted Universe 25 through his earbuds.

Now the cheap player's battery had run out. Gordy couldn't help being in the prison yard where his horrible fake father was bashing his poor cellmate even as he blasted threats at his cheating wife and the little bastard she'd foisted on him.

I'll-find-youse-both-when-I'm-outta-here-You'll-both-be—

He'd make her pay—then the kid. First he had to shut up his cellmate. Maybe that'd silence the thousands of other voices clamouring in his head. But as he raised his bloody fist to finish the job it was like the world fell away beneath his feet. He was gone—and Gordy blinked out with him.

I gasped in the darkness, horrified by what would become of Gordy but glad he'd been saved from the prison maniac. Maybe the scores of minds toppling like dominoes was a good thing. It might at least stop some of the escaped convicts and crazed civilians from murdering each other in the suburbs surrounding the prison and along the shoreline farther down the river. I felt awful for wishing everyone would drop into oblivion before anyone stumbled onto our hiding spot.

Someone came closer along the river path. An old bugger named Thomas who hated visiting the city and partaking in Christmas. At the insistence of his daughter he'd done both because she and her idiot husband wanted to show off their fancy new waterfront apartment. Thomas had been hiding in bed and grumbling at the prospect of jumping grandkids when his family and about a million of their tight-packed neighbours all seemed to start yelling.

Thomas yanked out his hearing aid, thinking some wi-fi gizmo was causing interference. But it made no difference. How was he being deafened when he was already almost deaf? Unless ... he was finally losing his marbles and these voices were inside his head. Thomas let himself out, still in his dressing gown and slippers, intending to walk around the block to make sense of things. When that didn't work, he just kept going.

Home was over one hundred kilometres away. Thomas knew he wouldn't make it. But at least the universe saw fit to let him see his birthplace one last time. It was only a flash—pulsing minds working momentarily like a relay down the coast—but in that second Thomas was gazing on the blue water and tasting the salt air of his beloved bay.

I had an idea as the old man shuffled away. Maybe I could find Mum using the same method. Sending my mind to the west, I hooked into a frightened primary school teacher and scoured her mind for any thoughts she was receiving from the Blue Mountains, trying to find Mum in the maelstrom. It didn't work. I tried again. And again.

My mind pinballed that way for hours. Like using a kaleidoscope to find a needle in a haystack. Bus smash. Train wreckage. Another crashed plane. Escape frenzy. Paracetamol overdose. Chainsaw attack. Falling blackness. Horrors piled up and I lost count of how many died or crashed with me as their witness. Still I didn't stop. Six, sixty, six hundred or six thousand degrees of separation: someone had to be able to show me my mum.

Suddenly minds lined up—freaked house husband in Seven Hills to hyperventilating florist in Penrith to suicidal butcher in the lower Blue Mountains suburb of Greenglen—and I was in Mum as she slurped wine and splashed ochre across a huge canvas.

Can't-sink-down-Try-calling-Danby-again-Gotta-hang-on.

Then she was gone. I bit my knuckle so I didn't cry out in frustration and jubilation. Hours for a second's insight! But at least I'd found her! It had been worth it for the sense of her it gave me. She was taking a mental battering but she was physically okay. She was doing everything she could to distract herself and hold on for my arrival. I couldn't let her down. But I couldn't get us going again until I was sure we weren't about to encounter an escaped prisoner along the river.

Shuffling beams of light caught me through the branches. My mind jumped to a woman weeping as she pedalled her bike along the river path. She wasn't looking for us or anyone. She was trying not to be found. I let myself breathe when her headlight skimmed away.

As much as I wanted to find Mum's mind again, I had to keep my focus on our immediate vicinity. No harm had been done by the bike woman getting so close. But I shuddered to think what would happen if I missed a murderer stumbling through the bush towards us.

Hour after hour, I stayed alert and kept watch. No one came through the trees, but weighed-down souls staggered regularly along the river path. Their names and stories were different but what they shared was the deep fear that they couldn't last much longer.

My head dipped and then jolted. I risked checking my phone quickly. Its glare startled me. So did the time. It was one in the morning. I'd been hiding like a frightened forest creature for half a day. I was exhausted but I couldn't risk falling asleep. I might slip back into the dark and empty place. I might wake up with some psycho killer looming over us.

No sleep till Shadow Valley. That was the vow I made before I passed out.

ELEVEN

I woke up gasping and sweaty and terrified. A dream of a screaming world faded from my mind as ash drifted down through the trees like dirty snow. Weak brown light filtered from a rusty sky speckled with tiny bats. Down by the coppery river, a cormorant circled, wings outstretched, searching for the sun. I checked the phone. Six past six. Still no network.

Evan was breathing steadily in my arms. I eased out from under him and stretched my legs painfully. A rabbit scampered behind a tuft of grass. Frogs started a croaking chorus. What I didn't see or hear was any human activity. I held my breath, closed my eyes, opened my senses as wide as they'd go. No one. Not nearby. Not far away. Just the warm smoky wind rustling dry leaves and birds calling tentative greetings to the strange morning.

I jumped up, joints popping and bones creaking, giddy with the rush of blood to my head but joyous at the thought that the telepathic fever had burned itself out while I slept. I looked down at Evan. Was he still catatonic? Or now just asleep?

'Evan?' I said. 'Wake up, sweet pea.'

He didn't stir. I shook his shoulder gently. Nothing.

I'd have to wait for someone to wander past. If I could tune into his or her mind, they'd tell me what was going on. If I couldn't, it'd mean the mind-sharing thing was over.

I sat back down. For once I had nothing to distract me from my actual physical world and its sharpness and solidity surprised me. Trees armoured with gnarled black bark. Tiny sapphire-flecked wrens flitted so weightlessly they barely stirred the branches.

My heart lurched as something crunched towards me. Maybe an escaped murderer, infinitely more dangerous now if I couldn't read his mind. Then a black bird followed its yellow beak out of the scrub. When my heart restarted, I plucked a dandelion and puffed on it to count the seed paratroopers floating away. I got to thirty. Then I did another.

As I sat and sat, it sank in that it wasn't only minds or voices that I couldn't hear. The mechanical background music of civilisation had been silenced. Motors, brakes, sirens, choppers: surely there had to be some of that if the recovery process had started. Or was the devastation so great that survivors couldn't get themselves organised? Surely someone would be along the path or river soon.

·•·

Next thing I knew I was wet and warm. Evan had pissed his pants and it'd soaked into me too. I checked my phone. After two! I couldn't believe that I'd drifted off for hours. At the same time I felt like I could sleep for days.

I still couldn't find anyone anywhere.

My insides went cold. I didn't want to think about it. Couldn't help myself. Maybe it wasn't that I *couldn't* read minds. Maybe there were no minds *left* to read.

'Bullshit!' I shouted, jumping up, daring someone to hear, hoping someone would. '*Bullshit!*'

The only response I got was pigeons flapping from a nearby tree. No one yelled back, 'Hey, over here!' or 'Who are you?' or 'Come out with your hands up!'

This was stupid. I had to find out what the hell was going on and where the hell everyone was. There might be an emergency assembly point just out of earshot and I was missing vital instructions on how to revive loved ones and where to go for food rations and crisis accommodations.

To find out anything, I'd have to leave Evan for a while. I thought he'd be safe in the foliage. But what if he woke up and wandered off? I might never find him. I puzzled over it for a second. Then, Lord forgive me, I used the sleeves of my jumper to tie him to the tree trunk. I'd give myself thirty minutes to get back.

The river path was empty in both directions. I paused to drink at the fountain and then walked east along the river. It wasn't long before the track took me inland and through a pine forest. When the path opened out again it led up a low hill.

This was Woo-la-ra. Aboriginal for 'the lookout place'. The sign made it clear it wasn't a sacred site but rather a man-made mound built around a toxic waste dump and planted with native grasses. Whatever was buried under me couldn't be much worse than air that was as grainy as an old film and rough in my throat as I trudged up the hill.

On the path's final rise I stopped.

'Oh, Christ.'

A heavily tattooed young guy wearing only red Speedos was sprawled on the dirt track. He was face up, pasty arms thrust out, feet crossed at the ankles. A crow had perched on his chest.

'Hey! Get off him!'

The bird screeched into the sooty sky. Despite the crow's predations, the dude looked peaceful. His eyes were closed and his long hair framed a thin, bearded face. Next to Bogan Jesus was a little graveyard of stubbed-out cigarettes and a drained bottle of Jack Daniels.

'Hello?' I said.

But I knew he was past resurrection. The guy wasn't a Goner. He was gone. What I'd taken as gnarly tattoos were streaks of post-mortem marbling coloured in by early decomposition. There was a livid purple tideline where his body rested on the ground. Now I heard the buzz of flies and saw the empty pill bottle clenched tight in one fist. A warm gust brought a whiff of him strong enough to cut through the smoke. I retched and stumbled into the tall grass and didn't inhale again until I was up the hill and upwind.

Woo-la-ra's peak was manicured, arranged with park benches and silver plaques pointing to distant landmarks. But what should have been a panorama of Sydney offered only glimpses of a landscape being set in amber.

I squinted at the city in the distance, sailing in and out of the sallow haze, Sydney Tower like the tallest mast on a ghost ship. A fireball bloomed near The Rocks, creating a shadow flash of the shattered Harbour Bridge in the gloom. Then an oily squall drew a billowing black curtain across the skyline. From here to that dark horizon, blaze after blaze poured more toxic ink into the atmosphere.

My clearest view was of the apartment edifices just beneath Woo-la-ra. People hunched motionless on balconies with dead phones and tablets. More bodies dotted the gardens and walkways fringing the complexes. Action figures strewn by some careless kid. Streets and paths and lawns were clotted with cars. Drivers slow-cooking in the heat and humidity.

My eyes followed the main road into Olympic Park. There were hundreds of people. Not one moved. Even from here I could see some were dead. But most looked like they were in stand-by mode as eddies of smoke swirled around them. The ones who were still upright spooked me most. I kept thinking they were faking, that they'd suddenly spring back to life.

Weren't the living dead supposed to shamble around? Rip us apart for food? Symbolise all that was wrong with humanity? I didn't know what to make of this. Should I fear these figures or be fearful for them?

Goners. I chided myself for thinking it again. They weren't doomed. Like Evan wasn't. Surely they'd all wake up when they got hungry or thirsty enough, wouldn't they?

To the north yachts and cruisers drifted on the river, while on the far shore nothing stirred in a McMansion development.

To the west there stood a sky-high brown wall where the Blue Mountains should have defined the horizon. I didn't know whether that smokescreen had been created by fires in the outer suburbs or blazes in the distant bush. Maybe it had all burned overnight and Mum and Shadow Valley were already cinder.

No! I couldn't think that way any more than I could let myself think about the sick feeling swelling in my guts.

'No way, uh-uh, statistically that can't be, there're others, has to be, I—'

I was muttering. Exactly what the last girl on earth would do when she went stark raving mad. I could not think like that. I would find other sentient people. I would find help for Evan. I would get to Mum and she would be fine. If I didn't believe those things I might as well grab some dirt next to Bogan Jesus.

Parramatta's modest skyline offered hope. On the other side of the nature reserve and parklands, past a shiny silver refinery and industrial estates, the city's glass-and-steel towers stood intact. Nothing there seemed touched by fire. That might not last. All the more reason to get Evan and get going.

·•·

I untied my little brother and carried him back to the kayak. Maybe I should paddle out to the speedboat floating east. Get it started and we would get to Parramatta faster. I quashed the idea. Told myself it was stealing. But I really was too freaked out by the prospect of climbing aboard only to find a zoned-out or blue-tinged body.

With Evan in the cockpit, I pushed the kayak into the shallows. I was about to climb in behind him when I spotted the monster. A crocodile—coming downriver. I couldn't believe my eyes. I'd seen the chaos at the zoo but could an escaped croc have swum this far up the harbour already? I tried to haul the kayak back to shore with mud sucking at my every step. The croc's black torpedo body was almost on me when I realised my mistake. I never thought I'd be relieved to see a dead body. But that's what it was: a half-submerged biker in black leathers and helmet. The man floated past me face down within arm's reach. Then another corpse bobbed by. She was also mercifully face down. Blonde hair billowing, arms and legs splayed, tracksuit puffy with air pockets: the girl looked like she was skydiving.

I fought to regain my breath. Steadied myself and the kayak. Yanked my feet out of the mud and took us onto the river. As I paddled slowly west, more bodies floated past. But I was less disturbed by the watery dead than by the living left on the land. Men in prison jumpsuits, guards in uniform, mums and dads in casual clothes, boys and girls in bright new outfits—they were like litter around the cafe, playground and grassy hills. When I cried, nothing came. I'd run out of tears.

I took in the traffic glut on the Silverwater Bridge with weary resignation. People had remained cocooned by their air conditioning and stereos until nothing worked anymore, nothing made sense, nothing was all they could embrace. Those who had got out didn't get far. Faces pressed against the pedestrian fence, like primates passed out against their cages, bars held in their clenched fists. Their eyes were closed but I still felt accusatory stares, imagined them hating me for surviving when they'd succumbed. In fact, I would've welcomed hatred, anger, anything. But not a mind flickered. Not on the bridge. Not in the shadows of its abutments. Not in the surrounding suburbs.

At least the people of Pompeii had been able to huddle together when the end came pouring down. Most of these guys hadn't even had that comfort. They were spread out as though obeying some unseen grid because when privacy had evaporated personal space had been the only thing left.

The river closed on the other side of the bridge. A few desperate souls had crashed out knee deep in mud and clutching mangrove trunks. I saw where the high tide had reached up their bodies. They'd been lucky not to drown. Then I saw the unlucky one. He was just head, torso and arms wrapped around a branch hanging low to the water. Nothing left beneath the waist. I wondered whether he'd been run over by some frantic speedboat. It didn't matter. I just wanted to put the sight behind me. I paddled faster and was glad there was nothing in my stomach to throw up.

The refinery monstered up from behind the swampy shore. Shiny towers and silos. White storage vats. Spiral staircases. It looked like something out of a sci-fi film but there was nothing more down-to-earth. Civilisation's blood had been processed here, pumped in as crude oil, sent back out as petrol and diesel and whatever else. Signs on channel markers—'Danger!— Submarine High-Pressure Pipelines!'—warned that right below us lay a network of veins and ventricles. Surely when the Christmas Day shift lost their shit someone flipped the safety switches? Surely even if no one had, there were automatic mechanisms to stop the place going supernova?

I paused mid-paddle in a moment of preternatural silence. It was like the universe was considering my questions. Then came the answer. Sirens whooped. Warning lights flashed. Workers didn't scramble to emergency stations to avoid catastrophe. No one was going to save us but me.

My paddle bounced off something rubbery in the water. Fat guy. Big and bloated. As I went to push him away with the blade, he rolled so that a pudgy arm flailed up at me. I yelled as a grey snout ripped a chunk from the corpse and the river churned with thrashing fins and tails. Sharks thudded against the kayak's hull. Black eyes rolled in grey bullet heads and razor teeth flashed from gummy mouths. The sharks weren't large but what they lacked in size they made up for in numbers. I held the paddle over my head so it wouldn't be bitten in half and the boat rocked hard in the pink frothy water. If we capsized we'd be wedged upside down in the feeding frenzy. We'd be sardines.

I heaved the paddle at a space between the sharks. Managed to propel us forwards. Scooped the water again. Got us closer to the edge of the carnage. The refinery wailed so loud it shook the mangrove leaves. I imagined some tiny static spark igniting a cylinder or tank. An explosion in the pipes underneath us. A scalding fireball shooting us high into the air. Me and Evan blinking like cartoon characters at the apex of that burning fountain before we plummeted amid the snapping sharks.

Bright flames whooshed from the tip of a refinery tower. I closed my eyes. Buried my head in Evan's neck. Braced for death.

There was no pain. No blinding light and searing heat. Just silence as the sirens cut out. I dared to look up. Plumes of flame fluttered above silver-latticed stacks. I looked at the water around me. The snouts and jaws and fins and tails were gone. Best I could guess: the flames were the refinery's fail-safe and the sharks were following the bodies down the river. I wasn't going to stick around and be proved wrong. So I paddled as hard as I could to get us away.

But I knew this wasn't really crisis averted—life was crisis now.

Once we were clear, I slowed my pace and the rest of the journey to Parramatta was almost peaceful. Ahead and behind, visibility dwindled and even the mangroves disappeared in the haze. Future and past seemed to vanish. My existence was reduced to soft splashing through brown water and brown air. I was grateful for this blurry space. I knew there were hundreds of suburbs on either side of the river where millions of people were in danger of dying. But being inside that cloud let me block it out. Just for a little while.

TWELVE

The world came back gradually. Mangroves gave way to industrial estates and then backyard fences. I passed under an old iron bridge and Parramatta's skyline massed into solid rectangles above the river. We entered the city and cruised into the centre of a watery cul-de-sac.

A sleek ferry wharf jutted from one shore and on the opposite side an apartment building stood on a sandstone cliff. Straight ahead lay a weir and pedestrian bridge. Above them, the river continued through the city, enclosed by concrete and parkland.

There were a dozen Goners on the wharf. Most were laid out loose and peaceful. A few sat stiffly with limbs at mannequin angles. One guy, whose tattered clothes sketched his story for survival, stood by a pylon, mouth set in a grimace, arm outstretched like he was reaching after a departing ferry. When I tried to find minds, here or in the city beyond, all I heard was my heartbeat, the cry of seagulls, and water lapping the kayak.

Surely there had to be other people. Maybe I just wasn't in range of whoever was out there. For now, I faced going it alone in this flatlined place. Wandering among the Goners was the second freakiest thing I could think of doing. The freakiest was being so paralysed with fear that we floated here until we died of dehydration.

I paddled to the wharf. A plaque read: 'Gi walawa and nalawala at Baramada'. The Aboriginal-to-English translation underneath seemed just for me: 'Please stop here and rest at Parramatta'. The tourist map was more direct: 'You are here!' it declared, pinpointing my place on the planet. It confirmed that when the river came out the other side of Parramatta Park it dribbled into a suburban creek. My kayaking days were over. I had no idea how I'd get us from here to Shadow Valley.

I tied the kayak to the wharf, pulled myself onto the concrete platform and lifted Evan out after me. I stood still and quiet, eyes darting between people on the gangway and benches and on the pathways beyond. A few were dead, skin changing colour, clothes matted with dried blood, flies buzzing around them. But the rest were still alive. I could hear the people closest to me as their stomachs gurgled and their chests rose and fell with raspy breaths.

Standing there among the living dead slammed reality home. There really might not be anyone else left like me.

'Why?' I croaked. 'Why me?'

Had a higher power singled me out for some greater purpose yet to be revealed? Had I won the genetic lottery with a one-in-eight-billion genomic quirk?

I heard an ugly noise. Realised it was me laughing. Maybe I hadn't been mystically chosen so much as simply forgotten by the creator. Maybe humanity had run its natural course and my freaky DNA had made me the last member of a soon-to-be-extinct species.

All I knew beyond doubt was that I was starving. If I had to fulfil humanity's destiny by dying, I would damned well do it after dinner.

A cafe called Starboard overlooked the wharf. It seemed as good a place as any to hole up. I tucked Evan under my arm and dragged him through the miserable congregation of catatonics. As best I could, I tried to keep my distance. I knew they were as harmless as Evan but I also thought if someone snapped back to consciousness I'd probably die of fright.

Up on street level, there were Goners everywhere. On the nearest corner, a woman sat on the kerb, red dress hiked up around her thighs, mouth resting on her knuckles like Rodin's thinker. Beyond her, a canyon of glass, steel and concrete was carpeted with stalled cars and frozen people.

Someone had beaten me to Starboard, judging from the smashed glass doors. I eased Evan down against a blackboard that wished customers a Merry Christmas. Edging closer, I peered into the cafe's dark interior.

A figure knelt on a table, arms raised to the heavens.

'Hello?'

As my vision adjusted, I saw it was a he and he wasn't praying or pleading for mercy. This guy had hooked his fingers over the top of a wall widescreen and connected himself to it with headphones. He was now as blank as the TV.

Stepping into Starboard, I saw the Plasma Guy was about my age, heavy set body wrapped in oversized streetwear. His eyes were clenched tight and his nose was pressed against the screen. I knew I should try to prise him down, but I told myself I'd overbalance the table and hurt him. Truth was, the idea of touching him freaked me out.

He was alive—I could hear him breathing softly. When I worked out how to wake up Evan I'd wake him up too.

I carried Evan inside and lay him down in a booth seat. Regular customers smiled from photos collaged on the 'Star's Board!' I tried not to think about the black holes that had replaced each of those people. Instead, I turned my attention to the menu board that had kept them coming back. Asian salmon salad. Lamb and goat's cheese pizza. Organic beef burger with the lot. It all sounded good. But the glass cabinets had been cleared out. Even the cookie jars were empty.

A tall fridge was unlocked and still stocked. I grabbed a bottle of warm lemonade and gulped it down. The walk-in pantry offered some basics: tins of fish and baked beans and crushed tomatoes, boxes of crackers and cereals, packets of pasta and cooking chocolate. I didn't have to worry about starving. There should be food wherever I went—houses, convenience stores, entire shopping centres—at least until all the used-by dates had been reached. It wasn't like I had competition.

I ate tuna with corn chips and salsa and drank nearly a litre of apple juice. It made me feel better immediately but also guilty and worried that I couldn't give Evan anything. I checked my phone. Seven o'clock. Over thirty hours now since he'd had the

Chocopops and milk. Maybe Evan's inactivity would buy him bonus time. Didn't every earthquake disaster story come with the good news of a small child plucked alive from the rubble after weeks without sustenance?

I moved into the booth next to Evan. When I had blacked out back at Beautopia Point, his voice had rescued me. That was where I should start. Maybe he'd respond to a few of his favourite things.

'Chocopops, Evan.' I held his hand and held in my mind an image of a plastic cup overflowing with the sugary breakfast treats. I pictured a booger splattering a robot. 'Snots 'N' Bots.'

I repeated the words, aloud and in my mind, and wove them together, visualising a strong rope lowering into the darkness. *Chocopops Snotsnbots!*

Visualising climbing down the rope and swinging at its end, I tried to grab him from the imagined abyss. He was inches away but miles beyond my reach.

'Chocopops, Snots'N'Bots,' I said beside him in the booth, lightly shaking his shoulder. 'Come on, Evan. Please.'

He couldn't hear my thoughts or words. I slammed my fists against the table.

Peeling Evan from his damp and smelly clothes, I washed him with a bottle of mineral water and wrapped him in tablecloths. At least he was clean and dry. In the little staff bathroom, I cleaned myself and hung my jeans to dry. Not that it was the highest priority but I would find us new clothes tomorrow.

Through the cafe's windows rectangles of sky darkened between buildings as night descended. There was nothing more to do now. But at first light I had to set about hydrating Evan. Buy more time to figure out how to wake him up.

I reached for my phone. Stopped myself with a snort. I couldn't search the internet for the answer. Google was gone. The Cloud was up in smoke. Even if I could locate a bookstore, I doubted I'd just be able to pluck *IV Drips for Dummies* off its bestseller shelves.

But a doctor's office! That's where I might find a textbook and the necessary solutions and bags and needles and tubes. I laughed at myself. Sourcing the right information and the right equipment was one thing. Poking a hole into little brother and pumping him full of saline or whatever was an entirely different matter. I might puncture an artery and he'd bleed out—or I'd put air in his veins and give him the bends. Thing was, if I didn't try Evan would dry up and die.

Exhaustion seeped into me. Sleep promised an escape. I made a rough bed of cushions under the table and curled us up in there. Evan breathed wispily and I willed morning to come so I could start saving him.

I awoke to a white flash so brilliant it seared through my eyelids. Then came a sky-ripping crack and a rumble that shook the cafe. I grabbed Evan, ready to run. Then there was another flash, another crash, and a storm broke over Parramatta.

Relief washed through me. I lay back down, stroked Evan's hair, letting myself drift into the sound of the rain. I hoped the deluge was drowning the fires. As I slipped into sleep, I thought maybe people caught in the downpour would wake up now, like born-again Christians baptised into a new life with Jesus.

Buddha's wisdom greeted me when I opened my eyes again. Starboard was lit by another eerie dawn.

'Do not dwell in the past, do not dream of the future, concentrate the mind on the present moment,' read a banner on the ceiling.

My eyes moved to a second message.

'I existed from all eternity and, behold, I am here; and I shall exist till the end of time, for my being has no end,' someone named Kahlil Gibran had once said.

And a third, from George Bernard Shaw: 'You see things; and you say, "Why?" But I dream things that never were; and I say, "Why not?"'

Maxims were all across the ceiling. Account managers and personal trainers had stared up at these quotes as they waited for their lunch orders. My eyes drifted to the gossip magazines set by the counter to cater for more trivial tastes.

'THE END FOR JEN & GEORGE?!'

'HELLBANGA'S VATICAN SCANDAL!'

'B-LO'S NEW LOVE!'

I couldn't imagine these celebrities as Goners. It made more sense that they were all somehow immune and partying behind velvet ropes in a VIP survivors' lounge.

I listened to Evan's chest. Felt the pulse in his neck. Touched his forehead. He seemed fine. Then it struck me: there was a way to tell if his brain was okay. I turned his face to the windows and pushed his eyelids open and watched his big pupils shrink from the light. Yes! They weren't 'fixed and dilated'—which was what

147

television doctors said gravely when someone was going to be a vegetable—and I gave him a hug.

But to save him I had to leave him for a while. I hoped he'd be safe under the table. I slid out and peered up at the Plasma Guy. He was still kneeling on his table, a steadily breathing statue on a pedestal. I was glad he'd made it. Outside it would be a different story. There were dead people and they would've started to smell. I spied a little stand of chewing gum, tore open a packet and munched pieces, sucking in menthol-flavoured air. I didn't know if that'd be enough so I found a tea towel, dabbed it with floral hand lotion and wrapped it around my nose and mouth like a Resist protestor trying to beat facial recognition. I pulled on my jeans and grabbed a bottle of water from the fridge. I was as ready as I could be.

The sky had dulled to tarnished silver and grey drizzle had stripped the world of colour. At least the storm and wind had cleared some of the smoke. Now the planet, or my little part of it, looked like a wet ashtray. At least when I inhaled I only smelled a strange mixture of menthol and moisturiser.

The deluge hadn't woken anyone. From the riverbanks to the city corners, everyone was where they'd been last night— just drenched. All except the woman in red. During the storm her weight had shifted and she had toppled into the gutter. Now she was submerged in a little pool that had formed where her body and other debris had blocked the drain. I didn't run to her. The time for heroics had been the middle of the night. That's when she'd been drowning in a puddle of rainwater while I'd entertained fantasies about baptismal resurrections.

'I'm so sorry,' I whispered. 'I'm so sorry.'

I allowed myself a moment of revulsion and shame. But I'd be lucky if she was the worst thing I saw today and if this was the worst I felt. I had to put her out of my mind and get on with my mission. All that mattered was finding IV stuff and getting back to Evan. Once he was stabilised I could put my mind to waking him up and getting us to Shadow Valley.

I'd read about people who disassociated when faced with trauma. They floated outside themselves to avoid going insane, even though that usually happened later when all the bad memories came flooding back. I didn't know whether it was possible to will such a personality split, but as I stepped onto the street I tried to step out of myself. It worked—for about four seconds.

The financial district—blocks of Goners between cars and beneath office towers—was more than I could handle. Just thinking about venturing among them made me tremble so much I thought I'd crumple into a pile next to the grandpa at the bus stop, his best suit soaked, drizzle pooling in the brim of his fedora.

I couldn't force myself to brave this claustrophobic nightmare but I couldn't give up and retreat to Starboard. There had to be another way. I clenched my fists, took a deep masked breath and visualised the tourist map down on the ferry wharf and the ribbon of river running through the city. There'd be more space and air and light there. It'd still get me to the main shopping district. That's where I'd find a doctor's surgery or a medical centre.

A lot of people must have thought the waterway and its banks were a possible escape route or safer place. They'd poured down here and passed out on the paths and lawns. Some had ended up in the river. Their bodies bobbed against the concrete weir wall in a frothy slurry of leaves and rubbish.

I wandered in slow motion, feeling like an intruder, imagining the Goners were watching me. A heavy woman in a tracksuit had collapsed with her legs folded tight under her. Junkies and drunks who passed out like that risked amputation as blood flow was cut off. I tilted the lady onto her side and straightened her out. Maybe that made amends for not helping the drowned woman. But I couldn't save the guy who'd ended his suffering by putting a plastic bag over his head.

A labrador sat by a blind man like a miserable wet sphinx. For a second, I thought she had crashed with her owner. Then she looked my way.

'Hey!' I said, pulling my bandana down and sticking my hand out. 'It's okay. It's okay.'

She let me ruffle her big golden head. I choked up at the comfort it gave me.

'Good girl,' I said. 'What a good girl.'

I stood up, stepped back, patted the front of my thighs. 'Come on. You come with me now.'

The dog watched me with big mournful eyes.

I tried for a while longer but she wouldn't leave her master's side. I poured some of my water into a takeaway container and set it down for her. I'd bring her some food when I'd taken care of everything else.

Bandana back on and head down against the horror, the path under my feet became a mosaic of murals and plaques about the Burramattagal clan who'd been the original custodians of this place. Archaeologists had uncovered stone axes and shark-tooth pendants here twice as old as the pyramids. The sun had risen and set over their river millions of times and then one day everything changed with the arrival of visitors from another world. The spectral figures wore strange fabrics, spoke a foreign tongue, piloted huge ships and wielded weapons of lethal magic in the name of unknowable gods. But the Burramattagal people's deadliest enemy was even stranger. Smallpox—invisible, unimaginable—killed two thirds of them within a few years of European settlement. Their dead had been too numerous to bury.

I wondered if we'd been struck down by something like that, the ultimate case of never kowing what hit us. I glanced at the river, with its mucky coating of plastic rubbish, at the parklands, covered with Goners and corpses, and at the Parramatta skyline, all glass and steel, and wondered how much of our world would remain to tell our story in one hundred centuries from now.

Sandstone stairs took me up to the Lennox Bridge on Church Street. The road was blocked where a bus had crashed and rolled. The front end rested on a crumbling balustrade. I prayed it'd hold as I ducked and crawled under the bus. Halfway across I glanced up, saw I was inches from bloated faces pressed against splintered windows, oozing bloody gunk through cracked glass.

Scrabbling out the other side, I tore off my bandana, used it to wipe slime from my cheeks and hair before dropping it to the road. I staggered to the footpath, spat out my gum and retched. When I straightened up, calmer, I saw Church Street was bumper-to-bumper traffic.

It was easy to see whether there was anyone in cars with smashed windshields and wide-open doors. Mostly, they were empty, though a few contained corpses and Goners. But the majority of vehicles were locked up tight and their windows were fogged with condensation. I was glad for two reasons: the people inside were still breathing and I didn't have to look at them.

The footpath was another story. I had to hop over a muscle-bound guy wearing only a red singlet. A few metres later I took a big stride to clear an Indian man whose white kurta was streaked with soot. Then I was stepping over a goth girl face down with a phone clutched in each pale hand.

I wanted to run. To get away from these people as quickly as possible. But wherever I went there'd be more of them. What I needed to change wasn't my location but my perspective. I had to banish all the zombie movie clichés I'd absorbed. These people didn't want to eat me and they didn't need to be shot in the head. They weren't just harmless. They were *helpless*. If anything I should be thinking of some way to save them. Even Mr Muscle back there.

Off the bridge I came to a smorgasbord of Thai, Indian, Lebanese, Malaysian and Italian restaurants. Being closed on Christmas morning hadn't spared these places the chaos of panicking drivers making rubble of outdoor terraces and dining rooms. But a cafe called Noosphere clearly had been open and it was a mess of overturned tables and chairs, sprayed food and smashed cutlery. A guy in kitchen whites slouched in a booth. Another man was spread out on the counter.

I stepped through the shattered doorway, fascinated not by the destruction but by the fact that this place's decorative focus actually had been death and disaster. Noosphere's back wall was a gallery of oversized reproductions of famous front pages. My eyes went from WWI's horrors at places called Somme and Paschendale to its sequel's opening salvos in Poland and Pearl Harbor; from the various collapses of Wall Street to the actual collapse of the World Trade Center; from the assassinations of JFK, RFK and MLK to the untimely deaths of Marilyn Monroe, Elvis Presley and Michael Jackson; from the Tet Offensive and Watergate to the exploding Hindenberg and the disintegrating Space Shuttle. But the centrepiece was *The New York Times* dated April 15, 1912: '*Titanic* Sinks Four Hours After Hitting Iceberg; 866 Rescued By Carpathia, Probably 1250 Perish; Ismay Safe, Mrs Astor Maybe, Noted Names Missing'. I imagined my headline. 'Civilisation Sunk By Telepathic Plague; Eight Billion Perish, Including Hellbanga And B-Lo. One Known Survivor A Nobody, 16'.

There would be no headlines and no stories. No one was left to report the Snap and no one was left to read about it. But staring at that big wall did give me an idea about what had happened to us. Not the stories themselves. Rather the frequency of 'good' to 'bad' news. Only three 'positive' events had made the cut: the conquest of Everest; man walking on the moon; the fall of the Berlin Wall. Our media teacher Miss Doran had said old news editors lived by the motto 'If it bleeds, it leads' and she'd said our tendency to post many more negative than positive comments on blogs was a modern equivalent. What I thought was that maybe we'd internalised that outlook for so long that when everyone became broadcasters and receivers what was bad about us was just that much louder than all that was good.

I picked my way along Church Street, jumping over bodies and clambering over cars. When I reached an intersection, I climbed onto the roof of a mini-van. Every corner told its own horror story. In TribalZoo, set up like an old-school barber's shop, a ripped dude still cradled the tattoo gun he'd used to turn his face and chest into a scrawl of blood and ink. Across the road, Hiphop Asylum had been looted. A body lay collapsed in the doorway in a pile of parkas and hoodies. Opposite, no one had touched the Commonwealth Bank, or the homeless guy who sat outside it, surrounded by shopping bags, cracked caveman feet stuck out in front of him. I watched him a while, thinking that because he probably battled disembodied voices daily he might've had some resistance. But he didn't stir under his dreadlocks. Neither did anyone at the Liquor Barn on the final corner. The place reeked of booze and vomit and blood and looked like a departure lounge for an eternally delayed flight to hell. People had hunkered in the aisles, flopped in its doorway, roosted in its windows and spilled onto the footpath as they tried to escape by drinking themselves to death. Some had made it. Those who hadn't didn't know any different and looked like they might be sleeping this one off forever anyway.

It'd been well over a day since I'd seen another conscious person. Just in the few blocks around me there were hundreds of Goners and I had no doubt there were thousands more in the surrounding city grid. I feared that zooming out from this intersection would simply add more zeroes: tens of thousands and then hundreds of thousands and then into the millions.

I stepped from the mini-van's roof onto an adjacent car bonnet and then onto the road. I sank to my knees. The Snap had sent me running from the madding crowd. Now I'd give anything not to be utterly alone.

Be careful what you wish for. That hadn't been written on Starboard's ceiling. Maybe it should've been.

THIRTEEN

Dance music blasted from a few blocks east. I recognised the tune immediately. You hadn't been able to go anywhere a few years back without the song oozing from earbuds, cafes, clothing stores. Even Evan, then three, could sing all the words and do the official dance, which had created another flurry of false hope for Stephanie.

It got me to my feet and I shuffled through the clutter of cars towards the sound. My fear of finding a random car stereo triggered by some electrical spasm evaporated when a hoarse male voice belted out, 'Party Dude!'

Just by itself that moronic two-word chorus would've been the sweetest sound I'd ever heard because it meant I wasn't alone. What made my heart really skip a beat was that I couldn't hear the mind of the singer. He was like me—and if there were two of us there had to be others.

I'd hated the song. I loved it now.

His head bobbed above car roofs, half a block away, and I went up on a Mercedes, about to start shouting and waving.

Then I dropped to the bitumen, crouched behind the car, trying to process what I'd seen.

The Party Duder was enormous. Big square head, close-cropped hair, tattooed body rippling out from under a sprayed-on T-shirt. He was taking belts from a bottle of tequila and thrusting in time to his boombox.

Anger boiled in me. The catatonic woman bent over the car bonnet was defenceless. I had to stop him. Attacking wasn't an option. He was twice my size. Angry abuse wouldn't work. Not without other people to shame him. My eyes fell on a full bottle of beer amid the debris on the street. Back in year seven I'd been the best pitcher in my softball team. I picked up the missile and ducked from Merc to Daihatsu to Honda to Saab until I was in range. I eased up slowly, wound up, ready to knock his block off. Then my mind got in the way: if I missed, this bastard might get me—and then Evan would die.

As I hesitated, the Party Duder finished in time with the end of the song.

'Awesome!' he yelled in the silence.

'Hey girl.' He laughed. 'If you liked that, you're going to love this!'

All at once I saw the gun and the puff of smoke and a spray of dark blood in her blonde hair. The gunshot was so loud and sharp in the empty city that I startled and let the bottle drop. It smashed with a distinct pop in the gunshot's echo.

I ducked, kept low, ran.

'Hey! Who's there?'

For a second the Party Duder sounded busted and embarrassed.

'Don't go! I was just mucking around!'

My only response was the *slap-slap* of my boots on the wet bitumen as I scurried back to the intersection. Then I heard the crunch of metal as he came up and over cars and after me.

'Run!' he yelled, laughing. 'Run, little rabbit!'

I rounded the corner into Church Street. I couldn't outpace him. He was bigger and faster. Besides, there was no way I could get any speed up with all the people and vehicles in the way. My best chance wasn't to run but to hide. But getting into a car or a store would make too much noise. I knew he hadn't seen me so I dropped to the footpath and arranged myself face down among the Goners.

From the corner of a squinted eye, I saw the Party Duder storm up onto the mini-van's roof. His chest was heaving and he was waving his gun.

I imagined his view from up there. A choked street. Hundreds of people. If I could keep my nerve, he wouldn't find me.

'Come out, come out wherever you are!'

The Party Duder dropped onto the road, peered through windshields, checked under chassis.

I closed my eyes, tried not to breathe, prayed he wouldn't hear my heart thumping.

'Are you . . . under the Toyota? Naaaa. How about . . . in the taxi? Hmmm.'

His voice got louder, the slamming doors and crunching glass closer.

The Party Duder stopped somewhere near me. A lighter flicked. I smelled cigarette smoke. Heard a satisfied exhalation.

'Nice try,' he said. 'Hiding in plain sight.'

I wondered whether by playing dead I'd killed myself—or whether he was bluffing and trying to flush me out.

I didn't move.

'But bitch, you're not smarter than me,' he said. 'If you'd been out here all night, like the rest of these zombies, you'd be soaked through. But you're dry, aren't ya?'

I pushed my cheek harder into the gravel as if I might pass through the road.

'I'm talking to you, girl,' he said. 'Brown jumper, dirty jeans, boots. Roll over, gimme look atcha.'

I didn't move.

'How about this? I give you to the count of three and then pow. You get what she got anyway—just the other way around.'

Before I rolled over, I made myself three promises.

'One,' he barked.

I wasn't going to say a word.

'Two.'

I wasn't going to look away.

'Three.'

I wasn't going down without a fight.

I turned over, sat up and stared up at him.

'Jeez, you're a kid,' he said, leering. 'What's your name, baby?'

Party Duder's words were crammed together, thick with booze and whatever else. His eyes were rusty but shiny, like old ball bearings. He was being all gangsta, holding the gun sideways, but his hand shook so much he might miss me.

'Whatcha name? Huh?'

Sweat rolled off his spray-tanned slab of face and his stubbled jaw flexed.

'Oh, baby, we're gonna party. Party Dude!'

His nostrils flared and veins pulsed in his temples. He blinked rapidly, like he was trying to focus. This man was coming apart. His contents were under too much pressure. Maybe he'd simply explode. Drop dead of a brain haemorrhage. I wouldn't be that lucky.

When his party ended, I'd be dead—and he'd kill Evan without even knowing it. Another reason to claw this shithead's eyes out before I died.

'Tell me your name, bitch.'

I stared. Said nothing. Tensed to launch myself at him.

Party Duder flicked his cigarette away, stepped closer and steadied the .45 at me. Even tweaking this hard he wouldn't miss now.

'You better tell me before I—'

Thunk.

I registered the noise. Party Duder's puzzled look. The flash of a silver stud just above his top lip. I hadn't noticed his facial jewellery before. The piercing must've been pretty fresh. Blood was welling from it.

The nasty glint in the Party Duder's eyes dulled and his granite physique crumbled. His arm dropped, the gun slipped from his fingers and he crumpled face first onto the road.

In his place stood a dark-skinned guy. He was lean, a few years older than me, dressed in jeans, sweatshirt and a red baseball cap. I had no idea what was in his head but his hand held a cordless nail gun. My eyes slid to the Party Duder's .45 now within arm's reach on the bitumen.

'Don't!' the guy said. 'You don't have to do that!'

I stared back at him in shock. Wondered how accurate his power tool could be. I guess the answer to that lay bleeding with a shattered skull just a few feet away.

'I'm not going to hurt you,' he said. 'Look.'

The guy lowered the nail gun to the street and brought his hands up empty. 'Are you okay?'

His voice was shaky and his hands trembled.

Scrambling for the .45 seemed rude after his show of good faith. Not to mention the whole saving my life thing. I heard myself answer as if from far away: 'I think so.'

The guy broke eye contact and I followed his gaze to the body beside me. Blood pooled around the Party Duder's punctured head.

'Oh my God, is he—he—' the guy said.

'Dead.' It was still dawning on me that I wasn't. I climbed to my feet. 'You killed him.'

The guy's eyes glistened. He took off his cap and ran his fingers through his black hair. 'Oh, shit, I didn't mean— I mean—it looked like—I thought he was going to—'

'Hurt me?' I didn't think this guy was a threat. He seemed on the verge of a panic attack. Not that I blamed him. 'He was going to *kill* me.'

The guy wiped tears from his cheeks. 'I should've given him a warning.'

I shook my head. 'You'd be dead. Me too. You did the right thing. Thank you.'

We gazed at each other as our shock lifted. Sizing each other up. Making sure we weren't mistaken. We didn't need telepathy to know we were both wondering whether we could see further than each other's eyes.

'I can't hear you or whatever,' he said, finally.

He broke into a big grin. I beamed right back.

'Me either.'

'I'm Nathan.' He stuck his hand out. 'Nathan Kapur.'

I grabbed it and we shook.

'Danby, Danby Armstrong,' I told him. 'Pleased to meet you.'

We burst out laughing at the formality but the sound echoing around the street soon sobered us. Guffawing in a dying city was wrong. A maniac lay dead at our feet. Any noise we made might bring more.

'When I heard the music,' Nathan said quietly, 'it was like, great, I'm not the only one. But then you were running and he was chasing and I just followed.'

'You always carry a nail gun?'

'I found it yesterday on the street,' he said, not getting that I was joking. 'Having it made me feel safer.'

Nathan chewed a fingernail as he looked back at the Party Duder.

'I really didn't mean to—' he said.

'Kill him?' A red mist rose in me. '*Screw* him!'

Nathan's eyes went wide.

'Screw you!' I screamed at the Party Duder. It wasn't enough. I kicked his body hard and ribs cracked. 'Screw you, you evil piece of shit motherf—'

Nathan came closer. 'Hey,' he said. 'Hey.'

Simple human need closed the gap between us. We hugged. He told me it was all right as I shuddered with angry sobs. Then he was sniffling into my shoulder and it was my turn to say he'd had no choice. Gradually, we calmed and I pulled free.

'I have to go.'

'Can I come?' Nathan looked stricken. 'I mean, can't we stick together?'

'Yes, of course.' I was sorry to spook him. The thought of being alone again horrified me too. 'What I meant is I have to help my little brother.'

Nathan listened as I rushed through my plan to stabilise Evan and then somehow get back on my way to Mum's place in Shadow Valley. When I finished, he grinned.

'I'm not sure I can help with the second part,' he said. 'The roads are in pretty bad shape. But I can definitely do the first part.'

'What?' He had my full attention. 'You're a doctor?'

Nathan nodded and shook his head. 'Yes, no—medical student, second year.'

'Then you can—'

'An IV's no problem,' Nathan said. 'But if I'm right about something we might not need to worry about that.'

I blinked at him.

'I might—*might*—be able to wake your brother up.' He looked from me to the Goners all around us. 'You and me, Danby, I think we might actually be able to save a lot of these people.'

FOURTEEN

Nathan and I stayed shoulder to shoulder as we advanced through the living dead. Him sweeping the street with his nail gun, me pointing the Party Duder's .45 at shadows: we were the least intimidating post-apocalyptic militia imaginable. Luckily the only movement we encountered was our own shadowy reflections shifting across car windows and shop glass.

'Hardware store first, then pharmacy,' Nathan had said. 'Can I explain while we walk?'

I'd nodded and picked up the Party Duder's gun. 'Let's go.'

'Obviously, I don't know what happened to the world,' Nathan began as we crept deeper into the city along Church Street. 'But I think I know how it's left people. See this guy?'

Nathan made a beeline for a man in overalls standing in the intersection, hands spread in front of his face like he was trying to ward off the attack of an invisible bird.

'I know,' I said. 'It freaks me out.'

Gently, Nathan straightened the man's arms until he stood at attention. Then he stood back like a window dresser admiring his work.

'Why'd you do that?' I hissed.

'I wanted to show you,' Nathan said. 'It's called "waxy flexibility" and it's a classic symptom of catatonia.'

'That's good news?'

Nathan rubbed his hands together excitedly. 'It is. Catatonia can be reversed.'

'How?'

'They used to use electroshock—'

I bristled.

'—but more recently they've had a lot of success with Lorazepam.'

He saw I didn't know what that was.

'It's a fairly common benzodiazepine. Have you heard of Valium? It's like that.'

Valium I understood: girls at school swore by popping a few to smooth out their comedowns.

'But doesn't Valium make you sleepy?'

'Usually, yes, but it has the opposite affect on catatonics,' Nathan said. 'They've done studies.'

'Studies?'

'Danby, the results are good,' he said. 'Something like an eighty per cent success rate.'

'How long does it take?'

Nathan pinched the bridge of his nose. 'Minutes, maybe an hour.'

That didn't seem very definite. I looked at him.

'It'll vary,' he said. 'But it doesn't take long. I was about to get what I needed to break into a pharmacy and try it when I heard the music.'

I was so excited I was skipping. I felt like a kid at Christmas: not that that expression would ever be used again to herald something good.

'There's our first stop,' Nathan said.

The HomePlace outlet's windows had been smashed in the chaos. We climbed in and hit the aisles to help ourselves to what Nathan reckoned we needed to get past the DrugRite's security shutters and plate-glass doors.

'So you said you don't know what happened,' I said as we lugged our newly liberated backpacks through the narrow spaces between cars. 'But what do you think happened?'

Nathan glanced at me over his shoulder. 'I've only got theories.'

'I've only got time.'

'At first I thought it was me,' he said with a laugh. 'That I was losing my mind.'

I chuckled darkly. 'Same here.'

'Then I thought maybe it was a toxic leak, a viral outbreak, something making everyone hallucinate,' Nathan said. 'But the little I could get from the screens showed it was happening all at once all around the world. There's no way a weather system or transmission vector could spread whatever it was that fast.'

Nathan pushed himself up between cars to clear a very obese and very dead woman wedged between panels. I followed up and over, careful not to inhale until I was clear of the corpse. Not that it made that much difference: everywhere we walked there was the sickly sweet tang I'd first smelled coming off Bogan Jesus. I pulled the chewing gum from my pocket, popped a piece into my mouth. 'Here,' I said, offering some to Nathan. 'It helps a little.'

'Thanks,' he said, squeezing out some gum, and returned the packet. 'Okay, so what I thought was that an idea could conceivably travel that fast, especially through social media. So that made me think we were experiencing some sort of mass psychogenic illness.'

'What's that?'

'An epidemic of shared delusion. In the Middle Ages crowds would suddenly start dancing and it'd spread to hundreds or thousands of people. The mania would sweep across the countryside for days or weeks and some people would literally dance themselves to death from exhaustion. No one's ever been able to explain it. You still see it today. Schoolkids or factory workers all become convinced they're sick and everyone comes down with the same physical symptoms even though it's all in their heads. Usually it's in the undeveloped world, so you might put it down to lack of education or superstition, but it also happened after 9/11 in the United States. There was a small and contained anthrax attack in New York but thousands of people all over America developed real symptoms even though they hadn't been exposed to anything.'

'Hang on a minute,' I said.

Nathan stopped. Sweat glistened on his brow and he waved his baseball cap to fan his face.

'Look around,' I said. 'We didn't imagine this. We didn't make this up. We really could hear what people were thinking.'

He nodded. 'We could. That's where science ends. After that, it's just me thinking out loud, if you'll pardon the pun.'

I smiled. 'Go for it.'

'Telepathy officially didn't exist,' he said. 'But we all knew what it was like when someone said something we'd just been thinking, how sometimes it'd feel too one-in-a-million or too meaningful to be coincidence. It really felt like getting a glimpse behind the curtains of our world, sensing that everything and everyone was connected.'

We reached a wall of traffic, vehicles arranged across the street like ramparts. A four-wheel drive had gone up onto a sports car. Other drivers who'd tried to go around had gotten stuck or smashed into shopfronts on either side. Nathan and I climbed onto a Lexus.

'There,' he said, pointing to the DrugRite at the end of the block.

We slid back down to the road.

'Where was I?'

'Behind the curtains, glimpses of telepathy.'

'Okay,' he said, 'think about everything you ever said, everything you ever wrote, posted, texted, drew. What were you doing?'

'Expressing what I thought.'

'You got it.'

'So what's changed that more than anything in our lifetime?'

I knew the answer. I felt its absence acutely. 'Connectivity.'

'Say human evolution's not just about passing on genetic

material but about passing on what we think. Then—boom—radio, movies, television, computers, the internet.'

We reached the DrugRite, its metal shutters padlocked to the pavement. I turned and Nathan reached into my backpack for the boltcutters we'd liberated from HomePlace.

'Keep an eye out,' he said as he bent to the padlock.

As I surveyed our audience of Goners, he kept talking.

'We used to talk to one person face to face. A century later we're tweeting, blogging, texting, messaging and updating for hundreds or thousands or millions. We're trying to let everyone know everything we're thinking and doing as we're thinking and doing it. Telepathy didn't exist but we were trying to make it real.'

'You're saying we hit the fast-forward button on evolution?'

Nathan shrugged. 'There were always articles about how constant connection was rewiring our brains? What if they were right? I mean, really right?'

The padlock snapped with a *ching*.

'Let me do the other one,' I said.

He stood up and handed me the boltcutters.

I knelt by the remaining padlock, grunting as I squeezed the blades against the steel. 'Evolution's supposed to be about selection for survival, right?'

Ching.

'Right,' he said.

'Well, why would we develop an ability that's about to make us extinct?'

Nathan shrugged. 'Like you said, maybe we fast-forwarded evolution, developed this power or sense or whatever, way before we were ready for it. If prehistoric man had moved from fire to gunpowder in the same day, do you think we'd even be here?'

I slowly rolled up the metal security shutter. Nathan started assembling the glass-cutter from HomePlace. We'd decided it was smarter than smashing our way in. The last thing we needed was to draw the attention of any other Party Duders.

'So, why us?' I asked, hunkering down beside him. 'You and me?'

'Why could we tune into other people but they couldn't tune us?'

I nodded.

He shook his head. 'Beats me.'

'Did you crash out for a second?' I asked. 'Go into that nothing place?'

Nathan looked at me. 'Yes, right at the start. It was horrible.'

'It was,' I said. 'But we both bounced back. We've got that in common.'

'True. But it'd make sense for that to be a function of our immunity—or whatever you'd call it—rather than a cause.'

I went quiet for a moment as he worked. 'Before this happened, did you have any flashes?'

Nathan listened as I quickly described the odd occurrences leading up to Christmas. My sanitised version of Mollie's party stopped at me hearing thoughts. I left out my freak-out and my diagnosis as a mental case. I didn't want to scare off my new friend. My *only* friend.

Nathan shook his head. 'I didn't have anything like that.'

But I'd come up with a new brainwave.

'I know!' I said. 'A few weeks ago I went off all screens, all social media, all devices, everything. It was only for six days. But maybe that had something to do with it?'

Nathan grinned as he stuck the cutter's suction cup to the plate glass. 'If that was the reason then we'd be surrounded by babies and senior citizens. As for me? I was on screens 24/7 right up to when it started.'

'Well,' I harrumphed, officially out of theories. 'I'm a Virgo.'

Nathan's eyes widened. 'Wow, me too!'

I'd been joking. 'Really?'

'Gemini,' he said with a smile. 'You're on the right track. There has to be a reason—or maybe several contributing factors—but right now with just you, me and the dead guy we don't have enough of a sample to tell us anything.'

Nathan extended the cutter's arm enough for the blade to slice a circle the size of a manhole.

'Here goes nothing,' he said.

We didn't know whether the DrugRite had an alarm with its own power supply. He turned the blade through a screeching circle. Together we used the suction handle to lift free a large glass disc. No siren or flashing lights.

Nathan smiled.

We crouched down and stared into the dark pharmacy.

'So,' I asked. 'Who goes first?'

'Rock, paper, scissors?'

I laughed and nodded. It wasn't a game two telepaths could use as a decider.

Climbing into the DrugRite was like passing through some air-lock portal into a space station. The daylight behind me seemed distant, Nathan talking was a far-off transmission and dust motes drifted as if in zero gravity. I breathed deeply. The atmosphere wasn't sour with smoke or decay but scented with the calming citrus of carpet cleaner. This place was exactly how it'd been preserved three days ago: a time capsule. It made me want to curl up in a ball and wish my way back.

'Danby, a little help?' Nathan said.

I snapped out of my daze. He handed the backpacks to me through the hole and carefully stepped into the DrugRite.

We switched on our flashlights, played the beams across the aisles, headed to the back for the hard stuff. Nathan strode behind the pharmacist's counter and scanned the shelves.

'Jackpot!' he said, holding up a yellow-and-white box. 'There's at least fifty boxes of Lorazepam here. Twenty tablets in each.' He scooped them into his backpack. I moved to join him. 'Let me get this and the IV equipment,' he said. 'Why don't you get the other stuff we talked about?'

As I browsed for electrolytes, painkillers and first-aid kits, I glanced back at Nathan. His flashlight was still darting as he searched the drug shelves.

· • ·

'He's dead,' Nathan said as he stepped into Starboard.

My heart thudded. 'Oh, no.'

Plasma Guy was still in his prayerful pose but he'd soiled himself. The smell cut through the liniment we'd rubbed under our nostrils in the pharmacy. Evan was still breathing steadily under the booth. I peered at Nathan as he draped a tablecloth over the corpse.

'What happened to him?'

'Could've been dehydration, shock, an underlying condition,' he said. 'Arms raised like that, it might've strained his heart.'

I should've gotten him down. My neglect had contributed to another death. But I'd feel guilty about it later. All I wanted now was Evan awake so we could get the hell out of Parramatta.

We carefully lay Evan on a table. Nathan lifted my little brother's eyelids and a shone a little torch into them.

'Pupils responsive,' he said. 'That's good.'

At least I'd gotten that right.

Nathan slipped a thermometer into Evan's armpit and listened to his chest with his stethoscope. Then he wrapped a cuff around his arm and pumped it up. When the thermometer beeped, he checked its little screen.

Nathan looked at me gently.

'I've seen this in the others,' he said. 'Evan's pulse and respiration are really slow, his blood pressure's pretty low and his body temperature's two degrees below what it should be.'

My hand went to my mouth. My eyes were glassy.

Nathan shook his head and smiled. 'No, no—it's a good sign. It means his body's conserving energy. Like a hibernating animal.'

He nodded to reassure me. 'Seriously, Danby, it's a good thing.'

I wiped my eyes, managed a smile. 'I'm glad but I don't want him like this for another second.'

Nathan's eyes darted away from mine.

'What's the matter?'

He pushed the palms of his hands against his temples, like he was trying to squeeze something out of his head. 'I've been trying to remember.'

'Remember what?'

'The studies,' he said, glancing back at me. 'They used a low dosage of Lorazepam. But—'

'You don't know how much to give him?'

Nathan shook his head, stared at his shoes. 'I'm sorry.'

'That's just great,' I said. 'What do we do now?'

Nathan looked wounded. 'I'm doing the best I can. Ordinarily, I'd consult the internet.'

'I didn't mean it like that.' I touched his arm. 'I'm sorry.'

He brightened. 'Look, a low dose is anything from one to ten milligrams. We can experiment.'

'You're kidding.'

'No, not on Evan.' Nathan pointed past me at the street outside. 'We try it on someone else.'

My stomach sank. Not because what he was suggesting was wrong. Because I knew any objections I raised would only be to make me feel better before I let him convince me to play god on guinea pigs. I'd save us both the time and angst.

'Who do we choose?'

Nathan's shoulders relaxed. 'If we can find someone his size—'

'Not a chance,' I said. 'If something goes wrong, I don't want some kid's death on my hands.'

'It's a mild sedative,' Nathan said. 'The risk of overdose is minimal.'

'But if it works, then we've got a scared child to deal with.'

Nathan nodded. 'Do you know how much Evan weighs?'

Actually, I did. Stephanie had gotten me to take him to his last medical appointment. 'Eighteen kilograms.'

'What about you?'

'About fifty-five.'

'So, one-third,' Nathan mused. 'We look for a woman your size. We give her a one-milligram intramuscular injection and then another one every ten minutes. Whatever brings her around, we use one third of that dose on Evan. It should work.'

'Should work?'

'It will work,' Nathan said. 'Trust me.'

It's not like I had a choice.

FIFTEEN

We walked from Starboard into the business district that had spooked me earlier. The shadows seemed deeper. But I felt safer. There was strength in numbers, even if we only numbered two. And we had our weapons.

Nathan paused to check every Goner with his stethoscope. I didn't know why because none were women my size. Evan's vital signs might be strong but the Plasma Guy's death had spooked me. I wanted to get on with finding our test subject. Nathan let his stethoscope hang back around his neck and joined me in the middle of an intersection.

'Doing a sample,' he said. 'Seeing what we're up against.'

I nodded and led us between cars. 'Tell me, but let's walk and talk?'

'There are forty people back there. Seven dead. Most of those have clear injuries or are elderly. It's a good result.'

'Really?' I looked at Nathan in disbelief. 'A good result?'

He nodded. 'Thirty-three people in reasonable health. It's better than good. It's remarkable. Some have probably been offline since Christmas Day but everyone's been down at least since the Big Crash.'

I stopped on a corner where a large lady in a polka-dot dress sat serenely in front of an unplugged vintage television. 'Big Crash?'

'About six o'clock yesterday morning?'

That dream of the world screaming. 'It woke me up.'

'You *slept* through that?' Nathan smiled—and then shivered. 'Everyone pulling each other into nothingness. The only thing worse than the noise they made was the silence they left behind.'

'Christ.' I had no idea it'd happened all at once. Just like I didn't yet know who Nathan really was or the extent of the horrors he'd been through. 'It sounds awful.'

'Yeah,' he said. 'But my point is that these people all seem okay. If they're in some sort of hibernation mode, they might last a lot longer than we'd ordinarily expect. We might be able to help hundreds, thousands if the Lorazepam works.'

Saving the multitude was secondary for me when my mum might be on that same clock. But this wasn't the time to bring up my selfish aims. Instead I nodded and pointed.

'How about her?'

The girl had wanted to stand out from the crowd. Now it might save her life. Pink hair flaring against the granite facade of an insurance building. Brightly inked arms folded defiantly. Fishnet-stockinged legs and purple boots thrust out from a lime-coloured tutu.

We crouched either side of her. Nathan set his nail gun on the ground and listened to her heart and breathing, checked her pupils, temperature and blood pressure.

'Yeah, she's good,' he said. 'Sit by her.'

I felt ghoulish, a disaster tourist posing for a photo, as he stepped back to check us out side by side.

'You're the same size,' he said, adding a smile. 'You girls could share a wardrobe.'

Nathan shrugged off his backpack. He took out the Tupperware container he'd filled with loaded syringes back at Starboard. In the kitchen, he had popped two five-milligram Lorazepam tablets from their blister pack into a soup ladle and then carefully measured fifty millilitres of bottled water into the stainless-steel container. He used a candle to bring it to the boil, stirring until the pills dissolved. He then dropped a ball of cotton wool into the mixture and spread the solution evenly over ten syringes. Nathan carefully talked me through the ratios several times. I understood first time around but I humoured him. His nervous patter about the process was as much for his own benefit as for mine. Talking about it clinically made it sound closer to medical science than junkie quackery.

I guessed we'd find out which it was now. Nathan removed a syringe's orange safety cap, flicked air bubbles upwards.

'Swab a spot on her upper arm,' he said.

I tore open the little packet and dabbed the girl's bicep with the sterile wipe.

'Okay, one milligram of Lorazepam in a five-millilitre solution,' he said, as though someone somewhere was taking notes.

Nathan slid the needle into the girl's flesh.

I expected her to flinch. She didn't.

'Time,' he said.

I pressed 'start' on my phone's countdown timer. 'Go.'

He dropped the plunger in a fluid movement and the drug disappeared into the girl.

Watching the digits drop from 10.00 gave me time to tell Nathan about the compromise I'd come up with that served my needs *and* the greater good.

'If this works,' I said, 'I want to wake Evan up and get going to my mum's place as soon as I can.'

Nathan looked at me dejectedly. 'I was hoping you'd help me to—'

I nodded. 'I think we might be able to save tens or even hundreds of thousands of people.'

There was a touch of condescension in his weary smile. 'Danby, even working around the clock we—'

'You had your maths moment back there,' I said with a smile. 'Now it's my turn. Pop quiz hotshot: what's ten to the power of five?'

Nathan blinked, surprised, calculated. 'One hundred thousand.'

'So what if every person we woke could wake other people up?' I said. 'We start here and head west to my mum's, setting off a chain reaction as we go.'

Nathan's eyes shone with the possibilities. 'There are hundreds of pharmacies that'll have Lorazepam! If every person we wake up wakes up just one person. And each of those people wakes up just one person and it keeps on like that, it'll equal—'

'A lot,' I said.

He hugged me. I put my arms around him for a moment and then pushed free. I was all for human comfort but I hardly knew this guy.

Nathan smiled, a little sheepish. 'Seriously, Danby, that's a great idea.'

I was glad he liked my theory.

Except that nothing was happening. My cunning plan all hinged on our punk princess. But she slumbered on, immune to Prince Pharma's kiss.

Nathan listened to her heart and nodded.

I swabbed her other arm and he delivered the second dose.

We sat and waited, listening to the wind whistle through the streets, gazing at the endless smoke clouds tumbling over the tall buildings. The phone display went to 07.00 and then 04.00.

'Can I ask you something?' Nathan said.

'Sure.'

'We don't have to talk about this,' he said. 'But do you know if your mum's okay?'

I stared at a few seconds tick by. Enough to make sure I wouldn't cry. Then I told him what I knew.

'So I don't know,' I concluded with a sigh, 'if she's up and about because Shadow Valley's maybe protected because it's more remote. Or if she's, y'know, like everyone else.'

Nathan gave me an encouraging smile. 'Either way it sounds like she's safe.'

I nodded. 'What about your mum and dad?'

'They're a bit farther away,' he said. 'Sri Lanka. I'm hoping for the best. Not much I can do about it.'

'I'm sorry. Do you have anyone here?'

Nathan smiled grimly. 'I was renting in this horrible place. Wow, "share house" takes on a whole new meaning now.'

I laughed. 'Well, you're welcome to stay with us.'

'Thank you,' he said. 'Your mum won't mind?'

'Of course not.'

Talking like this—like Mum would be fine, like I was casually offering him a crash pad—made me feel better.

My phone's alert sounded. The countdown was all zeroes.

Two doses, twenty minutes and not so much as a twitch— let alone a thought behind the test girl's mascara-smudged eyes.

Nathan saw how edgy I was getting.

'Don't worry,' he said, sounding worried himself. 'It'll work.'

I swabbed, he dosed. We both eyed the phone.

It wasn't even at 08.00 when he reached for the Tupperware container.

'I'm giving her another shot,' he said sharply. 'We're being too cautious.'

'Hang on!' I grabbed his arm. 'Wait.'

I wondered if he knew what he was doing. Maybe he'd mis-remembered not the dosage but the name of the drug. Maybe he'd killed her. I leaned in to satisfy myself the girl was breathing.

'Aaaaarrrrrrgh!'

She made a sucking noise, gasping for air.

Terrified, I jumped back as her eyes popped open, pupils shrinking in the light.

Her throat and tongue were so dry she couldn't speak.

Escaped!-Got-out!-Where-was-I?-Nowhere-Empty-Gone!-Alive!-I'm-soaked-So-thirsty!

She didn't see me in front of her until I pressed a bottle of electrolytes to her cracked lips.

Where'd-she-come-from?

'Everything's going to be all right,' I said, trying for my most soothing voice, looking deep into her frightened eyes. 'My name's Danby. I'm here for you. You're not alone. What's your name?'

Cassie.

In that moment Cassie's mind went from fuzzy to focused— and I realised how unlucky we were to choose her.

When the Snap happened, she had been on her way to her friend James's house for Orphan's Christmas. Her head went haywire and she thought it was an acid flashback. But then the bus rolled across the bridge. People sitting at the front died, and she was inside their minds as they did, but she climbed out the rear emergency exit without a scratch. Physically, she was in one piece. Mentally, she was coming apart. There was too much—everything happening everywhere and everyone overlapping. Getting to James's place and smoking, snorting, slamming, shooting—that was the only way to calm this shit down. Cassie stumbled through shouting streets until she couldn't go on. She thought she'd sit awhile but when she slid down the building's facade it was like the footpath opened and she kept going to the centre of the earth.

Cassie's mind reeled as Nathan materialised over my shoulder.

183

Should-never-have-done-ouija-I'm-dead-This-is-hell-He's-the-devil.

'You're not, it's not, I'm not,' he said. 'My name's Nathan.'

Cassie looked past us and recognised the sliver of city. I saw what she saw: stalled cars, shut-down people, smoke draped over rooftops.

End-of-the-world-has-to-be-a-dream.

'Cassie,' Nathan said, 'this isn't a dream.'

How-do-you-know-my-name?-Stupid-black-bastard.

We flinched as her mind thrashed.

Why-can't-I-read-their-minds?

'We don't know,' I said angrily. 'Our minds only go one way—'

Me answering her unspoken question spiked her panic.

Get-out-of-my-head!

'You get away from me!' she shrieked. 'Leave me alone!'

Cassie wanted to bolt to James's place and blot out this bullshit. But first she wanted us out of her head.

'Calm down!' Nathan shouted.

His outburst didn't send Cassie's mind into shocked silence. But the .45 she saw tucked in my waistband did. Either way, she shut up long enough for Nathan to explain that everyone else was catatonic and Lorazepam might bring some or even most of them around.

Cassie's eyes narrowed. 'How long's it been—'

Nathan gripped my arm to make sure I let her finish.

'—since it all happened?'

'Two days,' he said.

I dreaded her vocalising the next question.

'How many other people have you woken up?'

'You're the first,' he said.

Always-the-guinea-pig. But Cassie thought it without anger. Her friends often got her to taste drugs from new sources. She didn't mind at all.

Container-full-of-syringes-Must-be-the-stuff.

'You gonna give me more of those?'

Nathan looked at me. I shook my head. We both knew why.

Cassie's first stop on her way to James's place was going to be a pharmacy. I could hear her running through her shopping list.

Ritalin-Oxycontin-Adderall-Morphine-Pethidine.

'Lorazepam,' I said. 'About one milligram per twenty kilograms of body weight. You can get it when you get your other party supplies.'

'You greedy bitch,' Cassie sneered. *Should-I?-She-won't-do-nothing.* The ugly impulse hit me an instant before her spit spattered my cheek. She grinned at me triumphantly. *She-won't-shoot-me.* 'Suck on that.'

I turned to Nathan in shock—and was more shocked that he winked at me.

'She won't shoot you,' he roared. 'But I will.'

Cassie's face blanched when Nathan reached for the nail gun.

'Nathan,' I pleaded, playing along. 'Please—you promised no more blood.'

Please-don't-kill-me-I'm-sorry-please.

Nathan let the moment stretch before he lowered the nail gun.

'If I see you again, you're dead,' he said, gathering up the syringe box and his backpack. 'Danby, let's go.'

We got away from Cassie as fast as we could. I was thrilled the Lorazepam had worked but shocked by the mind we'd just encountered.

'Wow, we hit the jackpot with her,' I said.

'You sure can pick 'em,' Nathan replied with a laugh.

'"She won't shoot you—but I will."' I mimicked in a Schwarzeneggerian growl. 'What the hell was that about?'

'You think I'd let her get away with calling me a "black bastard"?' I reached out and touched his arm. Nathan grinned. 'And I wanted to put the fear of God into her. It worked, didn't it? She's not following us.'

We didn't have to look back to know she hadn't come after us. Cassie had seethed at us until we disappeared among cars. Then she set about resuming her original mission. She was stalking off in the opposite direction to find drugs and find her friends. Once she woke them up, it'd be chemical ecstasy from here to eternity. She vowed to get herself a gun—and if she saw us again we'd wish we hadn't revived her.

Evan was where we left him in Starboard. So was the Plasma Guy.

'Let's do this outside,' Nathan said.

We carried Evan out of the cafe and gently lay him on the grass verge above the ferry wharf. While Nathan checked his vitals, I swabbed his shoulder.

Nathan held up a syringe. 'This should be enough.'

I nodded. He injected Evan's arm. I started the phone countdown.

We were trusting in science, but sitting there holding Evan's and each other's hands, I reckoned we probably looked like spiritualists.

'What's it like?' Nathan asked. 'Your mum's place?'

I appreciated him trying to take my mind off the terrible wait.

I told him how much fun it was going through Mum's crazy clutter of stuff, how good an omelette tasted when made from her chickens' eggs and fresh vegetables from her garden, how beautiful it was sitting on the verandah and counting shooting stars on a clear night, how funny it was when the wind carried her neighbour's cockatoo screech of 'Hi-Ho!' across the paddocks.

'Sounds awesome,' Nathan said.

I smiled. 'You'll love it.'

My phone alert went off. Evan remained inert on his bed of grass. I blew an ant off his chest. We watched him in silence for what seemed like an hour.

'What's happening?' I said when I couldn't take it anymore. It was a stupid question.

'I don't know,' Nathan said. 'Give it a bit more time.'

'Shouldn't it be working by now?'

It was another stupid question. Then I realised there was a stupidly obvious question that I *hadn't* asked. How might Evan's condition affect the working of the drug?

'Okay, I'm going to try another milligram,' Nathan said.

'Wait!'

I told him about Evan, rushing through his symptoms and the various vague diagnoses doctors had come up with. Nathan listened quietly and calmly.

'I'm so sorry,' I said, 'I can't believe I didn't mention it. I guess I just think of him as normal.'

But I wondered if I'd subconsciously kept it secret because I thought Nathan might not want to help Evan if he knew.

'Don't worry about it,' Nathan said. 'His condition shouldn't make a difference.'

I knew he didn't know that but I appreciated him trying to make me feel better.

Nathan listened to Evan with the stethoscope.

'He's fine,' he said, holding up a second syringe. 'Shall I try with half of this?'

I nodded. He squirted the excess medication into the grass and administered the shot. We held hands again and took up a silent vigil.

Evan didn't wake up.

SIXTEEN

Law Of Small Numbers was above an electronics outlet on Parramatta's shopping strip a block from where Nathan had saved me from the Party Duder. We left the glass door street level entrance intact and ventured down a side alley and lugged Evan up the fire-escape stairs. Nathan grinned at me as he smashed a window and reached in to unlock the back door.

We set Evan and the backpacks down on a brown couch in the office's reception area and scoped out the rest of the small suite. It took all of sixty seconds.

'See what I mean?' Nathan asked.

I did. Nathan had done his tax here with Kee Law, Certified Practising Accountant, and he'd told me it was the dullest place on earth. There was a kitchen, a bathroom, the waiting area and the number cruncher's office with adjoining balcony. Filing cabinets and framed certificates, franchise furniture and potted palms: this was the last place anyone wanted to be at the best of times, let alone the end times. Up here we could stay hidden but command a view of the main street along which survivors might travel. We'd get to choose whether we revealed ourselves to them.

'It's perfect,' I said.

'You should try to learn this,' Nathan said as he got the essentials for an IV from his backpack.

I stroked Evan's forehead. He was still wrapped in a towel. We hadn't passed a kids' clothing store on our way from Starboard.

Nathan removed a framed diploma from the wall above the couch and hung a fat bag of saline from the picture hook. Next, he tied a tourniquet around Evan's upper arm and rubbed a finger on the small blue vein that rose on the back of his hand. He swabbed the area, inserted a catheter and taped it in place. He connected the catheter to the saline bag's tube and turned the little tap to start the drip.

'Not much to it,' Nathan said. 'Evan's being hydrated. It'll feed half a litre of fluid and salts over the next hour. He can go like this for as long as it takes us to figure out how to wake him up.'

'Thank you,' I said. 'For everything.'

Nathan smiled. 'All part of the service.'

In the bathroom I pulled on new jeans and a shirt that I'd liberated from the smashed clothing boutique across the road. When I emerged Nathan had laid out plastic plates of crackers and cheese and anchovies and olives and pickles beside bottles of mineral water on the reception area's coffee table.

'Awesome,' I said. 'Thanks.'

We crunched and sipped for a while.

'So,' he said around a mouthful, 'what's your plan for getting to your mum's?'

I'd been thinking about it. Trail bikes could get us through most traffic and terrain. But I couldn't ride one any more than I could drive a car.

'You know how to ride a motorbike?' I envisaged me and Evan and Nathan on a single bike—like families you saw in Asian cities.

'I was about to ask you that,' he said. 'We could try to learn?'

I shook my head. Teaching ourselves to ride on debris-strewn roads seemed like an idea doomed to something worse than failure. And the noise we made might attract unwanted attention from people like the Party Duder. 'Bicycles might be safer.'

Nathan nodded. 'We could strap Evan into a kid's seat.'

'Even if we have to go slow, stop to revive people here and there, we could still get there in a day.'

Nathan sat back from the table. 'What time is it?'

I glanced at my phone. 'It's after four.'

The clouds made it dark earlier. By the time we found bikes and got going it'd be like night. I didn't want to leave Mum any longer than I had to but I'd be useless to her if I ran my bike into a wreck in the gloom—or if our headlights attracted some crazy person who killed us.

I sighed. 'Do we start our good deeds now and leave first thing in the morning?'

Nathan frowned. 'What worries me is who we might wake up.'

We could both see that our debut Revivee was using the gift of life to rifle through the pockets of a dead dealer acquaintance—despite having already filled her backpack with prescription narcotics.

Nathan shook his head in disgust. 'She can't hurt us. But what worries me is what might happen to us if we revive someone who's really bad or really mad.'

I flashed to those afternoons I'd spent with Mum making the 'Turn Your Trash Into Treasure' flyers that she sticky-taped to telegraph poles up and down the mountains.

'What?' Nathan asked when he saw me smiling.

'We don't have to be there when they wake up.'

·•·

Nathan looted the laptop and battery-operated printer from the electronics shop downstairs. Together we worked up the wording.

YOU MUST READ & REMEMBER

DRINK WATER/ELECTROLYTES & <u>STAY HYDRATED</u>.
WHAT YOU REMEMBER <u>DID</u> HAPPEN.

- THIS IS A <u>REAL</u> <u>EMERGENCY</u>.
- MOST PEOPLE YOU SEE ARE <u>NOT</u> DEAD.
- BUT THEY <u>WILL</u> <u>DIE</u> UNLESS YOU ACT.
- YOU CAN REVIVE <u>MOST PEOPLE</u> WITH AN INJECTION OF **LORAZEPAM**.

  IT IS HOW <u>YOU</u> WERE REVIVED.
- EACH BAG CONTAINS 6 SYRINGES, EACH WITH 5MG OF LORAZEPAM.

- USE **APPROX** 1MG per 18KG BODY WEIGHT, EG—
  - 6MG (1 SYRINGE) = LARGE ADULT
  - 3MG (½ SYRINGE) = MEDIUM ADULT/TEENAGER
  - 1.5MG (¼ SYRINGE) = SMALL CHILD
- SWAB SHOULDER, THIGH OR BUTTOCKS AND INJECT.
- IF UNSUCCESSFUL AFTER 20 MINS, REPEAT WITH ½ DOSE.
- OVERDOSE IS UNLIKELY BUT NOT ALL PEOPLE RESPOND.
- LORAZEPAM & SYRINGES CAN BE FOUND IN ANY PHARMACY.

TO MAKE SOLUTION:

- CRUSH TABLETS IN BOTTLED/BOILED WATER.
- HEAT AND STIR UNTIL DISSOLVED.
- DRAW LIQUID INTO SYRINGE THROUGH CLEAN COTTON WOOL.
- INJECT SHOULDER/THIGH/BUTTOCKS.

REVIVE AS MANY PEOPLE AS YOU CAN.

COPY & DISTRIBUTE THESE INSTRUCTIONS IF POSSIBLE.

'How many should we print?' Nathan asked. 'The instructions should bounce from mind to mind anyway.'

'The more the better,' I said. 'Just to counteract Chinese whispers. People thought I was a soul-sucking ghost and an alien cockroach.'

Nathan laughed. 'Say what?'

We sat across from each other at the accountant's desk and I told him about Dad and Stephanie and getting away from Beautopia Point. I talked as I added electrolyte powder to bottles of water from the kitchen. Nathan listened as he made up syringes of Lorazepam solution. The printer churned through a ream of paper. When I finished my story, he gazed at me silently.

'What?' I asked. 'Are you okay?'

Nathan capped the last syringe. 'What's amazing is that you're okay after all of that.'

I didn't know that I was. I didn't know whether I should be proud I'd survived—or scream for the very same reason. But I nodded. 'Let's make these up.'

We began assembling what we'd dubbed our RSKs—Revival Survival Kits. Six loaded syringes, another six Lorazepam tablets, a bottle of electrolyte drink and a roll of powder sachets, a packet of painkillers and a ream of instruction flyers—all sealed into large zip-lock sandwich bags.

'So,' I said. 'Where were you when it happened?'

Nathan busied himself in an RSK.

'I wasn't that far from here,' he said. 'I was just coming off the night shift. Then everyone was going nuts. It was horrible. I—I—'

Nathan blinked and seemed far away.

'Oh,' he said, 'you stupid girl.'

I tuned to Cassie and saw what he saw.

Cassie had reached her friend James's apartment building in Olympic Park. She'd found Sammy face down but alive in the garden outside. It'd only taken her a minute to mix up Lorazepam and stick it in his butt cheek. She'd left him there while she went up and did the same for James, who was stretched out on his faux-zebra rug with empty bottles and bags licked clean of powder. Cassie didn't know how long it'd take for her friends to wake up. But she was going to pass the time with a little taste of the heroin from that dead dealer. I pulled myself away from her as she sank into her opiate oblivion.

'She could be dosing everyone in that building with Lorazepam,' I said bitterly. 'And instead she does that.'

Nathan reached over to put his hand on my wrist. His fingertips were warm on my skin. I moved my arm a little so our hands could slide together. Our fingers interlocked, gentle at first, then tighter as we made a fist together across the desk. The connection was soft but strong.

'We can't control what people do,' he said. 'We just have to do our best to help them.'

I nodded. He smiled. We uncurled our fingers. There was no awkwardness. We went back to preparing RSKs.

'So,' I asked, 'how do you reckon we should do this?'

We agreed to begin a few blocks east. We'd look for people with good vital signs and who looked like they could help others. We'd swab our person, set out the syringe we needed from our stashes, and put their RSKs where they couldn't help but see them. We'd repeat the process, moving up the street, until we'd both found ten people. Then it'd be hit and run, injecting from farthest to nearest, as we raced back to the office. Plan was to be back in our hideout long before anyone came around.

'All done,' Nathan said, sealing his last RSK. 'You ready?'

As I'd ever be.

I used a stethoscope to listen to a heavy-set guy crumpled in the doorway of a pawn shop. In his Hawaiian shirt, shorts and sandals, he looked like he was on his way to a barbecue. He stank of stale booze but had a strong heartbeat and was breathing evenly. I reckoned this big fella weighed about one hundred kilograms. I hunkered down with my backpack, set a full syringe atop his RSK. Once I'd swabbed his hairy bicep, I used a marker pen to circle the sterile skin. Then I looked around for my next patient. It felt unfair, terrible, to bypass a boy crouched by a fire hydrant and an old man in the gutter. But we'd agreed fit adults would respond best and be able to revive others—and that would include their younger and older loved ones.

Across the street Nathan opened the driver's door of a white hatchback—and slammed it against the smell. But he got lucky with a silver sedan and started prepping the driver stuck behind the wheel. My next candidate was a thirty-something woman in a sundress sprawled on the back seat of her station wagon. She had pulled a straw hat down so hard over her eyes that it had torn. I guessed she was seventy kilos and squirted a syringe down to size before prepping her and laying out the RSK.

By the time we reached the middle of the block, our backpacks were empty. Nathan tapped his wrist. I glanced at my phone and held up six fingers. He nodded. We were on schedule. If this worked, whoever woke up would have maybe an hour to orientate themselves before it was fully dark.

We gave each other the thumbs up.

Steeling myself against squeamishness, I crouched and slid

a syringe into the circled bicep of a woman wearing a fast-food uniform and a badge that identified her as Jackie. She'd crashed at the wheel of her hatchback. Nathan went to work on an Asian woman laid out beside a delivery van. I hurried along the footpath to a woman in her pyjamas and heard Nathan racing between cars to find his next mark.

Within minutes, I was finishing where I started, jabbing the Hawaiian shirt guy, throwing the last used needle in my backpack.

'How'd you go?' Nathan said, joining me.

'Good. You?'

He nodded.

We jogged along the block, jumped over Goners, tore down the alley, clattered up the fire stairs and slammed the kitchen door behind us. I'm not sure why we were so frantic. Our minds were alert to anyone coming online. So far no one had.

I flopped onto the couch beside Evan, felt his forehead and listened to his breathing.

'How is he?' Nathan asked, panting and pacing around the coffee table.

'Seems okay.' I checked my phone. The battery was almost gone. I'd have to find a replacement—or a power source. 'It's six ten.'

'Ten minutes.' Nathan nodded. 'We did a good job.'

'Not much good,' I said, 'if I doesn't—'

But then it started to work.

So-hot-So-thirsty, Jackie thought as she woke. In front of her on the steering wheel was her RSK. She didn't question where it came from, just ripped it open, unscrewed the drink bottle and drank deeply.

Oh-God!-What-happened?-Did-I-have-a-stroke?-No-Jesus-look-at-this—

Cars were banked up all around, shadows draped over steering wheels, people sprawled along the street. Now she began to remember. Some of them had been like that before she'd been sucked down.

Tony!-Baby!-Where-are-you?

Her hand shot out and turned the key in the ignition uselessly.

Ran-the-battery-down-with-the-stereo-and-air-con.

Panic flared in her.

Is-everyone-dead?

Then she saw the flyers in the RSK and pulled one out.

You-must-read-and-remember.

Nathan and I heard hope bloom in Jackie. Then she was out of the car, clutching the RSK, mind streaking ahead of her cramped legs. She hoped Tony was where she'd last seen him—in the lounge room of their house, face pressed against the TV, working his way through a case of beer. If he'd passed out there, he might still be okay. She didn't care what he had done, what he'd thought. She needed to forgive him, for him to forgive her.

Then we heard Ray, my Hawaiian-shirt guy, come online, and, in quick succession, others began to stir and come around in various states of discombobulation and disbelief.

'Nine,' said Nathan, tallying them.

'Eleven,' I corrected because James and Sammy were sitting by Cassie—who was snoring on the zebra-skin rug. The boys' minds were overlapping amiably now they'd followed their friend's example and shot up some smack.

Everything's-gone-man-But-like-we're-kings-now-Others-over-in-Parramatta-Fast-food-chick-Reading-about-Lorazawhatnow-Oh-check-this-stuff-out-Pharmaceutical-grade-speed.

'They don't count,' Nathan said, sitting on the couch next to me.

By six thirty, fifteen of our people were awake. All that steadied them—and then it was only just—were the drinks that eased the terrible thirst and the RSKs that gave them hope.

Someone's-in-charge-helping-It's-gonna-be-okay, the woman named Traci thought, crying softly. *Mum-Dad-I'm-gonna-come-home-now-and-help-you.*

Then, as though their minds were stretching, getting the blood flowing, their thoughts rose up, got louder and started to crossover.

'Now we find out if they can handle it,' I said softly.

Nathan put his hand on mine. 'It might be all right.'

What-happened?-Who're-you?-Traci-Cory-Ray-How'd-we-get-here?-What's-it-say?-Revive-people-So-thirsty-The-convenience-store-have-more-drinks-God-are-they-all-dead?-I-remember-Oh-God-it-was-like-this-Hearing-your-mind-It's-different-now-Not-so-loud-Who-wrote-this-left-this-bag?-Junkies-out-there-No-man-it-wasn't-us-It-says-they'll-all-die-We-have-to-save-God-I'm-aching-Gotta-find-my-wife-kids . . .

Like magnetised iron filings, the thoughts clumped together, even as the people thinking them stood warily apart, sizing each other up across cars and the street.

No one spoke out loud. But no one screamed.

Gotta-find-Tony-I'm-Frank-Who're-Sammy-James?-They're-spaced-out-God-can-see-why-they-do-it-So-relaxed-I-need-a-drink-Stay-sober-My-name-is-Ravi-All-I-remember-is-Music-wasn't-loud-enough-That-guy-didn't-wake-up-Grab-his-bag-got-more-stuff-No-it's-mine-I-need-it-for-my-kids!-Okay-stay-calm-Says-we'll-find-this-stuff-any-pharmacy-Whoever-woke-me-up-should-have-let-me-die!-Cut-the-self-pity-Don't-tell-me-what-to-think-Please-don't-don't-do-this-again!-Think-the-best-Lorazepam-I-could-sell-this-stuff-To-who-you-idiot?-You-can't-talk-Ray-you're-the-criminal-Guys-gotta-work-together-At-least-think-together-Man-there's-so-much-smoke-Is-everything-still-Look-don't-worry-about-any-of-that-I'm-finding-my-family-using-this-Lorazepam.

Nathan beamed at me. Our Revivees were like I'd been when I came back from the void. They had more control over tuning each other in and out and their new groupthink was more like a passionate town hall debate than a black-metal moshpit.

'Can't afford to get sucked into it all again,' I said, echoing what Ray had just thought as he struck out east on his own. *Gotta-find-Lyn.*

'Bigger problems now than who's the biggest wanker.' Nathan parroted Jackie, also heading east but sticking to her side of the street. *Tony-baby-hold-on.*

'Be positive, guys.' That was Traci. *Another-pharmacy-on-way-home.*

'I think they're getting it,' Nathan said brightly. 'You and me, Danby, I think we're saving the world.'

'Do you?' I asked. 'What about Anne?'

We locked onto my sundress Revivee, heading for her rich sister's house and wine cellar. *My-time-now-You-losers-do-whatever-you-want.*

'Cory?'

One of Nathan's. Young guy. *Man-I-use-this-stuff-I-can-revive-the-hottest-chicks-and—*

Disgusted minds rounded on them both—*How-can-you-think-that?-Time-like-this?*—but they didn't care.

Just-being-honest-You-can't-talk-you're-Whatever-just-leave-me-the-hell-alone-I'm-reviving-my-family-You-should-do—

Nathan shook his head. 'At least they're not killing each other.'

He was right. But I was disappointed that our Revivees were all on singular missions. 'Not one of them trusts each other enough to join forces,' I said. 'Not one of them's considered reviving a stranger just to be kind. No one's changed at all.'

Nathan squeezed my hand gently. I felt myself relax a little under his gaze. 'They're strangers, they're frightened. Of course they want to help family and friends first. Give them a bit of time to do that and then maybe they'll learn to think cooperatively and constructively. Let's see how they go?'

I nodded.

By the time I'd swapped Evan's IV bag, Nathan's faith in humanity looked like it was being vindicated.

The woman named Ravi had made it to her home in Westmead and found her husband Wayne huddled in the cupboard. A few minutes later, he was awake, the two of them crying, him sorry for screaming her away, her sorry for running off. They peered out through the curtains in their lounge room, frightened by the orange glow of fires on the eastern horizon but glad they were alive and together. Ravi and Wayne's minds still clashed sometimes, and every tangential thought threatened some trivial derailment, but they recognised their survival depended on setting bullshit aside and were groping towards true togetherness. It was deepening their love—and making them more determined to do whatever they could to save their family and friends.

Others were on the same track. Traci had made her way back to her family home. Her elderly father was dead but she'd revived her mother, sister and niece. Now the four women were wordlessly making up more syringes with the supplies Traci had collected and were sharing mental strategies to help the extended family. Jackie hadn't found Tony at home but before she headed out to see if he was holed up at the pub, she injected Sally, her neighbour, and the single mother's toddler son, Angus, and left them half her supplies. Now Sally studied our instruction sheet so she could make up more doses for her brother and his family.

'I've gotta tune out.' Nathan yawned and pushed the coffee

table out of the way to stretch out on the carpet. He pulled his baseball cap down over his eyes. 'I need to rest a while.'

The patch of carpet between Nathan and Evan's couch was irresistibly inviting. Being between two other humans seemed like the safest and most natural place left in this world. No matter that one was my catatonic little brother and the other was really still a stranger. I kneeled beside Evan and stroked his forehead for a while. Then I eased myself down beside Nathan. I couldn't help be conscious of how close our bodies were. I wanted to be even closer but I was wary of how he might interpret me curling into him for comfort.

I turned off my flashlight. The darkness in that windowless reception room should've been total. But my mind couldn't help going out to Revivees.

My heart sank as I saw Anne had claimed her sister's Parramatta mansion. Her Lorazepam went unused as she drank fine vintages and tried on designer dresses while the lady of the house lay slumped catatonic on a chaise longue.

Cory was cruising a mall, shining his light app on crashed out girls, telling himself he was only mucking around, that he wouldn't really do anything bad. Robert, a man Nathan had revived, made me even sadder. He had found the DrugRite and was collecting barbiturates to make a mercy-killing cocktail he would inject into his wife and kids before he used it on himself.

My stomach twisted with guilt. These people wouldn't be inflicting themselves on the bereft world if it wasn't for me and Nathan. But Ray, my Hawaiian shirt guy, wouldn't let me succumb to despair because, of all of them, he had really changed.

Ray was walking east, determined to make it to his wife's apartment in Strathfield and make amends. Christmas morning had been his first chance to see the twins since he was paroled and his big opportunity to talk Lyn around and convince her that the anger-management classes in prison had worked. Ray vowed not to stuff it up. But hanging around the halfway house on Christmas Eve, listening to the tinny TV sounds of men alone in their rooms, was too much to handle, and so he and Benny from the next cubicle had pooled their meagre resources and bought six bottles of cheap wine. There was no harm—they just drank and laughed and listened to music until the dawn sky was as pink as their eyes.

But when Ray woke to the plane exploding into the bridge it was like a nightmare chasing him into the day. Horrible visions, sounds, feelings, sensations jumbled through him—a riot in Silverwater Jail, suburban mums and dads baying for blood, jolts of pain as bones broke and skin split in a bus tumbling across a bridge—and then Ray was with Liam and Doc as they wailed amid Christmas wrappers at their frantic mother.

Don't-yell-Mummy-I'm-scared-So-loud-Where's-Daddy?

Lyn screamed—at the boys, at herself, in his head—and her fear and fury rippled through him so violently he vomited over the side of his narrow cot.

Shut-up-boys-Be-quiet-Can't-think-Ray-you-bastard-Drunk-Always-drunk-here-I—

Then she was gone—like Ray had accidentally changed a

television channel—and he was in Benny's head next door as the poor gimp blasted Led Zep on headphones and pounded a bottle of port. Ray's mind raged randomly through intoxicated and insane minds in other rooms and out into surrounding streets that were like war zones. Inside his own skull was worse than any prison cell. But at least he could escape his room. So he bolted from the halfway house to the LiquorBarn. The place was a shambles of broken glass and booze and blood-soaked bodies. Wild-eyed freaks surged in and out, grabbing whatever they could. Ray was one of them until he got his hands on two bottles of wine.

Ray staggered clear, guzzling warm chardonnay as he weaved between people. The first bottle didn't really help. The second one made his legs so rubbery he had to sit down. His mind tripped to his family again. Lyn huddled with their twins in the empty bath. Like this was an earthquake.

Mummy!-Please!-Don't-want-to-die!-So-loud!-Ray-where-are-you?-Everything-pushing-Love-you-Liam-Doc-but-get-away-shut-up-no-no . . .

Lyn hugged the boys even as she tried to repulse their minds. Then it was like the tub beneath them caved in and they were tumbling into the abyss.

'No!' Ray protested from his pawn-shop doorway but he was going down with his family into the enormity of the earth.

Ray replayed his mistakes relentlessly as he walked east. 'Those who cannot remember the past are condemned to repeat it'—he remembered reading that on the ceiling of a cafe where he'd asked about a dishwashing job. That connection tugged at me and made me wish I could reach out and reassure Ray everything would be all right, tell him his renewed lease on life was helping me believe things might be okay. As he climbed around the remains of a burned police car, I felt proud when Ray mentally gave thanks to whoever had given him a second chance to be the man he should've been the first time around. By God, Ray was going to save his family—and then he would revive as many people as he could and really pay back his debt to society.

Ray couldn't hear me but he wasn't alone. Minds out there helped him where they could. Ravi and Jackie weren't quite a GPS but between them they knew these suburban backstreets better than he did. Their advice meant he avoided a few dead ends. But it was more than that: they gently kept him on the right path whenever he thought about finding just one drink. These guys, these strangers, were better than any Alcoholics Anonymous group. They could see past everything to the good person he really was.

'Ray?' Nathan said in the dark.

'Ray,' I agreed.

'There's hope.' He briefly found my cheek with his hand in the darkness. 'I'm so glad we found each other.'

As I lay there, I gave thanks for Nathan. But I felt sick for him when I remembered what he had started to tell me before Cassie had rudely interrupted him. *The night shift*. Of course: medical students interned in hospitals. As bad as my flight from Beautopia Point had been, Nathan had probably had it worse. Patients, doctors and nurses battling their own and each other's demons in wards and waiting rooms. I wondered how long Nathan had tried to save others before he realised he'd be lucky to save himself.

'You never told me,' I said, 'what it was like for you?'

Nathan sighed in the darkness. 'I'll tell you everything in the morning,' he said. 'I promise. I'm just so tired now. Goodnight, Danby.'

I felt him roll onto his side.

'Goodnight.'

A moment later Nathan was snoring lightly.

We'd saved some people. Now they were saving each other. Our plan wasn't perfect but it was working.

What I wanted to know was how many other people were out there like us. If the ratio was 1 in a 1000, there would be 25,000 people in Australia. Even with a dismal percentage like that there'd still be eight million survivors worldwide. From Mr Mooney's history class I recalled that the global population had been around that at the start of recorded history. But this wasn't the new 4000 BC. I had found Nathan and he had known about Lorazepam. Others would be doing the same thing. Tens or even hundreds of millions would survive.

The big challenge in these early days would be finding each other. Without transport and telecommunications, it was like the world had been wound back. People who were suburbs away might as well be in other states. But that was where the telepathy might work in our favour. They didn't know it but the Revivees were already our radars. If they ran into anyone like us then Nathan and I would know about it. But we would also be frustratingly unable to communicate *our* presence. What we needed was to revive someone who would stay with us—and whose mind wouldn't drive us crazy. Through them we'd be able to broadcast to other Revivees.

Before I fell asleep, a chilling calculation occurred. If the sample of me, Nathan and the Party Duder held true across the wider population then 33.3 recurring per cent of those who were immune would also be psychotic murdering rapists. I was sure that civilisation couldn't survive that.

SEVENTEEN

When I awoke my eyes were inches from beige carpet. I didn't know where I was. Rolling over, I saw Evan with his IV. Everything came back. We were in the accountant's rooms. This was the reception area.

'Nathan?'

The place was so small that if he was in the office or the kitchen or the bathroom or even on the balcony he would've heard me.

A note was stuck to the wall. I stood up and peered at the scrawl.

4.30 a.m. Evan has fresh IV. Gone to help someone. Back as soon as I can. Hope we'll still be friends.

I looked at my phone. Just before seven. Nathan had left me in the dark. To help someone. I flashed to me asking him if he had anyone. He'd deflected with the joke about the share house. 'Someone' meant someone special. I wasn't jealous. Just angry. That he hadn't told me. Mum was my priority. He could have his. But now he'd abandoned me—us. Anything could go wrong and I wouldn't know it. If he brought her back here, how would we cope with a shared mind?

I sent my senses wide open out there. I skipped over Cassie and her friends, coming around after a night on the needle in a pub. I saw Ray, thirstier than ever but still sober and within striking distance of Lyn's place. I flitted past Jackie, still searching for Tony. Other minds spun through mine—Traci, Ravi, Cory, Anne and the rest of our Revivees and the people they'd woken up—but no one had eyes on Nathan.

Then I locked onto a girl named Tregan and dropped straight into her experience in a bush clearing. Her head lolled. Her brain ached, her heart beat heavy in her temples. Her tongue was sluggish, her skin flamed with sunburn and insect bites. But she barely felt the pain for the exhilaration.

I'm-back!-I'm-alive!-I'm-alive!

Then Nathan came into view and she felt only fear.

'Slowly,' he said, cupping her neck, holding a bottle to her parched lips. 'Tregan, drink slowly, it's electrolyte, I've already hydrated you, you're going to be okay.'

'You,' I heard her say, looking from his sweaty face to the empty IV bag among the weeds. There was a syringe, too. 'What—what—what—?'

Flashes hit Tregan: driving with Gary on the Great Western Highway, their minds overlapping, the argument, the plane screaming over the city, her fiancé slamming on the brakes to avoid a flipped tow truck, her throwing open the door to stumble into the bush, the weight of the world caving in on her.

'Nathan,' she said. 'What have you done to me?'

Drug-like-Datura-DMT-could-cause-hallucinations-Bastard-kidnapped-me-God-has-he-hurt-Gary?-Sick-he's-sick-but-I-never-thought—

Nathan stepped back, hands raised.

'Tregan,' he said. 'I'm sorry for everything before. But this isn't what you think.'

When-people-say-that-it's-always-exactly-what-you-think.

'When people say that it's always exactly what you think,' Nathan said.

How-did-he-do-that?-Bad-dream-has-to-be . . .

'It's not, Tregan,' Nathan said, crouching down. 'I wish it was a bad dream.'

Made-himself-smaller-less-threatening.

'I crouched because my legs are aching,' he said. 'I've been riding and looking for you.'

Better-play-along-crazy-psycho-stalker. 'How'd you find me?'

'Soon after it started I could see flashes of you and Gary,' Nathan said. 'Enough to have an idea where you were.'

Be-clinical-Tregan-He-thinks-he's-telling-the-truth. 'You're crazy,' she said. *Shit-not-helping-Wrong-thing-to-say-Sorry—*

'I'm the one who's sorry,' Nathan said. 'For everything that happened before. I was sick. You helped me see that. I got help. Got meds. I'm still on them. I promise.'

God-where's-Gary-If-you-hurt—

'I didn't do anything to him,' Nathan said. 'For godsake listen to me!'

Get-out-of-my-head-Leave-me-alone!

'I need to tell you something.'

I need to tell you something.

For Tregan, those words brought back everything frightening about Nathan. I didn't want to share her memories. I wanted to avert my mind. But I had to know who he really was.

At first Tregan's shy classmate had just seemed to come out of his shell as a really brilliant and funny guy. She was glad to have him as a friend and study partner. But then he started talking about sleep being for the weak and how they were soul mates meant to save the world. Classic manic episode. Gary, who was in third year, agreed with her diagnosis. Nathan had no insight into his condition, couldn't see that he was a walking DSM-VI entry. Talking to him about getting help only played into his paranoia. When Tregan ignored his ceaseless social media entreaties he would appear outside her apartment at all hours. She finally got a restraining order and Nathan disappeared from her life—after one last belligerent online rant. Title: *I Need To Tell You Something*. Last she'd heard, via another student, he'd gotten a medical deferral, had sought treatment and was working nights at a convenience store.

'Please listen to me,' Nathan said.

Tregan backed away from him. 'You—you—drugged me.'

Nathan shook his head. 'Lorazepam.' He tossed a bulging RSK in front of her. 'I revived you. Everyone's in a catatonic state.'

Tregan flashed to the moments before everything had gone black. Too much information. People falling into nothingness. She'd followed them. Already she was theorising.

Social-defeat-in-mice-can-result-in-catatonia-Lorazepam-Remember-those-studies—

Tregan looked at Nathan sharply, aware he was hearing her.

'It's all in there,' he said, 'Everything you need to help Gary and other people.'

Is-he-telling-the-truth?

'I am, you know it,' he said. 'Hear those people out there?'

She could. Echoing minds. Easier to focus than before. People injecting catatonics. Reviving them before it was too late.

'We woke them up the same way,' Nathan said. 'Tregan, you want to save lives, here's your chance.'

Other Revivee minds saw and heard all of this through Tregan.

This-guy-Nathan-He's-the-one-who-woke-us?-Can't-read-him-He-can-hear-her-She-thinks-he's-psycho—

'I'm going,' Nathan said, standing up, offering his hand. 'Find Gary, revive him, do whatever you can.'

Tregan took the bag—but refused his hand.

Stand-on-my-own-two-feet-you-crazy— 'Can you really hear me?'

Nathan nodded.

Worst-thing-ever-stalker-inside-my-goddamned-head-Oh-Nathan-no-I'm—

'Just like you can hear them out there,' he said. 'But I'll tune out. I'll leave you be.'

When Nathan picked his way back through the bush, Tregan followed at a wary distance.

When she emerged from the trees, Gary's car was where it

had been, one of scores of vehicles strewn across the highway. Tregan saw her fiancé behind the wheel.

Oh-baby-please-be-okay. She hugged the RSK to her chest. Tregan wanted to run to her man as much as she wanted to flee. She knew what could have gone wrong for him: shock, dehydration, infarction, aneurysm, desperate self-harm or the mindless violence of some passing maniac. What if she couldn't revive him? Or if she did, only for them to pick up their awful telepathic argument where they left off? Whatever happened had to be a private moment—or as private as it could be in this public world.

Nathan didn't need to be told once. 'I'll get going.'

Tregan watched him climb onto the mountain bike. *He's-really-going-Don't-know-if-that's-better-or—*

'Are you with someone?' she asked. 'You said "we"?'

Nathan met her eyes. 'I've got a . . .'

Girlfriend.

'Friend.'

God-even-he's-got-someone-What-if-Gary-won't-wake-up—

'Do you want me to wait?' Nathan asked. 'Just in case.'

Stop!-Stop!-Stop-listening-to-me-I'd-rather-be-alone-than—

I saw Nathan flinch, knew her every thought was hurting him.

'No.' Tregan forced a smile. 'Go.'

'I'm sorry,' Nathan said. 'For everything. Good luck.'

She watched him disappear into the maze of traffic.

I was about to tune away when Tregan's thought hit me like a shotgun.

Better-her-than-me.

Her was *me*.

I paced the reception area, clenching and unclenching my fists, stomach heavy with the dread that I'd replaced Tregan as Nathan's obsession. A shiver danced through the hairs on my arms as I thought about the times we'd held hands and hugged.

'I've got a . . . friend.'

Tregan had thought he was going to say 'girlfriend'. So had I.

Jesus.

Nathan had said he and I were saving the world. Did he think all this horrible stuff had happened to throw us together? What would he do if I tried to leave? I had time to escape. I couldn't carry Evan far but even if I got us into another building a few blocks away Nathan wouldn't find us easily. I knew how to change Evan's IV. I could try Lorazepam again. If that didn't work, I could revive a doctor—a *real* doctor—who could rig up an electroshock. All of that sounded possible—but terrifying because I didn't want to be alone.

I had to calm down. Look at Nathan through my own eyes instead of Tregan's.

He hadn't actually lied to me. Technically he was still a medical student—he'd merely omitted the more recent bit about being mentally ill. All he'd said was that when the Snap happened he was coming off the night shift. My imagination had provided the picture of him valiantly battling to save humanity in an emergency ward. Before he'd gone to sleep he'd promised to tell me everything in the morning.

Now he had. But Nathan had gone further than just telling me the truth—he'd consciously shown it to me in a way that went beyond words. He could have injected Tregan and been gone before she woke up. Nathan had stuck around. He'd wanted me to see him through her eyes and know the worst. He'd wanted me to have the chance to get away. As for him holding my hand or giving me a hug: it was what normal people did in even mildly distressing situations, let alone in the aftermath of the apocalypse.

What I knew about Nathan for certain was that he'd saved my life. Without him I'd be dead and worse at the hands of the Party Duder. Without him Evan would be wasting away in Starboard. Without him a few dozen people wouldn't be up and walking around. And that included Tregan.

I looked at his note again. He'd known what I'd think. He'd wanted to reassure me.

'Hope we'll still be <u>friends</u>.'

We would be.

But I knew what my friend had been looking for in the DrugRite after he'd gotten the Lorazepam: his medication. I had to make sure he kept taking it. And then I realised, who was I to talk? I hadn't brought my prescription with me—

I rummaged excitedly in Nathan's stuff. Found two boxes of pills. But he wasn't on Lucidiphil. What he was taking was Lithium and Lamictal. How different could they be? These drugs had to be at least a contributing factor to our immunity. Our anti-psychotic meds had reacted with our brain chemistries just enough to set us apart from everyone else.

I laughed nervously at what that might mean. The lunatics had taken over the asylum—with me as an honorary member.

I couldn't wait to tell Nathan when he got back. It could be the start of something. Maybe we could give people drugs like these to stop them broadcasting thoughts. If people didn't send there'd be nothing to receive. We might be able to do more than revive people. We might be able to reverse the telepathy.

My mind went out to see if I could track Nathan's progress back to me through Revivees. No one could see him, but flitting from mind to mind confirmed how well our plan was still working. Lovers and siblings and parents and children had been restored to life. Cuts and bruises had been tended, fluids and simple meals given, and people were venturing into the dawn to find pharmacies and resupply themselves. The evolving mental collective was sharing knowledge about how to measure doses, which streets were impassable, where fires were burning out of control. People were thinking about how to help more family and friends but some were also planning to assist strangers. If this kept growing exponentially then thousands of people would soon be revived.

But I still couldn't help seething at the selfish ones out there. Anne was boozing in her stolen mansion. Cassie and her crew were preparing more heroin. Cory now claimed a fancy department store as his property. Sadness swamped me when I saw that Robert had changed his mind about euthanising his wife and kids only to discover they had burned when every house on his street had been incinerated. I wished I could tell him how sorry I was that we'd revived him to face this horror.

But Ray kept my hopes up. He had reached the strip of shops near Lyn's apartment building. The pharmacy on the corner was intact. It was a miracle because the deli, bakery, cafe and liquor store had all gone up in flames. Ray felt sad for the dead drunks burned around the entrance but was glad that the inferno had boiled away temptation—almost.

Maybe-a-beer-at-Lyn's?-Just-one-won't—

'No!' I said. 'Don't.'

I couldn't help Ray but the support from elsewhere—*One's-too-many-You're-doing-so-well-You-don't-need-it*—helped him set aside his thirst.

Ray stepped into the pharmacy and shone his flashlight around. I yelped with him when the circle of yellow light fell on a round blue face. A young dude had tied his arm and injected himself with too much of something. For a fraction of a second Ray—and all of us with him—worried this was Lorazepam gone wrong. Then he shone the torch on the packet of morphine tablets beside the corpse.

Steadying himself, Ray went behind the chemist's counter. A helpful thought materialised in his mind.

It'll-be-on-the-last-shelf.

That was Gary. He had tuned into Ray while helping Tregan make up syringes of Lorazepam from the RSK that Nathan had left.

Ray found the Lorazepam where Gary said it'd be. Eight boxes. He didn't have the maths to know how many people that'd help.

Enough-for-maybe-two-hundred, Tregan chimed in. *Thing-is-to-act-quickly-Dehydration's-the-killer.*

That was another thing Ray liked about the shared mind. It could make you a better person at the same time it made you a smarter person.

I heard the music when Ray heard it. He froze, wondering if he was imagining things, and I froze with him, remembering the Party Duder. But this was different. Jangly guitar. Mournful singing. Ray thought maybe he was hearing it from someone else's head. Maybe one of his comrades in consciousness was listening to Bob Dylan on a boombox. I was a step ahead of Ray. A quick scan told me that everyone else was hearing it via him and were just as puzzled. I searched for a mind behind the song. I couldn't tune into whoever it was. Neither could anyone else.

Ray thought maybe it was that guy, Nathan, who he'd seen through that girl, Tregan. He knew the fella was a bit mixed up but he wanted to thank him anyway.

I knew that wasn't right. Nathan would be on his way back here. Regardless, he didn't strike me as the troubadour type.

'Ray, be careful!' I shouted uselessly to the dreary little office.

I wished he could hear me. He was listening to everyone else.

Someone-with-answers-Go-see-so-we-know-who . . .

They weren't afraid.

They hadn't been subjected to the Party Duder.

Ray stepped out of the pharmacy and blinked into the glare of a uniformed police officer. He was a youngish specimen, face bruised, thinning hair matted with blood, torso broad beneath his dirty blue shirt.

I sighed with relief. But Ray was shitting himself. Even now a cop was his worst nightmare. He couldn't read this man's mind but he didn't need to. He knew the type. Had all his life. His soul shrivelled in the pig's stare. He felt like a prisoner again, powerless before the Man. Ray let his plastic bag of pills and syringes drop to the glass-strewn footpath and raised his hands. Smashed pharmacy, stolen drugs, a dead junkie inside. This looked bad. He could kiss parole goodbye. But that didn't make any sense, not now, surely. Ray was just doing what he had to do.

Don't-do-anything-stupid-Just-tell-him-the-truth-Law-doesn't-apply: Ravi, Jackie, Tregan—they all shared my relief and the belief that this would be okay.

'Officer, I wasn't—' Ray said.

The Cop stared.

'I was just getting dru—medicine for my family,' he continued.

Inscrutable, that was the word to describe this policeman.

The Cop certainly wasn't playing the guitar and singing. Ray could still hear the song nearby. But he didn't see anyone when he risked a nervous glance along the cluttered street. Maybe when the muso came into view he could help talk sense into this meat head. Ray recognised the tune now. Not Bob Dylan at all but Johnny Cash's 'The Man Comes Around'.

Bang-bang-bang—someone joined in with a drum. Ray flinched, turned back to the Cop, wanted to say something but only had enough breath to wheeze out: 'Oh'.

The Cop stared blankly but he had his service revolver drawn. Ray looked from the smoking muzzle to his Hawaiian shirt. Hibiscuses bloomed dark blood as burning burrowed in his stomach. Then Ray's legs went and he was at the man's feet, head twisted at a strange angle, no feeling anywhere.

The Cop plucked our instruction sheet from the shopping bag and crumpled it in front of Ray's clouding eyes.

'No more of this,' the killer said, leaning down close, breath hot and fetid. 'Legion, no one comes to life except through me.'

The Cop straightened up and we watched helplessly as he raised his heavy black boot. We all screamed when he stomped and Ray's part of the world died.

EIGHTEEN

I ricocheted around the little balcony, searching the street below and the terrified minds all around, terrified that the Cop could read my mind and would come after me, terrified the Cop would get Nathan before he could get back to me. The air around me was thick with smoke and the stench of death. How many more people had died overnight? Were dying right at that moment? Rather than worry about myself I should have been out there. Administering injections. Setting up IVs. Doing whatever I could. But instead I paced, bit my nails and checked and re-checked Evan, and looked at the time on my dwindling phone every few minutes.

Finally, Nathan's red baseball cap bobbed between cars. He was on foot, carrying his bike over his shoulder, nose and mouth hidden behind a bandana. I'd never been so glad to see someone. I waved crazily and after a while he saw me and waved back.

Nathan clomped up the stairwell to me. He pulled down his bandana and smiled. I grabbed him, hugged him tight, not caring he was soaked with sweat.

'Danby, I'm sorry about—'

I hauled him through the kitchen door.

'It doesn't matter,' I said. 'I'm just glad you're all right.'

We had a lot to talk about. I'd wanted to tell him my theory about our medications. But that seemed old news now.

'Did you feel like that was especially for us?' Nathan asked as he paced the reception area with a bottle of water. 'For everyone in Ray's mind, I mean.'

'Definitely,' I said. 'But why? And what was all that stuff about Legion and coming to life?'

'Because he's crazy like that bastard who attacked you,' Nathan said. 'I know he was paraphrasing bits of the Bible. There's a part where Jesus encounters a possessed man and asks, "What's your name?" and the demon inside the guy answers, "Legion, for we are many."'

'So, we're the demons in this scenario?'

Nathan shrugged. 'The other thing—"No one comes to life except through me"—sounds like Jesus saying, "I am the truth, the way and the life—no one comes to the Father except through me."'

Nathan read my tiny frown and smiled.

'Hindu father, Catholic mother—I'm an atheist but I read religiously.'

I shook my head in frustration. 'Why would someone who believes in God be against reviving people?'

'Some fundamentalist Christians believe the Old Testament says drugs of any kind are Satanic sorcery,' Nathan said.

'What freaks me out more is that it felt like he'd tracked Ray to the pharmacy.'

'Do you think he can tune into us?' I hated how panicked I sounded. But the reception room no longer felt like a safe haven. It felt like we were under surveillance.

Nathan shook his head. 'We can't hear him. He shouldn't be able to hear us. I hope that's how it works.'

I wanted to believe. 'But,' I said, 'anyone out there could be next.'

The Revivees were of that mind. They feared that reviving people might incur the Cop's demented justice and that they'd never see him coming—at least not in the new way.

A few were loudly disavowing Lorazepam and pleading to be left alone. But I was glad that most weren't about to bow down, not when the lives of everyone they'd ever loved were at stake.

'What do we do?' Nathan asked.

I looked at him. 'I'm not sure if Jesus said this, but we're damned if we do and damned if we don't, right? If we wake people up, he might come kill us. If we don't wake people up, we're letting people die.'

Before he had a chance to reply we had a lot more to worry about than just the Cop.

Cassie and her friends had fixed after seeing Ray die. Typical fascist pig behaviour, was what they reckoned, before they started mumbling and went into their respective nods. Now she was waking up, wet and warm on the couch.

What-the-f—

She spat, clothes soaked, eyes stinging inside a suffocating rainbow aura.

Petrol-Who-the—

A blurry figure sloshed a jerry can over James.

'Ah, man,' he shouted, falling off his barstool as he snapped into consciousness.

Now Sammy was drenched.

Cassie saw enough to know she didn't believe her eyes.

A Surfer blocked the doorway. Board shorts, singlet, thongs: he looked like he'd just come up from the beach.

'You want to be wasted,' he said in a spacey voice. 'Here you go.'

As the Surfer backed out of the pub, he reached down to the trail of petrol with a Zippo lighter.

'No!' *No!*

Cassie jumped off the couch. James slipped as he tried to stand. Sammy launched himself at a window as the pub exploded.

'Jesus,' I said.

Nathan's mouth moved but no words came.

Cassie and James were gone. Sammy rolled amid broken glass on fractured bones, his burning skin stretched on the scorched footpath like chewing gum on a hot day. The last thing he saw through his flames and agony was the Surfer shaking his head sorrowfully from across the street. Sammy wanted to scream—that he was sorry, that he needed help—but when he opened his mouth his last air whooshed from his body in a fiery plume.

'Why?' I gasped.

Nathan's shoulders heaved. I was having trouble breathing too.

'Two separate attacks,' he managed. 'Suburbs apart.'

'Do you think—I mean—will—are there . . . *more* of them?'

Nathan shook his head as he paced. 'I don't know.'

I blinked at him. 'What do we do?'

'If we leave now, we're out in the open,' he said. 'No one knows we're here. We should be safe.'

'You don't sound sure of that.'

'I'm not.'

We went into the accountant's office and peered through the venetian blinds at the street below. Plenty of Goners but no movement. Except for a cat shrieking west on the far footpath. The yowls and growls of unseen others played my nerves like an untuned piano.

If the Cop and the Surfer and whoever else could hear our thoughts then the first we might know of their approach could be them coming up the stairs.

'Are you sure they can't read us?'

I wanted Nathan to reassure me. I knew he couldn't.

'We have to go,' I said, unable to shake the image of killers closing in on us.

Nathan nodded.

'We need to get you a bike, heavy tyres, seat for Evan,' he said absently, like he was trying to remember a shopping list. 'There's a lot of glass. Get a puncture kit, pump. The bike shop's five blocks towards the highway. We'll have to walk them out of the city. But I could ride okay in a lot of places on the highway.'

Nathan began unhooking Evan's IV as I threw stuff into a backpack.

In the wake of the Surfer's massacre, most of the Revivees were mentally waving white flags.

I-won't-use-the-stuff-Won't-loot-Please-don't-hurt-me-or-my-family.

We-can't-run-They-can-track-us-Don't-wake-anyone-Not-worth-dying . . .

They sounded like people bargaining with God. There'd been a lot of that when the Snap happened. I wondered who or what was on the other end of their prayers now.

Not everyone was surrendering.

You-cowards-I'll-take-you-bastards-on-Come-get-me-you . . .

I was tuning Tim, Jackie's brother. When she couldn't find Tony, she'd gone to his place. Took ages to break in. Jackie had to laugh when she saw him huddled with his guns and dressed in his army surplus clothes. Tim the Prepper had gone down as surely as everyone else. But he was still her brother and he might be able to help her find Tony. She had the syringe in Tim's arm when Ray's death flooded her head. Jackie injected her brother anyway, hoping the Cop didn't see, or, if he did, that he'd let it slide because she'd done it so close to deadline.

Now Tim was crouching below the lounge-room window with his assault rifle. Once he knew what was going on he told Jackie they were gonna find enough Lorazepam to wake up the whole street. Tim hated his neighbours. But he hated being told what to do more.

No-don't-you're-making-it-worse-for-everyone: scared minds were piling into his. But he wasn't defenceless like he'd been Christmas Day. Now he could fire back at the chickenshits.

Cowards-can-shoot-a-drunk-Set-fire-to-junkies-Let's-see-how-they-handle-a-real-man-who-can—

Nathan and I screamed as the wall behind Tim exploded in a booming cloud of wood chips.

That's-ninja-shit. Tim toppled onto the floorboards. They'd come in total silence and known exactly where to aim. *Thigh-back-shoulder-Be-dead-in-minutes-bastards.*

Jackie crawled across the floor to him.

'Go,' he said through a mouth of blood. *Take-some-of-these-assholes-with-me.*

Tim pulled himself up, fired randomly out the window, as Jackie scrabbled away, the house erupting all around her.

'Go!' I shouted to her.

Nathan shook his head violently. 'Sssssh!'

He was right. We didn't know who was where and who could hear what. I kept packing but my mind was with Jackie.

Jackie launched herself over Tim's back fence. She dodged through another backyard. Darted between cars on the choked roads. Slowed as she reached Parramatta's business district.

I heard her plan not to plan. If they knew everything she was thinking then she wouldn't think about where she was or where she was going. If she didn't know, they couldn't know.

'Clever girl,' I said.

228

'Hope it works. Almost ready?'

Nathan had Evan wrapped in a blanket. I threw the backpack over my shoulder. I'd crammed it with boxes of biscuits, bottled water, Lorazepam, first aid, IV stuff and the nail gun. We had enough to keep us going for a while if we got stuck somewhere and couldn't resupply.

But now we couldn't look away from Jackie. Against all survival instinct she'd walked with her eyes so squinted she was nearly blind. Head down, seeing only indistinct shapes through the mesh of her eyelashes, she bypassed blurry bodies, felt her way between vehicles and skirted building facades. Now, too scared to go on, satisfied she was lost, Jackie crawled into a darkened shop. Fragments of glass dug into her hands and knees, but she only cried out when she felt the lacy hems of dresses brushing softly against her cheek. As much as she didn't want to know, Jackie knew she was in a clothing store.

Nathan and I pinpointed it to a boutique called Bravo Apparel. We couldn't read this from Jackie's mind. We didn't need to because we were watching from the balcony when she randomly chose the store opposite our refuge as her hiding spot.

Jewellery-store!-Gift-shop!-Computer-outlet!-Tattoo-parlour!

Cowering under a desk in the dark back office, Jackie thought of every business she could not related to clothes. But if they were after her then that'd still tell them she was in some sort of shop. So she conjured up emotional memories, fired them off like the flares fighter jets used to confuse heat-seeking missiles. Jackie was back in Girl Guides. Eating popcorn at the movies on her first date with Tony. Getting married on the beach in Bali. Anywhere but there.

'Holy shit,' Nathan whispered.

I followed his stare to the end of the block. A beast of a Biker, dressed in dirty denim, machine gun over one shoulder, strolled between vehicles. Behind him trailed the Cop and the Surfer. They also had guns. The three of them weren't in any sort of hurry.

We tiptoed back into the office and shared a sliver of venetian blind. The trio came into view below as they moved in on Bravo Apparel. They didn't speak and they didn't use hand signals. We couldn't read their thoughts but I was sure they were sharing a mind.

The Biker, the Cop and the Surfer stopped outside Bravo Apparel.

'Don't,' Nathan whispered.

I took my hand away from the .45 in my waistband. He was right. Even if I hit one of them from up here, it'd only tell the others we were here. Guilt corkscrewed my stomach again. We'd brought Jackie back to life so she could face this death.

The men walked into Bravo Apparel. I didn't want to be inside Jackie's experience but I couldn't look away. No one could. From under the desk, she heard boots on floorboards and coat hangers rattling on a display rack. That's when Jackie and everyone else knew the outcome had never been in doubt. Whoever was out there hadn't needed to run to chase her.

They'd zeroed in on her hiding spot as surely as if she had a homing beacon in her skull.

The door to the office opened and the room filled with the smell of stale sweat and the sound of men breathing.

Hail-Mary-full-of-grace.

Jackie's heart pounded so loud in her ears it drowned out her prayer.

'Do you mind coming out?'

The voice was surprisingly gentle.

'Out you come, Jackie,' he said. 'Please.'

The polite way he said it gave Jackie hope. She lifted her head from the carpet and crawled out from under the desk, blinking up at the Biker as he shone a flashlight on his big hairy face so we all got a good look.

'No drugs, no looting and no guns,' he said pleasantly.

Jackie nodded. 'Yes, I'm sorry, anything you—'

The words died in her throat when the Cop and Surfer appeared like spectres from the shadows.

'I'm not talking to you,' the Biker said, pressing cold metal against her cheek. 'Last warning.'

Jackie winked out of existence a second before we heard the muffled boom from inside Bravo Apparel.

The Biker walked out of the boutique, tucking a revolver into his jeans, taking his machine gun from his shoulder. The Cop and Surfer followed and they each took a shop to search on that side of the street, using the butts of their weapons to smash glass doors. Farther up the street, more unreadable people appeared, all of them armed, all of them scoping out shops, scanning first-storey windows, staring down alleys and peering into and under cars.

This wasn't how it had been with Ray, Cassie and Jackie. They weren't following thoughts to thinkers. This time they were after people they couldn't hear and see.

They were looking for us.

NINETEEN

'They know we're around here,' I whispered. 'We need to go right now.'

Of course they did. Our Revivees' memories of returning to consciousness all centred on the same street just a few blocks away. It made sense that whoever was doing the dosing was holed up nearby. There were a dozen or more of them out looking for us. God knows how many others on the way. Before long someone would smash the street door and come up our stairs. Even if we killed him or her, we wouldn't be able to do it without telling every one of his comrades who and where we were. Our only chance was to go down the fire stairs and quickly and quietly get very far away.

Nathan put Evan into a fireman's carry and we crept through the kitchen door. I stepped softly onto the landing and peered down the alley. They hadn't got this far yet. But it wouldn't be long.

'Wait here,' I said when we reached the bottom of the fire escape. 'I'll check the street.'

I hurried across the cobblestones to the rectangle of smoky daylight that opened onto the next block. I took a deep breath and poked my head and the .45 around the corner. The street was empty of our enemies, just cluttered with cars and debris and the dying and dead.

I nodded back to Nathan and he started towards me with Evan.

Then he was down on one knee, mouth snarled in silent pain as he lowered my little brother to the ground. I scrambled back to him.

'What's wrong?' I said.

Nathan rubbed his ankle. 'Twisted it.'

'Can you walk?'

I helped him up and he tested his weight.

'I'll be okay.'

'Take these,' I said, handing Nathan the .45 and the backpack.

I hauled Evan up over my shoulder.

'Can you manage?'

I didn't know if I could but I nodded. 'Go.'

Nathan limped to the corner.

'The river's five or six blocks,' I said. 'Can you make it?'

'Can you?'

We lurched out onto the street. But we hadn't even gone half a block before Nathan was hobbling and I was struggling under Evan. We'd be finished when one of those bastards came around the corner and saw us. I pointed to an empty taxi, closed my eyes, tilted my head and rested a cheek on the back of my hand.

Nathan nodded furiously at my pantomime.

'I'll drive,' he whispered. 'I look the part.'

I actually snickered as I eased a passenger door open. His joke made this less real. It was like an action-movie wisecrack. Buddy heroes never died in those flicks.

We put Evan down on the floor and I hid him under the backpack. Then I crawled onto the back seat and lay face down. Nathan snicked the door closed behind me, circled the vehicle and slid into the driver's seat. He pulled his cap low, rested his forehead on the steering wheel and held the .45 down by his legs.

'If you shoot anyone,' I whispered. 'They'll all come.'

'I know,' he said. 'But I'm gonna mess up anyone who messes with us.'

The heat in the taxi was stifling. We'd bake to death if we had to keep this charade up too long. Hibernation state or not, I wondered how long the millions who'd crashed out in cars could possibly survive.

Movement around the corner—doors slamming, glass tinkling—but our block remained maddeningly still and silent. With every passing second they didn't come closer, I regretted our plan. *My* plan. Playing possum hadn't fooled the Party Duder. Maybe if we'd struggled on—carried Evan stretcher-style—we could've made it to the river. I imagined what anyone looking would see inside the taxi. A driver and his passenger both in their seats and in each other's personal space with no evidence they'd tried to distract themselves with devices or drink or drugs. It wouldn't add up.

I groped my phone from my pocket and pushed myself up.

'What are you doing?' Nathan hissed.

'Getting into character.'

I held the phone to my chest and hung my head over its blank screen. At least I was in the posture of a million other Goners now. If the Biker and the rest of those bastards were concentrating on buildings, only glancing at cars, it might be enough to fool them.

As soft as I tried to make my breathing, it still sounded like rasping sandpaper to me. My heart was even noisier. If they didn't hear it hammering, then surely they'd see my pulse throbbing in my temples, know I was faking because my blood pressure was supposed to be lower and I looked like I was about to shoot steam from my ears. Sweat trickled from my hair, ran down my flushed forehead, slid off my nose and splattered on my phone. Another droplet followed, slipped down my face, quivered maddeningly on the end of my nose. I wanted to shake ever so slightly to rid myself of it. But if anyone saw me move then—

'Oh,' Nathan said. 'Oh.'

Heavy feet crunched broken glass. Car doors groaned open and thunked shut. Their sounds grew sharper, louder, closer. They were coming our way. Without saying a word. Through squinted eyes, I saw shadows moving around the car ahead of us. This was it. They were almost on us.

'These aren't the droids you're looking for,' Nathan whispered.

His joke offered no comfort this time. It made me realise our mistake.

We weren't Jedis. They weren't stupid stormtroopers.

They didn't know where we were. But they knew *who* we were. What we looked like. When we'd shown ourselves to Cassie we'd shown ourselves to them.

'Danby and Nathan, if you get out of the car you won't be harmed.'

The Biker. I recognised that honeyed tone. He was close. Other footsteps came closer. I heard bullets being chambered. I pictured the goon squad surrounding the taxi with their guns. I saw it as if from outside my body. I guessed that's where I was about to be.

'Danby and Nathan, if you get out of the car you won't be harmed,' he repeated. 'I promise.'

We held our poses like kids playing hide-and-seek who try to avoid being caught by keeping their eyes closed. Then, after a few moments, Nathan said in a small but calm voice: 'Here or there, Danby?'

I knew what he meant: in the taxi or on the street. Either way, this was the end. We were trapped by killers who hadn't shown any mercy. Just minutes ago Jackie had made the mistake of hoping and we saw how that went for her. I let one hand drop from my phone to touch Evan's cheek. It was warm and smooth and that was as nice a last feeling as I could've hoped for. I wasn't scared. I'd burned out on being afraid. I just didn't want there to be any pain.

'Here,' I said.

'Okay.'

'Danby and Nathan, if you—'

'Shut the—' Nathan roared as he reared out of his fake catatonia '—hell up!'

I expected a cacophony as he emptied his gun and they emptied theirs. But there was just a loud bang as something hot punched into my head.

I slumped onto the seat. Blood filled my eyes. It streamed across my face and pooled around my neck. Strange thoughts came. I was awash and sinking. But this wasn't my life leaking out. It was death flowing in. I'd always been a tiny boat adrift on an endless sea. The ocean claiming me was inevitable. I felt a smile form when I realised I was holding my phone so tightly it was like it was fused to my finger bones. Future archaeologists would find so many of us like this that they'd conclude the little black rectangles were funerary objects meant to spirit us into the afterlife. Afterlife: now *that* was a funny word. When life's over, take *afterlife*! It was like bonus time. Afterdeath: that was more accurate. Whatever. Wherever. I'd be there in a second. And that was fine. Except it wasn't. I couldn't die yet because—because—because . . .

I needed to make sure Nathan was okay. Because—because—

Evan—I had to—

Then I was gone.

3 the raised.

TWENTY

I was at peace. How could I not be with her watching over me? Ancient dark eyes. Silver hair cascading around milky shoulders. Standing in her gown in front of a classical temple and a fiery sunset. She was more than beautiful, more than mortal. She was an angel. I was in heaven. Then my head started hurting like hell.

I'm not dead: that much I knew.

What I didn't know was if I was glad to be alive. The pain in my skull had at least jolted me back to reality. My guardian angel was actually an old oil painting hung on a plaster wall. My head was bandaged and I was tucked into an ornate four-poster bed under an elaborately embroidered canopy. I pushed myself up against the pillow and looked around the room. The painting wasn't the only thing from another time. Every piece of furniture glowed from within like a priceless antique. Silver mirrors shone with candlelight from a crystal chandelier. Heavy red velvet curtains hid the windows. There wasn't a machine of any kind in view. Not even electrical outlets in the walls.

My head throbbed. I didn't know who I was. I didn't know where I was. I didn't know *when* I was. The idea of pulling back those curtains filled me with dread. Would I see ladies wearing hoop skirts? Gentlemen in top hats? Horse-drawn carriages? Was that what I was supposed to see?

All I knew was I had a head injury. I'd been put into this bed to recover. I'd come out of some strange dream I couldn't quite remember. A name appeared in my mind: Mary Shelley. I knew she had a nightmare and was inspired to write a book in Switzerland in 1816. I could even see her explaining the work to elegant friends in a drawing room while a storm raged outside huge windows. How could I know that? Was that me who'd been there and then? How else would all the details be so vivid?

I threw back the sheets, lurched from the bed, stumbled across the room and yanked open the curtains. Daylight dazzled. Then my eyes adjusted. Below me was an expanse of lawn enclosed by a white picket fence. Beyond that was a fleet. Not tall ships at harbour. Four-wheel drives parked between ghost gums. The vehicles were being loaded and fuelled by a small army of men and women in modern clothes.

My involuntary thought—*I-can't-read-their-minds*—brought everything crashing back.

I'd been with Evan. Trying to get to Mum's. I'd met Nathan. We'd tried to help people. Then those bastards started killing people. I remembered Nathan's shout and that single gunshot and feeling like my head had been blown off. Then bleeding and fading to black.

Other flashes came. The taxi door opening. Strong hands lifting me out. My blood everywhere. A blur of cars and streets, a stone gateway, green garden. After that nothing until the portrait of the lady.

I sat back dizzy on the bed and my mind spiralled out. The Revivees were terrified. Hunkering down. Fleeing for their lives. They were convinced reviving anyone new would sentence them to death. Everywhere they looked—in spare bedrooms, in their sooty yards, in yawning doorways of neighbouring houses and up and down their smoke-cloaked streets—they imagined assassins ready to step from the shadows. They feared that even simple tasks—eating tinned soup, washing and dressing cuts, burying the dead—might somehow invite wrath. Anyone who considered reviving loved ones or picking up a weapon was howled down for endangering everyone. The most selfish had gone to ground in fear that they were about to pay for sins, actual or imagined. Their names and lives came back to me. They didn't know anything about Evan. They didn't know about me. They couldn't tune us. I shut them out.

I had to get up, get out of this room, get back to Evan and Nathan, get us all to Mum's. But my head throbbed. The room started to slip and slide. My face went pins and needles and it was hard to breathe. I had to get to the door. But when I tried to stand up blackness pulled me back to the bed.

My eyes opened on another young angel. It said so on his rock T-shirt: 'Grievous Angel'. But he was real. I couldn't read his mind but his face was handsome concern by candlelight.

'Are you feeling better?' he said.

I nodded.

'I've given you something to help with the pain,' he said, leaning in, breath warm and smoky. 'Would you like a drink?'

He held a straw to my lips so I could sip from a cup of cool water.

'Where am I?'

'Safe,' he said. 'You're safe.'

I felt the bandage around my head. I knew I'd be all right. I could think, move and see. 'Evan?' I said, fighting back tears. 'My little brother, he was—is he okay?'

The man nodded. 'He's fine.'

Relief swept through me.

But if that was true then why was Grievous Angel's expression so grave?

Nathan.

'My friend, he was with me and—'

'I'm sorry.' The guy shook his head and touched his fingertips to his heart. 'The bullet hit him here. Went straight through.'

'Oh, no,' I heard myself say.

'Then it got you here.' He ran his fingers along the side of his head. 'It didn't penetrate the skull but it ripped your scalp. It's nothing the stitches and time won't heal. You were very lucky. I'm sorry about your friend.'

Nathan was dead. It was my fault. If I'd thought the scenario through I would've known we couldn't hide in the taxi. If he hadn't saved me in the first place he might still be alive.

'Where is— Where's Evan? He needs IV, fluids, he was in the taxi, he—'

My throat was closing.

'It's okay.'

The guy touched my wrist and his face lit up with a smile. Then with theatrical loudness he bellowed, 'Okay!'

The door flew open and Evan bounded across the room to my bedside.

I pulled my little brother tight to me. I was fully awake and alert, the opiate cobwebs and cotton wool blown away. That was good, that was great, because I wanted to feel all of this.

'Danby!' Evan giggled. 'Squashing!'

I relaxed my grip, held him by his shoulders. He smiled at me, eyes bright and clear, looking no worse for wear, dressed in new clothes that smelled like a department store.

'I was so worried,' I said, tears flowing freely, feeling for his mind, wanting that connection I'd felt back in Beautopia Point. I couldn't tune into him now but what mattered was that he was alive, safe and conscious. 'I'm so glad you're all right.'

I looked at the guy over Evan's shoulder. Sitting in a plush armchair, expertly rolling a cigarette and dressed in black threads: he looked like an indie rocker. I wondered whether I should know who he was and whether we were in the eccentric castle he'd bought with his music millions.

'Did you wake Evan up?'

He smiled up at me and nodded.

'How?'

'I'm not quite sure myself,' he grinned, tucking the finished smoke behind his ear. 'But I'll be happy to show you when you're up to it.'

'Did you do this?' I asked, pointing at the bandage. 'Sew me up, I mean.'

He nodded. 'I had some help.'

My little brother wriggled out of my grasp to push a toy truck along the windowsill.

'I don't know what—thank you so, so much.' My words were infinitesimal, too tiny to even be called inadequate. 'Who are—'

'Jack,' he said, reaching over to shake my hand.

'Danby.' I didn't know if I should offer my surname. They probably no longer mattered. 'How long have I been here?'

'Just since this morning,' he said.

Relief swept through me. I hadn't lost that much time. Mum should still be okay. And now that Evan was conscious it would be easier to get to Shadow Valley.

'Is this your place?' I asked.

'Yes.' Jack laughed. 'Well, actually, it belongs to all of us. You're in Old Government House in Parramatta Park.'

I'd been here before on a primary school excursion. It was the colonial mansion where Australia's early European rulers had lived and worked, and it had been turned into a museum for their documents, maps, furniture, clothes and artwork. My most vivid memories related to the poor children who'd had to grow up here. I remember thinking I would've hated sleeping on a hard little bed with only raggedy dolls, wooden animals and tin soldiers to play with. Their single schoolroom had been just as dull—a blackboard of religious instruction, uncomfortable chairs and musty old books. No computers, no projection screen.

'Yummy,' Evan squealed. 'Fri-rice!'

'That's all he wanted,' Jack said with a laugh. 'There's someone cooking in the kitchen. You can have whatever you like.'

It hurt when I laughed.

'What's funny?' Jack smiled.

'"Whatever I like?"'

The world had gone mad and then it had gone to shit and here he was talking to me like the hipster owner of some historic hotel.

'Hey,' he said with a smile, 'we probably can't do green chicken curry.'

My veins filled with ice.

Green chicken curry. The dish I'd ordered on my last visit to Rubber Thaime.

I finally understood the total violation everyone had felt on Christmas Day, why they'd all suffered so much more than I had. I felt trespassed upon, laid bare, raped. This guy was in my mind.

Jack's mouth became an O of surprise and he held up his palms.

'Hey, hey, no—I'm not reading your thoughts,' he protested. 'I can't—any more than you can read mine. Evan said something about "green chicken curry for Danby". That's all.'

Evan was back at my bedside, pushing his toy vehicle up a little mountain made by my knees under the covers.

'*UH*-oh!' he said as he let the truck roll back into a crevasse. 'Green chicken!'

I sank back into the pillows. 'Sorry,' I said. 'Just spooked me.'

'Do you want to eat?' Jack asked.

'What I want to do is get to my mum's place.' My voice sounded far away. 'That's what I want.'

Jack stood up. 'It's too dark to go anywhere now. We'll talk about everything in the morning.'

I didn't want to wait. I wanted to march west, drag Evan behind me, damn the Biker and all his bastards to hell. But I was struggling to keep my eyes open. I wondered if this was shock—or a side effect of the painkillers.

My little brother smiled at me from his chair.

'He'll stay with you.' Jack was closing the door behind him. 'You get some rest.'

Sickly orange light filled the windows. Evan slept in the chair by the bed. I propped myself up on my elbows. My head didn't hurt and my mind felt clear. But I was starving. The door was open and wonderful smells drifted into the room: bacon, toast, coffee.

Swinging out of the bed, I stood up a little shakily. The dresser was stacked with T-shirts, jeans, underwear and socks, all still store folded or in plastic wrappers, and my boots stood beside new sneakers along the skirting board. A metal basin brimmed with water. Toiletries and a towel were laid out. Even my phone had been cleaned up. I instinctively clicked it on. Still no service but a full battery. There were even packets of chewing gum. Same brand I'd had in my pocket. My host had thought of everything.

Evan slept on. I let my nightie fall from my shoulders and

looked at myself in the cheval mirror. I was clean and the bruises on my arms and legs from car crashes and kayak bumps and the rest of it were already yellowing. I unwrapped my head bandage and lifted crusty gauze and padding. Black stitches stuck out like insect legs from the gash that started above my left temple and carved its way to just over my ear. Maybe that's why I'd thought of Mary Shelley. Frankenstein's creator. It wasn't too bad. I looked kinda punk.

My face flushed red in the mirror. I'd been wearing jeans and a shirt in the taxi. I guess only an idiot would stitch a person up and then tuck the patient into bed in blood-soaked clothes. I looked at the nightie at my feet and wondered if Jack had taken it upon himself to be the first man to ever see me naked. The idea didn't trouble me as much it would have a few days ago—and not nearly as much as when I'd thought he was in my mind.

Splashing my face with cold water got me thinking about the important stuff. I didn't know why we were here, who our host was or how he'd revived Evan. And I needed answers to make the best decision about what to do next. Jack and all those people out on the lawn looked pretty organised. Maybe they could help us get to Shadow Valley.

I got dressed. Tried on new sneakers but stuck with my boots. Grabbed some gum and pocketed my phone. Tied my hair back. Evan was still curled up. I let him sleep.

I stepped into a gloomy corridor, floorboards creaking underfoot, walls lined with paintings of the Australian bush looking like English countryside. I glanced through doorways into deep rooms. There were roped-off displays of furniture, clothing and assorted colonial treasures but no other guests. Following the breakfast aromas took me down a wide staircase to a chequerboard hallway and then to a grand dining room.

Jack turned from the windows and greeted me with a smile.

'Oh,' I said, melting.

The long table between us was piled with platters of bacon, eggs, mushrooms, tomatoes, baked beans. Coffee steamed from a silver pot. Condensation jewelled a crystal jug of milk. Ice floated in a tall pitcher of orange juice. Roses erupted from a centrepiece vase. My stomach rumbled.

Jack laughed. 'How's the head?'

My hand hovered over the bristle of stitches. 'Pretty ugly.'

'Only half right,' he said, grinning as he pulled out a chair for me. 'You must be starving.'

Jack poured a glass of juice that was the same colour as the sky outside.

'Just so we're clear—' His frown lifted as he smiled slyly. 'One of the women got you cleaned up and changed.'

'I wasn't worried, I was—' I stammered, not sure why I was going red. 'Given the circumstances, it's fine, really, it's—'

I drank the orange juice to shut myself up and cool myself down. It was a wonderful icy sunburst.

Jack waved at the food on the table. 'Do you want everything?'

'Please.'

Jack sauntered around, piling a plate. Whenever I thought he was going to catch me watching him, I made a point of studying our surroundings. Bentwood chairs stood sentry beneath each window. An intricate rug was squared before the cavernous fireplace. Sideboards gleamed with serving bowls and wine glasses. The polish and precision gave the room a military air, the effect heightened by the portrait of a white-haired gent in a redcoat uniform above the marble mantelpiece.

'Governor Arthur Phillip,' Jack said, setting my breakfast down. He took a cigarette from behind his ear. 'Is it okay if I stand by the window?'

'Sure.'

I wasn't going to be put off by a little tobacco smoke. Not after what I'd smelled out there.

'Please, dig in,' Jack said.

I did. Greedily.

'You know the history of this place?' Jack asked, lighting up. Then added, 'Sorry, I hate it when people ask me a question when I'm eating.'

I chewed a mouthful of toast.

'That dude,' he said, pointing at Phillip's portrait, 'built here in 1790 because the soil at Sydney Cove was shit and the First Fleet was starving to death.'

Jack nodded out at the park's gentle slopes and the silver twist of river. 'It was that fertile land out there that saved them.'

I scooped up baked beans.

'The Aborigines supposedly didn't have agriculture,' he said. 'That's why they could be deemed "uncivilised". So this area was occupied with a clear Christian conscience—like the rest of the country.'

He blew a plume of smoke out the window. 'Know why the land was fertile?'

I shook my head.

'Because the Aborigines had done firestick farming here forever.'

'Ten thousand years,' I said, remembering the plaques on the river path.

'Right,' he said. 'I knew you'd get it.'

'What?'

He paced back from the window in a blue cloud to ash his cigarette on a silver platter. 'The irony. The agriculture the Aborigines supposedly didn't have was what saved the invaders—and that's what sealed the fate of the indigenous people. Actually, irony doesn't cover it.'

My appetite was fading fast. I wasn't sure what purpose his history lesson served. 'What happened was terrible.'

'I'm not trying to guilt you out.' Jack sat down with a sigh and ran his fingers through his thick hair. 'I didn't know any of this until I found out from the caretaker.'

'The caretaker was okay?'

Jack gave me a little nod. 'He's up and about.' He stubbed out his cigarette and poured us cups of coffee. 'I knew the basics of our history. But I didn't really understand until he filled me in on all the gory details. Milk? Sugar?'

I shook my head.

'If you'd looked out these windows two hundred years ago, you would've seen a vast town of convict tents.' Jack piled sugar into his coffee. 'Poor bastards turned into criminals because they'd stolen a piece of bread to keep themselves or their kids alive.'

I took the coffee for its warmth.

'Shipped to the end of the earth as slaves. Convict labour built this house. Built this country.'

Jack turned to Phillip's portrait.

'Don't get me wrong,' he said. 'Him and the rest of them weren't bad dudes. They weren't evil. They were doing what they thought was right. For God and country. But let's face it. Dispossession, extermination, oppression, slavery: that's what our country and our whole world was built on.'

My appetite was gone. I pushed my plate away.

Jack pulled out a pouch of tobacco and got rolling again.

I sipped my coffee. 'Are you saying what happened was payback?'

'Who knows?' he said. 'If I'd asked you on Christmas Eve whether you'd unlive your whole life and unbuild your society to right all those old wrongs, would you have said "Yes"?'

I didn't know what the hell he was getting at.

'I don't know,' I said, keeping a lid on my frustration. 'All I know is I have to get to my mum.'

Jack nodded. 'I'll help you with that.'

'You will?' My heart sped up. 'Really?'

Jack fixed me with his stare. His eyes were intense, golden and green, but his smile exuded easy confidence. 'Sure I will,' he said. 'But first I really have to show you something. Won't take long, okay?'

Stepping out of Old Government House I was greeted by

the sight of Evan and a little girl kicking a soccer ball across the lawn. My little brother rarely played well with others. I tried to tune her mind but got nothing. Jack grinned. Was this what he wanted to show me?

'Who is she?' I asked.

'Michelle,' he said. 'She's six. Her mother and father ran off. Nice, huh? I found her down by the river.'

Jack pointed down the hill, towards the edge of the park. 'This way, to the city.'

He began walking. Turned around when I didn't follow. I didn't want to go back to where I'd nearly been killed any more than I wanted to risk leaving Evan behind.

'What about him?' I said.

Jack looked from me to my little brother—and then to a big guy in sunglasses standing in the shade of a tree and cradling a shotgun.

'Nick over there will guard them with his life,' Jack said.

The man gave us a nod that said there was nothing he couldn't handle.

'Evan's safe here,' Jack said soothingly, assurance flowing from him again. 'We'll be safe out there.'

As we walked down the hill, I saw why Jack and the others had set up base here. There was only one road into the park and it followed the fence and then the river before looping on itself and leading back into Parramatta. Compared with the city streets, that mile or two of bitumen was relatively clear of cars and people. Off the road, there was room to move, plenty of space between the vehicles and victims strewn across the grassy slopes. I guessed that while some people had fled into the park to be alone, the panicked hordes hadn't driven in here hoping to reach someplace else. I gazed at the fleet of off-road vehicles. Men and women filled petrol tanks from cans and checked engines and loaded cargo areas with cartons. Their minds were closed to me but I saw they were broadly similar specimens: young and fit and intent on their tasks. The military got all sorts of immunisations. Maybe one of their jabs had protected these guys from the worst of it. My medications hypothesis could stretch to accommodate that possibility. I stifled a sob as I thought of Nathan, who hadn't lived long enough to hear my theory and tell me where it went wrong.

'Are you guys the army?' I asked.

Jack smiled at me. 'I guess we are now. But what we really are is lucky. All of those four-wheel drives you see were already inside the park. Getting the right vehicles off the city streets would've been near impossible. We need all the grunt we can get if we're going to get out of here.'

'Get out?' I asked. 'This place seems . . . good.'

Good: I regretted the word as soon as it left my lips. Could I be more stupid or insensitive? Within a stone's throw of where we walked I could see two obviously dead people and ten times that number who'd die unless they got help. The air around us was streaked with smoke and the sky was straight out of science-fiction. It was very far from good—but it was like Eden compared with the city streets we were about to enter.

'I didn't mean "good",' I said. 'I mean it's—'

'No, you're right,' Jack said. 'This place would be perfect. Old Government House was built for a world without electricity, the river connects us to the coast and there's plenty of rich soil to raise animals and crops like they did back in the day. We'd be able to defend against fire and if the city and suburbs didn't burn around us they'd supply us with clothes and medicine and tools and stuff like that for years to come.'

I wondered who the 'we' and 'us' were but didn't say anything.

'They're the reason we can't stay,' Jack said, hand sweeping across the field of the dead and dying. 'It's not that they're a biological hazard. You won't get sick from them, unless you eat them or drink water from where they've been festering.'

My breakfast bubbled in my stomach.

'Mass burials or cremations after disasters aren't to protect people from disease,' he said. 'Bodies are buried or burned for morale, for a sense of closure, to get them out of sight so people can get on with things. But mostly? It's to save survivors from the smell.'

The sour tang of decay was getting stronger as we got closer to the city. Jack produced menthol gel and rubbed streaks of shiny stuff under his nostrils. He handed the tube to me and I smeared it on my upper lip as we passed under a stone archway and onto a city footpath. Just here, on this one stretch of street on one edge of Parramatta's urban grid, there had to be one hundred dead people.

My brain ached when I tried to add up how long it had been since Christmas, instinctively wanting to measure the time in years or decades, rebelling at the reality that it'd been just four days. Even if Nathan's hibernation theory was right, the dying had to accelerate soon.

'Relatively speaking, it's not too bad now,' Jack said, inhaling cautiously. 'But in a few weeks there's going to be millions of bodies, all of them rotting. The sight of it, the smell of it, will be impossible to live with. The smoke in the air's bad now. The clouds of flies will be worse.'

'How,' I said, 'do you know all of this?'

Jack looked at me. 'One of the guys back at Old Government House worked in disaster relief back after that big tsunami.'

Frustration swelled in me. I didn't know how he could equate the disasters, how he could miss the obvious. 'These people aren't dead,' I said. 'They don't have to die. We can revive them. We can—'

Jack shook his head. 'No, we can't, Danby,' he said. 'Not if we want to live.'

Fear radiated through me. Jack wasn't armed. We didn't have a shotgun-toting guard. I'd followed him blithely into territory ruled by the Cop, the Surfer, the Biker and other maniacs, something he was belatedly acknowledging. As if on cue, there was movement down the next block, big men heading from the city centre, heads bobbing our way through stalled traffic.

'We should go back,' I said.

'You don't have to worry about them,' Jack replied calmly. 'What you have to worry about is—'

I looked at him. 'What?'

Jack sucked on his cigarette. 'Hard facts.'

'How,' I said, cracking, 'can the freaking facts get any harder? What are you talking about?'

He let the smoke ooze from his mouth. 'I'm talking about accepting that just about everyone is going to die. About accepting we can't do anything about it.'

Before I could argue, Jack strode across the road, squeezed between cars, skirted around a woman in a wheelchair, ducked under a guy who'd hanged himself from a tree branch. When I caught up to him on the footpath, I saw that the guys approaching us were hefting cartons. Jack shepherded me up onto the steps of an office building so they could pass.

'Bottled water, tinned food, medical supplies,' Jack said. 'We don't know what we'll find out there—it's better to be prepared.'

We were close enough to reach out and touch any of the men but none of them looked our way or acknowledged our presence.

'Hey,' I said to the red-haired guy who was last in line. 'Hi.'

At first it was like he didn't hear or see me, like it had been with Boris in Beautopia Point. But he slowly turned my way.

'Good morning,' he said dully. 'I'm glad you're feeling better.'

'I am,' I said. 'Thank you. How are—'

But he zoned me out and walked on towards Old Government House. Had he and his comrades been ordered not to fraternise with civilians? Were they in shock?

'What's with them?' I whispered.

'Nothing,' Jack said. 'They're just . . . adjusting.'

He stepped back to the footpath. I stayed where I was.

'What's going on?' I demanded. 'What are we doing here?'

If we really didn't have to fear the Biker and the other killers, then we should be reviving people. Instead, we were just touring the necropolis. Looking around, I reckoned a quarter of the people around us were already dead. The liniment couldn't entirely mask the stench of death and the clouds of flies already seemed blacker. I just wanted to grab some Lorazepam, dose a few people and tell them what to do, then go get Evan, strap him onto a bike and get riding for Shadow Valley.

'I can't tell you,' Jack said. 'I have to show you. Just come with me to the next street?' Jack looked up at me, hand shielding his eyes from the sky's yellow glare.

When Jack and I reached the next intersection, I realised where we were. If we turned left, we'd be headed back to the river and bridge. If we went right, we'd pass the Party Duder's remains and the taxi where Nathan lay dead. I was relieved when Jack walked straight ahead into fresh territory—not that it held any fewer horrors than anywhere else. Corpses and Goners filled this street like every other, forlorn under awnings, in doorways, beside cars.

'Wait here,' Jack said, stepping over someone's daughter and into a convenience store. I watched with confusion and excitement as he grabbed a shopping bag and started filling it with sports drinks. So he was going to revive people.

Jack stepped out of the store and turned his attention on the Goners around us. I followed him breathlessly to a shaggy haired twenty-something guy stretched out by a sports store window. Jack crouched beside him. I guessed he was going to show me he could do for this man what he'd done for Evan. That was it: he'd found a different method to wake people up, one that also switched off the telepathy and made their minds safe from the Cop, the Biker and the rest of those bastards. Had to be!

But all Jack did was touch the man's cheek for a moment. Then he stood up and walked on.

'What's wrong?' I asked. 'Is he dead?'

Jack didn't answer, just shook his head. I knelt down and touched the man's neck, lowered my ear over his mouth. He had a pulse, he was breathing.

'Hey!' I yelled. 'He's alive!'

'I know,' Jack said from where he was bent over an athletic young woman with a yellowish tan. 'But he's got leukaemia.'

The man's face was pale but his body seemed strong and muscular. Nobody could diagnose such a disease just with a look and a touch. By the time I reached the jaundiced girl, Jack had already moved on. She was alive, too, chest rising and falling.

'Hey, what are you doing?'

Jack ignored me. He felt the hand of a burly teenager leaning against a deli window and reached down to touch an African-American guy folded up on the footpath. Then he stood by a bald guy stretched out under a bus-stop seat.

'What the hell are you doing?'

'Triage,' he replied.

'What?' I was doing my best not to cry.

'From the French verb *trier*, meaning to separate or sift,' Jack said. 'We have limited time and resources and we have to devote them to people who need to be saved.'

'Need? They all—'

'The guy with leukaemia won't last long without modern treatment,' Jack said. 'The girl back there took an overdose of paracetamol three days ago that's ruining her liver.' He pointed at the teen. 'Anyone in advanced dehydration will need IVs and recovery time that we don't have.' Jack gestured at the black man. 'He's already in the first stages of muscular atrophy, and he'd need physio just to walk.' He looked down at the bald dude at his feet. 'But this guy? He's been in the shade and open air, he's stretched out and he looks strong. What we need to know is if we need him.'

There it was again: *need*. Didn't we need everybody?

Jack touched the man's stubbled cheek.

'His name's Bruce and he's a nightclub bouncer,' he said, looking up at me. 'He knows jujitsu, he's a home handyman and mechanic. All of that's good because there's muscle memory involved.'

Anger flared in me at this cheap trick. 'Did you go through his wallet?'

Jack stood up, showing me his empty hands. He was suddenly very close to me.

'I only have to touch them.' His soft voice was like honey. 'Keep an open mind.'

A small voice inside me wanted to call bullshit but he radiated that calm reassurance stronger than ever. Jack held my eyes a moment longer and then he leaned down and whispered something into the bald man's ear.

Bruce the bouncer woke up.

TWENTY-ONE

Bruce didn't kick or thrash or cry out. He just opened his eyes and slid himself out from under the bus stop, body creaking as he got to his feet and stretched. A brown waterline ran the length of his body. He'd been lucky not to drown in the storm but looking at his dull eyes I wondered whether he'd been underwater long enough to suffer brain damage. He didn't seem to see me as he took the sports drink Jack offered.

'Holy shit! Is he—'

I turned from Bruce to Jack and back to Bruce. 'Are you okay?'

I needed to ask because I couldn't hear his thoughts.

Bruce cracked the drink and took sensible sips.

'I think so,' he said, blinking at me. 'Bit stiff. Hungry.'

I stood stunned.

'Go and have something to eat,' Jack said. Like he was sending an employee off for a lunch break.

Bruce nodded and lumbered away, navigating through cars, heading back the way we'd come.

I wanted to whoop so loud it'd wake the dead. Not that I needed to because Jack pretty much had that covered.

'That was . . . amazing!' I said. 'What . . . how . . . how did you do that?'

'You've had the show,' Jack said with a worried smile. 'I hope you can handle the tell.' He started off along Church Street with me dazed at his side. 'I was just outside Central Station when it started. I thought someone had dropped acid in my coffee. There are a lot of people who think buskers are fair game for any sort of bullshit.'

A *busker*? My hand shot to my stitches as I wondered if a botch job was festering there. I got an even sicker feeling when I remembered that Johnny Cash song. Had Jack been minstrelling just a few blocks from where Ray was murdered? Fiddling while Cassie and her friends burned?

Jack crouched by a redhead, pressed a hand to her flushed forehead and stood up.

'What's wrong with her?'

'Some sort of infection,' the busker-doctor said. 'She's pretty sick.'

'You don't know that,' I said, already wanting to disbelieve what I'd seen with Bruce. 'You don't. You're making it up.'

Jack shrugged, shook his head and walked on.

'But if you're telling—I mean, you can bring her back, right?' I said, following him. 'We can get her antibiotics.'

'She'd need round-the-clock care for days,' he said over his shoulder. 'And besides she's—'

'What?'

263

Jack stopped and leaned against a Honda to size me up. 'She's a fashion student and part-time model.'

It was like he'd punched me. 'What the hell difference does *that* make?'

Jack rummaged for his tobacco.

'When we're done,' he said, 'if you still want to wake her up, we'll come back. Okay?'

I looked at him hard. He didn't blink. I guess I must have.

Jack slid his cigarette into his mouth and kept on.

'So I was outside Central Station,' he said. 'A man's gotta eat so I was playing the people pleasers. Beatles, Stones, Floyd, Oasis, Springsteen, y'know?'

He let silence drop. Crossed the street. Checked Goners. Rejected them all. Reasons he didn't share. 'Plenty of people coming into town but I'd only made about ten bucks since before dawn,' he said. 'Christmas spirit, right? I was about to call it quits and head down to my beach squat.'

Squat. A few days ago he'd been a homeless busker and now he was living in a historic mansion, performing emergency surgery and raising the nearly dead? Jesus had said something about the meek inheriting the earth. But Jack wasn't meek. I hoped to God he wasn't about to tell me he was Jesus.

'I wasn't homeless, if that's what you're thinking,' Jack said, spooking me, and leaving a hipster where he lay outside a MobiFfone outlet. 'I have—had—secret places all over. Railway tunnels, empty terraces, vacant offices, even a cave with harbour views. Plenty of homes and didn't pay a cent for any of them. That's a lot more than a million mortgage slaves could say.'

I checked the chap in the cardigan and skinny jeans. Strong pulse. Breathing. If I'd had Lorazepam with me, I would've blasted him right there.

'Jack, wait,' I said. 'This guy—'

'Triage, Danby,' he said, wandering back to the MobiFfone storefront to look down at me and the man. 'He would be good. He's a nurse. We could use him. But he's allergic to a lotta stuff.'

'Allergic?' I sputtered, standing up, hands on hips. 'So what?'

'He'll blow up like a balloon as soon as he gets stung by a bee or eats something that contains traces of nuts.'

'But he can avoid those things, he can carry an EpiPen,' I spluttered. 'He's still a person.'

Jack looked around and let out a long sigh.

'They all are. But our job now is to help the people who can help other people the most.' He flicked his cigarette butt into the street. 'Just because we *can* save someone doesn't mean we *should*.'

I was incredulous. Searching for the punchline. Any indication he was kidding.

'I'm sorry,' he shrugged. 'But it's the way it has to be.'

It was like being stabbed in the heart. He'd closed up my head wound only to inflict this worse one.

'But Jack, you can't—'

He shook his head against negotiation.

'This is *the* essential new fact of life,' he said. 'Not my life, not your life—*human* life. *This*—triage, sifting, selection of the fittest and the most useful, whatever you want to call it—is how *we* survive. I don't mean "we" as in you and me. I mean "we" as in the *species*.'

I wanted to walk away. There was nowhere to go.

'No, it's . . . it's . . . *terrible*.'

'Not any more terrible,' Jack said, 'than what you and your friend were doing.'

My bewilderment became anger. 'What? We chose people who were strong because they'd be able to revive their . . . their—'

Family and friends was what I was going to say.

As the phrase formed in my head, I realised what Bruce *hadn't* done when he woke up. He hadn't expressed concern for a partner or child or parent. None of the people—carrying cartons or attending the vehicles at Old Government House—had loved ones with them. Just as no one was fat or weak or very old or very young. What they had in common was adult strength and cooperation beyond communication. I'd seen it before, stalking these streets, hunting Revivees down and then coming for Nathan and me. My stomach heaved and I doubled over and vomited up my breakfast.

Jack didn't say anything but I felt him standing by me.

When I'd spat my last, I straightened up, head spinning with what I suspected.

'You,' I said. 'What did you do? What have you done to them? What have you done to Evan?'

Jack held me with a steady gaze.

'I've given them—and him—the best chance for life,' he said. 'Let me explain, please.'

'No, no, no,' I said, sliding down a car panel to sit on the footpath.

Some elaborate con job. That's what this was. Bruce was in on it. That's why Jack was passing over so many people. He was looking for confederates. The guys with the cartons and in Parramatta Park had to be actors. But why would anyone do this now? No sane person would. I didn't care what angle Jack was working. I wasn't going to play some stupid game.

'No more of your bullshit,' I said. 'No more about who we need and . . . and . . .'

Jack crouched down by me.

'I know this is hard,' he said softly. 'All I ask is you hear me out.'

I sat there, head in my hands, elbows on my knees, for I don't know how long. Eventually I gave him the slightest nod. Stuck in this dying city, with him as my only companion, what choice did I have?

'For me it started with "The End"?' Jack said. 'By The Doors?'

I knew it. One of Mum's favourites. What did that have to do with anything?

'I swear to God,' he said, with a smile, 'that's the song I was playing when it started.'

What did he want me to do? It was a bit late to call *Amazing Coinkydinks*. I glared at Jack. His amusement faded.

'Anyway, everyone around me started coming apart, spilling themselves everywhere, punching the shit out of each other. Cars smashing. People jumping out windows. I was in it all, y'know?'

Of course I did.

'Total chaos. Assholes everywhere. Didn't take long before I realised I was different. They couldn't hear me and kinda couldn't see me. Then that plane came in and I ran for a tunnel I knew.'

Jack unfurled his tobacco. 'Want one?'

Why not? My head couldn't spin any more. Smoking might block the stench all around us. Worrying about dying from lung cancer seemed like wishful thinking. I took his cigarette like a soldier accepting a small mercy from an enemy captor.

'The tunnel's almost impossible to find unless you know it's there,' he said. 'I knew I'd be safe from people, at least physically. I watched it all from the dark. Buildings burn, boats sink. God, the roads.'

I coughed. The tobacco was evil and disgusting. It fit the moment.

'People up top were too much,' Jack went on, 'and I couldn't shut them out. I tried singing at the top of my lungs and playing my guitar like a maniac. But it didn't help. Then it was like—I don't know—like I was falling *through* the tunnel, disappearing somewhere beyond light and dark, if that makes any sense.'

'It does.' Puffing out smoke I felt connected to a fellow survivor despite myself. 'I had that too.'

'You did?'

I wondered whether this was Stockholm Syndrome. He wanted us to talk and bond.

'Only for a few seconds,' I said. 'Seemed to last forever.'

'Exactly,' he said. 'It was like the blink of an eye and eternity wrapped together. But when I resurfaced I could kinda control whose mind I was in. But it got worse and worse for everyone else. Then they were all screaming and then they were all gone.'

Nathan had called it the Big Crash. I was glad all over again that I'd slept though it.

'I didn't know what that silence meant,' Jack said. 'Whether I just couldn't hear them or if the whole telepathy thing had stopped.'

It was like he was telling my story.

'What really scared me was that I was the only one left. That thought freaked me so much that I just stayed in that tunnel. I'd still be down there if it wasn't for one person.'

Jack took a deep drag on his cigarette and waited for me to meet his gaze.

'You,' he said. 'You saved me.'

I had no words.

'Danby, you appeared to me in the darkness, and you know what you said?'

I trembled ash from my cigarette. Just when I thought things couldn't get weirder.

'You said, "Everything's going to be all right. I'm here for you. You're not alone."'

Jack smiled with something like embarrassment.

'It took me a moment to realise you were talking to someone named Cassie. That I was seeing you through her. But what mattered is I wasn't alone. *You* were out there. We had like minds. Just by being there, you'd saved me. I had to find you and save you.'

My stomach rolled. 'Save me from what?'

'From—' Jack hesitated, looked at me and then all around. 'From everything.'

I stubbed out my half-finished cigarette. If I wanted to kill myself, I'd find a quicker way than cancer. But if Jack had meant for his story to soften me then it had worked. He seemed vulnerable and I felt responsible. That didn't make sense. Nothing did. Sense had stopped. Maybe he was putting me under a spell. Maybe I was back in the hospital bed while Dr Jenny and her orderlies worried about my restraints snapping.

'Let's see who else we can help?' Jack said softly.

We walked, silent for a while. The footpath ahead was clumped with corpses engulfed in a buzzing fug of decay. Cricket bats, iron bars, club locks lay all around, sticky with blood and hair. It looked like these people had beaten each other and themselves to death. Jack edged around the tangle while I held my breath and climbed over a Hyundai to avoid the bugs and bodies.

'When I came out of the tunnel, I saw a sight just like this.' Jack scanned Goners and cars. 'Trying to drive would be a waste of time so I just started walking west to where I'd seen you.'

Jack halted at an intersection. I stood by him. Neither of us spoke. The street opened into a wide pedestrian mall. The Town Hall was strung with Christmas tinsel and crowned with a big Santa. Its community noticeboard said tickets to the New Year's Eve Ball were selling out fast. Across the way a granite church with cathedral pretensions rose from the centre of a little park. There must have been a thousand Goners. They sat on the mall's pavers, on street furniture and in the amphitheatre. They were sprawled across lawns like sunbathing office workers. They'd thronged the church to beseech a God unwilling or unable to deliver them from evil.

Jack walked into the crowd and started checking people. I pictured him like a shopper in The Grocery: perusing, test-touching and selecting or dismissing products. A nerdy guy in headphones was woken up against his tree. A tattooed woman set down her tablet, drained a sports drink and strode around the corner. Another three people, all young and strong, rose from the multitude and went in the direction of Old Government House.

I joined Jack as he bent to a slender girl stretched out in the shade. He brushed aside her tangle of auburn hair and whispered to her. The girl's eyelids fluttered open. He cupped her neck and helped her sit and drink. After a while she stood up and stared around.

'Hi, I'm Danby,' I said loudly, hoping to snap her out of her daze. 'Who are you?'

Her hazel eyes dialled from off to on.

'Lauren,' she said. 'I'm a nurse.'

Jack had been denied his nurse before. Now he had one. Like a kid ticking off another card in a collect 'em all set.

'Not your name or what you do,' I said. 'Who are you?'

Lauren blinked at me.

Jack looked annoyed, like I'd broken some unspoken etiquette.

'You go on,' he said to her. 'We'll be there later.'

271

She strolled through people in desperate need of her skills, bare feet finding clear patches amid the crumpled figures and broken glass, like a pretty party waif drifting home through a battlefield.

What disturbed me was that Jack hadn't told her or any of them where to go. At least, not out loud. He and I weren't mentally connected but he had something going on with the people he raised. When Lauren disappeared around a corner, I tried to keep an even tone.

'All right,' I said. 'Tell me.'

'When I started walking out of the city, I recognised some of the people on the streets,' Jack said. 'I'd seen a few of them, day in, day out, rushing here and there, glued to their phones and tablets, and here they were, dead or dying, still with their faces in their gadgets.'

We sat side by side on a low brick wall.

'I saw this stockbroker douchebag,' he continued. 'I remembered him from Resist in Martin Place. I was performing protest songs, you know, amping up the morale, or trying to, and this guy came across our lines with a few of his buddies. They all smelled of a boozy lunch. This douchebag, he said to me, "Want a revolutionary idea? Get a job!" And he dropped a McDonald's application form in my guitar case. This really cracked him and his mates up. While they were walking away I made up this little ditty about them and everyone started laughing. But it really pissed off the douchebag and he marched back. I was hoping he was gonna hit me because that might start a riot and it would have been *on*.'

Jack grinned at me. I'd been fourteen when Resist was at its peak and wanted desperately to join its ranks. In a rare exercise of parental control, Dad had forbidden me from going anywhere near the occupation. He agreed most protestors were peaceful but reckoned there were always radicals looking to start trouble. But I still daydreamed about running away, meeting a boy with ideas as big as my own and changing the world together. A few weeks later we saw what happened. I might have been among the dead if I'd been there when the bomb went off.

'But instead of hitting me,' Jack went on, 'this douchebag leaned right into my face and said, "One day we'll exterminate your kind in death camps." My kind?'

Jack laughed. 'Teenagers? Guitarists? Activists? Hatred poured off this guy. He was deadly serious.'

Jack shook his head like he still couldn't believe it.

'You don't forget someone like that,' he said. 'So I'm walking through Ashfield and there he is! In the gutter outside one of those fortress apartments. Expensive clothes all torn. Face scratched to hell. One hand wrapped around his phone and the other one up in the air. Like he's in some fancy restaurant closing a deal and summoning his waiter.'

Jack chuckled again.

'I couldn't resist,' he said. 'I high-fived the asshole. But everything changed when I touched him. Suddenly I know this guy inside out and back to front. His name is Mike—the Mikester, the Mikenator—and he pulls down five hundred thou a year. He doesn't think that's nearly enough. What really spun me out is that he was still down there inside himself. All I had to do was speak and he'd wake up.'

I saw why Jack had given me repeated demonstrations before he told me his story. Otherwise I wouldn't have believed a word.

'How?' I asked. 'How it that possible?'

'I've always been a real people person,' he said, blowing smoke at the sky.

My mouth dropped open.

'I'm kidding,' he said. 'I don't know why. The best way I can describe it is like they're behind a soundproof door that's locked from the inside. But somehow they can hear me and they open up and come out. Does that make any sense?'

It sounded similar to what I did with Evan back in Starboard when I envisaged myself trying to rescue him down in a hole. The big difference was that Jack could make the connection.

'What do you say?' I said. 'To make them wake up?

Jack glanced at me, as if deciding whether he should share his secret. 'Oh—I say ... well ...' He looked sheepish. 'I say, "Open your mind."'

I looked at him. 'Seriously?'

He nodded.

'So if I say it, will it work?'

Jack shrugged. 'You can try.'

I hopped off the wall, took a few steps and knelt by a scrawny guy in shiny sunglasses. Jack watched me with a pained expression. Was he worried I'd fail—or succeed?

'What do I do?' I said.

He dragged on his cigarette. 'Just touch him. Find him. Focus. Then say it, I guess.'

I closed my eyes, as though it'd sharpen my other senses, and rested my hand on the guy's forehead, like it might be more receptive closer to his brain. I tried to hear and feel the man's consciousness or soul or essence or whatever. All I heard was his scratchy breathing. All I felt was his clammy skin. 'Open your mind.'

I opened my eyes. His stayed shut.

'Getting anything?' Jack asked.

I looked over at him and shook my head. I performed my hocus-pocus again. Nothing.

'Can you help him?' I asked.

It felt terrible to leave this guy now.

I stepped back and Jack took over.

'You've got good taste,' he said, hand where mine had been. 'Hugh here's not in the best of health but he is a chopper pilot. That will come in handy.'

Jack leaned in and whispered.

Hugh stirred but didn't wake up like the others.

'He'll need an IV and antibiotics,' Jack said. 'But he'll be okay.'

A shadow fell across us and the helicopter pilot. When I looked up, the red-haired minion who'd said he was glad I felt better leaned in to scoop up the man whose career choice had saved his life. When they had gone, Jack grinned my way sympathetically.

'It's not as simple as just waking them up,' he said. 'You should be glad you can't do it.'

'Yeah.' I wasn't but I felt he was. He wanted to stay The Man. 'Sure.'

'I'm serious,' he protested. 'With great power comes great responsibility and all that.'

I snorted. Now he wanted to be Spider-Man?

'When I woke up that stockbroker guy, Mike, it was like I had hacked him,' Jack said. 'It was like I was me but I was also inside him.'

I took a swig of my sports drink. 'We all had that, seeing through other—'

Jack held up his hands. 'I wasn't just hearing or seeing what he heard. I *was* him.'

I shook my head.

Some part of me had known this was coming but I still didn't want to believe.

'I didn't believe it either,' Jack said. 'That Mike guy? Almost as a joke, I willed him to carry my guitar and amp and backpack. And he did. Then I realised I didn't just know and control him but that I could access everything he knows. It wasn't a sudden flash. It was like this stuff has always been in my mind. I don't even have a bank account but now I could talk for hours about credit default swaps, short selling, hedge funds, all of that financial shit that's so meaningless now.'

Jack sounded *pleased* with himself, with this new world. He'd wanted Resist to spark revolution. The Snap was something like that. Re-evolution maybe. With him as some kind of ringleader.

'Still I didn't believe it,' he said. 'Maybe I'd heard one of his asshole friends call him Mike. Maybe it was a coincidence that he'd come back to consciousness when I spoke to him. Maybe he was carrying my stuff because he was in shock. All that financial mumbo jumbo in my head? I could've been making it up, right? It wasn't like I was going to stop to check an economics textbook.'

Jack snapped his fingers. 'So I try it again and the next guy wakes up too. Pastry chef, speaks French, lived in New York for eight years. Suddenly, I can make a croquembouche, speak French with a Parisian accent and find my way on foot from the Bowery to Brooklyn. The next one's a truck driver. If I raise him, I'll know how to drive an eighteen-wheeler but I'll also know what it's like to be a serious meth-head. So I left him. But I kept walking, kept touching. It's amazing, Danby. Every person I raise, I learn more. I'm learning how much I didn't—'

'What've you done to Evan?' Zombie to minion wasn't any sort of improvement. 'What the f—'

'He's fine,' Jack said firmly. 'He's safe.'

'Was that him or you? Last night with me? Playing with that girl?'

'Both,' Jack said. 'Evan's still himself. He's still in there. I'm just holding him up for a while.'

'Holding him up? Can you let him go?'

Jack held up his hands. 'Let me finish what I was telling you?'

I blinked at him. Gulped painfully. Nodded.

'God didn't say to Noah, "Grab animals at random." He said, "Get two of each." Imagine if Noah's kids had rocked up with, like, fifty giraffes and said, "Dad, can we keep them?"'

I couldn't even force a smile.

Jack studied me, took a deep breath, held it for a moment like he was about to dive in.

'First I saw that selfish bitch Cassie. Then her party animal friends. Then there were five and ten and fifteen more minds out there. I could see what you and him were trying to do. But I also saw it couldn't work.'

'It was working,' I said.

'Not really. You saw what they were doing.'

'Not all of them,' I protested. 'Not even most.'

Jack looked at me like I should know better. 'Not just the ones who were getting high and looting and the rest of it. Reviving family, friends and neighbours? Sure it's heart-warming but are those the people who're gonna bring us back from extinction?'

'It was working,' I repeated. 'We just needed time.'

'We don't have time,' he said. 'Tax accountants, human resource managers, brand strategists, advertising executives, hotel concierges—they're no more necessary than fashion students who sideline as catalogue models.'

I narrowed my eyes at him.

'I'm sorry,' he said. 'But you know it's true. What we need are people who can build houses, grow crops, deliver babies.' Jack glanced at my head wound. 'Sew up injuries like that, repair engines, raise livestock, all of that. I've checked thousands of people to find firemen, mechanics, engineers, the paramedic whose knowledge helped me stitch you up. Carpenters, plumbers, metalworkers, chemists, a horticulturalist, strong guys to do the heavy lifting.'

Bile rose in me. There was no way for me to avoid the conclusion my guts had reached back at the MobiFfone shop. Jack was neglecting to mention a few people in his collection.

'Don't forget your Cop, Biker and Surfer and the other thugs,' I sneered. 'You—you—you *killed* people. Had them killed. However it works. You're a *murderer*.'

Jack met my stare. 'I had no choice.'

'You're full of shit.'

I wanted to hit him. Bust his nose all over his face. Break his smile into little pieces. Bury his eyes under bruises. If looks could kill he would have spontaneously combusted under my glare.

'You really think so?' he said. 'How long before your dozens became hundreds and then thousands and then tens of thousands? That was the plan, right? How long before all those entangled minds went crazy again?'

I shook my head so hard my vision swam. 'You don't know that's what'd happen.'

Jack's smile and nod said he knew I'd considered that very possibility.

'Even if it didn't,' he went on, 'do you think the people you revived and whoever they randomly woke up were going to organise themselves to produce food, clear roads and rebuild infrastructure? You know they weren't. They were going to take care of themselves and their immediate circle and they were going to compete for what was left. Best case scenario it's a few months before people are killing each other for tins of food. Killing us. Dragging everyone down. Better to stop it before it was too late. Better to really start over.'

What cut me deepest about Jack's crazy talk were the stabs of sanity.

'You didn't have to kill anyone,' I said. 'You could've—'

'Asked people to stop reviving their friends and family? I had to set an example strong enough to shock you all. We have to face the truth, Danby.' Jack sized me up. Bit his lip. Decided to say what he had to say. 'The people who died would've only ended up hurting themselves or other people.'

'You're crazy!' I balled my fists, nails digging into my palms. 'That's not true.'

'It's not? Well answer me this: how long was a fast-food cashier with a history of severe depression going to last? How long before her redneck brother was shooting people for looking at him the wrong way?'

Jackie: shot cowering under a desk. Tim: blown away defending his own home.

'How were drug addicts going to contribute to the greater good?'

Cassie, Sammy, James: burned alive for being selfish slackers.

'How long do you reckon it'd be before he drank a case of wine and made his family pay for thoughts they couldn't help thinking about him?'

Ray: gunned down trying to save Lyn and their kids.

'And me? And Nathan?' I asked. 'You shot us.'

Jack averted his eyes, reached for his tobacco.

'You were an accident,' he said. 'I thought he was a threat.'

'A *threat*? Nathan was my friend! We were together!'

Jack looked at me sharply.

'Not like that,' I said. 'We were working together.'

He nodded. 'I get that now. But see it how I saw it. The first time I saw you, through Cassie, you were afraid he was going to hurt people again. "Please—you promised no more blood." Those were your exact words. He had a nail gun, for Christ's sake.'

Our cruel defensive joke. Meant to scare Cassie into leaving us alone. 'Jesus, no,' I protested. 'He wasn't serious.'

Jack arched his eyebrows. 'The other time I saw him was through the girl he stalked so badly she went to the cops. She was frightened of him—and she was glad you'd taken her place. "Better her than me." Remember?'

'No,' I said weakly. 'She didn't know—I mean—he was sick but—'

There was nothing to add. We'd both been in Tregan and felt how scared she was of Nathan.

Jack sighed, ran his fingers through his hair. 'I wanted to give him the benefit of the doubt. I wanted to end it without violence. My guy promised you wouldn't be hurt if you came out.'

I wanted to scream. 'We were supposed to believe that? After what happened to the others?'

His eyes darkened. 'Your friend was the one who yelled and came up with a gun. I can control the minds but there's also muscle memory involved. The Cop was trained to shoot first, think later. I'm sorry it turned out the way it did.'

I sat in silence, trying to absorb everything.

'But I'm not sorry about what I'm doing here,' Jack said after a while, waving a hand at the street. 'It's no different to the disaster plans governments had in place.'

He met my cold stare without blinking.

'You think if an asteroid had been about to hit earth that the official survival bunkers would've been open to you? To Evan? To your family? No, they would've been filled with politicians, billionaires, scientists, academics, celebrities. What would they have done if you tried to get in? They. Would. Have. Shot. You. At least this way we get to rebuild from the bottom up.'

I swallowed painfully when I remembered what the Cop— what *Jack*—had said about Legion. 'Do you think you're . . . God?'

Jack shook his head. 'It's more like being . . . Google.'

There was no expression to match my emotions.

'Then what about that religious stuff?' I asked after a while. '"No one comes to life" and all that?'

Jack shrugged. 'More than half the people you woke up had some Christian background. I thought if I put the fear of God into the mix, they might take more notice.'

Nathan and I had feared a zealot. Jack's practicality was somehow scarier.

My mind skipped out to the other Revivees, still flinching at shadows.

'Are you going to kill all of the people we revived?' I asked.

'Of course not,' Jack said. 'They just have to keep to themselves.'

'What about me?'

'No!' Jack looked wounded. 'I want you to come with me.'

'I have to get to my mum in—'

'I know,' he said. 'In the Blue Mountains.'

Ice water ran in my veins. He knew because Evan knew. I was glad my little brother's knowledge of Mum's hideaway wasn't any more specific than that.

'How far up is she?' he asked.

'Not far. Why?'

Jack grinned. 'Well, I'm heading to Clearview. I can get you there at least.'

Clearview! A cute village in the lower mountains. It'd put me within twenty kilometres of Shadow Valley. I tried not to let my excitement show. Or my suspicion that he was delusional about going anywhere given the state of the roads.

'But you need to make up your mind,' he said. 'Because I'm leaving in a few hours.'

•●•

I trailed Jack through the streets as he raised people here and there. Given what he'd told me and how much human suffering stretched in every direction, it was stupid that seeing the labrador stiff and dead on a car bonnet was sadder and more shocking than anything.

'Oh,' I said. 'Girl, I'm so sorry.'

Jack grimaced as he returned to me. 'We had to put it down.'

'Put it down?' The dog's fur was matted with blood where she'd been shot. She had died snarling. 'Why?'

'It attacked one of the guys.'

'I saw her a few days ago,' I said. 'I meant to go back and feed—'

I wiped my eyes.

Jack put his hand on my shoulder. 'It's not your fault. C'mon, Danby.'

As he led me away, I knew he was wrong. Starvation must've driven the dog to leave her master. And that must have driven her mad. All I'd needed to do was remember to get her a can of food.

Gloom seized me. I didn't come back to my surroundings properly until I came upon another familiar corpse. Having to step around the putrefying Party Duder meant we were walking along Church Street. My throat tightened. My feet felt mired in mud again. The taxi where Nathan and I had made our only stand was just ahead on the other side of the street. Even from here I could see his red cap slumped over the steering wheel. No pretending this time.

I couldn't fathom why Jack wanted to show me my friend's dead body.

Was he offering some sort of closure? Was he showing off his handiwork?

'What are you doing?' I asked.

Jack turned to me. 'What do you mean?'

He didn't know. Hadn't realised where we were. Maybe it was no surprise he wasn't thinking about Nathan. He literally had a lot of other people on his mind.

My eyes drifted past Jack and my guts turned to cold slush. Nathan wasn't in the taxi. The corpse wore my friend's cap but that's where the similarities ended. Under the veil of flies the guy's skin was darker and he had a big belly.

'Danby?'

I forced myself to look back at Jack casually.

'I mean I need to know . . .' I said, stepping closer, keeping his focus on me. 'Evan. You said before you were holding him up for a while. Can you let him go? Any of them?'

Jack sighed. 'I tried with that stockbroker douchebag,' he said. 'He dropped back into catatonia and then I couldn't wake him up again.'

'Great!' I said, pushing past Jack, striding up the street, leading him away. 'Jesus!'

'Wait,' he said, following me for a change. 'Danby!'

When we were well clear of the taxi I stopped and let him catch up. I needed a moment to catch up to this new reality. Nathan, alive!

'There has to be a way to return them to normal,' Jack said. 'But I'm going to have to work out how to do it slowly. I'll do everything I can to help Evan. I promise.'

I'd turned on the theatrics to get him away from the taxi but I didn't have to force tears now. Evan: he relied on Jack like a life-support machine. Nathan: of course he was darker and swollen because I'd been cruelly tricked by decomposition.

My head and shoulders slumped and I didn't pull away when Jack put his arm around me.

'It's going to be all right,' he said soothingly. 'Trust me.'

Then I wasn't sobbing sad. I was sobbing happy. We stood in the intersection and I stared over his shoulder up at the windows of the Law Of Small Numbers office. For just an instant—even through the blur of my tears and against the sky's sallow glare—light and shadow played at the edges of those venetian blinds. Nathan was up there watching. I was sure of it. He had managed to drag himself to our hideout. I hoped he was able to fix himself up with the medical supplies we left behind in our mad scramble to escape.

'Nathan's all right! We have to help him!'—that's what I almost said.

Something stopped me. I wasn't sure if Jack was telling me the truth about how Nathan had been shot. But I wasn't going to risk my friend's life to find out. He had to stay hidden and stay away from us. God knows what Nathan thought of me hugging this guy. I needed to give him some sign. I let one hand creep up Jack's back and made the thumbs-down signal. It's all I could think of. I wasn't sure Nathan would understand what it meant. I wasn't sure I knew myself.

'Can we go back?' I said, pushing free. 'I need to see Evan.'

'He's fine,' Jack said. 'I promise.'

'I believe you,' I said, 'but I just want to see him.'

Jack nodded.

·•·

'You think we brought this on ourselves, don't you?' I asked as we made our way back to Old Government House.

Jack looked up at me from where he was laying hands on

a lanky guy spread among ferns in a big concrete planter. 'Did splitting the atom create nuclear weapons?'

He let the question hang.

'No.'

'The Sync—that's what I call it—didn't create all this destruction,' Jack said. 'What was in our minds did that. Cosmic consciousness? It should have been *the* great evolutionary leap. It should've ended all violence and war, ensured social justice, given us the means to save our environment, everything we supposedly wanted.'

I watched in silence as Jack whispered and the lanky guy blinked awake. He stretched and drank and walked away. Jack resurrecting these people was beautiful—spiritual even. I wondered whether I was in the presence of someone who'd be remembered—*worshipped*—thousands of years from now.

'We were given the ability to walk in other people's shoes,' Jack said. 'The opportunity for true empathy. But what did we do with this incredible power? We worried about hiding our secrets. Searching out the sins of others. Who thought I was fat? Who trash talked me? Who thought I was pretty or ugly or smart or stupid or sexy or successful? Who was sleeping with who? Who was ripping-off who? Not that that stuff doesn't play a part in who we are. But it's all most people saw, all most people cared about, even at the end. We were blind to the miracle.'

Jack walked on. 'It was like the internet raised to infinity.'

I caught up to him. 'What?'

He glanced at me, rubbed the stubble at his jaw.

'The internet placed the world's knowledge at our fingertips, right? What did most people use it for? Porn and online dating, playing shoot-'em-up games, spending real money to buy virtual farms, pop-culture trivia, pirating movies and music, showing strangers what they ate for lunch and pouring hatred on people they didn't even know.'

Jack nodded in anticipation of my objection.

'I know, I know—that's not *all* we used it for but my point is the internet didn't create the desire to actually understand ourselves and the world more deeply. All we wanted was to skim the surface ever faster. We wanted to always be connected. We got our wish with the Sync—it was like some kind of "Mindbook"—and look what it did to us.'

'But Jack—'

The air flashed and the ground rippled as a boom shook the buildings around us. Glass facades shattered from office towers above our heads. It was like the world was ending all over again. Jack pulled me into a doorway just as a glass stalactite exploded into the footpath where we'd been standing.

When everything stopped jangling and rumbling, Jack stepped from our alcove. He looked back at me ashen faced.

'Are . . . are . . . you all right?'

I nodded, stepped onto the footpath and saw what had him rattled. There was a huge spray of splintered glass right where we'd been walking. Beyond it every Goner on the street glittered with shards and blood. Across Parramatta hundreds of people would be terribly injured. There was nothing I could do to help any of them. All I could hope was that Nathan had been out of harm's way.

'Thanks,' I said to Jack, meaning it.

He nodded, colour returning to his face.

'What the hell was that?' Jack gazed in awe at the oily mushroom cloud reaching into the atmosphere east of Parramatta.

'The refinery at Silverwater.' I was glad to tell him something he didn't already know from his megamind. 'I passed it on my way here. It nearly blew then.'

'Jesus,' he said. 'I thought someone had launched a nuke.'

My heart trembled at the thought. Some crazy person somewhere probably *had* launched nukes. The people bleeding out around us might be blessed. They were dying fast and they didn't know it. We might survive all of this only to end up riddled with cancers from radioactive fallout blanketing the world.

'A refinery could burn for months,' Jack said. 'All the more reason to get away.'

'How?' I blurted. 'How can we go anywhere when the roads are all blocked?'

Despite everything, Jack's eyes twinkled.

'One road isn't.'

TWENTY-TWO

Railroad.

I had to admit, Jack's plan was smart. During my short driving career, I'd been in hundreds of minds all trying to find the solution to the same problem: how to get out of the city. Jack's answer hadn't occurred to anybody. I certainly hadn't reimagined the railway as a highway.

We stood in the doorway to Old Government House's family room, watching Evan and Michelle playing with plastic dinosaurs on the rug. I couldn't reconcile how he could be both of them—and everyone else—but I didn't want to make things more complicated by thinking about it too much right then.

'But I saw a train crash,' I said. 'At least, I saw the wreckage.'

Searching for Mum, several minds had shown me carnage on the western line we'd be following.

'Where?' Jack asked.

'Near Penrith.'

He nodded. 'We'll deal with it.'

Deal with it: just that simple.

'And then?' I asked. 'What happens when you get to Clearview?'

I was still saying 'you'—telling myself I hadn't decided anything yet.

'First ensure everyone has the basics—food, shelter, security,' he said. 'Next try to find more survivors. Then work out how to transition everyone back to their own minds.'

That all sounded so goddamned reasonable.

I wanted to run from Jack. I wanted to stay with him. He made me feel safe. He scared the shit out of me. As split as my feelings were, I didn't really have a choice. Without him, Evan was as good as dead, and there was no doubt Jack was our best chance for getting to Shadow Valley. Getting Jack out of Parramatta was also the best way to keep Nathan safe if Jack still secretly considered him a threat. As ruthless as Jack's means had been, he had a survival plan for society. He didn't need me for it to work but I thought I knew why he wanted me with him. Anything that anyone else said or did was only his echo and his shadow. But me? I was beyond his control. Not that it made me feel exotic or mysterious. Jack really might be settling for the last girl on earth. But that didn't matter. What mattered was that it gave me some power.

'I'll come with you,' I said. 'But on three conditions and you have to promise.'

Jack dipped his head for me to go on.

'You don't kill anyone else.'

He looked at me. 'What about self-defence?'

Jack had a point. If Nathan hadn't killed the Party Duder I would be dead. Evan too. I nodded. 'Promise under no other circumstances?'

'I promise. What else?'

'When we get to Clearview, you revive everyone, no matter who they are or what they do.'

Jack sighed. 'Even people who've got no chance of recovering? I bring them back just so they can be conscious they're going to die?'

Bloody hell. 'You bring back everyone who's got a chance of living,' I snapped. 'There has to be a role for everyone. Even if it's just washing dishes or planting seeds.'

Jack nodded. 'Done.'

I took a deep breath. I didn't know if he'd go for three.

'I go alone to find my mum.'

Jack's eyes narrowed as he went to object.

I put my finger to my lips.

'Whether she's like you and me or I have to revive her with Lorazepam—'

'But I can—'

'This is not negotiable. Mum's a firebrand. A free spirit. Very private. She'd rather be dead than have someone pull her strings or tell her what to do. I go alone. She decides whether she wants to come back to Clearview. If she doesn't, we leave her be. We—you and I—stay out of her head.'

Jack laughed.

'What?'

'Even at the end of the world, I can't get a girl who'll take me home to meet her mother.'

'This is serious,' I said. 'You have to promise.'

'What about you, Danby?' Jack frowned. 'Do you promise to come back no matter what?'

'I'd never abandon Evan,' I said. 'I promise.'

'Then I promise, too.'

Was this how diplomats felt when they struck peace deals with dictators? If Jack was true to his word, I'd stopped more needless violence and I'd cleared the way for more people to be saved. But our negotiations had been much more personal than that. An unidentifiable tremor ran through me at what he might expect down the track.

·•·

The four-wheel drives were rumbling and ready to go. Packed with passengers and supplies, the convoy pointed at the north-western edge of the park. Jack led Evan, Michelle and me to a silver Pathfinder in the middle of the line.

Nick had traded his shotgun for the steering wheel. I saw he had a horrible snake tattoo on the back of his neck. Another man mountain with a rifle sat in the cargo area among cartons and Jack's guitar and amp.

Through the tinted windows, I saw men down by the park gate, chainsawing trees, unrolling barbed wire and driving mini-bulldozers to form earthern ramparts. Even this far away, there was no mistaking the Biker, the Cop and the Surfer among them.

I gasped.

'Don't worry,' Jack said. 'They're staying here. They'll secure the park and the house in case we have to come back.'

He had no reason to suspect Nathan was still alive. But I worried his skeleton crew of thugs might stumble upon him if they plundered Parramatta for supplies.

'No killing,' I said.

He turned to me. 'I gave you my word.'

Half of me was glad the killers were being left behind to suffer flies and firestorms. The other half knew it wasn't fair because the real culprit was in the front seat. If the Biker and his cohort died here then they were as much victims as Ray and the rest. My head and heart ached with the contradiction—and at leaving Nathan behind in this hell.

The convoy started to roll. The lead vehicles bumped across the grassy field and we followed the path they wove between vehicles and bodies. A minute later we were through a gate and had bounced up a service road that took us onto the railway connecting Sydney with the Blue Mountains. Our chunky tyres crunched over the blue-metal gravel, big wheels straddling the tracks as though the axle width had been calculated for the task. We weren't setting any speed records but it felt like a miracle to see Parramatta's skyline, now dwarfed by the refinery's black mountain of smoke, recede in the rear window.

Tension began to drain from me as I sank into the leather seat in the cool gust of the air conditioner. But I shifted and felt stifled when it dawned on me that we had more than a dozen vehicles in our convoy and they couldn't have all been conveniently vacant. I tried to banish my guilt. It was as useless as wishing I could revive the Goners I saw in the weeds along the railway embankments.

I had to look at the positives. Nathan was back from the dead. He'd surely find other survivors. Evan and I were alive. We were heading in the right direction. The few cars that had encroached on the tracks were easily nudged aside by the powerful lead vehicles. The railway was a fire break, inside which we passed safely through swatches of burning suburbia.

We might make it to Clearview. From there I had a good shot at Shadow Valley.

My mind went to Tregan and Gary at their camp on the shore of a reservoir. They had a tent, sleeping bags and a small stash of groceries from an abandoned campervan and were hoping such minor looting wasn't punishable by death. Every sound in the trees behind them ignited panic. Other Revivees were also convinced they were being stalked by unseen killers. I wished I could tell them the danger had passed. I wished I could fully believe it had.

My imagination went to Nathan. I pictured him so alone in that dreary office. Unaware I had left the city. Unable to communicate his presence to the Revivees. I felt like the worst person for leaving him. I told myself again it was the right thing to do. Then I had a thought that almost made me cry out in agony. We had left the back door of the accountant's office open when we fled. The movement of the venetian blinds could've been caused by a breeze. The flyblown body in that taxi might really be my dead friend.

Jack popped open the glove compartment. 'You want some music?'

Anything to distract me from my mind's bleak places. 'I guess.'

'Carly Simon, Bette Midler, Barbra Streisand, Adele,' Jack said, rummaging through CDs. 'Bit of a classic hits selection.'

I could imagine the woman who'd driven this car. Someone's daughter, lover, sister, mother, she'd likely been alive in this very vehicle a few hours ago when she'd been dragged out and discarded, only for her driver's seat to be filled by someone's son, lover, brother, father, his mind now enslaved. Violent dispossession, systematic extermination, brutal oppression and forced labour: Jack had tried to prepare me for the foundations of his new world.

'Adele,' I said.

A few moments later 'Rolling in the Deep' filled the car.

My eyes filled with tears as dead suburbs rolled by.

I didn't know how Blacktown had gotten its name but it described what I saw of its commercial district. The streets were a mess of melted cars, twisted steel and broken masonry. But they were mere foothills around a volcanic mega-mall cascading fire and smoke.

We stopped inside the scarred bones of Blacktown's railway station. This concrete skeleton had withstood the firestorm but charcoal corpses were falling to pieces on its platforms and stairs. The heat was overpowering our air conditioning.

'Why are we stopping?' I said.

'We're stuck,' Jack said, turning off the music. 'Debris.'

'What are we going to do?' I tried to keep the panic out of my voice.

We'd bake inside the car if we stayed here too long. Evan and Michelle were already clammy against me.

I leaned forward to look at Jack. His eyes were closed in concentration. Nick opened his door, got out, and put on gloves. Up ahead, big men were already out of their vehicles, getting to work in the rippling haze. Through smoke and snowy ash, they banded together to heft blocks and girders clear of the tracks.

'Don't worry,' Jack said finally. 'We'll be on our way in a minute.'

We emerged from Blacktown's city centre into an unburned strip of suburbia. Rows of townhouses on our left. People didn't stir on their balconies and in their backyards as we passed. Sports fields on our right. Movement I thought was me seeing things. Maybe a visual echo of soccer players about to kick off. But the trio of people jumping and waving were real.

'Jack!' I grabbed his shoulder. 'Look!'

'I see them.'

The convoy slowed. A woman ran towards us. Yelling incoherently.

'Can you hear her?'

Jack meant her mind. I told him no.

'The others?'

I shook my head.

Nick leapt onto the railway tracks to aim a revolver at this scrawny woman in a dirty floral dress. The big bruiser stormed from the back hatch to point his rifle at the poor wretch. I whiplashed in my seat. Saw more gunmen scrambling from vehicles.

'Don't!' I said to Jack.

'Stop!' the guys with guns shouted in unison.

The woman skidded in the dust and reached for the sky. She was close enough that I could see her confusion. What looked like a rag-tag UN convoy had appeared on the railway line. She'd thought her prayers were answered. Now she was facing a firing squad.

'Don't shoot!'

Out on the soccer ground her two friends held stiff arms aloft in surrender.

The moment stretched. I hitched my breath against the barrage of gunfire.

'Chill,' Jack chided. 'I promised.'

Jack crunched down the embankment, a .45 tucked in the back of his jeans, flanked by his guards. He closed on the woman quickly, they spoke for a moment and she dropped her arms to hug him. She led him to her companions and they pumped his hand like he was a politician or preacher. Then they all seemed to study their feet. That's when I saw another person lying on the field amid backpacks and shopping bags.

Jack knelt by the figure. A second later, he helped a teenage boy to stand.

'Hallelujah, praise Jesus!'

I heard the woman clear across the field as she threw her arms around the kid.

The two men chattered at Jack. He held up his hands to calm them and talked for a while. The slender dark-skinned man nodded. But his squat offsider jabbed angrily at the suburban sprawl beyond the park. Jack spoke some more. Whatever he said seemed to mollify the guy.

Jack led the group back, minions spread out behind them. As they drew closer, I got a better look at the woman's bedraggled companions. The sleepwalking boy with a sports drink had inherited his mother's gaunt features and frizzy hair. I figured the taller man was Somalian because his fine features and colouring were like those of my old maths teacher. But the argumentative dude—sullenly kicking up dirt with his thongs, pale belly shining from the bottom of his blue singlet—was a cartoonist's idea of a hangdog Aussie.

Jack guided them to our car.

'Danby, this is Tina, her son Joel, and their friends Jamal and Baz.'

'I wanna thank you,' Tina said, eyes shimmering as she clasped my hands through the window. 'For saving my Joel.'

I looked from the woman to Jack. 'I didn't do anything.'

'Yes, you did,' he said. 'You saw them first.'

Jack smiled at me warmly. He was being generous with the credit. His eyes in the lead vehicle must have spotted them before I did. Maybe this was him acknowledging my influence. If I hadn't been with him, he might've driven on. Or worse.

'Your boy might take a while to come good,' Jack said to Tina. 'He's been through a massive trauma.'

'I feel okay,' the kid said—or Jack made him say. 'Tired.'

Tina hugged her son. 'I'm just glad to have him back.'

Jamal's mouth was tight. His eyes were heavy. I wondered who he'd lost and how much survivor guilt he bore. 'We couldn't find that injection stuff,' he said. 'The fires were too hot. Those men were killing people. But we prayed, and God, He has delivered you to us.'

Baz sniggered. He was like a creepy neighbour. When I looked at him his eyes darted to Evan and Michelle and to the supplies packed in the back of the Pathfinder.

'Youse have done all right, haven't ya?'

Tina reeled on him. 'I've had it with you! No one's making you come. Stay here if you're so desperate to find her. But you won't, because you aren't— You're all talk.'

Jamal nodded, arms folded.

Jack looked at me, eyes widening. I forced a smile, hoped stopping wasn't a mistake.

Baz's face went red and he balled his fists. 'Now listen here, just because I—'

'We've heard it,' Tina cut him off. 'We know.'

'Guys, chill out,' Jack said.

Baz spun around. For a moment he looked like he wanted to hit Jack. Then his weasel eyes flitted to the armed men all around.

'Yeah,' he said, stepping down. 'Whatever you say.'

Jack nodded. 'We've all been through a lot but we're in this together. Let's get you into a car, get you something to eat and drink and get our nurse to look you over.'

'You did the right thing,' I said when we were underway again. 'That was good.'

Jack chuckled. 'I guess we'll see.'

I settled in with Evan and Michelle.

'That guy, Baz? Didn't he want to come with us?'

Jack twisted around to look at me. 'When he saw what I did for the kid, he demanded we go and wake up his wife.'

'Oh.' So Baz wasn't any more of a bastard than anyone else. 'What did you tell him?'

'I told him we'd send someone to get her.'

'Will you?'

Jack faced forward with a sigh. 'He didn't really want me to. That's what he wanted me to say so he could leave with a clear conscience.'

My stomach clenched at what I may have in common with Baz.

As we bumped across ridges of gray gravel, pulled west by ribbons of shining steel, Jack strummed his guitar softly. I welcomed his warm instrumentals in the face of the great silence that spread out around the convoy. After we found Tina and friends, I expected we'd find more clusters of people who'd avoided the Big Crash. But no other survivors waved at us from windows and rooftops and backyards.

Jack set aside his guitar and busied himself scribbling in a leather-bound notebook. I hoped he wasn't composing a song about the way of the world that he'd want to try out on me. I couldn't hold in a giggle.

'What?' he asked looking over his shoulder grinning.

Think fast. Don't insult him.

'Oh, it's just, with Tina on the scene,' I said, pointing at the vehicle ahead of us. 'I guess I'm not the last girl anymore.'

Jack frowned. I made an exaggerated sad face. Blood rose in my cheeks. My silly spur-of-the-second joke had been meant to sound self-deprecating. It'd come off as an awful and needy overshare.

'No,' Jack said, face all earnest. 'That's not the reason that I want you—' He saw my stricken expression and he made himself laugh like he was in on it.

'Yeah,' he said, facing forward. 'Better lift your game. Tina, hmm.'

Jack's flush had tinged his ears pink. My joke had blindsided him. I felt bad he was embarrassed—and guiltily good that I had gotten under his skin.

'So our new friends?' I said to break the tension. 'I wonder how they're doing?'

'They're fine,' Jack said.

Of course—he really could tell me. He was in that car with them as surely as he was in this one with me. 'But that Baz guy? He's a real glass-half-empty asshole.'

I thought about Baz and my theory as the convoy rumbled onwards. Maybe it wasn't his fault. Maybe he had a mood disorder. Maybe he—and Tina and Jamal—had been on meds like me and Nathan.

'Jack, can I ask you a question?'

'Hang on.' He kept his head in his writing for a few moments and then closed his notebook. 'Okay, shoot.'

'Have you ever been . . . mentally ill?'

Jack smiled darkly. 'You think I'm crazy?'

'You saw Nathan through Tregan?'

He nodded.

'Well, you heard him say he was on medication. I was, too. Just before Christmas I had what they said was a psychotic episode and they put me on this stuff. So I thought maybe that's what Nathan and me and you and them have in common.'

The vehicle rattled around debris. Jack considered what I'd said. 'What were you on?'

'Lucidiphil.'

'And Nathan?'

I told him.

'It's a good theory,' he said. 'But Lithium carbonate's a salt. Lamictal's a sodium channel-blocking anti-convulsive also used to treat bipolar disorder. Lucidiphil's a fourth-generation anti-psychotic that blocks dopamine and serotonin receptors.'

Jack shrugged off my look of disbelief. 'I know that stuff because one of the guys is a pharmacist. The point is they're three very different drugs. If everyone on psychiatric medication was immune, half the world would be up and about.'

I nodded. It made sense.

'To answer your initial question,' he continued with a grin, 'I might be crazy but I've never been prescribed anything.' Jack made shower-scene-from-*Psycho* screeches. 'Do I have to worry about you? You said they "claimed" you had a psychotic episode.'

I looked out the window. 'It was a misdiagnosis,' I said, not caring if he believed me. 'So what's your theory on what sets us apart? What makes us special?'

'Special?' Jack smiled. 'That's what they used to call educated convicts who were set free to help build society.'

I laughed at that. 'More fascinating facts from the mind of the Old Government House caretaker?'

Jack nodded. 'What makes us special? I know a lot of stuff but I don't know that. Could be it's a quirk of DNA. Chosen by God. Destined by fate. Maybe we're just— Whoa.'

The convoy stopped.

'What is it?' I asked.

'Take a look,' Jack said, stepping out.

Penrith's skyline wasn't far off. But between here and there was where a diesel engine hauling cargo had collided head-on with a commuter train. Carriages lay scattered along the embankment. Chains of coal cars had bucked off the track and battered through houses. Craters smouldered in streets and backyards. Even with most debris spread on either side of the railway, we still faced a dead end of bent steel and ripped track and downed pylons.

'This is what you saw?' Jack asked.

I nodded. 'I had a glimpse of the train driver, right at the start, and I got echoes later on, but I had no idea it was this bad. You didn't see it?'

Jack closed his eyes. 'I guess it was out of my range. But now I'm here I remember. Really faint, from other minds, like flashes from a dream you're not sure you had.'

I looked around. The roads were barely visible for the smashed cars, chunks of train and collapsed walls and roofs. Even monster trucks wouldn't get us through that mess. I supposed we were close enough to hike to Clearview but then we'd have to leave most of the supplies. We were stuck. Just when the Blue Mountains were visible as a shadow rising from the hazy air.

'What do we do?' I said.

He looked at me. 'We'll deal with it.'

Jack was prepared. His army unpacked tools and oxy torches and began cutting and dismantling. Like a well-rehearsed emergency crew they carted twisted iron from the tracks and chained bigger pieces so the most powerful vehicles could haul them free. Watching them work around us made my head spin. I didn't know whether Jack had to micro-manage his minions or whether he could just set and forget.

Jack and I hauled a concertinaed metal sheet clear and let it slide down the embankment. When he wiped sweat from his brow, his gloves left muddy smears on his forehead. My stitches stung with heat and perspiration.

'Getting there,' Jack said with a grin.

Enough wreckage had been cleared to create a corridor that would soon be navigable. Jack handed me the water bottle.

I gulped it down but remained parched. 'I'll get us some more drinks from the car.'

Evan and Michelle were side by side on the back seat and happily entranced in *Snots 'N' Bots* on a tablet. Seeing them like that gave me pause. The kids didn't have any skills suited to this or any occasion. They were too small for grunt work. Evan hadn't turned out to be a savant. Michelle was unlikely to be some pint-sized genius. Evan had been raised for my benefit. But why did my little brother need a playmate—any more than they needed to play a video game? My best guess was that Jack was trying to ease my fears. He was showing me Evan doing something familiar and what it'd be like when my little brother and Michelle were back to themselves. I didn't know whether it was sweet—or sick.

I grabbed bottles of water and headed back to our work site. But Jack was standing on a far embankment and staring into the distance. As I headed his way, passing minions lugging axles, I walked by Baz and Jamal conspiring in the shadow of a signal box. They went quiet when they saw me. I had the feeling that if I could tune into their minds I wouldn't like what I heard.

I handed Jack his bottle. 'How's it going?'

'We need to check that place out.'

I followed his gaze down the hill. Inside a razor-wire perimeter stood a clump of brick buildings amid gum trees. The parking lot was filled with camouflaged trucks and earthmovers: a fleet of vehicles especially made for driving over and clearing just about anything.

'Combat engineer regiment,' Jack read from a sign by the abandoned checkpoint and empty gatehouse. 'I'm going to leave some people here to get those vehicles. We also need to collect any guns and ammunition and explosives from inside.'

I rounded on him. 'Why? Isn't that a bit over the top for self-defence?'

Jack swigged his water and looked at me wearily. 'Has it occurred to you that we should take it so someone else doesn't?'

It hadn't. I didn't much like the idea of a Party Duder armed with a bazooka. 'Sorry.'

'We don't know who else is out there,' he said. 'Are you ready to go?'

I looked back with him along the railway. The last segment of curled track had been pulled free.

The way forward was clear.

TWENTY-THREE

The convoy slowed as it rumbled through Penrith station. Bodies were scattered across its platforms. I couldn't tell who was alive and who was dead. The town's office blocks and massive shopping plaza hadn't been touched by fire yet.

I was breathing hard.

'You okay?' Jack asked.

'I'm fine.'

I wasn't fine. What was particularly not fine was that there were thousands around us who could be helped. I should demand that Jack stop and do his voodoo. Tell him to let me out so I could find a pharmacy and start dosing people with Lorazepam. But all that mattered to me was getting to my mum. I wasn't going to say a word.

The convoy trundled out of Penrith and across an iron truss bridge that took the railway over the Nepean River. The foothills of the Blue Mountains finally took their correct shape and colour. We drove through Emu Plains, the last patch of flatland suburbia, and began the gradual rise up into the bush.

The few houses nestled here amid eucalypts had tall television antennae. This far out they'd needed them to get a clear signal.

I sent my mind out to check that Jack was being true to his word. What I *didn't* find turned my stomach inside out. Tregan and Gary were gone.

'What are you doing?' I said.

'Nothing,' Jack snapped. 'Really.'

Scanning for Robert was no use either. Cory and Anne were nowhere to be found. But then I hit faintly on Ravi and Wayne—and learned from their minds that everyone was safe. The Revivees weren't being menaced by the Biker and the Cop or anyone else. But they were breaking up like a broadcast getting fainter over distance. That made sense. We were at the outer edges of the telepathy and there was no one to act as relays between us and the Revivees.

Jack was rigid in his seat. I wanted to ask whether he could still control the Biker and others. Then I saw Nathan. He was in my mind, a shimmering figure, seen through the eyes of a woman named Joanna.

Help!-I'm-alive!-Thank-God-But-where's-Daniel?-My-family?

Joanna's last memory was falling forever in the hallway of her Westmead apartment block. Now she was blinking back into life and looking at Nathan hunched over her neighbour Tatiana.

Who's-this-Indian-dude?-What're-you-doing?-Don't-hurt-her-What's-this—

Joanna's fingers were curled around a plastic bottle filled

with orange liquid. Beside her legs was a clear plastic bag containing syringes and a printed flyer. Other people were also surrounded with drinks and bags.

So-thirsty.

The drink was warm and salty but it refreshed every cell in her body. She saw bottled water and first-aid kits in the hallway. A bundle of rifles leaned against an apartment door. The scene was fading from my mind. But before it disappeared entirely, Nathan was back with Joanna, leaning in to look at her.

'I'm not going to hurt you,' he said.

Joanna didn't fear him anymore. She'd been dead. He brought her back to life. Now he looked like the one in trouble. His breath was coppery. Pupils like pinpricks. He winced with every movement. She guessed this guy was only on his feet thanks to some powerful painkillers.

'I'm Nathan,' he said, forcing a smile, giving a thumbs up. 'The flyers in this bag will explain what you need to do. What they don't say is that there are people in the west who want to hurt us. They're even more dangerous because we can't—'

Then Joanna's mind vanished from mine and Nathan was gone again.

Nick slammed on the brakes and we shuddered to a stop. The convoy ahead halted in a cloud of dust.

'Oh my God,' I said. 'Oh my God.'

Jack's jaw was tight and cords stuck out on his neck. He massaged his temples.

I held my breath, held Evan and Michelle closer to me, afraid of what he would do. I didn't think Jack knew that Nathan's thumbs up was a message for me. But it didn't matter. Reviving people, arming them: Nathan might as well have declared war.

'I feel terrible about this,' said Jack.

He turned to me grimly. I shook my head. If he was going to turn the convoy around and go after Nathan he would have to kill me first.

'I'm glad your friend's alive,' he said. 'But it's my fault he's so badly injured and it's my fault that the first thing that woman hears on waking is she's got a target on her head. I wish I could tell them they're safe now. But I want to tell you I'm sorry.'

Jack ran his fingers through his hair. I relaxed my grip on the kids and took a long breath.

'You could send the guys you left behind to talk to him.'

I didn't really want him to do that. But I wanted to see how Jack responded to the suggestion.

He shook his head. 'They'd be the last people Nathan would trust.'

That was right but I wondered if it was the real reason. Maybe Jack no longer controlled the Biker, the Cop and the rest. Maybe they'd dropped back into catatonia like that stockbroker guy. Maybe Jack still had them in his grip but wasn't going to tell me so he could send them out to hunt Nathan.

'Why?' I asked, leaning forward so my head was by his shoulder. 'Why the change of heart?'

'"Why the change of heart?"' he repeated, adding a laugh and a shake of his head. 'You still don't get it?'

My toes curled in my boots as I wished I could take the question back. Whatever he was going to say, I didn't want to hear it.

'You,' he said.

I held my breath.

'This morning I wanted to convince you I was right. But you showed me I was going about things the wrong way.'

I exhaled slowly. I'd egotistically thought Jack was going in a different direction. I tilted my face to look into his eyes. They looked candlelit.

'You mean it?' I asked. 'You won't hurt Nathan and the others?'

Jack's warm smile faltered and he knitted his eyebrows. 'I'm sorry you still think you need to ask that.'

'I'm sorry,' I said.

'It's okay,' he replied. 'Everything's happening very quickly.'

Jack broke eye contact and turned his attention to the railway track curving up into the bush. 'All that matters,' he said, 'is that we get things right from here.'

I wondered whether Jack's about-face was as abrupt as it seemed. He wasn't the Party Duder. He was intelligent, idealistic. He couldn't have killed those people without feeling something, wondering if it was necessary.

'When we're established up in Clearview,' Jack was saying, 'we'll see if we can reach out, find some way we can clear everything up.'

Reach out? Clear everything up? Jack was pretty good with those understatements.

'What's done is done,' I said. 'Let's get going.'

My mum was waiting. I hoped.

Since Jack had first told me where we were going and how we were getting there, I'd equated driving up the Blue Mountains railway with bouncing up a rocky ridge at an absurd angle, like some stupid commercial where owning an off-road vehicle meant world domination. Instead, we were steadily ascending a gentle slope behind Sydney's westernmost houses. The people who lived in them looked like everyone else. A woman floated in a backyard pool. A grandfather sat on a terracotta roof. A kid lay inside a trampoline's safety net.

Getting into the Blue Mountains proper didn't mean leaving such sights behind. As we crossed the bridge that straddled the Great Western Highway we saw where cars had bashed into each other, crossed lanes and crashed head-on. The surrounding drab green bush held swatches of colour. Each was someone who'd abandoned a vehicle. Many people would have made it deeper into the trees where they'd now stay forever.

The terrain became more rugged though our route remained gentle and almost level as the railway hugged the mountainside. On the driver's side we were inches from ancient sandstone strata while on the passenger's side we were but feet from a cloud-draped gorge.

One by one a tunnel swallowed the convoy's vehicles. The engines roared louder against the rock walls and ceiling, and through the windshield the world closed to a halo of yellow headlights and red tail-lights. I didn't like rumbling through the centre of the mountain. A billion tonnes of timeless geology pressing down reminded me of being in that nowhere place after the Snap.

The end of the tunnel appeared as a bright archway. A second later we were out and the Pathfinder's roof was being pummelled. At first I thought we were caught in an avalanche and that the spray of pebbles would be replaced by sandstone boulders. Then I realised we'd emerged into a furious downpour from a low black sky. Water poured down the cliff faces in curtains, our wipers no use against the water sluicing across the windshield.

'No!' Jack yelled. We lurched towards the cliff edge. Our wheels spun across slippery tracks and sleepers. He thrust his hands against the roof. I clutched Evan and Michelle tight. Time elongated as Nick wrestled the steering wheel. A horrible protesting shriek came from our tyres digging furrows in the gravel. Then the *vrrrr* of the vehicle shooting sideways and the *cru-thunk* of its panels hitting the sandstone wall. The kids and I were hurled against our belts and bounced back into our seats as I yelled swear words. Evan and Michelle stared ahead like nothing had happened. The engine sputtered out.

'Oh, shit!' Jack said.

During the frenzy the Range Rover ahead of us had been spinning towards the cliff edge. While we'd crashed into safety, the other car was spearing backwards into empty air.

The other driver's mouth and eyes were wide in horror. Tina and Jamal and Baz and Joel tore at seatbelts and door handles, faces pressed to the tilting windows like people at the portholes of a sinking ship. Then the car's back end tipped and it flipped into a tree trunk before slipping into the grey and green fog of the rain-swept ravine. There was no blood, no fire, no sound above the rain, just an empty space ahead of us in the convoy.

'Shit,' Jack said. 'No.'

'They might have survived!' and 'We can't just leave them!' and 'We have to go down and check!'—they were the things I should have said. But I didn't. I knew they were dead. Or as good as. Even if they were only critically injured, just trying to get to them could injure or kill more of us. I knew all of that as hard fact in a split second. I also knew I was glad it had been them and not us. I didn't know if that was triage thinking but I thought that as much as I'd influenced Jack he had influenced me.

'It's okay,' I whispered, hugging the kids, though neither needed my comfort. 'It's okay.'

'He couldn't—I couldn't!' Jack said angrily. He slammed his fist into the dashboard. 'I couldn't get both of us under control.'

'It wasn't your fault,' I said, leaning forward to touch his shoulder. 'You did everything you could. And you saved us.'

Jack's tension eased and he let out a long sigh. He reached up to put his fingers over mine. A jolt surged through me. I wanted to break free but couldn't. Like someone who can't let go of a livewire.

'Thank you,' he said softly, smiling back over our joined hands, 'for being here with me.'

I nodded dumbly. Wondered if the flow of energy in his touch was how he charmed people back to life. I felt warm all over. And weirdly empowered by the realisation that for all Jack's power, I was the one with power over him.

Relief and disappointment swirled in me when he lifted his hand from mine so he could face forward and I could sit back in my seat.

Nick turned the key in the ignition and the Pathfinder roared back to life.

··•··

The people in the Range Rover had come so close to seeing Clearview. Within minutes of the convoy starting again, we were flanked on both sides by the safety of rocky ridges and then we pulled into the town's quaint railway station. The rain eased as we chugged past the long platform. It was wet and clean and clear of bodies. No one was crashed out in the colourful gardens or on the pedestrian bridge linking the station to the town. In the past four days, I hadn't seen any place untouched by the madness. But Clearview's station ignited a tiny spark down in the darkness that had filled me. Maybe the farther we got from the density of the cities, the more places and people we'd find who'd been spared. Maybe Mum and Shadow Valley were okay.

As much as I wanted to believe that, if it was true I should be able to tune into Mum by now. She was only twenty or so kilometres away. But I got nothing when I tried to send my mind to Shadow Valley. I had to face the fact that I'd probably have to revive her with Lorazepam. But Nathan appearing to me had shown that it could still be done. Mum should be fine so long as I got to her soon.

We passed by the station and onto a service road. A minion from the first car used boltcutters on the chained gates and pushed them open. Our vehicles rolled onto a street called Railway Parade. Neat weatherboard houses nestled behind hedges and rose gardens and pine trees. Dogs barked furiously. I hoped they were confined to backyards. If a labrador had gone rabid then I hated to think what fiercer mutts might do. We crested a hill and were met by a sign welcoming visitors.

Clearview—Gateway to the Mountains.
Pop. 545, Elev. 236 m
Winner of Tidy Town Award (Western Region)

Clearview was still tidy. Spookily so. Nothing looked out of place. Nothing had burned. The next street was the same.

We veered left into Main Street. Ahead and behind us, other vehicles peeled off. I guessed Jack was sending people out to scout. Not for the first time I wondered what the inside of his mind looked like. Fed by so many sights and sounds, I imagined it as a NASA control room.

Another big sign with a sepia photo described Clearview's origins as a mining town. The original shops still stood but the economy had long been aimed at well-heeled tourists. Wholesome Cafe offered gluten-free organic everything. Chardin's Way was bright with New Age books. Bric-A-Brac Shack bustled with retro whatsits. High Life had weatherproof essentials for trekkers and Off Road was a one-stop mountain-bike shop. The DrugRite was padlocked shut and that was good because its Lorazepam should be untouched. Yuletide had dusted these ye olde shops with plastic snow. They retained their festive good cheer, were closed and intact, as though the owners had yet to return from holidays. I tried to picture

Clearview's population safely in their houses, working their way through Christmas leftovers and enjoying their presents. As much as I wanted to, I couldn't believe that. Anyone here would have to be Revived or Raised.

'It didn't escape, did it?' I said.

'There's a row of houses burned out down there,' Jack said, flicking his head back the way part of the convoy had gone. 'Look closer, Danby.'

I did. He was right. Some of the cars parked at the kerb outside this row of shops were banged up. We passed an untouched real-estate agency and gift store but the vintage boutique and artisan bakery windows had been smashed—and then boarded up. Someone had been cleaning up Clearview.

We were probably being watched. At any moment that person—or persons—might decide they didn't want gun-toting invaders messing with their tidy town. I imagined bullets ripping through the Pathfinder and us. My stinging head reminded me I'd already survived such a scenario. I might not be lucky a second time.

Jack's men and women jumped from cars and trained their guns on shopfronts and houses and the park opposite the village. I clamped a clammy palm over my mouth, not to suppress a fearful gasp but to stifle a hysterical cackle. Jack hadn't told me he'd picked up any special forces soldiers. All this springing into action might be him recreating movie silliness rather than real military tactics.

'Shit went down here,' Jack said gravely.

That was too much—straight out of a B-grade flick.

I guffawed into my hand, eyes bulging and streaming.

'Are you okay?'

Jack's rubbery expression of concern didn't help. He looked like a handsome Shar-Pei.

I wiped the tears from my cheeks.

'Just a little delirious, I guess.'

'You sure?'

I nodded and forced myself to take this seriously.

Jack smiled uncertainly and turned his attention back to Clearview.

Shit had indeed gone down. Jack pointed out a pool of dried blood on the footpath outside the locksmith. The road sparkled with bits of broken glass but bigger pieces of debris had been swept into piles in the gutters. In the park, on tables and on the ground, dead tablets and phones glinted under the silver sky.

Our driver stopped the Pathfinder.

'Listen,' Jack said.

I heard it: *chugga-chugga-chugga*.

'There,' I said.

Artificial light shone from a mini-supermarket up on the corner, where a generator on the footpath coughed out blue smoke. A four-wheel drive had already disgorged minions who waited under the shop's awning.

Nick stepped into Clearview's rain-slick main street. We left the guard in the back to look after Evan and Michelle. Jack's people, all stern-faced, all locked and loaded, closed ranks around us.

Thinking of this as some film fantasy brought a smile to my

lips again. But it died when I realised that if this was a movie then Jack and I would be the *villains*—the megalomaniac and his wench, enclosed by expendable gun thugs.

Being surrounded by heavily armed people didn't make me feel safe. A sniper bullet could find us. I wasn't amused anymore.

'Go easy,' I said to Jack. 'Whoever's here is probably terrified.'

'There are bodies by the school,' he said. 'Six, under a tarp, next to an open grave. There's another freshly covered grave.'

I shivered like someone had just walked over mine.

Jack turned and held his hand out to me. I wasn't sure if I wanted to experience that strange connection again.

'I'd rather have a gun,' I said.

He smiled. 'I'll get you one.'

I accepted his hand. There was no supernatural buzz. All I felt were his fingers light around mine as he led me towards the supermarket, as casually and naturally as if he was taking me onto a dance floor. Trailing him again, I wondered if Jack saw me as a follower. Nathan and I had walked and worked side by side. I liked that better.

When we reached the shop, Jack's vanguard parted so we could approach the entrance. He guided me next to Nick and another hard-looking guy. Both had assault rifles pointed at the pavement, pockets bulging with ammo clips.

'Wait here,' Jack said, releasing my hand.

I should've curtsied, told him, 'Yes, Your Grace' or said or done some other snarky thing to let him know he wasn't the boss of me. But I was too scared to do anything but nod.

Jack stepped into the supermarket doorway. Framed against

the light he'd made himself an easy target. But he looked utterly unafraid. I thought again of movie scenes—army commanders striding confidently through bullets and bombs while lesser mortals cowered in the dirt.

'Hello?' Jack yelled. 'Anyone here?'

He waited a few seconds. No answer.

'I'm coming inside,' he said, taking the .45 from his jeans and setting it on the floor. 'I'm unarmed.'

As much as I didn't want Jack as my Fearless Leader, I didn't want him shot dead by some nervous wreck hiding in the fresh food section. I was frightened for him—but also for Evan and everyone else he had raised. I had no idea what would happen to them if he died.

'Jack,' I whispered. 'Send someone else in.'

He shook his head. 'I've got this.'

My pulse raced. I didn't know if he was being brave or stupid. I did know I wanted him to stay outside with me. 'Please,' I said. 'Be careful.'

Jack grinned and nodded and stepped inside.

I waited under the awning, standing with his guys next to the noticeboard advertising the craft market and book club that'd never happen. I didn't know if I should make small talk, ask them what was most rewarding about minioning. Then I remembered: anything I said to them, I said to Jack. They could give me the lowdown on what was happening inside.

'Jack,' I said to Nick, feeling kinda silly. 'How's it going in there?'

Nick smirked.

'No one home,' Jack said.

I turned to see him in the doorway, tucking his .45 back into his jeans and eating jelly beans from a plastic bag. 'Have some, they're good.'

I walked past Jack into the supermarket. It might be empty but it hadn't been that way for long. The linoleum floor was wet and streaked with muddy footprints. Someone had been busy in here. But they hadn't been looting. The shelves were stocked with cans and boxes and packets and tubs. The fridges and freezers were beautifully frosted and frozen. There looked to be enough food to sustain our small army and whoever else we revived or raised for weeks or months.

I grabbed a shiny red apple from the fresh food section and bit into it with something like ecstasy. Its sweetness soured when I gazed up at the little 'Employee Of the Month' gallery behind the cashier's counter. Teenage faces stared back at me from shiny gold frames. Guy R. —'Mr September'—hadn't let his braces stop him from grinning for the camera. Zoe L.—'Ms October'—wore an exquisitely bored expression under her peroxided mop of hair. Chris M.—'Mr November'—looked like he was smouldering for a fashion shoot. I smiled when I imagined local girls loitering whenever Chris had a shift. I pictured Guy and Zoe rolling their eyes and telling themselves they weren't jealous. Local kids, my age, working part time to buy Shades or cars or overseas holidays. I hoped Jack would be true to his word and wake everyone in Clearview. These guys might still be saved.

Now Jack ate an ice-cream as he hovered in the doorway

with a pudgy minion. When the man left, Jack looked back at me.

'Man, this is so great,' he said, wiping his mouth. 'Let's go find out who we need to thank?'

I followed him from the supermarket. Our guards fell in behind us as we crossed into the park. We skirted a playground and wandered into a picnic area, where Jack climbed onto a table. Anyone in the shops, or the houses facing the park, or the bushland surrounding Clearview, had a clear shot if they wanted it. One of Jack's people put his amp at his feet and handed him a microphone. There was no missing him now.

'Hello,' Jack said with a feedback shriek. 'We're not here to hurt anyone.'

His voice echoed across the town.

'We've come up from the city and we are here to help.'

I tried to imagine what I'd do if I was watching Jack from a hiding spot. I wasn't sure if I'd lay low or make myself known.

'We can revive people,' Jack said. 'We can wake up your family and friends.'

The reverberation of his words faded. The generator chugged on. The wind whipped through wet branches. Thunder rumbled farther down the mountains.

'See if you can find someone to help,' Jack said to his men and women, letting the microphone catch his commands, a bit of theatre for whoever was watching.

Jack's people spread out, headed up footpaths and between hedges, calling out from verandahs before going through front doors. It was like heavily armed Mormons had descended on Clearview.

Yapping came from a yard screened by hedges. It ended in a yelp and whimper. The town's other dogs burst into a renewed chorus of howls.

Across the street, a muscle-bound minion appeared from a gate. 'This lady needs help!' he boomed over the canine racket. The man's big hands gripped pink-slippered feet and he was trailed by another huge guy lugging the sagging bulk of a middle-aged woman in a dressing gown. Her face was shiny and green, like something out of a bad zombie movie.

'Jack,' I whispered. 'She's too far gone.'

I was surprised he couldn't smell her decay already through his minions.

'She'll be fine,' Jack said, making sure the microphone caught him, playing to whoever was out there. 'Bring her to me.'

As the guys carried the woman closer, I saw that her deathly pallor was a mud mask gone dry. Poor thing had had her hair up in rollers, been about her beauty regime, when the world had turned really ugly. Jack stepped down as his men lay the woman carefully on the picnic table. Around Clearview the dogs simmered down as though they were wondering what would happen next.

Jack handed the microphone to a minion and leaned in. A wind shift caught his words and his whisper crackled through the amplifier, 'Open your mind.'

Only now it sounded different. Harder. Less coaxing. More commanding. I wonder whether Jack hadn't told me everything. Whether I hadn't said abracadabra in the right way when I tried it.

Jack helped the mud-masked woman sit up. A minion brought her a drink and she sipped it as she blinked from me to him and to the people who'd taken over her town.

'What's your name?' Jack asked, holding the microphone close enough to catch her answer.

'V-V-Vera,' she said—or he said through her.

'How do you feel, Vera?'

'What happened?' she asked. 'Is everyone okay?'

'We're going to explain everything,' he said. 'But are you all right?'

'I'm still thirsty, my head hurts, but, yeah, I think so.'

Jack looked around Clearview. I don't know if he was waiting for applause. Maybe someone to throw coins into a guitar case. What I knew was that if I was watching from a house or a shop or a tree I'd probably think what I'd seen was up there with what Jesus did for Lazarus.

'Over here! Over here!'

The ragged voice came from a dreadlocked dude who'd popped up from behind the stone parapet on the roof of the real-estate agency. He waved his hands in the air to show he wasn't armed.

'I'm coming down! Don't shoot!'

If he'd had a gun he could've made a stand.

But now Clearview was ours.

TWENTY-FOUR

Marv was a thick-set ball of muscle in his fifties who all in a blur introduced himself, asked our names, shook our hands, burst into tears, crossed himself, got his emotions under control and implored us to follow him to the other side of the park and save his wife and daughter. He didn't ask how Jack had raised his neighbour, Vera, who was being helped from the park by two minions. I guessed he didn't much care.

Marv led us to his house, talking in a torrent, days' worth of conversation flooding from him. Seconds after it started, village gossip had gone into hyperdrive. Jane, his wife, had gone from placidly opening Christmas presents to fuming crazily about everyone she knew. Their daughter, twelve-year-old Lottie, was angry beyond words that her mum spied on her social media accounts. And both Jane and Lottie were totally freaked out that they couldn't hear Marv's mind when he could read theirs. With the clamour increasing, Marv had literally run out on them—told himself that jogging the bush circuit would clear his head.

It didn't work. A million voices screamed up from the Sydney plateau. Omega Point's lookout had a view of the city some seventy kilometres distant. Marv saw carnage on the Great Western Highway just a few kilometres below the lookout and his mind was in a lot of those cars as they crashed. It was terrifying and horrible. But he was a little bit blessed. Other people's heads were being shucked open and their souls were being sucked out. At least no one could see and hear what Marv was thinking. But still the cacophony got louder and the pressure piled up and then it was like the sandstone lookout crumbled beneath him. For a while, Marv was no one and nowhere.

Marv-please-we-need-you.

And just like that, he was back, Jane's terrified voice pleading for him to come home, wherever he was, that she was sorry for being so bitchy, that Lottie had locked herself in her room, that despite everything they both needed him.

Marv had jumped away from the metal handrail, realising he'd been leaning against it in limbo, just a weight shift away from toppling into the rocky bushland far below. He had no idea how long he'd been like that, only that it was enough time for a massive train accident down the hill near Penrith and for a plane to crash into the distant Sydney Harbour Bridge. Smoke rose up across the city and the world screamed louder and louder.

Marv shouted that he was coming. Jane and Lottie couldn't hear him but it didn't matter.

Everything would be okay when he got home. They had survived his cancer together and they'd survive this, too. If they could all just get calm, hunker down for a while, everything would be hunky dory.

Marv had sprinted. As he ran, voices and visions and vibes seemed to emanate from the rocks and trees and from the earth itself. Marv wondered whether this was the Dreaming, whether this was how his ancestors had perceived the country, whether he was hearing and seeing and feeling all the living and dead who'd ever walked this land. Marv had no sooner perceived this strange beauty than it was vacuumed up by Jane's screams as she and Lottie slipped away into darkness.

We stopped outside a bungalow surrounded by a tropical garden. 'When I got back here I saw they weren't dead,' Marv said, crossing himself. 'Just, like, asleep or whatever. I locked myself inside because everyone else was going crazy. I just tried to keep myself to myself. After a while, well, it was like they'd all dropped off.' He looked back at Clearview. 'When I finally got the guts to come out, it was like a ghost town. Well, not a ghost town, but you know what I mean?'

We nodded. I heard the hum of a generator from his backyard as we paused on the front steps.

'Jane and Lottie?' Marv said. 'I just couldn't wake them up. I tried everything—I slapped them, threw ice water in their faces, put ammonia under their noses. Nothing worked. So I rigged up a generator, that's my trade, sparky—electrician— and kept the air con on to keep 'em cool. I figured the less they sweated, the less they'd dehydrate, y'know?'

Marv glanced past us, back out at Clearview.

'A lot of people had run outside, were in the park, in the

streets,' he said. 'I took 'em back to their houses with my people mover.'

He gestured to the pick-up truck parked out the front of his property, its tray lined with a mattress and pillows and criss-crossed with bungee ropes. On the nature strip stood a big wheelbarrow lined with blankets. I pictured Marv collecting friends and neighbours, carrying them carefully to his vehicle, talking reassuringly to them as he delivered them back to their houses and families.

'I thought they'd have a better chance inside, y'know?' Marv continued. 'And, if they weren't gonna make it, well, at least, y'know they'd pass away in their own homes. I did my best but some had already, y'know—accidents, fights, shock, some did 'emselves in.' He crossed himself again. I thought it'd probably started as a comforting ritual and quickly become a nervous tic. 'I buried seven in the schoolyard.'

Marv sighed, brushed dreadlocks from his face.

'I tried to get the cars off the road,' he continued, 'for when the emergency-service vehicles came. I boarded up a few places where people had done damage. I've been taking stuff from the supermarket, pet food mostly, to put over fences and keep the dogs alive. But I've kept a list of everything I've taken, for the authorities. I wasn't stealing.'

'We know you weren't,' Jack said. 'What you've done here is amazing.'

Marv paused by his front door, key in the lock.

'Can you really help Jane and Lottie?' he asked.

'I can try,' Jack said. 'But can you help us?'

Marv nodded before he'd even heard what was required of him. I got the sense he was happiest when helping out.

'If we supply more generators, can you hook them up for us?'

'Sure, sure,' he said. 'Give me enough time, I could get this whole place rigged up for solar . . . You know, if we can get the panels and if the sun comes out again.'

Marv swung the door open and arctic air gusted from the entranceway. He'd clearly thought keeping his loved ones close to refrigerated would preserve them the longest. It made sense. People trapped in snow routinely seemed to defy the survival timelines. He led us along a hall to a room where a slender woman lay peacefully beside a waif of a girl on a king-sized bed. Mother and daughter looked like they'd just stretched out for an afternoon snooze. We eased into the room and I saw the gentle rise and fall of the sheet and the mist of their breath. 'I've been turning them,' Marv whispered. 'Y'know, to stop bed sores.'

Marv's throat made a clicking sound and he crossed himself. 'One of the dead people? Ah, well, ah, Mrs Whitaker, from a few doors down, she—she—she died because of me.'

He looked from me to Jack, wanting to confess, fearful whatever he was about to say might go against Jane and Lottie.

'I didn't know if maybe people who're in comas or whatever might be able to take a little water,' he said. 'I couldn't risk Jane or Lottie so I tried with old Mrs Whitaker. I got a tube down her throat. God forgive me when I put the water in . . . she . . . gurgled and stopped breathing. I think I—'

Marv hung his head. 'I drowned her.'

Jack clasped Marv's heaving shoulders.

'Look at me,' he said commandingly.

The stout man wiped his nose with the back of one hand and pinched water from his eyes with the other as he blinked up at Jack.

'We've all done things we thought we had to do, haven't we, Danby?'

Jack was asking for my absolution as much as he was offering his to Marv.

'That's right,' I said. 'It's not your fault.'

After a moment, Marv nodded.

'After Mrs Whitaker,' he said. 'I put my faith in God, helped where I could.'

Jack smiled. 'God helps those who help themselves. Let's take a look at your ladies.'

The rapt way Marv looked at Jack unsettled me. But I was more unsettled at the way I felt when I looked at Jack.

Jack knelt on the carpet beside the bed. He gently touched Jane's forehead and murmured in her ear. What I got of the words sounded the same but somehow different. I couldn't say how. Not that it mattered because all I heard next was Marv's cry of jubilation when Jane opened her eyes.

Marv, Jane and Lottie hugged each other and wept happy tears. Even though this family reunion wasn't what it seemed, I couldn't help blubbing along. Jack was misty-eyed, too, though it might've been because of the emotional surge he was forcing out of mother and daughter for Marv's benefit.

Marv glanced up at us as a man and a woman slipped into the bedroom with a duffel bag.

'Hi Danby,' Lauren said. It was the nurse from Parramatta, and the guy who'd been hanging with Jack in the mini-supermarket doorway.

I nodded. I wasn't sure how much I was supposed to play along with this pantomime.

'Marv,' Jack said, 'Lauren and Benny are going to make sure you're all okay. They're nurses and they're going to run IV lines, get the girls fully hydrated, that sort of thing. You guys rest. We'll wake up everyone else that we can, okay?'

It seemed to take all of Marv's energy just to nod as he sagged onto the bed beside Jane. I reckoned he hadn't slept in days.

TWENTY-FIVE

We stepped out Marv's front door, back into the humidity.

'I'm glad for him—them—whoever,' I said. 'But I gotta get a bike and go.'

Clearview was secure. Jack was raising people as promised. Now Mum was my mission.

'A motorbike?' he asked.

I shook my head. 'I don't ride. A mountain bike.'

Jack looked at me seriously. 'Someone can take you wherever you need to go on a motorbike. It'll be faster.'

He was right. It'd be the difference of a few hours. That wasn't the deal. Granted, I'd made my demand when I trusted him less. But I knew Mum would be much more likely to return with me if I didn't have to explain that my companion was a human puppet controlled by my new friend in Clearview. Besides, if the Great Western Highway and Shadow Valley Road were in really bad shape, cycling could prove quicker and safer. I didn't need to ride pillion behind a minion. I needed to get supplies and get going.

'It's not that far and I've got to do this for me and her,' I said. 'All I need is a bike and some Lorazepam and—'

Jack nodded. 'I'm having someone get everything you need right now. You'll be on the road in a little while.'

I realised I'd selfishly assumed he'd look after my little brother like he had when I was coming round from being shot. 'Will Evan be okay with you?'

'I'll take care of him like he's my own,' Jack said. 'I know you can take care of yourself but I'll still be worried until you're back here safe.'

'Thanks,' I said, meaning it.

'All right,' he said. 'Your stuff's being brought up to the house.'

The house: a grand but gloomy terrace on a corner block overlooking the park and the village. As we walked along the iron perimeter fence, I saw Evan and Michelle were already sitting on a garden seat in the front yard. Heads down in their tablet, neither of them looked up as we approached.

An armed minder opened a gate with a brass sign on it that read 'Griffin House'. Jack smiled at some private joke and led me up the garden path crowded with thick rose bushes. Dark marble steps rose to a shadowy portico. There were bars on the heavy leadlight windows. Our way was blocked by a big wooden door inlaid with a gnarly relief carving of a griffin. The place had the vibe of a medieval fortress. All it was missing was a moat. I didn't know why he was bothering with this house. There had to be any number of other places that were available since their owners had deserted or died.

Jack sized up the door. Looked locked up tight to me. I wondered whether he had psychic talents he hadn't revealed. Was he about to use his mind to tear it off its hinges? Then Jack did something even more unexpected. He reached into his jeans pocket and took out the one thing I didn't associate with a homeless busker: house keys.

Skeleton keys. Had to be. Made sense if he was busting into houses a lot. But I knew that wasn't what this was. Jack slotted a key into the lock and pushed the door inwards. The house was dark and cool.

'Jack?'

He didn't look around or answer. Just stepped inside.

I followed him along the hallway. The creaking floorboards and ticking clock emphasised the stillness. We passed a sitting room, a guest bedroom and a book-lined study, all decorated with antiques, a showcase so neat I was reminded of Old Government House.

Jack rounded a staircase and we went through a darkened dining room into a country kitchen whose leadlight windows made a colourful mosaic of the static sky. Fruit flies hovered over a bowl of brown bananas. An empty bottle of red wine stood with a purple-rimmed glass beside a bare sink.

'Upstairs,' was all Jack said.

We found him in the front bedroom. Eyes closed, in a leather chair, hands folded over a dog-eared doorstop of a Bible. A bull of a man, head bristling with silver stubble. His suit and tie and shiny shoes made me think he'd just returned from church when everything went wrong.

'Danby, meet the Major,' Jack said, staring blankly at the man. 'Dad, this is Danby.'

I took a sharp breath.

'Is he? Can you—' I could smell the answer. That shitty odour of recent death.

'Save him?' Jack shook his head. 'He's gone.'

'Oh, Jack,' I said, stepping closer. 'I'm so sorry.'

I hugged him. He rested his head on my shoulder gently. I felt sorry for him, felt safety in our closeness, felt reluctant to break the embrace I'd initiated. But as much as our discovery of his dad was terrible, I was terrified I'd find the same thing in Shadow Valley.

I eased myself free. I had to get to Mum.

'Did you know?' I asked. 'That he would be—was—'

'I prepared myself for this.' Jack smiled grimly at the wall decorated with framed medals and commendations inscribed to Major Miles Griffin. Photos showed a much younger man saluting a white-haired superior, standing on the deck of an aircraft carrier, gloating over the toppled statue of Saddam Hussein. No pictures of his son—or other children or his wife. 'He won a lot of battles. But he had a bad heart.'

Jack didn't seem upset, just resigned to reality.

'"You're never to set foot in this house again,"' Jack bellowed in imitation. 'That's what he said last time I saw him. He was wrong about that.'

'If he really meant it,' I said gently, 'he would've changed the locks.'

Jack smiled thinly and lowered his eyes. 'I guess you're right.'

There was heavy stomping up the stairs and two big guys walked into the room. Without a word, they lifted Jack's dad in his chair and carried him out still clutching his Holy Book.

'Where are they taking him?' I asked.

'To the church. He actually had a plot picked out,' Jack said. '"Be prepared" and all that.'

Jack opened the balcony doors against the smell.

'Let's talk out here.'

Everywhere I looked Jack's people were saving Clearview. Men and women went door to door. I assumed they were checking physical conditions, assessing what people needed and who Jack should visit first. They were also bringing out the dead, setting them on the nature strips outside houses. Another team was on collection detail, wrapping corpses in plastic sheets and bundling them into the back of a pick-up truck.

'This must be hard,' I said quietly. 'Seeing the place like this, knowing some of the people.'

'Not really,' Jack said. 'I wasn't here that much. It never seemed like home.'

Jack smiled at me brightly as a woman wheeled a bike along the front fence below us.

'The sort of thing you had in mind?' he asked.

'Awesome,' I said.

The mountain bike had chunky tyres, a big light affixed to its handlebars and bulging panniers hung from the luggage rack behind the seat. The woman wheeled it through the gate.

'You know I want to go with you,' Jack said.

I nodded.

'But even if you'd let me, there's too much to do here.'

The moment he said that, I wanted him to come.

'I'm worried you won't come back,' he said.

'Of course I'll come back. Evan's here. You're here.'

Jack shook his head. 'I don't mean like that. Come inside.'

We stepped back into the bedroom as the bike woman was leaving. She'd set the two bike panniers on the bed.

'All the medical stuff you need's in that one,' he said. 'Two syringes, five milligrams of Lorazepam each. Is that enough?'

If Mum needed it, that would be plenty. 'Should be fine.'

'There's a first-aid kit, pain relief, broad spectrum antibiotics, IV stuff, y'know, just in case she needs that level of help,' he said. 'I can give you a quick run-through.'

I touched his arm, anxious to get going. 'I can do it.' Jack looked at me disbelievingly. I nodded. 'I know how to run an IV, seriously.'

Jack smiled and opened a pannier and lifted out what looked like a glowstick on steroids.

'This is a flare,' he said.

'Haven't used one,' I said. 'Enlighten me.'

'You snap this cap off, hold it away from your body, twist here and aim at the sky. There're five in there. If you get into trouble, or if you need help, fire one every hour and we'll find you.'

Now I understood. Jack wasn't worried about me not wanting to return. He knew I wouldn't leave Evan behind. He was concerned I wouldn't *make* it back. It was a reasonable fear. I might fall off the bike and break my neck. I could be bitten by a spider or snake. I might run into people like the Party Duder.

'What about that gun?' I asked.

'There's a revolver in there,' he said, with a smile. 'Ammunition too. But do you know how to—'

'I've fired a gun,' I said. 'If I hadn't, I wouldn't be here.'

Jack chuckled. 'There's a helmet, protective clothing and I—'

I kissed him quickly on the cheek. Anything to shut him up. I had to get to Mum.

'All great,' I said. 'I have to go.'

Jack put his fingers where my lips had been and smiled. I wondered whether I'd made a mistake. Given him the wrong idea. I didn't even know what idea I had about him. Books and movies where heroine and hero were struck by instalove had always pissed me off. Especially when they managed it in life-and-death circumstances. But I couldn't deny Jack had gotten to me—even if I was as much freaked out as fascinated. There'd be time to sort out my real feelings later. Much later. The last thing I needed was for him to think this was a romantic scene.

Jack reached into his back pocket and held up a small envelope.

'What's that?'

He tucked it into a pannier. 'Promise me something?'

I nodded.

'Don't open that until you get to your mum's.'

A letter.

Jack steepled his fingers together under his chin.

It took me a second to realise he'd asked me a question. My mind was still on the relationship we weren't going to have.

'I asked how long will you be?'

'Oh.' Mum might need nursing. Even if she didn't, we'd need time to talk. 'A few days?'

'New Year's Day,' he said. 'If you're not back then, I'll come find you.'

I wasn't sure if it was a question or a statement.

'Okay,' I said.

Jack stepped closer. I worried he wanted to kiss me. But he just took my hand and held me with his eyes.

'Until next year then,' he said. 'Be safe.'

Jack squeezed my fingers and turned and left the room.

Until next year then? Be safe?

I stepped out onto the balcony and watched him stride out of the yard and into the park. He didn't look back.

TWENTY-SIX

I changed into the bike clothes the woman left on the bed. Checking myself in the dresser mirror, I looked like a human tadpole: body in padded black lycra and an oversized helmet head. Might look dumb but I'd be happy for the protection if I came off the bike. I didn't fancy wandering the bush with gravel rash or a fractured skull.

I was down the stairs before I realised I had my phone in hand. Pure instinct. I'd spent my life leaving the house with it or one of its predecessors. I laughed when I wondered how long it'd be before I stopped carrying it everywhere. But this model had been with me when I thought I was going to die. Maybe it was a lucky charm. I tucked it into one of the panniers slung over my shoulder.

'Evan?'

He looked up as I wheeled the bike to the garden seat. Michelle stayed ensconced in the tablet.

'I'll be back soon,' I said, planting a kiss on his little cheek. 'I love you.'

Evan hugged me tight.

'Back fast,' he said. 'Love.'

I pulled away.

What the hell had just happened? Had the real Evan broken through? Had Jack made Evan say what I wanted to hear? Or had Jack used Evan to tell me how he felt? Tell me he loved me?

My stomach flipped when I thought about what was in that letter. I wasn't in a hurry to find out what it said. I was glad I'd promised not to open it until I got to Mum's.

Evan's eyes dropped back to the tablet.

Stunned and shaking, I steered the bike through the gate and onto the street. I hauled my leg over the frame and stood with my fingers light on the handlebars, the tips of my shoes in the dirt, my padded bum hovering over the padded seat. Seconds stretched. It was like I was waiting for a starter's gun. Instead I heard the rumble of the mini-digger gouging the oval, the rev of four-wheel drives running along Clearbrook's back streets and the insect drone of motorbikes racing away on minion errands. Jack and his people were in motion. I didn't want to move. My body ached and my mind was exhausted. What passed for daylight was fast draining from the sky. The smart thing would be to rest and rejuvenate and go tomorrow. Riding tired I might fall asleep on the bike and die in some ravine. Not riding now could mean Mum deteriorated beyond help overnight. My choices only ever seemed to be between bad or worse.

I pushed down hard on the pedal, started along the one road that led out of Clearview. Once I was climbing the last rise to the Great Western Highway, I felt much better. The cool wind on my face woke me up and warm blood pumping around my body helped soothe my various aches. I stopped at the top of the hill to get a glimpse of what lay ahead.

The highway had been strangled. Cars and trucks were pointed in all directions across the road and breakdown lanes. There were bodies in cars, between cars, in trees, between trees.

Getting through the maze of vehicles would be tough. But not as tough as ignoring the souls trapped inside the cars and strewn around them. To make it to the Shadow Valley exit I would have to pass by thousands of people. I'd probably have to carry my bike over bodies. Some dead, some alive. Most of the time I wouldn't know who was who. What I would know all the time was that in my possession I had enough Lorazepam to revive one or two people and the means to rehydrate them. I'd be denying all of them that chance at life so I could deliver it to my mum.

I had to accept all of this as hard fact before I went down to the highway. I'd be on a road to mental ruin if I thought about what happened to those people, imagined the immensity of their terror, felt sorry for them and berated myself as selfish. It would slow me down, paralyse me. The deal I struck with myself was to help them once I had helped Mum. Find a pharmacy. Stock up on Lorazepam. Inject as many people as possible on my way back to Clearview. Jack said he wasn't worried about Nathan reviving people, so it wasn't like he could really object. With that plan in mind—selfish now, selfless later—I let the bike roll down the hill.

When I reached the highway, I blinkered my consciousness, focused on the rhythm of pedalling, on breathing evenly, on steering between vehicles. Keeping my mind on small things helped block out the big picture. My goal was to find a way through this mess of metal. Nothing else mattered. Not even whatever was in that letter. Not that I could stop myself thinking about it.

I'd pedal ten or twenty car-lengths before I had to stop and walk through whatever narrow gap presented itself between vehicles. When there was no way forward, I wheeled the bike back and found a new route. Even when I got a clear run, I kept my cadence slow so I could safely guide the tyres away from the worst concentrations of broken glass and around the flotsam and jetsam from the fleet of vehicles. I kept my eyes on the road and on the next obstacle to avoid. That way I didn't get distracted and despair at the faces behind fogged-up windows and the people laid out on roofs and bonnets.

But more than once I had to stop for bodies. The first was just a pair of legs in striped stockings sticking out from under a VW. They reminded me of the witch killed by Dorothy's falling house and I backed away from them like they had some evil magic. It took me precious minutes to find a new way through the maze. After that, I just lifted the bike over the Goners and corpses.

There was no way through the black dead-end caused by a crashed petrol tanker that had incinerated a stretch of traffic in both directions. So I hoisted my bike over one shoulder and carried it up a muddy furrow the rain had carved into the roadway embankment. High and clear of the carnage, I picked my way through brush and around trees, happy to keep the highway in my peripheral vision. I didn't need a closer view of the burned stick figures amid the charred vehicles.

After struggling a while under the weight of the bike and panniers, I saw through sweat stung eyes that the highway below wasn't just clear but empty. The black horror behind me had bottled up traffic in both directions; stopping cars getting further up the Blue Mountains as surely as it had turned around vehicles fleeing to Sydney.

Just ahead the big yellow M of civilisation rose above the trees. As I hefted the bike down the embankment, I remembered the first time I'd seen those plastic golden arches on this road. I'd just turned eleven and it was the first time Mum was allowed to take me to Shadow Valley. That day also marked the first time Mum had been to the Beautopia Point house and met her replacement. Dad was all misty eyed and magnanimous. Stephanie flittered around offering tea and cakes. Mum was so dialled down it was like she was applying for a job. Everyone making so nice had been exquisitely awkward. I'd excused myself and waited in the passenger seat of Mum's Jeep.

'Wow, just wow,' I remembered Mum saying when she climbed behind the wheel.

Driving away from Beautopia Point she made a Pac-Man motion with one hand. 'Man, could you be more superficial?'

I was giddy with anticipation. Robyn finally ripping on Stephanie!

But she didn't go there.

'Reach, engagement, demographic, sales indicators!' Mum laughed. 'He's talking about junk mail stuck to a toilet wall that people read when they're taking a poo!'

I guffawed. Mum hadn't always made me laugh. When I was really little she was just warm and cuddly. Sometimes silly or sad. So sleepy once, she went to the hospital to wake up. Then Dad said she had to go away to get better. When I was nine, just after Stephanie arrived on the scene, he told me Mum was feeling good again—and she wanted to see me . . . if I wanted to see her . . . but that I didn't have to . . . if I didn't want to. Dad looked worried that I would. Of course I did.

Mum and I first got together in a park with Dad waiting in a cafe across the road. I was nervous at first but soon it was like being with my fun new school friend Jacinta. Mum didn't try too hard. She pushed me on the swing and roundabout and when she asked about my friends, my classes, my favourite music and movies and books, I could tell she was genuinely interested. Mum used a tripod and timer so she could get shots of us making funny faces with her old film camera. While we ate the picnic lunch she'd made, she told me she was painting again and wanted to move to the Blue Mountains and start a small business selling old stuff. Sounded like fun to me. As for what had happened to her, and between her and Dad, there never was that awkward moment when she cleared her throat, put on the serious face and voice, declared it was time to listen up. We were just all of a sudden talking about drugs and depression and divorce. She accepted blame for bad choices but also said some stuff had been beyond her control.

'Sometimes, Dan, shit happens,' she said.

I giggled not because she used a rude word but because I understood she was telling the truth. Grown-ups like Dad and Stephanie always pretended everything went to plan. But sometimes shit did happen.

'What you do with the shit that happens is what matters,' Mum said. It wouldn't win her Parent of the Year but it made sense to me.

When our hour was up, Mum told me I could call her Robyn if I liked and that she hoped we could be friends. It was only later, after I hugged her tight and said, 'See you next week, Mum,' that I realised not once in our hour had Robyn checked a phone. By the time I was ten we got whole afternoons together without Dad supervising from a distance. After another year, Robyn had gotten her place in Shadow Valley and hadn't relapsed, and it was agreed we could have the occasional weekend together.

We were looking forward to that first sleepover. Beautopia Point was in the rearview mirror. Shadow Valley was ahead. Before we got there, I wanted Robyn to let loose about Stephanie.

'Dad's so daggy,' I agreed. 'But what about her?'

Mum changed lanes abruptly to a clamour of honking horns. 'What?'

'Stephanie?' I rolled my eyes theatrically and sighed dramatically. 'God, she's such a—'

I let it hang there for Mum to finish.

'Bitch?'

'Right!'

347

'No, sorry, kiddo,' Mum said. 'I know you *so-so-so-so* want me to hate her but she ...'

I looked at her.

'She seemed nice,' she said. 'Poor thing was so nervous. Today must've been hard for her.'

Mum shrugged off my scowl. 'I'll try to find something wrong with her next time.'

I pouted. 'If it's not too much trouble.'

'But your dad,' Mum said, pulling onto the highway. 'He wanted to write great lit-ra-char. He said he wasn't going to write something people read on the toilet! Now look what he's doing!'

I looked at her. 'At least he's kinda making shit happen,' I said.

We dissolved into laughter.

Mum coaxed her antique car stereo into playing a grunge mix-tape. I couldn't really hear the angsty anthems above the sputtering of the Jeep's engine but I enjoyed Robyn's spirited singalongs. We were chugging happily up the highway when Mum punched the pause button and stopped raging about 'Killing in the Name' to stab a finger at McDonald's yellow arches gleaming above the tree line ahead.

'Know what I really love about that view?'

I'd spent enough time with Mum to know she abhorred the fast-food franchise for all the usual reasons (fatty, salty, sugary, lazy, stupid, corporate greed) and for an unusual and unreasonable one (coulrophobia) so I was ready for sarcastic anti-capitalist, anti-consumer and anti-clown commentary.

'What I love is that it's the last McDonald's for fifty kilometres,' she said, taking her riff in a different direction. 'There's not another one up here. Once we pass this we're in the real Blue Mountains, served without fries, supersized by nature.'

I laughed. '"Supersized by nature"? Really? Maybe you should work for Dad after all.'

· • ·

Now I passed that last McDonald's. Garish plastic Ronald stood sentinel by the door. Inside, a few people were slumped over dinky little tables and in the cushioned booths. The happy meals would outlast the customers by years. That's what I'd heard: the place's burgers didn't decompose.

I rode on. Greenglen's main drag looked like it'd been hit by a tornado. The pizza shop, liquor store, delicatessen, bank, post office, thrift store, carpet retailer, Chinese takeaway: they'd all been smashed by cars veering off the highway. The pharmacy had a four-wheel drive garaged in its shattered storefront. When I returned I'd have to pick my way through rubble in there to find Lorazepam.

But it wasn't the property damage that sent a shiver through me. Amid the stiff corpses and the Goners was a bushy-looking guy, machete clutched in one hand, throat torn open, three dead dogs around him—all of them in a pool of blood. When I stopped, ready to carry the bike around the bodies, I heard a squealing noise, like the echo of my brakes, back down the highway. Before I could work out how that was possible, the dusk erupted with angry snarls and barks. More rabid dogs. In the shadows. They might rip me to pieces before I got the gun from my pannier. I leaped over the Machete Guy and the dead dogs and jumped back on the bike. My legs pistoned and I bumped between car panels, bunny-hopped over a Goner, got the bike onto a clear stretch of road and rode for the horizon. My panting, my heart in my ears: they were too loud for me to hear how close the slavering jaws were behind me. Had the dogs been feral already, living in the surrounding bushland, or were they domestic pets driven insane by hunger and hatred for what humans had become? It didn't matter.

'Faster, don't fall,' I told myself.

If they ran me to ground I was dead.

It wasn't until I was well out of town that I risked a look back. Behind me, the highway was dark and empty and quiet.

I slowed and stopped. My blood was hot and hard in my head and my vision swam a little. I had a horrible thought: that I'd imagined the whole thing. I was nearly dead from exhaustion. I was at the end of my tether at the end of the world. It'd be surprising if my mind didn't snap, if it didn't start conjuring waking nightmares. Then I heard it, terrible and wonderful: barking, howling, yelping, silence. I wasn't crazy. At least not yet. There were dogs down there that wanted to savage me. As long as they were there and I was here.

Night came quickly. Blackness welled out of the ground. Pressed down from the clouds. The only illumination was my bike's headlight and I shone it on Jake's Stop 'n' Fill. This was the family-run petrol-station-cum-general-store that marked the turn-off to Shadow Valley. It hadn't been smashed or burned. The doors were closed and locked. I hoped that wherever Jake and family were, they were as peaceful and unperturbed as their property.

'Last chance to check your Facetics and Intermails on the World Wide Pond.'

Mum always made some variation on that joke when we stopped here to pick up her snail mail. She used an old lady voice, simultaneously making fun of her offline ways and my online addiction. But it was true. Once we started the descent into the valley, the bars on my phone dwindled. By the time we hit dirt road, with mountains rising all around us, there was no reception. Other people who lived down this way had satellite dishes for their phone, internet and TV. They all enjoyed the same connectivity as the rest of the world. Just not Mum.

As if to compensate, Mum's cottage provided old-fashioned information overload. Soon after she rented the place, she started her secondhand business. With money saved from selling paintings, she magpied her way through musty op shops, garage sales and flea markets, filling her Jeep and trailer many times over with movies and music, books and magazines, vintage clothes and decor, old toys and weirdo folk art. When Mum had her first stall on a sunny spring Sunday, hipster tourists flocked to her retro-rustic-chic inventory. She turned a healthy profit and the next day was back out trawling for fresh stock. After a few months, she started putting up flyers offering to buy people's unwanted stuff.

Mum acquired trashy treasures faster than she could sell them. By the first time I visited Shadow Valley, the place was already a junkatorium. In her hallway alone, string art creations and paintings of blue-faced ladies competed for wall space with blaxploitation film posters and framed cigarette advertisements. Books teetered in thigh-high towers along the skirting board. The picture rails were lined with armies of action figures. Tin robots clustered around deco lamps.

'Wow,' I said.

On that first visit I helped Mum weed her vegetable garden and collect eggs from her chook house. She told me the names of the trees in her yard and she taught me how to bake chocolate cookies in her warm country kitchen while fog and rain filled Shadow Valley. She enjoyed me poking through her stuff. We laughed at the big hair and bigger shoulder pads in yellowing *Cosmopolitan* magazines and she showed me how to work her old turntable and care for her musty record collection. After dinner, she dragged out her super 8 projector and we watched *Bride of Frankenstein* while she drank red wine and I sipped homemade lemonade. I loved all of it, not least because it was the opposite of my Beautopia Point house, where all the food came from gourmet packets and all the furniture and decorations looked like they'd been bought last week.

But that first weekend I realised how hard-wired I was to expect wi-fi everywhere. On the Friday I reflexively reached for my phone every ten minutes. It wasn't until Saturday afternoon that my inability to text or update had sunk in enough that I actually pressed the 'off' button. But as soon as we were climbing towards Jake's on Sunday afternoon I was excitedly awaiting the return of connectivity, much to Mum's amusement.

Thinking about all that gave me renewed hope about what I'd find at the end of Shadow Valley Road. If the telepathy worked like a radio wave—which recent experience with the Revivees indicated it did—then maybe Mum really could have been shielded from the worst of it. There might be thousands of places like hers all around the world, effectively cut off from civilisation and thus saved from its end. I pictured cave-dwelling hermits, pockets of Bedouins, remote Tibetan hamlets, baseloads of Antarctic scientists and space station orbiters all asking themselves what the hell had happened to everyone else.

The only way to find out was to keep moving. I needed to get to Mum's place as soon as I possibly could but I also needed to ride safely. What lay below me were a few kilometres of narrow sealed road and then many more kays of narrower dirt track, all of it flanked by rugged and completely dark mountain wilderness. I wouldn't be able to see much farther than a few metres. If I went too fast I might follow the headlight out into thin air and wind up at the bottom of a cliff. I wondered what'd happen if I came off the bike and broke my leg. Whether I'd crawl to Mum's rather than fire off a flare for Jack to follow. I forced myself to eat a muesli bar, washed it down with a big drink of water and then peed on the road.

'Here goes nothing,' I said to the night.

I let the bike roll, crunching gravel, fingers tugging lightly on the handlebar brakes. When I got to the bottom of the dip, I clicked through the gears and pedalled in long slow strokes up the next hill. I rode along a plateau for a while and followed the road as it wound down into Shadow Valley. I rode endlessly into the brilliant tunnel that the headlight carved from the night, everything beyond the tree trunks and canopy as black as deep space. Pedalling slowly, I hit a calming cadence inside that glowing cocoon.

My heart jumped when silver flashed at me from the edge of the darkness ahead. I squeezed the brakes and eased the bike to a stop. My headlight had flared back at me from the chrome and glass of a black Jeep Cherokee parked in the centre of the road.

'Hello?' I called.

No response.

I rode up and summoned the courage to cup my hands against the driver's tinted window.

I jumped back from the face smudged against the glass, hand clamped over my mouth. The window was blurred with condensation.

I should just keep going. But I felt terrible leaving whoever it was. I'd passed thousands of people in the past days but this was different. It was like how city people suddenly start waving at each other in cars on remote country roads.

I got off the bike and gingerly opened the door, bracing myself for a blast of decay.

There was none. The woman lolled against her seatbelt. Chubby features. Pink tongue protruding between grey lips. She was dead. But only just. Her shoulder wasn't cold when I pushed it so I could tuck her back in and close the door.

My guts twisted. This woman had tried to flee the voices. Hadn't made it. Hadn't been protected by her hibernating body.

I leaped back on the bike, mind racing, legs pumping, speeding up as the road levelled out. I didn't even register the two silver discs floating ahead of me until the entire kangaroo materialised in the headlight's halo. This time I slammed on the brakes and the bike skidded and went into a sideways slide. My scream snapped the big roo free of its nightlight trance and it bounded into the black bush just as the bike flipped and sent me flying.

I landed on my rounded shoulder and went into a roll. My lycra-wrapped body tumbled across the bitumen. I didn't feel any bones break and the helmet saved my head from splattering across the road. The bike banged and crashed into a tree trunk. For a second the headlight pulsed at me, as if saying it was really sorry about this, and then it dimmed, dwindled, disappeared.

The blackness was total. I lost all sense of direction. But I couldn't lay here and wait for daybreak. Those hours could be the difference between Mum living and dying. Except me riding or walking in utter darkness might be the death of me—and that wouldn't help her. I calmed myself and mentally inventoried the contents of the panniers on the side of the bike. Water bottle. Energy bars. Beanie. Basic first-aid kit. Gun. Lorazepam. Flares. *Phone*.

I groped cautiously like a blind insect towards where I thought the bike was. Finally, my hand found tyre rubber and I fumbled along the bike frame. I stood up, steadied the back wheel between my thighs and found the panniers still attached.

As if bonded by use, my fingers fell first upon the sleek rectangle of my phone. A week ago, I wouldn't have needed anything else to summon help. There had been reception on this part of Shadow Valley Road. I pressed the 'on' button and was rewarded by a glorious rectangle of light.

'Yes!'

My bright photo wallpaper showed me goofing with Mum. My battery bar was full thanks to Jack's recharge while I'd been out cold at Old Government House. I used the flashlight app to check the bike's headlight. A crack across its glass eye told me it was dead. The bike was also useless. The front fork had buckled enough to make riding impossible.

But if I rationed the phone battery, I could walk to Mum's. I unhooked the panniers, strapped them together and slung them over my shoulder as an impromptu backpack. Flashlight app revealing only a few metres of the world, I felt like a spelunker wandering through an immense cavern. I couldn't build up much speed but I figured safe and steady was the way to go. Even at my slow pace I'd be there before dawn. The road turned to dirt under my feet. Ten kilometres to go.

I scraped along the dirt and gravel track, muscles aching on the rises, fearful of slipping as I went downhill. I shone the light to be sure I had a straight path and then forced myself to walk in the darkness, sweeping a stick in front of me.

Eventually, I had to rest. The phone read 4.06 a.m. when I sat down. I turned it off to conserve the red sliver of battery remaining. I took a big drink of water and ate another muesli bar.

•••

Jack and I were curled up in one of the beds in his father's house. We weren't just comforting each other. We'd joined at a much deeper level. Our child was growing in me. The first of many that would repopulate our new world. No: that wasn't right. This wasn't our bed. Wasn't us. It was Mum's bed and she was alone. Trapped under the blankets. Her eyes were sunken in their sockets and her skin was baking paper stretched painfully over her skeleton. Her lungs rattled as she struggled to take air. Through her bedroom windows I could see Shadow Valley Road. She'd waited but I'd never arrived. Mum rasped and stopped breathing. Then, like some time-lapse film, she deflated and dessicated, hair turning to straw, lips and gums receding to reveal big horse teeth.

•••

'No!'

I jolted awake. The sky was filled with weak brown light. I'd dozed off. Unforgivable. I clicked the phone, saw it was 5.46 a.m. I jumped up. Started to jog. The panniers slapped around my shoulders.

I'd been running maybe ten minutes when the landscape started to look familiar. I saw the old hand-lettered 'Nuclear Free Zone' sign some hippie had put up by the roadside. The cluster of termite mounds that Mum called ant skyscrapers. Once I rounded the next hairpin corner, I'd be on that last steep slope to the bottom of Shadow Valley. As long as I didn't fall or collapse from exhaustion, I'd be at Mum's place in a few minutes.

Then I saw a dark bump amid sandstone chunks just off the dirt road ahead. I slowed to a walk. I tried to think it was a kangaroo that had been bounced off a bullbar. But dawn's dull light showed me there were colours in the greyish lump: dark hair, burgundy leather jacket, stained blue jeans.

I edged closer. A young guy. Face down a few feet from the cliff edge. I didn't know if he was dead or dying and it shouldn't have mattered. But it wasn't lost on me that had things gone worse with the roo last night *I* might be road kill this morning. I hated to think someone would walk past me without a second thought.

'Hello?' I shouted, as though I could scare him into waking up.

My voice echoed through the bush.

He didn't respond.

I came closer, hunkered down. His eyes were closed. His cheeks were pale. I couldn't tell if he was breathing but there was no post-mortem purple or decomposition. I'd become a bit of an expert.

'Hello?' I said, quieter this time.

When I reached to feel the pulse in his neck, my fingers brushed black-and-white goop on the shoulder of his jacket. Bird shit. Gross. I wiped it off on my bike pants and felt his throat. No heartbeat. What he did have was a cold knuckle of bone trying to push through skin under his stubbled jaw.

How the poor dude had snapped his spine made sense when I stood up and saw the shattered remains of a trail bike by the creek far below the cliff. Looked like he had been riding up from the valley and hadn't seen the bend until it was too late. He had lost control—and slid or maybe jumped—only to tumble into chunks of sandstone as the machine went over the edge.

Standing there, looking at his handsome profile, I had the feeling I knew him. Maybe he was one of Mum's neighbours, someone she said hello to at Jake's store or waved to as we rattled past his yard in her old Jeep. I felt guilty for the hope it gave me. If he'd been alive until very recently it could mean other people had been shielded.

I sprinted down the sloping road into Shadow Valley. The secluded properties I passed were still, but why wouldn't they be? It was dawn after all, right down to the rooster crowing and the cow mooing.

My mouth went dry as I saw the Wollemi pines that marked Mum's driveway. Adrenaline surged in me, anaesthetising my aches, cutting through my exhaustion. Her Jeep was parked in the usual spot between rows of Kentia palms. She hadn't tried to go anywhere. That was good, right? Just beyond that her cottage looked, as it always did, like a hippie postcard, rainbow colour scheme matched by the Tibetan prayer flags fluttering between trees. Curtains were drawn in the front windows.

'Mum?'

My voice echoed across the paddocks and off the hills.

'Mum!'

As I sped up the driveway there was a sharp *smack* from the house. The screen door swung open a few inches. Slammed shut again. There was a shadow in the hall.

'Mum! It's me, Danby!'

I leaped up the porch steps as the wind played with the screen door again.

The hallway's clutter now included an antique mannequin. I bustled past it.

'Mum?'

I'd pictured this moment so many times. Mum would meet me at the door, fold me into her arms and take me safely inside. It wasn't going to happen that way. I looked in the front bedroom, where I slept when I stayed. The bed was unmade, probably since I was last here in September, and dust motes swirled amid the knick-knacks. Mum's bedroom was just as much of a happy mess, and just as lifeless.

'Mum?' I kept calling.

She wasn't in the dining room or kitchen, either.

Through the kitchen window, past the chicken coop and vegetable gardens, stood Mum's studio, a red barn painted with yellow stars, next to her old outhouse. That made sense! She was in the studio! When she got right into her painting she'd work for days. I rushed down the back steps, sprinted across the yard and threw open the studio door.

'Mum!'

She was a few feet away, crashed out on her couch, wearing paint-spattered jeans and T-shirt. Her eyes were closed. Hands clasped together under her breasts.

'Mum, wake up!'

I knew that wouldn't help. What would help was the injection. Then she'd be up and about and as good as new. But that wasn't true. Mum's chest wasn't moving. Her face and arms were marble white.

I could still save her! Her respiration might just be shallow and she might be pale from dehydration. I rushed to her side, dropped to my knees, grabbed her wrist, put my ear to her mouth. No pulse, no breath. But she wasn't cold.

'Please, God, no!'

I pulled a syringe from the pannier, flicked off the lid, jabbed it into her upper arm. I had to start her heart, get her breathing.

I prised Mum's mouth open and breathed into her. Once, twice, started compressing her heart, counting off loudly.

'Please, Mum,' I shouted. 'Come on!'

If her mind could come back, the rest of her would. I gave her two more breaths, tore the lid off the second syringe and slammed the Lorazepam into her arm. I compressed her heart to get the blood flowing. Blew breath into her lungs. Pumped her heart again. Tried to tell myself I heard her mind. Felt her pulse. Convinced myself the slow wheeze of escaping air was her exhaling.

I screamed.

I hugged her to me. This was worse than everything combined. I needed her. I couldn't lose her. But I had. She was gone.

'I'm sorry,' I cried, slumping down against the couch. 'I'm so sorry.'

TWENTY-SEVEN

I cried so hard it was like bleeding.

I hated the world, for folding in on itself, for taking Mum and everyone, for not taking me. I hated myself, for not getting here sooner, for not letting Jack bring me on a motorbike, for wrecking the bicycle and losing precious hours.

I'd shot at people—been shot. Smashed and crashed. Picked myself up and kept going. For what? For nothing. I hadn't been able to save anyone. I'd been the death of Stephanie. I hadn't been fast enough to stop Dad killing himself. I'd been unable to wake Evan. I'd come up with the plan that'd nearly killed Nathan. I'd revived people only so they could die horribly or live in fear.

I sobbed because there was no hope. There never had been. Nathan might be alive but I couldn't see many people risking death to revive strangers. In a few days it'd be too late. Jack might raise a few hundred in Clearview but I didn't know if his minions really counted as human. I wept harder at the thought of Evan. What made him my little brother might be gone for good.

Against reason I had hoped that Mum would be here for me, that she could tell me what to do, that together we would work this out, that everything could somehow be all right. I thought I'd been facing reality. But I'd been avoiding it completely.

This horror expanded ruthlessly, exponentially. Such nonsense: offering prayers, like any cosmic entity listened. Instead: karmic endgame, humanity's obituary, mankind's extermination. Cities and countries would burn and the soil and oceans would be poisoned by the fallout. The smoke that wrapped itself around the planet would choke the life out of whoever was left.

I'd wondered all along why I was spared. Now I knew. So I could find Mum like this. Know, *really* know, hurt and utter hopelessness before it was my turn to die.

'We belong dead,' I said. It was the last line from *Bride of Frankenstein*. 'We belong dead.'

I dissolved into suffocating tears and snot, clutching my chest because my heart ached so bad, hoping it was possible to die from grief.

TWENTY-EIGHT

It wasn't.

The Danby I didn't control, the part that kept my heart beating and my lungs sucking in air, whether I liked it or not, refused to let me off that easy. Gradually, my wracking sobs eased into hiccupy breaths.

My hands were pressed hard against my chest. 'Idiot,' I said. I realised I'd even gotten my grief wrong. My heart wasn't in there. I was clutching the left side of my goddamned body. Then it hit me. Where I was holding—that's where Nathan had been shot. Jack had shown me. He should be dead unless he was like me.

Situs inversus: that could be it. What had Dr Jenny said? One in ten thousand people? Whatever genetic glitch I had, Nathan might have it too. Same with Jack and Marv and Tina and Baz and Jamal and the Party Duder. It might've done more than rearrange our viscera. It might've been what stopped us from sending our thoughts and from crashing out. But one in ten thousand? If that was right then it was worse than I'd thought before. There might be just 800,000 people left in the entire world. That'd mean just a few thousand spread out over the huge expanse of Australia. As bad as this new theory's numbers were, having a hypothesis to hang on to made me feel more in control.

What I had to stop feeling was sorry for myself. Less than a million people worldwide: it was all the more reason to be thankful that I had found other people. Despite the misunderstandings and violence, we had each other in this goddamned mess. I thought how horrible it must be for other survivors who lived in smaller towns and cities. They might never find anyone. They might wander among the dead until they died.

My eyes drifted around the studio. Older canvases were stacked against the wall. Ashtrays were piled with cigarette butts. Four empty bottles of red wine. The water in Mum's bong was the colour of a puddle. I laughed. At least Mum had been out of it when she went out. My smile flatlined when I saw her last big canvas propped up on the easel. The painting was modelled on Edvard Munch's *The Scream*. The central tortured figure was on the Sydney Harbour Bridge, a halo of semi-circular arcs emanating from the top of her head, like the wi-fi connected symbol. The two background figures were fellow screamers, also with those nimbuses. A smudged jumbo jet came out of the maze-like sky that meshed with their halos. In the bottom corner, Mum had scraped the title 'Syncosis' into the thick, still-wet swirls of oil paint.

Being in Shadow Valley hadn't protected her. Not when the worst of it could be relayed between so many minds. Mum had tried to tame the crazy onto canvas. It hadn't helped in the end.

I looked at Mum. She was peaceful now. It was over for her. I knew she'd want me to keep going. Make the most of the shit that had happened.

But before I got out of here—before I went up the road, down the highway and past the dogs to revive people, reunite with Evan and Jack and somehow find Nathan—I needed to be alone in this quiet place. I needed to bury Mum in the soft earth. For me. For her. Billions were going to rot where they fell but not Robyn. As far as possible her passing was going to be normal, natural, respectful. And I'd get to remember it and her that way.

First, I needed to eat. I went out to the chicken coop and I collected eggs. I walked around the garden, picked tomatoes, spinach, an onion and zucchini. In Mum's kitchen cupboard, I found long-life milk. The cheese in her fridge still smelled all right. I cracked and chopped and cooked an omelette on her gas stove.

Clearing a space on the couch in her lounge room, I ate from a plate in my lap. I smiled as my eyes wandered around the room, from the whimsy of the not-for-sale collection of colourful slinkies dangling from the ceiling to her 'serious' bookshelf groaning with tomes about art, music, history, psychology and conspiracy.

Mum had left a bottle of red wine on top of one of her big floor-speakers. It was about two-thirds full. Why not? Even more than being planted in her backyard, she would've wanted me to toast her life.

I unscrewed the lid and sniffed. It smelled strong and earthy. I took a big gulp. Then another.

My eyes fell on the panniers on the floor and I remembered Jack's letter.

I dug into one satchel and then the other, spilling out the gun and a bag of ammunition and the first-aid kit and the flares and everything else.

There it was: Jack's letter.

I took another swig from the bottle and looked at the little envelope. I didn't want to open it. Not now. This moment was about Mum. And I was afraid of what Jack wanted me to hear.

Music! That's what I wanted to hear. That's what Mum would want at her wake. I knew how to make that happen. In the kitchen, I grabbed her boombox. When I plonked back on the couch and pressed play, Jimi Hendrix flamed from the speakers. I drank more wine and let her mix-tape play. Jim Morrison, Janis Joplin, Jeff Buckley: mournful as all hell, like she'd made it especially for this moment.

I pressed eject and saw her hand-lettered title on the cassette: 'Gone Too Soon'.

The mix went on: Amy Winehouse, Kurt Cobain, John Lennon.

How heavily we'd relied on dead people for our entertainment. We read their books, listened to their songs, watched them on our screens. They were our classics and what stopped that from being tragic was how they lived on through their works and influenced others to create. That chain had been broken. Moroseness engulfed me as it sank in that all our art was probably lost—*forever*.

I was glad when the batteries died mid-Michael Jackson. By then the bottle was empty and the room had started to spin. I ran for the bathroom, dropped to my knees and hugged the porcelain as I brought everything up. When I was done spitting and gasping, I closed the lid and reached up to push the button. As I flushed, I saw the framed cartoon of a kangaroo hopping out of a mushroom cloud.

'Don't worry about the world ending,' it read across the top. And across the bottom: 'It's already tomorrow in Oz!'

I laughed and then I had to puke again. I felt hot and disgusting. I peeled off my bike clothes, went to the kitchen and poured myself a glass of water. It eased the burning in my stomach, cleared my head a little. The velvet Elvis wall clock ticked on, blue suede shoes swaying off the seconds, sequined sleeves outstretched to tell me it was ten to two. The house was warm and I guessed it'd be even hotter out in the studio. The longer I left burying Mum, the harder it was going to be.

Mum's final resting place would be the raised garden bed where railway sleepers enclosed a person-sized patch planted with strawberries. I unwrapped the insect mesh and used a small spade to lift out the plants and their root clumps and set them gently on the grass. Then I set to work with a shovel to dig out the rest of the soil. Before too long I had a big mound of earth and a makeshift mausoleum.

I drank from the tap on the side of the rain tank and splashed water to cool and clean myself a little. Standing in the open wearing a T-shirt and underwear, I felt like a character in a slasher movie. One of those teenage chicks whose promiscuity provoked the eyes in the hills, the watcher in the woods or whatever monster was lurking in the shadows. The idea didn't scare me. Not with the more frightening reality that there was virtually no possibility of anyone being anywhere nearby.

I went back into the studio. Half a day's heat had taken its toll. Mum looked waxy and smelled like mouldering laundry. I didn't want to disrespect her by being repulsed. I slid one arm under her neck and scooped the other beneath her knees. I counted three and lifted her—hardly at all before I fell back with her onto the couch. She wasn't a big woman—I'd been taller than her for the first time last September—but I couldn't carry her dead weight.

Dragging was less dignified but I didn't think Mum would mind too much. I angled her torso off the couch, got my arms under hers and pulled. When her heels hit the floor, she let out a thunderous fart. I stood there, bent over, crying with laughter, glad I wasn't able to breathe through my convulsions. I knew if she was alive she would've thought it was hilarious. As I dragged her to the door I pretended we were both in on the joke and she was trying not to burst out laughing.

I don't know what I stepped on. Rusty nail, sharp stone, glass shard, bottle top: didn't matter. All I knew was it cut into the soft flesh of my left foot and I flinched instinctively and lost my balance. I dropped Mum and toppled sideways onto 'Syncosis'.

The big canvas fell to the floor and I landed on it, smearing the main screaming woman and Sydney Harbour Bridge. I lay there for a moment, feeling terrible that I'd ruined Mum's final artwork. But the only way to remove myself from the scene was by doing more damage. I placed one hand palm down on the already smeared jumbo jet blob and planted the other on the crazy mindwave halo coming from the screaming head.

As I stood, I saw myself in the mirror on the back of the studio door. I looked like some psychedelic human-zebra hybrid, my T-shirt and thighs stippled where rivulets of paint had ruptured, both hands covered with mucky black-and-white swirls. But I also had red on my cheek. My head wound was bleeding.

I righted 'Syncosis' against the wall, grabbed Mum under the armpits and dragged her through the doorway and into the garden. Burying her was going to be grubby work, but I didn't want to do it smeared in paint. I left Mum on the grass, arms and legs spread, as if she was about to make a snow angel, and ducked back into the studio to get a bar of vegetable soap, some rags and a scrubbing brush.

Over by the rainwater tank, I stripped out of my clothes. If some hockey-mask-wearing psycho was out in the bush, he was in luck with today's special nude bodypaint show—though with my bloody stitches maybe I looked like the monster. I wiped the bigger globs of colour off with the rag and then scrubbed myself as best I could.

Back in the bathroom, I dried myself with a clean towel, dabbed at my stitches with antiseptic cream and affixed a gauze pad over the wound. In her bedroom, I squeezed into a pair of Mum's jeans and put on one of her T-shirts. I slid into clean socks and put on a pair of her sneakers. I grabbed a shiny gold-framed photo from the wall. The two of us making funny faces on that first picnic day. Smiling really fiercely so I wouldn't cry, I clutched the picture to me and went out to continue her burial.

Outside, I saw that where I'd grabbed Mum I'd left fresh black-and-white splotches on her already spattered T-shirt. That was when I heard a noise in my head. It wasn't a big revelatory blast or even the sound of a bulb being switched on. It was the simple tick of a small piece falling into place.

I left Mum and went back inside to the bathroom. I picked my lycra pants off the floor. There, on the right thigh, was a similar smear to the one I'd left on Mum's T-shirt. Similar to the smear I'd thought was bird shit on the dead guy's jacket up on Shadow Valley Road.

I went back to 'Syncosis'. Set back on the easel, the plane blob was level with my eyeline. The dead motorbike guy had been tall, maybe six feet, so it would've been shoulder height for him. I closed my eyes against the now messed-up canvas and tried to remember it as I'd first seen it. Yes: I was sure—the jumbo jet, mostly white, outlined in black, had already been smeared. He'd been in here. I pictured the scene. This young guy manages to leave his house and check on his Shadow Valley neighbours. He finds that he can't do anything to help anyone. That includes Robyn, who's just expired in her studio, and as he leaves, his leather jacket brushes her big wet painting. Then, or soon after, he summons the guts to get on his motorbike and go further afield. Except when he roars up the hill he loses control on the sharp bend and breaks his neck as his bike plummets into the ravine below.

I kept turning the scenario in my mind as I dragged Mum to the strawberry garden. It didn't make sense. If Trail Bike Guy lived in Shadow Valley then wouldn't he know the road well? Other stuff was weird too. There hadn't been any gear spread out around the bike in the gorge. No sleeping bag or tent. He hadn't been wearing a helmet or a backpack. Maybe he'd just assumed he could get whatever he wanted by looting and taking shelter wherever he liked. *I* knew that was true because I'd seen what was left of civilisation but how did *he* know it from down here? What if he got up to the highway only to find everything had been incinerated? The timeline was weirder. The biker hadn't looked like he'd been dead longer than a few hours. The same went for Mum. It could've been coincidence. Right at that very instant there were probably millions of people drawing their last breaths. There was probably nothing that strange about any of it but I welcomed the chance to think about something other than the fact that I was shovelling dirt over my mum.

When she was covered completely, I replanted the strawberries, tamped dirt down between them, and piled a few bush rocks into a small grave marker. I smiled because I was sure that Mum would love her resting place. She reckoned coffin burials were insanely expensive—not to mention ridiculously inconvenient for the worms. I leaned the framed photo of us against the pile of stones and stared at it as I summoned a fitting eulogy.

'Shit!' The word exploded from me again, 'Shit!'

I'd been distracted from the picture by the glare coming off the gold frame.

Gold frame—I knew where I'd seen Trail Bike Guy before.

My head swam and my legs felt far away as I walked from the yard, staggered down the driveway and hauled myself up the dirt road.

Trail Bike Guy's stench hit my nostrils as I crested the rise. He'd started to swell in the heat. I didn't care how bad he looked or smelled. The cloud of flies parted angrily as I leaned down and rubbed my finger on the black-and-white smear on his jacket. It was definitely oil paint. He had been in Mum's studio. But I already knew that.

Seeing his face in profile, as I had before, wasn't enough to be sure. I dug one hand under his shoulder and put the other under his pelvis. With a grunt I heaved him onto his side and let him roll onto his back. His eyes were milky and dirty. They stared sightlessly at the silver sky. Even in death he was fashion-model handsome. The boy who'd been celebrated in Clearview's supermarket.

Employee of the Month.

Chris M.

Mr November.

TWENTY-NINE

I sat on Mum's verandah. Whatever sun there was set and night fell. I didn't move. I just thought about everything.

Eventually I took my phone out of my pocket and clicked it on. By its last power I looked at this device through new eyes. Even unattached to the internet, it contained my life—emails, addresses, photos. Dozens of those pictures were of me and Mum. Right here on this verandah. Out the front of her property. Mucking around next to the Nuclear Free Zone sign. Eating ice-creams in front of Jake's by the Shadow Valley Road sign.

I remembered asking Jack if he knew all about Bruce from looking through his wallet. But that wasn't right. If you wanted to know someone you'd go through their phone. When I was unconscious in Old Government House, Jack had taken mine and recharged it. I thought I'd kept Mum's location secret from him. That he only vaguely knew she was in the Blue Mountains because that's all Evan knew. But he had known all along where I was going. I flashed to me hesitating in Clearview, wondering if I was too tired to ride, hearing motorbikes race off on minion errands. One of those had been Mr November, getting ahead of me, coming here after Jack revived him.

But why? To see if she was all right? To maybe help her with an IV? Why not send one of the other minions instead of this new boy? There was only one answer. Jack didn't want me to recognise him if our paths happened to cross. He hadn't noticed him in the Employee of the Month gallery because he'd been too busy looting jelly beans and ice-cream. I wondered whether he'd even really had to look around the supermarket aisles at all. I thought he'd been so brave in going in there unarmed. It'd made me feel scared for him. But now I suspected those muddy footprints on the linoleum didn't all belong to Marv. I reckoned minions had been in the shop before we arrived to make sure it was all clear and that their leader could appear fearless.

I felt sick.

I lit a candle. My stomach twisted with dread as I tore open the envelope that held Jack's letter. By the flickering yellow flame, I unfolded a page from the notebook he'd scribbled in as we drove along the railway.

Dear Danby,

You saved me from fear & from myself.

I'm going to do everything in my power to keep you safe & happy. I've known since I first saw you that we'll be together. Together we'll make a better world for you & me & Evan.

While I'm not with you now, please know I'm with you in spirit.

You're not even out of sight & I can't wait to see you again!

You just joked that you were the last girl and that's why I wanted you with me.

But I don't think of you as the last girl.

You're the only one for me.

All my love,

Jack

PS: I hope your mum is fine. Please say `Hi!' and tell her I hope to meet her soon.

I read it again, anger mounting at his grandiose assumptions, at the saccharine sentiments, at the gutlessly indirect way he'd professed 'love'. But it was the horrifically jolly post-script that made me scrunch up his note and hurl it off the verandah like the filthy trash it was.

The bastard.

The bastard had sent Mr November here to make sure that I couldn't revive Mum. Not with all the Lorazepam in the world. If the guy arrived and found she was already dead then all he had to do was leave. If she was alive but catatonic then killing her would be as simple as covering her nose and mouth until she stopped breathing.

'No.'

I must've said it one hundred times. I didn't want to believe it.

But it was like I'd opened a door that I couldn't close and a blinding new light was shining on everything.

Jack didn't shoot Nathan by accident or because of the Cop's muscle memory or whatever. He wanted him dead for the oldest male reason there was—because he saw him as a competitor for love and leadership. I recalled how Jack had reacted when I said I was 'with' Nathan. Me getting shot? Unfortunate collateral damage. But it had given him the chance to *save* me and fix me up. Discovering Evan—the littlest hostage—was another bonus. Jack knew I'd never leave Evan.

A line from his letter echoed mockingly in my head: *Together we'll make a better world for you & me & Evan.* The way I heard it now was him saying that if we weren't together there'd be no world for me and Evan.

Once I agreed to go to Clearview, Jack had revived Joel and rescued Tina, Jamal and Baz. I'd been impressed by him, with myself for changing him. But whatever Jack heard in their car ahead meant they had to go. Even their deaths had the happy spin-off that I'd felt Jack had saved my life and Evan's.

My stomach lurched when I thought about the Major. Jack had been in no hurry to get to his dad, and he hadn't been surprised to find him dead. What I suspected was that while we'd been with Marv, a minion had taken Jack's key and slipped inside and finished off the old soldier. 'He had a bad heart' didn't have to mean the Major had died of a coronary. It sounded to me like his son had hated him and had killed him in revenge for being kicked out.

Jack was happy to get me out of Clearview. Nathan was reviving people. That had to be stopped. Jack couldn't very well head back east and carry out a pogrom with me around. Down here, I was out of the way, unable to hear the Revivees. I had no doubt that the Cop, the Biker, the Surfer—or others just like them—were out hunting down innocent people again. I guessed Jack's plan was to finish the job he started with Nathan and kill enough Revivees to terrify the rest back into compliance. I'd given him *days* to do it. When I got back, how would I know the difference? When I got back to Clearview he would sadly explain that the mortality rate had been much higher than expected.

'Why?' I said to the night.

Mum: he'd perceived her as a potential threat. I wondered if she'd still be alive if I hadn't told Jack she was a firebrand free thinker.

I was sure the story Jack was writing had already been recorded time and again in the pages of Mum's history books.

Jack wanted to rule the new world. He had unleashed a bloodbath to establish his new order and since then he had tried to convince me that I'd blessed him with newfound benevolence. Jack wanted me to choose to be at his side. I felt sure he meant it when he used Evan to tell me he loved me. It was in his letter in that roundabout way. *Love*—in his sociopathic definition of the word. It seemed absurd that a monster could want a mate. But there were plenty of examples way beyond old horror movies.

Didn't Adolf love Eva? Napoleon dote on Josephine? I bet if I checked Mum's library I'd find that Mao and Stalin and Pol Pot and the rest of history's genocidal maniacs all had 'better halves' too.

Queen, First Lady, Co-conspirator, Confessor: that was the role he wanted me to play. Jack was all about theatrics. The Legion stuff. The way he'd built up to raising Bruce. His fearless supermarket entrance. Waking up Vera to lure Marv. The goddamned dead dad moment that made me so sad and sorry for him. I knew what I was supposed to do now: drag my ass back to Clearview, my sadness about Mum magnifying my gladness for him. My freakin' saviour.

But I wasn't in Jack's story—he was in mine. And in my story shit had happened the wrong way for him. Mr November had been supposed to go over the cliff. If he had then I would never have known he'd been here. But the fact that he hadn't gone over the edge with his bike gave me hope.

Jack had told me that the very first person he raised—Mike, the Mikester, the Mike-anator—had returned to catatonia when he experimented with 'letting him go'. If that was true, why didn't Jack just send Mr November into the bush and switch him off? It seemed to me that he'd tried to make him kill himself. Was that because if Jack let him go he would revert to his normal self? But Mr November hadn't gone gently over the cliff. I thought I had seen minion self-preservation instincts kick in before when faced with self-destruction. The Range Rover driver's eyes and expression had reflected horrific awareness as his vehicle went over the cliff. Maybe he wasn't wrestling against the slippery railway line but against Jack in those final seconds. But I *hadn't* glimpsed fear in Evan or Michelle when we had slipped towards the same abyss. They knew—Jack *knew*—it was just for show.

I laughed in the verandah's darkness. Me and my theories. But I *knew* I was right. Jack's power over people wasn't final and forever.

Comforted by my new conviction, I curled up in Mum's bed and slept a dreamless sleep until late the next afternoon.

EPILOGUE

I know it's New Year's Eve but I don't know how many minutes or hours are left until midnight. It doesn't really matter. Either way, I know there won't be any celebrations anywhere. That's fine by me. There's nothing I want less than skies emblazoned with explosives and cacophonous crowds going crazy.

Silent stars materialising high over Shadow Valley are spectacle enough. It's probably only a break in the cloud rather than the blanket of smoke lifting. There's still too much to burn for me to hope for clear skies. But the glimpse of those distant yellow suns offers reassurance that the universe still exists beyond whatever's left down here. At least something's the same as it was a week ago.

I know the maths. The human race isn't quite done. There will be other people like me in Newcastle, Canberra, Melbourne, Brisbane, Hobart, Adelaide, Darwin, Perth. Maybe thousands of survivors in megacities like Tokyo, Seoul, Shanghai, Delhi, New York, Sao Paolo, Karachi. Jack can't reach those places. Beyond me and him, beyond Evan and Nathan, beyond the Revivees and the Raised, the human race will make it, even if in a newly evolved form and greatly reduced numbers.

But the world at large isn't my concern. What I need to do is take control of my part of the planet. I have to set free Evan and the rest of Jack's minions. If I can get those dozens and dozens of strong young men and women reviving people then we can work our way east and link up with Nathan—if he's still alive. I've got a shot at saving some of the city's citizens. I know the odds aren't great. But they're all I have.

I'm not the Last Girl on Earth. But in this corner of the world I am the Last Girl. I'm the one who survives to the end in the horror movie. I'm the one who has to fight the monster.

I turn my Christmas present on my wrist. I found it in a little ribbon-wrapped Santa box on Mum's bedside table. The silver's tarnished but shiny enough to just catch the starlight. It's a kitschy bracelet with the words 'Wonder Woman' stamped into it. The small card simply read, 'To Danby, You're my hero, All my love, Mum.' I'm going to make sure I'm worthy of my mum's belief. And I'll do my best to grant Jack his post-script wish to meet her.

The cosmos above me is calming and that's good because I need to be calm. Tomorrow, I'll head back to Clearview. Jack will be waiting for me. I'll cry real tears about Mum. I'll let him hug me. I'll hug him back.

I want him to think that he's won. That I could love him. That's the way to get him alone and with his guard down.

I'm Jack's weakness and tomorrow his weakness is going to kill him.

ACKNOWLEDGEMENTS

Thank you to Clare and Ava, who make everything worthwhile. Clare also for many reads, hugely helpful suggestions and endless patience when the conversation again turned to The Book. Noel and Wanda, who instilled love—and the love of the written word. Melanie Ostell, who first saw Danby's potential and whose agency ensured she made it to publication.

Allen & Unwin's uber-publisher Anna McFarlane, whose calm good nature made the apocalypse such a smooth undertaking. Cat McCredie, whose structural suggestions made every step of Danby's journey better. Rachael Donovan, for unfailingly answering every editorial question and sending Tim Tams. Melanie Fedderson, for her terrific cover and interior page designs, Marika Järv, for her perfect *Wall of Sound* artwork and Katie Evans, for her fine proofreading work. Liz Bray, for believing in *The Last Girl*, and Angela Namoi, for repping it to the world. Lara Wallace, Jyy-Wei Ip and Allen & Unwin's sales team for helping to put this book into your hands. Booksellers, for fighting the good fight.

Mic Looby, for a quarter-century's friendship and for reading, re-reading and making great suggestions. Great friends Luke Goodsell, Lachlan Huddy, Dan Creighton, Oscar Hillerström and Paul O'Farrell for early reads, enthusiasm and course-correcting critiques. Great friends Chris Murray, Michael Pickering, Amanda Ryding, Liz Doran, Michelle Newton, Shane Bugden, Guy Mosel, Rod Yates, Sam Barclay and Neil White for listening to me tell the story late into various nights and being goodly enough to say, 'Sounds awesome', rather than, 'Sleep it off, man.' Rachel Carbonell, Leonie O'Farrell and Charlotte Pache, for being ace. Zoe Stewart, for answering questions about medical students and *Situs inversus*, though any mistakes of far-fetchedness rest on my shoulders alone.

Dave and Tina, for love and support. Ray and Denzil, Susan and David, Sam and Max, Michael and Sarah, Charlie, Oscar and Leo, for being the best in-laws ever. Linda, Huw, Ella; Hali, Chris, Luka and Mila; Bek, Klete, Blake, Mia, Kayden and Rosa Lee; Matt, Eva, Finn and Matilda: for good times and making us feel welcome in the Mountains. Kylie, Damien, Eli and Zoe Taylor; Jude, Phil, Georgia and Evan Bailey, for making our last place feel like home.

Michael Adams has been a restaurant dishwasher, television host, ice-cream scooper, toilet scrubber, magazine journalist, ecohouse lab rat, film reviewer, social media curator, telemarketing jerk, reality TV scribe and B-movie zombie. This one time he watched bad movies at the rate of one per day for an entire year and wrote a book about the traumatic experience, which is called *Showgirls, Teen Wolves and Astro Zombies*. Michael lives in the Blue Mountains with his partner, daughter, one dog, two cats and an average of three supersized spiders. *The Last Girl* is his first novel. Find Michael on Twitter *@wordymofo*.

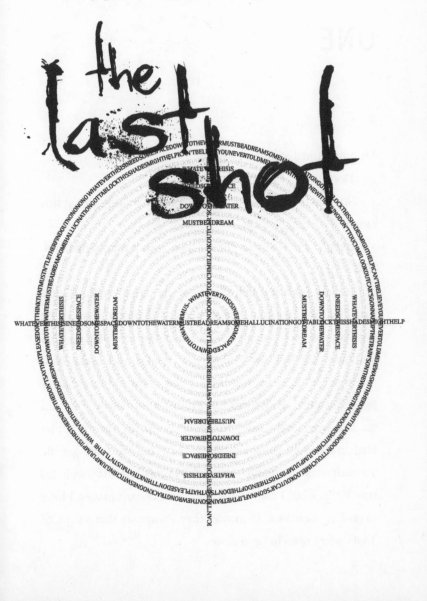

Turn the page for a sneak preview of the next book ...

ONE

My gun's aimed at Jack.

'Don't move,' I whisper.

Not that he can. Nor do I think I can miss him. Not at this range.

'Bang,' I say, lowering the weapon with a trembling hand. 'You're dead.'

My Jack is six feet tall, similar to the actual version. Other than that, any resemblance to persons living or soon to be dead is purely coincidental. Sketched on the door of Mum's old outhouse, this Jack has oval eyes, a smudge nose and a half-moon smile set in an oval head. I was going to draw a heart inside his pink-chalk torso but I didn't know where it should go. Left side? Right side? Nowhere at all? My theory is that Nathan survived being shot because he has the same genetic anomaly—*Situs inversus*—that I do. I don't know if that holds true for Jack but I can't risk it. His heart doesn't matter. I have to go for a headshot. In movies they always say that it's tricky. That's why I need to be in close.

I raise the gun again. Try to hold it steady.

It's an hour after the kinda dawn and Shadow Valley looks like it's immersed in weak tea. Sepia smoke and cloud hangs low from the mountains to blur the crowns of the gum trees behind Mum's studio. Haze and hillside merge on the back paddock to reduce nibbling kangaroos to shuffling shadows. But even with all the grit in the air, my target's perfectly visible, just a few metres away.

I need Jack dead to free my little brother. I'm gutted every time I think of Evan back there in Clearview. Not because I fear for his physical wellbeing—I'm certain Jack will keep him safe for my sake. But I wonder where the real Evan is right now. Is he stuck inside that awful nothing place, frightened and feeling trapped forever? What I want to believe is that Evan's somewhere happy—maybe in the mental equivalent of his cupboard cave, eating Chocopops and playing *Snots 'N' Bots* and feeling safe surrounded by his soft-toy friends. That I can't be sure of any of that—and the fresh realisation that I'll never see Mum or Dad or Jacinta again—makes my eyes well up. There's no holding back the tears that surge from me.

It's a while before I'm wrung out, before I wipe my eyes clear and see the target again. But I feel calmer, composed. It's like my anger and sorrow's become cold and concentrated. I raise the revolver—if cinematic memory serves, the little gun's a .38 of some sort—and point it at Chalk Jack again.

I picture the real Jack's smiling face. So confident. All that self-belief. It's going to be his downfall. The smug bastard was so sure of himself—of his power over me—that he couldn't conceive that I might turn the gun he gave me on him. What pisses me off is that Jack was almost right. If poor Mr November had died according to plan then I wouldn't have had a clue that Mum was murdered. Instead of still being here, training myself to be an assassin, I might already be back in Clearview in Jack's arms, feeling all tragic—maybe all romantic. He played me like his goddamned guitar.

My finger touches the trigger and then curls away from it.

The revolver sits heavier in my hand than the .45 did back at Beautopia Point. Then I was all jumped up on adrenaline. But those fight-or-flight chemicals are gone. Even though this gun is smaller—wooden grip, blue-steel barrel, six brass cartridges glinting in the cylinder—it feels like a dead weight.

Jesus—if I can't shoot at a crude drawing of Jack, what chance am I going to have against the flesh-and-blood version?

I'm no cool movie gunslinger. I'm not worthy of my Wonder Woman bracelet. I've been standing here wavering for what feels like ages.

But that's the point of this New Year's Day morning practice session. Get used to the gun, get comfortable with how it feels and how it fires. Because I'll only have one shot at Jack. If I don't get it right, Evan will be lost forever, Nathan's chances of evading the minions will dwindle and I . . .

I'll be dead.

Simple as that. Jack told me he loves me in a roundabout way. But I have no doubt he'll kill me if I threaten him.

I steady my aim. Best I can tell, I'm gonna put a bullet right between his eyes.

'Bang.' I lower the six shooter. Exhale slowly. Raise it again. Take aim. 'Bang.' My draw-aim-bang routine gets smoother with repetition.

Now I need to bite the bullet. Fire one, at least.

Thing is, I'm afraid of the real blast the revolver will make. Rationally, there is the slightest chance someone's still alive and sentient in Shadow Valley and that hearing a gunshot might make him or her reach for a rifle usually reserved for rabbits. Irrationally, I feel like the bang will disturb Mum's whole rest in peace thing down in the strawberry patch.

I'm being stupid. Wherever Mum is, it's not with her body in the dirt. Anyway, she'd definitely want me to have the skills to blow Jack out of this world—if only so she could have a turn kicking his ass in the next.

Chalk Jack smiles blankly from the dunny door. I raise the revolver, sight down the barrel at his head and curl my finger around the trigger. I don't back off. I don't tremble. I take a deep breath. Exhale slowly. Squeeze.

Crack!

The muzzle flares orange and the weapon tugs against my hand as the gunshot echoes through Shadow Valley. Smudged kangaroos bound into the safety of the denser murk. The noise fades. Silence returns. Mum doesn't rise from the grave. I don't take incoming fire.

I take the few steps to the outhouse to check exactly how dead I've made Jack. But his head's unscathed. I haven't even scored a body shot. Then I see it: a wound in the wood just below his left arm. No: that's an old knothole I hadn't noticed before.

Missed.

Returning to my spot, I steady myself and fire again. There's a flash, the shot rips the air and echoes off the hills. What I don't see is a bullet punching a hole in the door amid a flurry of paint flakes and wood chips.

Missed again.

I examine the little gun. There's not much to it. The barrel is no longer than my middle finger and the front and rear sights are no more than metal fins. I can't see how the gun could be askew or need calibrating. I also can't see how I can be such a terrible shot.

I take a big step closer. Now the revolver's muzzle is only a body length from him. God, I knew I'd have to be close—but this close makes my stomach turn when I recall how horrible it was when Dad put his gun to his face.

That memory is like ice cracking beneath my feet and I plunge into doubts that are like frigid black currents. What if I'm wrong about Jack's guilt? What if I'm murdering humanity's only hope? What if I'm right but Jack's really a life support system? What if—with one bullet—I kill not just him but Evan and everyone else he has raised? These questions could encase me in ice, freeze me solid.

I shake my head, try to surface, reclaim calm and clarity.

'No,' I say. 'You're right about this.'

I know I am. I've turned over the evidence in my head again and again. This is my fear trying to talk me out of what I have to do. Of course I'm doubtful. A week ago I was a sixteen year old unwrapping Christmas presents. Now I'm a sixteen year old doing a dress rehearsal for first-degree murder. No wonder my brain's trying to find some way out of this.

But I know there's only one way out for me and Evan and everyone—killing Jack.

Relax. Inhale. Exhale. Aim. Squeeze.

Blam!

I hit nothing again. At this rate, I'll have to hold the gun to Jack's temple. As much as he might love me, I'm not sure he'll stand still for that. I step closer again to the outhouse, intimate enough now to see a column of unconcerned ants spilling from a crevice near my target's inner thigh.

I aim and squeeze the trigger and the muzzle flares and my ears ring louder. Chalk Jack abides unplugged as unfazed ants march on across undamaged wooden planks.

A lot of *un*s also apply to me. Untrained with firearms. Unmoored by what's happened to the world. Unable to believe every single shot I've fired has missed. The toilet door fills my entire field of vision. Physics wasn't my strongest subject at school but I'm goddamned sure bullets don't go around corners.

Chalk Jack's smile no longer seems blank. It seems sinister. Mocking. My skin prickles into goosepimples. Maybe he is a God. I've invoked him with my crude totem and then insulted his divinity with my puny attempts to inflict injury. Maybe he can watch me through those vacant eyes as easily as he can bend the laws of the universe so my bullets miss him.

'No,' I say, as if my denial only has power spoken aloud. 'No.'

Jack isn't here. He can't see me. Chalk Jack's not real. He's just a representation.

Then it hits me that this isn't only true of my outhouse door drawing.

I look at the gun in my hand.

It's fitting that everything I know about it—that it's a .38, that headshots are tricky, that I'm supposed to squeeze not pull the trigger—comes from movies and television.

That's because I don't think the gun's actually a weapon at all.

I think it's a prop.